SHIELD OF SKOOL
Clovel Sword Chronicles: Book 1

OTHER BOOKS BY GORDON BREWER

RAY IRISH OCCULT MYSTERY
A SHOT OF IRISH
(RAY IRISH SUPERNATURAL MYSTERY BOOK 1)
DIE IF YOU WANT PRAISE
(RAY IRISH SUPERNATURAL MYSTERY BOOK 2)
DRINK WITH THE DEVIL AT MIDNIGHT
(RAY IRISH SUPERNATURAL MYSTERY BOOK 3)
NO REMEDY AGAINST DEATH:
(RAY IRISH SUPERNATURAL MYSTERY BOOK 4)
DEATH STALKS THE RUNWAY: RAY IRISH MYSTERY CASE
FILE #1
REAPER WALKS THE GARDEN: RAY IRISH MYSTERY CASE
FILE #2

PARANORMAL AND FANTASY
BEOWULF: CURSE OF THE DREYGURS
INFINITE LOOP
THE CURSE OF BLACKBANE

CLOVEL SWORD CHRONICLES SERIES
SHIELD OF SKOOL (BOOK 1)
BATTLE FOR THREE REALMS (BOOK 2)
DOWNFALL OF THE GODS (BOOK 3)
CLOVEL SWORD CHRONICLES: OMNIBUS EDITION

CLOVEL SWORD SAGA SERIES
CLOVEL SWORD SAGA: VOLUMES 1 - 2
SKELETONS OF NILGAVA: CLOVEL SWORD SAGA 3
THE BLEEDING MOUNTAINS: A CLOVEL SWORD SAGA 4

SHIELD OF SKOOL
Clovel Sword Chronicles: Book 1

GORDON BREWER

Brewer Internet Publishing LLC
2023

Second Edition

Thorn Bishop Press

Cover Illustration Art © Dusan Kostic | Dreamstime.com

Cover Illustration Design: https://www.fiverr.com/oliviaprodesign ©Gordon Brewer

ISBN-13: 978-1-945590-57-3

Visit the series website at

www.gordonbrewer.com

Dedication

To my son Teige, who decided I needed to finish writing this story, which I started some 20 years before. A special, and profound thanks to my wife who told me I needed a hobby and who spent long hours helping edit this work.

Contents

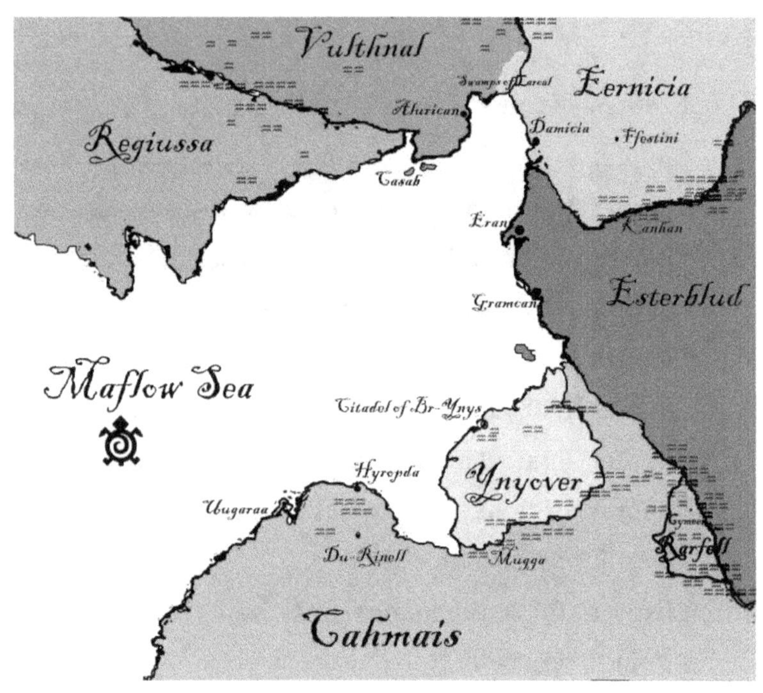

Vulthnal
Eernicia
Regiussa
Swamps of Lareal
Ahurican
Damicia
Ffestini
Casab
Eran
Kanhan
Gramcan
Esterblud
Maflow Sea
Citadel of Br-Ynys
Ynyover
Hyropda
Uugaraa
Gymee
Da-Rinoll
Mugga
Rarfell
Tahmais

Prologue - The Restoration

Long before humans arrived in Kamin, the ancients of the realms ruled the heavens. These ancients took no visible form, existing among the cosmos within their intertwined great spirit. They saw an unformed world of barren rock and seeking to create something pleasing to their many senses. These ancients wanted life upon this sterile world, so they opened holes in the sky, sending great rivers of water rushing from the heavenly seas to flood the terrestrial sphere. In those places not covered by the newly formed lakes of water, they splintered the great sphere, causing massive peaks to reach high into the heavens to stop the floods. When the ancients finished the blue sky, icy waters, and dust covered Kamin.

These ancients molded wild beasts and monsters from the gray clay of the underworld, sending them onto the sand and soil to prey upon each other among the forests and grasslands they created. Still not satisfied, the ancient celestial beings shaped the first humans, a deformed creature that came from the seawater mixed with the desert dust. They sent the humans upon lands to compete with the wild beasts and monsters. The misshapen humans could not compete, and a new form arose from the celestials, a specimen designed to battle the creatures and become a master of the sphere. Realizing such creatures remained just water and dirt creatures, not worthy of the realm they inhabited, the ancient beings liquefied the raw part of their spirit, injecting an eternal spirit into these humans. Some of these spirits were benevolent and just, leaving the ancients happy in the knowledge that their molded forms carried godlike qualities of honor and principle. However, many souls remained malevolent and spiteful, concerned only in vain praise of themselves for their cleverness or beauty. The ancient ones left this new world, returning to the Great Void where they left this new human creature in an ageless struggle of power and control.

From a tablet fragment - Temple of Skalds (Du-Rinell)

The bitter war of Necropa between the largest kingdoms of Kamin was finally over. The domains of Cahmais and Esterblud bled their young repeatedly during multiple invasions across the lands of Ynyover. Twelve consecutive seasons of constant battles and ruthless attacks by both powers left fertile areas of their lands in ruin and countless people dead and maimed. Even the center of spiritual learning, called the Citadel of Br-Ynys, was near ruin. With a fragile peace treaty finally agreed upon, the restoration began. The rebuilding of devastated cities and villages started as the *satgerts*, learned priests of the gods, helped lead the efforts throughout Ynyover.

The first morning of *Calanf*, the beginning of the winter season on Kamin, found the new satgerts lined up in two columns inside the Citadel of Br-Ynys. Their lines extended through the large central hall towards the closed doors of the grand banquet room. Dressed in scarlet red robes, these followers of the new Sacred Overlord were a collection of young and old, from the various lands of Kamin. Gathered together by their overlords and the learned elders of local temples, the lines consisted of multiple tribal affiliations, many of whom looked suspiciously at rival tribe members in the lines. Some of the aspiring priests, among the overwhelmingly male audience, cast sidelong glances at the spattering of female invitees. Voices in various languages and dialects carried across the hall helped along by the high vaulted ceiling. The satgerts came from great cities like Damicia in Eernicia, Gramcan in Esterblud, or Uugaraa in Cahmais as well as the many small villages and hamlets inside the kingdoms of Vulthnal and Regiussa. It was fortunate that heavy trade routes across the Matlow Sea allowed educated people to have at least a partial understanding of many languages spoken in the hall.

While the people waited, some of the younger members stared in awe at the giant twin doors in front of them. Each dark brown yan-yew door held engravings with the symbols of the ancient gods, known as the Guardians, as well as the new gods that replaced them. Those in the front of the line heard the loud grating noise of latches unlocking, which shattered the soft sounds of private conversations. The doors swung open. Without orders, the two columns began to move forward into the grand room of the Sacred Overlord, ruler of Ynyover. The priests filed past a small line of guards dressed in scarlet tunics overlaid with gold-colored breastplates. The sentinels stood on either side, each man holding long halberds; ax blades topped with a long, gleaming pike. After moving into the massive main hall, the satgerts began seating themselves on the benches that lined long tables. At tables arranged in a semi-circle around a platform in the middle of the room, the guests passed around metal cups filled with heathmead.

An old man sat on an ornate chair situated in the middle of the great hall. Dressed in a splendid robe of scarlet with a white sash draped over one shoulder, he watched the crowd moving to their seats. His lanky frame leaned forward, one hand holding a staff. A long white beard, matching the color of his long hair, hung down the front of the man's robe. When the last of the priests took a seat at the bench in the back, the scarlet-robed man nodded to his guards. Instantly, they pounded the shafts of their halberds three times on the stone floor. The crowd grew quiet. The old man stood, his body quaking from the effort.

"Welcome my friends," he spoke in his native tongue, his voice weak. His hushed voice caused those around him to lean forward slightly, straining to hear his words. Those in the group who didn't understand his language whispered their translation of his words.

"To those of you who may not know me, my name is Joenhip from the kingdom of Eernicia. I'm here to instruct you on our common history, the core training of our beliefs, and our shared visions of the gods," he stated. "With this knowledge, you will guide the people of your lands. Much like the destroyed sections you see outside our walls where craftsmen work, I will reinstate the learning and traditions of the satgerts." He paused to let them reflect upon his words.

"Because this is a great honor, it is my responsibility to bring our satgerts together as one voice within the temples across Kamin. I accepted this labor despite the reservations of some within the Majireef Council," he explained. "For those unfamiliar with the council, it is made up of the closest advisers to the Sacred Overlord. They believe I must guide others with the teachings of our new Sacred Overlord. I agree with such wisdom. Therefore, we must start at the beginning."

Murmurs broke out in the hall, with a few load groans as well. The young ones in the crowd looked around in confusion while some of the elders shook their heads in disbelief.

"Why do you waste our time? The skalds travel with the stories of our past. We're satgerts. We know the god's history," yelled a large man seated at a nearby table. The murmuring in the room grew louder.

Joenhip nodded to his attendant. Heavy pounding from the sentry's halberds striking the stone floor reverberated throughout the room, interrupting the discontented voices. He smiled patiently at the group while holding up one hand.

"I repeat that it is my responsibility to take you back in time to an era before our kingdoms existed." Joenhip raised his voice. "Let us remember the ancient times. Our ancestors sought shelter, away from the anarchy and turmoil that existed when the foul gods called the Guardians came into our world. I know that some of you will remember the names of these wretched creatures, but this does not mean you understand the history of our people and these gods. Bear in mind that, like the sea that sweeps away the sand of a beach, the truth fades from the memory of our tribes."

Joenhip stretched his hands in front of the crowd.

"Misleading and false beliefs led to the destruction that you see outside this fortress. Think of the destruction and deaths in your lands and mine. Each of us knows people who used the gods to their advantage. Consider the blasphemers who swept across the lands of Regiussa, attracting so many cult followers. Death Bearers defiled and destroyed temples after enslaving your brother satgerts. The barbarian hordes enforced a brutal subjugation over those who opposed their black flags and heathen ways. In forcing their profane views upon the population, there was no depravity these barbarians would not commit. My travels to those ravaged lands revealed the corpses of educated men swinging from the trees, grisly monuments to these Death Bearers. And we know this cult of death still exists in a few isolated areas, attempting to rise again. It will be up to each of you to help spread our teaching across Kamin. You will fight blasphemy by using knowledge of our past within the temples you command."

His piercing eyes and powerful passion grabbed their attention.

"As learned people, do we, once again, let the whims of madmen and zealots condemn us to death? Do we use the emotions of anger and hate among the rabble to fester and turn our lands into desolation and death?" Joenhip asked.

"I say no, we must remember the past and teach the younger satgerts in our presence. They may not understand the true history of the gods and heroes of our realm." Joenhip paused for a moment.

"We will base our learning and our mission from the same place in time and history." He told them. "Now, with your patience, I will give you the history of the Warrior's Code, which I've memorized from the tablets within the vaults of our great citadel."

The old man leaned back and closed his eyes to begin telling the story of the Kamin people and their gods.

~~~

Many generations ago, the Guardians emerged from the Great Void. They found the world filled with primitive people who inhabited the Kamin realm. These primitives bowed before the great god, Babulm, who created the three realms. Babulm made the Sky Realm as his home, a vast floating city of spirit temples. To those tribes he considered worthy of his trust, the sky god gave bits of his wisdom along with those of his brother and sister gods. Those leaders wise enough to accept this instruction built the first pillars of fire within the temples. Jultera, keeper of the flame, and Puanac, the god of the harvest, helped humanity emerge from their primitive ways, teaching them to develop crafts and trades to build their farms and cities.
~~~

Over the generations, Babulm left the Sky Realm to travel among the lands. He moved like an invisible whisper, going among the various tribes, where he spoke words of wisdom to worthy men. Those who received this knowledge became the first Kings. The era of the first overlords brought the tribes together, forming the great clans of Kamin. Weak aboriginal groups of hunters fell away as they become absorbed by superior cultures creating even larger kingdoms.

Across the lands and seas, the gods used their powers to benefit themselves and humanity. For the people who gave devotions, the Guardians provided a bountiful harvest from the land and a limitless catch from the sea. The people of Kamin offered great sacrifices of grain and animals, while the temples began to flourish. Learned people sang the praises of their benefactors. Those individuals who communed with the gods began to fill the temples as satgerts. The people were happy and lived to a great age as their gods kept their lands in a peaceful state, giving an order and balance to the world.

The balance could not last. As the seasons progressed, generations of people were born, grew old, and died as the countless life cycles went on. The Guardian's spirits became polluted as a sickness replaced their essence. They grew bitter at the very creatures they helped shape. In their diseased minds, humans became weak, pitiful creatures. The gods grew to believe people were barely above the other beasts that roamed the lands of Kamin. Just as a human might look at a stubborn *erba* as nothing more than a beast of burden, the Guardians began to see people in the same light. Unable to harness the power of nature, or the forces of the supernatural, the humans could never be the equal of a god. As the gods grew cold, they viewed their subjects with increasing disdain.

The god Aluric who controlled the underworld realm, made the fateful decision to bring chaos into the world. Aluric used his powers to create fearsome beasts, called *beorhs*. These creatures were the spirits of depraved humans, now turned into monsters filled with unbridled urges to savagely rape women or men while ripping their victim's flesh from the bone with monstrous claws.

Sending their creatures into the world, the god welcomed the slaughter innocents to fill the underworld.

Not satisfied with his depraved work, Aluric produced the *Clovel*, a fanged monster that walked on two legs, with massive extended arms that could rip a person apart. The ruthless deity built the savage beast from his lifeblood and sprinkled with the eternal water of the Exyts Spring, making it nearly immortal. Aluric sent out the creatures to prey upon the bands of warriors who traveled the roads to protect the innocent from his monsters.

Another Guardian entity named Kriell learned of Aluric's beasts and came to the underworld god. Kriell, the spirit stealer, relished the souls of humans for his consumption. Together the gods saw their opportunity to use the souls as slaves for their depravity.

Finding rapture in the suffering of innocents, more gods came from the Great Void to join in the new world of human slaughter. Even Babulm forgot his way as he participated in the abuse of his loyal subjects. Using powers of illusion and transforming, he and other sky gods traveled among the human realm to impregnate human women. In time, the gods created bands of demigod warriors who destroyed the lineage of the first kings. The demigods became the leaders of Kamin. Like their powerful fathers, the new leaders of Kamin sought supremacy over their brothers by invading territories of nearby kingdoms. The first large armies of humans, led by the half-breed gods, attacked with ruthless abandon. The pillage and destruction of once peaceful cities became great spectacles. Watching in amusement and aided by their half-god sons who commanded the people, the gods brought death and destruction over peace and harmony. It was a fearful world where humans desperately sought protection. They crowded within the temples, begging the priests for rescue, to stop the suffering. However, the priests abandoned their flocks. They believed themselves protected by their devotion to the Guardian gods.

Camulas, the god of war and master of souls, showed the priests the error of such belief. In his lust for blood, Camulas entered the temples in human form to inflict death upon his subjects. The war god instructed the underworld monsters to remain outside, trapping the unfortunates. Carrying his whip of god fire inside the white stone buildings built as monuments to himself and the other Guardians, Camulas killed everyone. The huddled men, women, and children fell under his fearsome weapon. The brutal god enjoyed walking barefoot on the temple floors, enjoying the warm blood as it gathered in massive pools around his feet. When he turned back to his vulture form, the deity nourished himself from livers ripped from the temple priests. Such was the wretched Kamin world of chaos that covered the land like foul smoke, waiting for a fresh breeze.

~~~

There was a pause. Joenhip looked among the rapt audience who had edged closer on their benches. Some of the younger people left their seats to find a place on the floor at the edge of the platform. He looked down at them, sad in the awareness that his life soon would pass from this world. As a *hakra*, or seer, Joenhip foresaw his end in a vague dream, yet he could never place the date of his passing.

Joenhip's eyes landed on a young boy with red hair who fidgeted in the stifling robe he wore. The boy looked to be the youngest in the group. He wondered if the boy was another orphan from a well-connected family sent to become a priest. He reached for a mug of Aberffraw wine after one of the Citadel's servants placed it on the arm of the chair. His hand grew steady as the drink warmed him. He cleared his throat, closed his eyes, and remembered the words of the scribe's chronicles.

~~~

In the lands of Esterblud, the leader of the Gramcle tribe gradually discovered one great seer. King Belwur heard of a young priest named Heptarc. Tales of the man's grand visions of the future spread across the lands. Rumors spread that he could perform miracles to keep the beasts from attacking people in the barrens of Gwendak. The noble king sent his finest warriors to bring this first prophet back to the fortress at Eran. Against the wishes of those advisors who maintained their allegiance with the

Guardians, the king held firm. He wished to see the man of miracles. His warriors left the coastal fortress dressed in their polished armor, astride their fine armored *ossanes* in their quest to find Heptarc.

When the Esterblud warriors reached the desolate lands of Gwendak, deep in the remote section of the Mythroloy Mountains, they came upon the young man residing near a crossroads. Standing outside of a rustic hamlet, Heptarc offered the riders a place to rest and food. Despite the ever-present danger of foul beasts coming from the underworld, their host wore no armor or chain mail, only a tattered brown robe. He carried a long-bladed machete hooked to his belt. Heptarc impressed them with his massive chest and powerful arms nearly bursting from his woolen robe. However, the Esterbluds found it hard to believe the golden-haired man with light eyes could be the great *hakra*. They scoffed at the idea that such a man was the destroyer of monsters.

Heptarc took no offense from the visitor's disbelief. He merely offered them drink from the nearby stream and the shade of the great twisted, *lellowtere* tree, which he used as an open-air temple. Around the tree were crudely made tables where incense pots held dried herbs and vegetation. Heptarc used prayers and rituals to placate and appease those gods who were not part of the bloody chaos.

Carcus, the leader of the visitors, decided to test the young man, asking for a vision of his future. Heptarc smiled at the grizzled veteran, saying he would need to sleep upon such a request. The patience and softness in his response misled Carus into believing Heptarc as a weak man. As the eastern sky turned red with the evening sun, the mild-mannered host offered the fighters the last bit of his food. He stroked the flames of the campfire and apologized for the meagerness of the meal. Telling the men he would bring back heathmead from the local tavern, Heptarc left. As they watched him go, a few fighters laughed, then declared the man to be a fraud or a fool.

The visitors spread out their bedrolls upon the ground around the tree, welcoming the coming night as the stars appeared in the sky. After a while, one warrior in the group complained about how long Heptarc was taking to get their drinks. The others joined in the condemnation of their host. During the banter, they failed to hear rustling coming from outside the light of their campfire in the stumpy brush nearby. No one spotted the gleaming eyes which waited and watched.

With a wild inhuman cry, the skeletal beorhs suddenly rushed the unsuspecting group. Several of the large, sinewy creatures fell on the closest man, ripping through his armor with their steely claws. Before the rest of the men could react, the beasts dragged the warrior off into the darkness. They could hear him screaming for their help before the pitiful cries became weaker, then ceased. With their sword drawn, the king's warriors formed a defensive circle around the fire. The beorhs watched and waited, their fanged, elongated faces showing the savage madness and evil which permeated these former humans. The creatures circled the area as they looked for weaknesses in the warrior's defensive ring. They attacked in waves, attempting to isolate individuals to drag away like the first. Despite the skill of the fighters who used their sharp blades to cut into the beasts, it did not take long before several warriors were captured and dragged off to their dreadful fates.

The waves of monsters threatened to overwhelm the men, and they heard a familiar voice yelling as Heptarc drew close. Using an ancient spell, Heptarc brought forth light as bright as the Kamin sun. The beam blinded those in the battle. The line of beorhs abruptly opened wide as the light sent many of them crouching in pain and fear. Carcus waited as his sight to recover and then looked again. He saw Heptarc approaching their circle. He was forced to shield his eyes from the light coming from a talisman that hung around the young man's neck shining like a miniature sun. The warrior watched in disbelief as the large man sliced through the cowering monsters with his machete. When he joined the circle of warriors, he led the men in a vicious battle with no quarter to be given by either side. Heptarc, covered by the blood of the fiends, paused when the talisman went out.

The satgert proclaimed the ancient words, and again the talisman lit up the night. Warriors followed the hakra as they slammed into the bewildered creatures, cutting them down. One beast tried to grab the young satgert only to be nearly cut in half by the sword of Carcus, who was closely following Heptarc. The men continued pushing on as they chopped the beasts apart in bitter vengeance for their lost friends.

As suddenly as the monsters attacked, they began to scatter into the night, each howling in anger and pain. However, the men continued hunting the beorhs. Carcus had trouble getting his warriors to return, so intent they were to destroy the beasts.

When the fighters eventually came together near the campfire, they found Heptarc there. The satgert busied himself by lighting the bowls of herbs, telling the men to rest and mend their wounds. His calm demeanor stood in stark contrast to the fearsome fighter they just witnessed. He retrieved the small barrel of heathmead that he left by the road. Sitting the cask by the tree, he assured the armed men they would have no more to fear from the monsters that night. While the warriors treated their wounds and drank the heathmead, Heptarc took his usual spot under the lellowtere tree. To the astonishment of the king's men, the young seer quickly fell asleep, still covered in the black blood of the monsters.

The next morning, Heptarc announced that he would return with them to meet the king. He explained that his visions told him of his future. The warriors were surprised to find Heptarc had already bathed in the stream, gathered his few garments as well as his incense pots and herbs. He rolled the items into his threadbare blankets for travel. As the men gathered their gear and mounts, Carcus asked again about the prediction of his future. The hakra simply gave a smile with a contented expression filling his face. They would be bound as brothers, dying together for a great cause.

The fighters returned to King Belwur, who listened to the stories of Heptarc's skills in battle and foresight. Still unconvinced, the king gave him a series of tests to prove the claims. When he too was convinced of the truth, Belwur personally took Heptarc to the temple of Jultera, which lay inside the walls of the fortress city. The Gramcle tribe held the god in special reverence for her fertility and wisdom. Within the temple, Heptarc gained a reputation for his mystic skills as he gathered knowledge from the other satgerts. It was said he communicated directly with the goddess Jultera.

Not content with priestly ways along, Heptarc learned the deadly art of weapons under the tutelage of Carcus. Soon, he began wearing the long tunic of his overlord's warriors. Eventually, Heptarc carried a long sword given to him by the king as a gift after becoming a trusted advisor. However, those people in the kingdom who benefited by the chaos and terror in the lands were not pleased with the rapid ascent of this man from the backlands. As with all people who seek power, the discontented people whispered in the shadows, spreading rumors and innuendo against the hakra.

Heptarc persuaded King Belwur to let him gather a group of dedicated warriors to rid the lands of monsters. Joined by Carcus, the fighters traveled throughout the kingdom, destroying the creatures let loose by Aluric and Kriell. During their travels, Heptarc's men became so efficient in their duties; they became known as the Slayers. Word spread about these warrior heroes, led by a new prophet. And, as the other kingdoms learned of this hero, King Belwur grew jealous of Heptarc, influenced by those against the satgert. Not long after, an advisor to the king suggested Heptarc l got to the lands of Cahmais. In a moment of weakness, the usually honorable king acceded to the whispers and sent his champion, Heptarc, to the dominions of King Aclac, one of the greatest kings of the Aberffraw tribe.

~~~

A loud murmur of anger erupted from a few of the new satgerts. They were people from the land of Esterblud. Sensitive to any slights of their overlord or their history, the new priests
~~~

complained loudly against the story. Joenhip raised a hand to silence the dissent while other satgerts raised their voices in the old man's defense. After a while, the sounds of the commotion calmed down enough to allow him to speak.

"Hear me out, for I know my words cast a good king in a bad light. Remember, all people, including our great overlords, can make unwise decisions. This is especially true when the advice comes from those ill-suited to provide proper counsel. We must always consider this point in the future." He looked over the crowd, eyeing each angry person who moved forward against him. "The words I speak are true. Written by the hand of one who served Belwur, the parchment resides in the vaults below. You will have a chance to see these archives in the future. Condemn me after you view the truth."

He took another drink of his heathmead while the sounds of murmuring quieted at his words, and he continued his tale.

~~~

When Heptarc and Carcus arrived in the lands of Cahmais, they traveled to the villages and stopped at temples along the way. During his stay, Heptarc learned of a demigoddess who was known for her sympathy for humans. Fascinated by the idea that such a god might exist, he went to a small village called Du-Rinell in the highlands of the Eilginn Mountains. During their travel through nearby villages, they found locals who praised a young woman for her ability to heal the sick and infirm. These villagers and farmers told the warriors about the great deeds of this demigoddess known as Mythrol. When they arrived at Du-Rinell, the two foreigners went to a timber-frame and wattle home where the sign of a hostel hung above the door. As they approached, they observed a line of people outside the door. Ignoring the protests of those standing in line, they pushed to the front. As they entered, the men encountered a small woman with red hair who wore the faded red robe of a healer. As they attempted to speak with this demigoddess, the woman grew angry at their methods, and she sent them away. Despite her small stature, the demigoddess carried terrible fury, forcing the larger
~~~

men to retreat in haste. When they left the building, Heptarc recognized some of the charms used by the demigoddess while she comforted the injured. He realized she held great powers as well as compassion, something few gods ever revealed. Heptarc decided to remain in the village and learn from her.

In time, Heptarc gained the trust of Mythrol, and they learned the secrets of the spiritual and the human realms as partners. While they grew closer, he discovered her powers included the ability to enter the realms of the gods, where she could learn the secrets of the gods in the Sky Realm or the underworld.

The satgert also heard about the woman's past, which explained her sympathy for her human side. The demigoddess despised the cruel god, Camulas, who fathered her by savagely raping her mortal mother. Growing up among the Guardians, Mythrol knew well of the god's butchery. She took it upon herself to mend those that the gods maimed and crippled. Disregarding her father's ban on using the healing power of the Exyts Spring, the goddess often went into the Sky Realm to bring back the medicinal water to speed the recovery of her patients. However, Kriell discovered Mythrol's actions. He intended to stop the demigoddess as she returned to Du-Rinell.

On that fateful evening, Heptarc waited near the unguarded gates at the village edge when he saw her red hair in the dim light. As she got closer, he could see her face alight with a smile. He smiled back, but then his face turned to worry when he noticed small, muscular figures with bright yellow eyes coming from behind a tree near where she walked. In the faint light, three *crubas* approached the woman from behind. The monsters from the underworld lifted their large reptilian heads, opening their massive jaws to help draw in the scents of their human prey. These foul creations of the Guardians hobbled along with their short legs, using their long, muscular arms to speed themselves forward. Yelling to his friend, Heptarc ran toward the demigoddess, yelling a warning to her. Mythrol glanced back before breaking into a run as the crubas closed upon her. Massive clawed hands reached out for her when Heptarc met the first beast. He impaled the nearest creature with his sword. However, another monster cut through his chainmail and leather armor. The massive claws ripped into his chest and arms.

Another creature joined the second cruba as they attempted to finish off Heptarc when Carcus joined his wounded friend in the fight. He crashed into the beasts with a flurry of sword strokes, slicing into the chest of one creature which screamed briefly before dying. Heptarc fell from his massive wounds at the foot of Carcus, who continued to strike against the monsters. Mythrol joined in the fray, dragging Heptarc away. Their friend finished off the last beast with a blow through its reptilian face.

Carcus hurried back to help his companions. He drew the uninjured arm of the injured man across his shoulder as he helped him back into the village. After reaching her home, the goddess used the sacred water of the gods to revive the hakra. To the amazement of Carcus, Heptarc was well enough to travel by the next morning.

Realizing the Guardian gods would seek out demigoddess for the simple act of helping them, the Esterblud warriors made a fateful decision. They would join together to seek out others with the power of foresight and visions. Together, the hakras and the loyal warrior would stop the monsters. The next day, they left on a path toward Ynys. It was during their journey that Mythrol explained the coming danger for all people of Kamin.

During a visit to the Sky Realm to retrieve the waters from the Exyts Spring, a water nymph came to Mythrol. A calm voice whispered just above the babble of the stream. The spirit told her of a great and powerful talisman which lay in the creek, hidden from those who would use it for wickedness. She learned about the dread which the Guardians held for this amulet. Mythrol asked why the nymph told her of this talisman. The water dryad explained that the evil ways of gods infected the realms of Kamin, where nature and spirits must co-exist. The spirits of nature suffered as much as the humans from the depredations of the monster. While the souls of the humans might wander aimlessly as ghosts for eternity, the spirits of nature were sought out by the Guardians. The soul-stealing gods drained the nature spirits of their powers, turning them into monsters to kill the humans.

The water spirit showed the demigoddess the secret location of a sizeable metal-like medallion. When she removed it from the waters of the spring, the sacred object filled her hands like liquid before regaining its solid, metallic form. Carrying it away from the spring, Mythrol could only guess at the powers that such an item might hold. The water dryad told her the medallion, known as the Skool, would one day restore the balance between humans and gods.

When the group reached the Citadel, where they found additional knowledge about the Skool, the couple bid farewell to Carcus. Their friend returned to King Belwur. Carcus spread the false news that Heptarc remained gravely injured, near-death and had lost the use of his injured arm. The ploy was designed to keep the king and his advisors from ordering the hakra's return. It worked, allowing Heptarc and Mythrol to discover more about the Skool. It also led to the unexpected relationship that grew between humans and the demigoddess during their time together.

Several seasons had passed in the village of Ynys before Heptarc and Mythrol sealed their commitment to each other. They met near a small shrine on the road to the Citadel of Br-Ynys. They also decided on their path against the gods. They created the new ceremony, which is used throughout Kamin between man and woman, making offerings to the gods of the Great Void, and sealing their actions with a kiss. They traveled into the desolate highlands beyond Du-Rinell, where they sealed themselves away from the world of humans.

During their time in isolation, the goddess bore Heptarc two sons and a daughter to continue their lineage as well as vital knowledge they were gathering. Heptarc, through the dangerous work of his wife, grew to understand the vulnerabilities of the Guardians. Using her ability as a demigoddess to cross the realms, Mythrol traveled into the underworld and the Sky Realm.

The secrets discovered by Mythrol during her secret journeys gave Heptarc the knowledge for destroying the beasts created by the gods. Using his natural skills in forging weapons from iron, he fashioned the instruments capable of defeating the monsters and those offending gods. You know about these weapons now, the same devices used by humans in their madness of wars and the slaughter of humans across our kingdoms.

~~~

Joenhip stopped his tale, visibly growing weak. His throat dry, he took another drink from the mug at his side. "It was Heptarc's abilities along with those of his wife who built the Skool. Heptarc became the only person able to carry the power of the gods in his hands. However, this is the story for another time."

"The details of the final battle at Du-Rinell and the great heroes who remade our world. I'll save this for our next meeting." The man looked across the crowd.

"Suffice to say; you should already know that Heptarc used the Skool and sword built by him from the ash of the monsters to open the Great Void. Within the Void, the triad of Heptarc, Carcus, and Mythrol brought forth the new gods to replace the Guardians and to protect humans," his voice fell to just above a whisper.

"In his final act, we know the great warrior and satgert sacrificed himself to keep the Guardians from returning," he continued. "For his sacrifice, our warriors from all lands honor the code of Heptarc and its four components: justice, vengeance, truth, and honor."

He put down the mug, apologizing to the group in the room. "Please forgive me, but I grow quite tired. I am unable to continue our lesson for the day. Let us continue tomorrow."

His thin frame leaned back again, and his shoulders drooped, suddenly overtaken by weariness. Gradually, the satgerts began to file out of the grand room, heading to the temple for offerings before their midday meal. Beyond the rustle of the woolen robes and shuffling of leather shoes on the stone floor, the crowd was strangely quiet. For many, it was the most detailed account of their realm's history that they had ever heard. Digesting the
~~~

words of Joenhip, the men, women, and youths kept thinking about their place in the new order. In the peace coming to the lands throughout Kamin, many could see a path to the example set by Heptarc, just as Joenhip intended.

The council may have brought the man called Satres from Cahmais to become the Sacred Overlord, but the fact remained that it was Joenhip who could bring order to the temples throughout the lands. As he stood up, using the chair arms to steady himself, the old man recalled his disagreement with Satres. Both men were charged by the treaty council to restore the Citadel of By-Ynys. Deciding to disregard the veiled threats from his new rival, Joenhip instead focused his attention upon the task of re-establishing spiritual devotion to the gods following the teachings of Heptarc.

Slowly walking back to his chambers, Joenhip waved away the two attendants who sought to help him. He shuffled along to his rooms, which the Sacred Overlord had thoughtfully allowed him to occupy on the main level. The years have made his joints ache, and walking stairs was an ordeal for the man. He stopped for a moment as he felt a queasy pain in his stomach. Attributing the discomfort to the food he ate earlier, and the man continued down the hall to an arched door where he entered his rooms. As he turned to close the door behind him, he noticed the attendants. Although he dismissed them, they were moving to take up positions just outside his door. He shook his head at a thought creeping inside. After closing the door, he turned to the table next to his bed when he felt another wave of nausea wash over him. He stumbled forward, falling on his knees at the edge of the bed. His face turned pale as he felt the cold comfort of the mattress while he stared at the desk so close to him.

Sweat broke out, covering his face, which now turned the color of ash. He opened his mouth to call out for help, only to gasp at the intense pain enveloping his abdomen. His hand shakily reached for the table, feeling for a parchment. Finding the smooth skin paper, he pulled it down to the mattress where he looked one last time at the map of Kamin. He knew death came for him, and he hoped, despite his beliefs, the warrior goddess would remember his past battles. While he didn't die in battle, perhaps the demigoddess of Haligulf would allow his spirit into the Sky Realm to meet with Duwdamon. Maybe the same gods would explain why Satres felt the need to poison him.

The Restoration of the Necropa had begun.

Chapter 1: Red Sky

A red sun peered under the high, wispy clouds in the Kamin horizon as morning awoke. The gentle roll of the outgoing Maflow tide lapped at the beach, swirling around dark granite boulders strewn across the red sand. The waves pushed broken timbers, shields, twisted bodies of humans and ossanes along with other remnants of a ship into grotesque piles, each a monument to the sea god's fury earlier. The lifeless bodies of the ossanes lay across the beach, their elongated heads, at the end of long necks, sweeping back and forth with each swell.

Out in the rolling waters just off the beach sat the remains of the Esterblud sailing ship, her back, the hull broke open, showing white ribs of ottwood jutting upward. The ruins of the broken ship appeared to be still screaming in a direct challenge to the power of Uugor, the sea god. She was an elegant vessel that carried the fight bravely; however, wood and iron were not a match for a god of such fury. Her single mast lay broken, pitched down at an odd angle with the torn canvas sail and a patchwork of lines flapping lazily in the morning breeze. Struggling for days, this creation of the human world found itself thrown against the jutting rocks that lay offshore, an unfortunate end to one of the man's defiant creations. Coming up from the tide line were two sets of footprints in the sand leading up to a pair of figures lying near each other in a large patch wild green eyegrass, under a single twisted tree.

One of the bodies began to stir, slowly rolling over with a slight groan as his muscles stretched, complaining at this effort. Urith opened his eyes to a haze-filled fog, staring at the red clouded sky above him. The red lines above him led him to focus on a vision inside the kingdom of the slain. One star still shining in the morning sky twinkled at him, the light a gleam from Duwdamon bidding the warrior close his eyes forever; to join the gods and great heroes in drunken oblivion within Haligulf.

Quietly, Urith laughed as his body and mind began to feel the sand under him, and the cold of soaked seawater clothes penetrated his very soul. He felt the beginnings of despair, as well. He was a favorite of the great King Penhda of Esterblud. The king led them in a victory over the Helter tribes during the tribal expansions against Cahmais. Now Urith disgraced the house of Penhda, dominate overlord of the northlands. It was a shame he felt wash over him like the waves, which nearly drowned him earlier. He could see the image of his long-dead elders above him, mocking him as they drank from the skullcaps of their conquered enemies. The stories, songs, and poems of the skalds filled his ears, laughing at his forgotten exploits and his largest failure. No Liege Body would come, and his name scorned within the kingdom. He blinked his eyes quickly as he tried to remove the visions of the sunken eye sockets of the elders staring at him, waiting to mock him for eternity after his timid death. Worse, he would see one of the Vanths, foul demigods of the underworld, coming to cast his spirit to the bowels of their realm as chattel to Caruun and the rest of the underworld beasts. Finally, the visions became too much for the man, and he yelled out to the spectators above him.

"Enough, I'm not finished yet. I am *Geniht* to King Penhda, not some slave used by the gods. You may mock me when dead, but not before."

Urith's rampage of grief filled the air over the sound of the surf, startling a few *vensars* flying to gather on the bodies. He wished he could destroy all of the nasty winged scavengers with their yellow beaks that would pick at the dead flesh of his friends. But it was a useless gesture. His head was beginning to clear as he turned over and pushed himself up, squatting on his knees as he surveyed the destruction around him. Thinking back as he pulled himself out of the raging water during the storm, he was able now to see how he came to rest near a twisted lellowtere tree surrounded by large patches of high cycgrass, which provided them some protection from the winds and rain during the storm.

Oslaf!

He suddenly remembered the young warrior he helped during the storm as he struggled to get the two men out of the waves. Each massive wave tried to drag them back into the sea during the night. After the deadly tiring struggle, both men dropped to recover and let the storm pass.

Looking around, he spotted the young man lying with his back to him. Afraid that his nephew had not survived, the man inadvertently held his breath until he noticed the boy's side moving with each breath. Visibly relieved, he staggered a few steps over to him. When he stood, Urith felt the heaviness of his long gray shirt; the padding still drenched from seawater. There had been little time save his gear when the ship broke apart.

Nevertheless, he thanked the gods for the garment, which kept him warm. The layered flaxen fiber of the underclothing provided defense against the sharp tips of spears and arrows penetrating his chainmail armor. Automatically feeling for the comforting touch of his Clovel Sword at his side, he touched the scabbard, knowing he was fortunate to get his sword belt on over his leather breeches before jumping into the surf with Oslaf. Looking down at the young man lying in the sand, the older warrior observed with specks of sand on his sleeping face, still peacefully oblivious to the destruction around them. Urith decided to let him sleep while he surveyed the damage and to look for other survivors. His muscles strained at his walk to the beach, aching as they tried to recover from the battering during the night.

His face remained unmoved at the sights, viewing the damage scattered across the beach. While he might have been considered handsome early in life now, a ragged scar ran down the side of his face. The thick callous line ran from his right ear to the end of his lip, leaving him a permanent sneer.

Sandy hair covered his head, falling on broad shoulders and down his muscular back, conditioned by many seasons of warfare and training. Taking a deep breath, he could smell the salt air from the sea spray as the ocean slammed on the rocks offshore near the broken ship. Exhaling, the survivor began his journey among the dead.

Urith moved from body to body in a futile attempt to find survivors among forms rolling back and forth in the waves. He quietly thought of his friends and relatives who lay waiting for the funeral pyres that would never be. The older warrior came upon the body of Guthlaf, his most trusted friend. He knelt at his friend's body, hoping that the gods had taken his friend's spirit to the great hall of warriors within the Sky Realm. Pulling his friend's sword from the stiffening hand, Urith began collecting the valuable weapons he would need to finish his duty. He took some comfort in knowing that his friend's death while fighting the powerful Uugor might give his friend the possibility of reaching Haligulf, the Hollowed Hall of the Slain. He sent a quiet plea to the sky god, asking that his daughter, Mivraa, would remember his friend. But, like his dealings with the gods before, he had reason to believe they would not listen.

Guthlaf had warned him of the dangers of the western route across Cahmais Magna to reach the kingdom of Ynyover. His friend advised them to use a traditional way following the merchant traders later in the season before the harvest festivals. However, their Overlord convinced Urith and Guthlaf of the need for this risky course to bypass potential spies from Cahmais. Now it was too late for the Esterblud leader to admit to his dead friend that the man was correct. Three days of northern gales had forced the ship to the south, continuing on a direct path toward Ynyover, near the Cahmais border. After the Esterblud longship had broken her back, those men not battered against the rocks by the pounding waves drowned by the strong outflow tide. The coast was a place where ships often died, and their crews became easy pickings for the locals who combed the sand.

Urith stood, looking across the bay at the high cliffs jutting out of the sea. He recognized the vast Citadel of Br-Ynys sitting perched at the top of the cliffs, its tall circular towers insulting him as he stood on the coastline. As he thought about his location, trying to come up with a route to the fortress, the warrior heard the sound of a low moan behind him. Whipping out his longsword while spinning around with the catlike reflexes of a black *bater*, Urith saw Oslaf moving toward him. The young man kept one arm firmly against his side.

"Have we failed?" The young face peered up at him, as his nephew held his side, slightly bent over.

The older warrior sheathed his sword and leaned over to help the boy, grabbing his leather shoulder strap with one of his hands to steady him. Just seventeen *Draenyna* or solstices old, the young warrior stood nearly Urith's height, although not as muscular. They had a similar appearance in their face, but Oslaf had deep blue eyes and dark blonde hair. The pair made a formidable team as the largest men within their village, if not within Esterblud.

"No, my friend, we have not failed," he spoke with a forced grin, "the gods have just made our task more difficult."

As he spoke, he used his free hand to lift the front of the shirt to reveal the expected blue and purple bruising, which stood out on his nephew's white skin. He could hear the labored breathing of the boy, and he had seen such wounds before. Oslaf might be in danger of bleeding in the lungs from such a rib injury. He would have to keep a close eye on him. Perhaps they might find a healer. Like the rest of the world around them, such fortune would depend upon the Fates.

"It looks like you may have hurt your ribs. If we are not careful, you will soon speak in blood," he stated.

He was surprised at the youngster's reaction as he saw the fear cross his face.

"Urith, I must not die this way. That will shame my

family," he hesitated and looked away. "I'm afraid."

The older Esterblud threw down the back of the shirt and jerked the younger one around, causing him to wince. The warrior's gray eyes bore into the very soul of Oslaf.

"You forget that you are of my blood!" his voice booming above the sound of the ocean waves. "Curse the gods, you are not dead yet, and I will not listen to you cry like an old woman."

His face pulled close into Oslaf's as he pulled at his young friend's shoulder to emphasize his point. "Now listen to me. The gods may decide our deaths in the end, but I've decided that we will not die on this beach today. Is that understood?"

The young warrior slowly nodded his head in stunned agreement, suddenly more afraid of his mentor than the Fates. He tried to look away, ashamed of his weakness in front of his guide as he gathered himself together.

"Now, go and gather anything useful you can find. Anything we need to continue our journey," Urith told him. "It appears all of the mounts are dead, so that means we will be walking."

While the Esterblud leader did not care much for the long-necked creatures they used for their transportation in the lands of Kamin, he knew they would need to find some of the beasts to get out of the area quickly. They would be in trouble if any mounted enemy should arrive.

"We will start by scavenging any food and weapons you can find. Check to see if anybody else survived. Then, we will scout for any ossanes that may still be around." Urith sent the young man off across the red sand.

The screeches and squawks from the *vensars*, their mottled black feathers rising in anger, suddenly got louder as more of the scavenger birds arrived. Soon they would peck at the eyeballs and exposed flesh of the dead. Both men moved quickly across the shoreline walking from one body to the next corpse, loathing the grim task of turning their friends over to reveal their open eyes and distorted faces. Death by drowning seemed unnatural to their warrior way of life. Oslaf moved carefully from his pain while he looked past the bodies, picking up any supplies and weapons which he took to a small pile out of the surf. Urith noticed the young warriors focus on survival with some satisfaction. Perhaps, he might survive this trip. However, so much now would be up to the Fates, he thought grimly.

"Do you know where we are? We haven't landed in Cahmais, have we?" Oslaf asked over the chatter of birds.

Urith shook his head as he prodded the last body lying on the shore, looking for a sign of life. He looked up at the large stone outcropping of cliffs jutting from the sea across the large bay.

"No, this is not the land of our enemy. While we were heading that way during the storm, I think we've come ashore in Ynyover, just outside the Cahmais border. Those massive cliffs on the other side of the bay hide the capital of Ynys and the harbor town of Grimma." Both men realized they had come ashore in the land of mystics. Ynyover was off-limits to virtually all armed outsiders, like themselves, without the approval of the Sacred Overlord. The small kingdom was a neutral area open to all believers since the Restoration of the Necropa – an event twenty-two Kamin cycles before that restored the Sacred Overlord over his country. However, any warriors coming to the territory required advance agreement among the overlords of the surrounding kingdoms of Cahmais and Esterblud. This was something they did not have.

"Then, we are in trouble, aren't we?" Oslaf asked as he viewed at the cliffs in the distance.

"Yes, our landing here makes it difficult," Urith agreed. "Without a formal announcement to the Sacred Overlord's envoys at the docks, we will be in peril. So we must tread cautiously. Even in the best of times, Esterbluds moving along the border between Ynyover and Cahmais will arouse suspicion. And with all the raids over the past seasons, you can bet the locals will not trust any strangers."

"But wouldn't the Sacred Overlord understand such an accident, since we were driven here the gods themselves?" the young man asked, turning to Urith.

"Perhaps, but our overlord isn't sure this man called Satres is a friend of the Esterblud. However, I'm confident that we are on the neutral side, and that is Ynyover just across the bay. Since we cannot swim across, we will have to go around following the coastline. It may not be the right entrance, but we will complete the charge of King Penhda."

He gave the youngster a reassuring glance.

"But we cannot worry about that right now. We need to gather any weapons we can find, and then we will need to find ossanes and food. We will have more visitors soon as villagers, and their militia will spot those birds. It would be better to stay out of their way."

"What if we run into them?" asked the young warrior as he put another shield on the pile of weapons he was collecting from the debris.

"If we do, they better be able to handle their weapons against us," Urith gave him a wink. "No need to worry, our good king and his skalds told us of places to go if we find ourselves in trouble. While we may have lost our maps, we still have our memories, along with the stories and songs to guide us. Be assured that we have friends in Ynyover."

Urith's words did not sound very convincing to Oslaf as he examined the bodies around them. The older warrior glanced again at the pale dead face of Guthlaf before turning away for the last time. He would have to make amends for the twenty dead men in his charge, he thought bitterly.

During his search, Urith found his chainmail armor and his long outer tunic caught under large wood planks at the edge of the waves. Immediately, he pulled off the leather strap that held his sword along with a long Esterblud triangular dagger. Unhooking another leather belt, called a baudrik, which ran diagonally across his massive chest, he laid the weapons aside. The Esterblud shook off the beach from the chainmail and pulled it over his head, letting the mail fall over his padded undershirt to mid-thigh, over his breeches. He then pulled on his green and red tunic showing the colors and symbol of the *Geniht*, King Penhda's guard. Spun from the finest Vulthnal wool, the long body of the garment protected from the cold of the night. He cinched up the trousers, pulling his sword belt through open spaces in the chainmail and tunic to hold the whole outfit in place. As he put the baudrik belt back on over the wool cloth, he watched as Oslaf slowly pulled up a pair of heavy battle axes from the bodies of their fallen friends. Urith looped one of the long spears he found on the shore through one of the several holes in the baudrik, flipping it behind his back for quick retrieval. Adjusting his weapons, he went back to the beach, looking for any additional items.

Oslaf watched his mentor as he pulled a heavy sword from the hands of a young friend called Ocase, whose body still moved around in the surf, rolling slightly with each incoming wave. He pulled a dagger from the dead boy's belt, sliding it into his leather belt at the waist, recognizing how Urith kept glancing over at him as he worked his way through the bodies.

"Oslaf, come here," called the man, holding up a waist-length chainmail shirt he recovered from the beach debris. The mentor had a vague recollection that the chainmail armor came as a spoil of war during their raids on a Cahmais island near their border.

Slowly pushing a hatchet into his belt, Oslaf gingerly walked over, trying to work through the pain of his sore ribs. When he reached Urith, they struggled to put on the mail, clearly built for a smaller person. Fortunately, they were able to pry open the back, which allowed Urith to hook the leather straps through the metal loops and bind it around Oslaf's upper body. The elder warrior hoped the tightness of the steel mail around his body would help to ease the pain while protecting him as well. After getting the armor on, he and Oslaf also struggled to put an Esterblud tunic over the mail.

"Come on; we've got enough weapons to keep any comitatus from getting too close. I didn't find any food or drink. How about you?" Urith asked. Oslaf shook his head as he adjusted his belt and weapons.

"It's a shame, but this is good land for us to hunt game so we should be able to find food and a stream nearby for water. Let's get to the top of that ridge and see what we can find." Urith indicated the direction with a nod, and Oslaf gave him a slight grin, trying to keep his focus on their situation.

They went to the top of the sandy ridge to get a better view of the unknown landscape in the distance. Urith carried his circular battle shield, which he found among the debris, along with his helmet and the battle-ax tucked under his belt. The pair was almost to the top of the ridge when they heard the distant sound of ossanes coming fast toward their position. Scrambling to get a look over the rim, they spotted six riders coming their way. Both men knew they were in a terrible defensive place with the sea behind them and a mounted enemy in front of them.

The six riders pulled up a fair distance away when they spotted the two strangers appear over the ridge in front of them, unsure if other warriors might be out of sight below. They spoke among themselves in the Aberffraw language; however, Urith could only make out a few words due to the distance. He watched their body language. It told him that their enemy was unsure of the fighting abilities of the Esterbluds. The older warrior quickly centered his attention on the rider sporting a golden helmet, topped with the white eagle feathers of the Aberffraw guard. The man wore the blue tunic of the royal guard while directing the others as their leader. The other men around the Aberffraw leader wore brown leather armor tops and canvas pants. Each fighter wore the pointed metal helmets of the comitatus. Urith noticed most of the men carried only spears and a short sword, which was no match against an Esterblud in a one on one fight. However, the Esterblud leader had no illusions to the danger they faced.

They remained outnumbered, and he had a wounded comrade with him. Urith knew well the fighting ability of comitatus when Aberffraw warriors led them during King Penhda's raids. They could be fierce in protecting their home soil.

"I don't like this. They are not all locals. You see that golden battle helmet?" Urith pointed out the man to Oslaf. "That looks to be an old enemy I met with our king in our Cahmais raids a few seasons back. Notice his helmet style and the similar armor on the ossane. Only elite guards of the Aberffraw king can possess such armor for themselves and their mount."

Urith found the apparent fact illustrating since the Ynyover comitatus were unlikely to be led by an Aberffraw. It meant some treachery was afoot between the Cahmais and Ynyover overlords. Led by the Aberffraw tribe, the Cahmais kingdom was the mortal enemy of the Esterbluds. Urith suspected the kingdom of Cahmais was trying to control Ynyover.

"Well, it looks like they are coming for a fight. Remember the heathmead tastes best in Haligulf," Urith grimly joked while their enemy began to brandish their weapons wildly. It was apparent the enemy wanted a brawl. He put on his black battle helmet while Oslaf did the same.

Unlike their enemy, Esterblud helmets covered the entire head and neck, with rounded slits for the eyes. The faceguard of the helmet sloped down to protect the cheekbones and mouth, giving the overall impression of an executioner's mask. On the top of the helmet's crest was an elaborately decorated image of an *Estercetus*, the sea serpent symbol of the clan.

Urith pulled his long Clovel Sword as he stood looking out at the enemy. He held the point of the sword down while he put the pommel end to his lips as he prayed to the gods. Down the longsword blade, which was half a human in length, were finely detailed engravings of the beasts and humans in battle. Along the edge was an inscription of the spells used by those who sent the Guardians out of the realms. On the pommel end was a cast iron ball, filled with the rare bone ash of the Clovel, a monster beast now mercifully lost to the Kamin world. The Guardians, also known as the Gods of the Great Void, once used Clovel creatures for hunting the humans. Only a warrior who had destroyed such a beast was worthy to carry this sword. Only two of these swords were known, and Urith had one. His youthful exploits against the deadly fiend were still sung about by the skalds of Esterblud.

He heard Oslaf beside him, giving the same prayer to the gods, and he was pleased. While he didn't believe in fearing the gods, as many within the Kamin realm, it pleased him to know those gods would guide him to Haligulf if he were worthy during the coming battle. He watched his nephew and began a chant in homage to the *Estercetus,* which would grow to a full battle cry when the attack came.

Seeing the black helmets now on the Esterblud warriors, two of the comitatus riders suddenly charged, apparently sure they would get to the spoils of battle first. The others hesitated, waiting for a signal from the Aberffraw leader who was observing the reaction of the Esterbluds. Urith moved back to an area just behind the crest of the ridge to provide them cover from a spear thrown by the mounted warriors. This position also allowed the sandy soil and steep slope to slow down the headlong rush of the comitatus riders coming. Both noticed the four remaining enemy riders slowed themselves, ensuring they would avoid an ambush if other Esterbluds remained hidden behind the slope.

The two lead riders kept charging at full speed when Urith stuck his sword in the ground, pulled up his spear, and took aim at the leading rider. With an experienced eye, he waited until the enemy was several ossane lengths away and threw the spear. His spear struck the enemy in the chest, slicing through the leather armor as the force of the impact knocked the comitatus warrior tumbling backward off the mount. The Esterblud fighter, pulling his sword from the sand, rushed to the top of the ridge as the other rider reached it, barely sidestepping a spear streaking toward his chest, then turning with an upswing thrust of his sword. Urith impaled the enemy in his side, just under his belt and through his leather jacket. The enemy screamed as he doubled over, clutching his side. His ossane continued past the Esterblud, heading down the slope as his dying master slid off the black mount, falling to the ground.

While Urith remained occupied with the first two militiamen, another two comitati were bearing down on him as they sped up their mounts to full speed as they came up the slope. The lead warrior rushed his charge, intent on impaling Urith with his spear. Suddenly another spear shot past him from behind as Oslaf let his weapon fly toward the rider. He had moved up on the ridge to the right side near a large boulder. His throws caused him to groan in pain from the effort, but the spear flew accurate enough to land into the chest of one rider. The enemy fell on the side of the other mount, sending the rider's animal off course. Trying to change his direction with a hard pull of the long-necked animal, the enemy threw and missed his target. Urith swung around his body and brought his sword down on the arm of the comitatus, slicing through the man's forearm at the elbow. The enemy grunted and then screamed from his grievous wound, trying to clutch at his wounded arm with his other hand.

When the enemy rider got to the top of the ridge, Oslaf took a running jump from the small boulder. He landed on the back of the animal, behind the man who still screamed from his wound. With a quick thrust of his dagger, Oslaf cut the wounded man's throat, then pushed his enemy to the ground. The Esterblud struggled for control of his captured mount but managed to turn the long neck around, toward the remaining enemy warriors coming. Oslaf suddenly dug his heels into his new mount, deciding to charge at the two remaining fighters who were closing in on the top of the ridge where the older Esterblud stood waiting for them. The enemy spotted Oslaf coming at them, and they pulled up their mounts in shocked disbelief at one person attacking both of them.

"No, get back here!" yelled Urith to the unhearing Oslaf as he watched the young man riding down the slope.

Urith knew young Esterblud was making a terrible mistake and ran forward over the ridge a few steps. Pulling out the spear sticking from the chest of the nearby corpse, he continued as fast as he could after Oslaf. He hoped to make the best of an imperfect situation and cut them off, knowing he was still too far behind to help. Urith heard the Esterblud battle cry coming from his nephew as the cry of their enemies rose in response, seeing him charge headlong into the other ossanes. He watched the enemy riders break apart, with one enemy fighter using his shield to ward off the charging blow of the sword. The other rider with his distinctive gold helmet brightly shining in the morning sun pulled around the passing Oslaf, turned his mount hard, and threw his spear at the boy, striking him in the lower back. The older warrior watched it all as he ran toward the melee.

"Come around and turn them back this way!" he yelled desperately, knowing no one could hear him in the distance. He hoped the young man would keep moving and turn the two enemies around back to Urith. As if Oslaf read his mind, he saw the young man pull the long reins controlling the mount, forcing the ossane into a broad sweep to the left. His move forced the enemy riders to change direction as a rambling row of boulders lay in their way. Losing sight of the warriors following Oslaf, the Esterblud changed his route to cut off the trio as he ran through a small gap between some of the boulders.

The Aberffraw leader and his militia rider regrouped after the first charge. They rode at breakneck speed toward the wounded Oslaf. The Esterbluld had trouble directing his mount while attempting to hold the spear stuck in his back. The youngster spotted Urith, who emerged on the other side of the boulders and took a hard turn toward him, spurring his mount on. Oslaf remained only a couple of animal lengths ahead of his attackers, and Urith could see the boy was fading as he struggled to keep the spear steady with each gallop of his mount. The enemy moved into view from behind the edge of boulders; the lead rider spotted Urith just as the Esterblud leader sent his spear at him. The enemy saw the spear coming and yanked the reins of his mount to the right, leaning over hard as he nearly dismounted himself, but he avoided the deadly weapon. However, the militia rider behind him was not as lucky, when the spear struck his white animal in the front chest. Man and animal went tumbling head over heels with the rider trying to kick away, only to get the total weight of the mount crashing down on him. When the dust settled around them, neither enemy nor animal stirred from their final resting place.

"Urith, look out!" yelled Oslaf as he passed the warrior.

"Get yourself into the rocks and wait for me there." The leader shouted as the enemy rider turned his animal back. Urith recognized his disadvantage. Fine chainmail with overlapping silver-colored plates of steel covered his opponent's upper body, arms, and thighs. Even the man's ossane had armor protecting its head and chest area; the steel gleamed dully in the mid-morning light. In another setting with time to think about it, the armored man and beast would impress Urith. He would have rightly guessed the fighter was a leader in the Cahmais kingdom.

With a yell, the Aberffraw leader swiftly pulled his longsword and attacked the Esterblud. Urith parried the downswing hack of the sword as the rider passed by him. The armored brown animal, well trained in battle, tried to run over Urith during the first pass with the golden helmeted master still after his prey, the young Oslaf. However, the Aberffraw was forced to break off to the right at the last minute when the young Esterblud pulled his mount into a small gap between the rocks, dismounting clumsily. Oslaf pulled at the spear, finally releasing it from his back after he landed on the ground. He turned bloody spear tip toward the gap in the boulder while hanging on to his mount by the reins.

Reconsidering his attack, the Aberffraw leader swung his animal around and decided to attack Urith, still exposed on the open ground. The Esterblud stood in a defensive stance, ready for the oncoming charge, and watched as his opponent dug his heels into the ossane to get his mount to full gallop. While holding his sword in his right hand, the warrior used his left hand to reach behind him and slowly pull out the battle-ax from his waist belt. The mount gathered speed and again attempted to run over Urith. The Esterblud warrior waited until the last moment, faking a dodge to the right and came back left as he swung the battle-ax across the armored head of the long-necked animal hitting it between the eyes. He could feel the downstroke of the enemy's sword coming at his head, and Urith ducked down almost quick enough, but he received a glancing blow that stunned him, knocking him to the ground. As he fell to his knees, Urith noticed the mount stumble, stunned from the impact of the Esterblud's ax. The rider futilely trying to keep the animal from dropping over on its side. Sand and grass filled the air as the mount stumbled, kicking up debris with its four cloven hooves.

Urith tried to shake the cobwebs out of his head while he struggled to stand. He didn't see the rider go down with his mount landing heavily on one leg. Urith only heard a thick groan after the animal and man fell. The Esterblud scrambled over to finish off the downed rider but slowed. He realized the fallen animal lay over the rider's leg. From the short distance away, Urith saw the enemy's leg jutted at an impossible angle, revealing a nasty injury. Each time the ossane struggled to rise, the Aberffraw warrior screamed out in pain while he fought to prevent the animal from injuring him further.

Urith left his disabled opponent and ran over to the tall boulders where Oslaf waited. He heard the beast's shrill bleating again, and he looked back to see the downed man pull his knife from his belt. After a couple of clumsy attempts, the enemy cut the saddle strap away to release the animal. The mount struggled to get to its feet before shaking itself. As the ossane slowly stepped away, it left its master holding his leg in agony.

As Urith came up, the young warrior was sitting with his back against a large boulder. He smiled weakly at his mentor, his face pale as his uncle sheathed his sword.

"It's been a tough day," Oslaf said, his eyes looking down at the ground. "I'm sorry for my mistake. I just wanted them so badly. You are right to be angry with me."

Urith shook his head. "No, you did well today. We all make mistakes in battle. You forget that you now have a trophy in your captured ossane and other spoils. You will learn from this. Now, we need to move soon. Let's get you back on this stinking animal."

He reached down to help the boy to his feet, carefully turning him around to lean against the rock while he lifted the young man's shirt to look at his wound. Luckily, the spear entered his lower back near the side, going through muscle near the hip, apparently missing any vitals since the Esterblud did not smell any foul odors from the open wound. He put the shirt down and carefully hitched up the belt to compress the bleeding wound, causing the boy to buckle, nearly falling from the pain. Urith then helped his nephew back onto the ossane. He turned and backed the animal and Oslaf out from between the boulders.

"The spear missed your vitals. It went in deep, so we will need to get some herbs for it soon before any infection starts. You get that black mount over there so we can travel quickly. We'll try to gather what we can before we go. And, I'll look at our guest," he sneered.

Urith went back toward the Aberffraw enemy, who was now sitting up; the man's leather booted foot resting at a twisted angle. His mount remained nearby, grazing on the high cycgrass as the man still held the cut reins in one hand. The Esterblud approached casually, watching the enemy reaching to retrieve his weapons. The wounded man only succeeded in getting his knife, staring desperately at his sword, which lay just out of reach. The Esterblud paused, then bent down and retrieved his battle-ax. He sheathed it in his belt. When he reached the enemy leader, he carefully wiped away the blood from his sword using the saddle blanket that lay in the dust nearby.

"If you understand my language, you should know that you have nothing to fear from me now," said Urith in Esterblud. He removed his battle helmet, sliding it under his arm. He liked the cooling breeze strike sweat on his forehead. The enemy warrior stared at the Esterblud carefully. Struck at the sight of the jagged scar running down the man's face, it gave the giant stranger an unnatural death grin. The wounded enemy guessed many others had seen that sneer when they died.

Still unsure if the stranger understood him or if he was ignoring him, Urith continued. "You have fought well. We Esterbluds don't kill wounded just for sport. Given how many comrades you seem to have, I would expect help will soon come for you". He pointed to the man's leg with his sword and turned to walk away.

"I understand your tongue." The wounded warrior spoke up unexpectedly as he pulled off his helmet showing the Esterblud a long narrow face with an aristocratic nose. His curly blonde hair fell to his shoulders while his blue eyes focused at the Esterblud.

"You have come a long way to die in this land." The man talked through the pain.

Urith stopped and turned back. "You are correct. We have come a long way after a week of storms. Finding an Aberffraw Guard on this coastline so close to Ynyover was a surprise. You are a long way from home as well."

The wounded enemy tried to smile despite the pain he felt. "It's interesting you would know the Guards. Have we met before? Your helmet looks familiar."

"Oh, I've seen the Aberffraw many times as most

Esterblud warriors have." Urith avoided a direct answer. "Now, can you explain why the elite guard of your king is within the neutral lands of Ynyover? Aside from breaking treaties, it seems you are just as far away from home as I am."

The man shook his head with a small laugh. "No, I'm closer than you think. Much closer," he said cryptically. "Nevertheless, you have shown great courage and honor in battle. I offer my thanks to you for that. What is your name?

The Esterblud warrior paused slightly, "I'm known as Urith of the Penhda clan."

The wounded man paused as well. "Ah, yes, I thought I knew the helmet of your lands. I've heard of you, the Clovel Destroyer. You took part in the raids on my homeland islands. We should have your head mounted on a pole for that," said the enemy bitterly. However, he sheathed his knife back into his belt, grimacing from the slight movement.

Urith shook his head, "You're as wrong as your king. It was not Esterbluds who started the fight over those islands. And it was you who began this battle. Now you know we do finish our fights. We are forced to since many of your tribesmen are quick to invade our lands."

"This is not your land, and I know more than you may realize. It appears you hold to the warrior code. Too bad, you fail to recognize those warrior ways are dying. But, in fairness, I will give you a warning. If you remain in this land of Ynyover, you and your friend will not live long."

The Esterblud's sneer-smile grew at the threat.

"Well, you're in a poor position to make such a threat. I doubt that the Sacred Overlord would be happy at such thinking. We are in a neutral land as storm survivors, and to hunt such survivors would go against the laws followed by all our tribes, even in your Cahmais."

"Laws or not, survivors or not, you will be hunted down and killed. You don't understand that the world has changed, and your countrymen are now spoken of as pariahs by the same overlord you seek to visit," said the wounded man, his tan face grimacing from the pain in his leg.

Urith's expression showed the surprise he felt at his enemy's claim. He wondered how much this adversary was saying was true and how different things may have become.

"I see by your face; you don't know the trouble you have stumbled into within this kingdom. As you have allowed me to live, I will return the favor when I tell you to leave Ynyover. Take what you can and return to your homeland."

Urith laughed lightly. "It appears that you and I are just following a path that has been determined by others. I suspect, like you, that I'm just a part of something already laid out before me by the Fates. Tell me, what is your name?"

The Aberffraw stared at the warrior above him.

"Yes, you should know the name of the one who may destroy you. Remember the name of Lyncus."

Urith nodded his head, turned around, and began his walk back up the slope to help Oslaf. "Until we meet again, Lyncus, I thank you for your information."

He moved back up to the path between the boulders to reach Oslaf, who had already gathered up two ossanes from near the fallen enemy. He knew that his nephew was in no shape for a long ride. However, they must leave the area quickly before more of the enemy arrived. Aside from the threat from Lyncus, he knew what a tempting target their ship would be for locals looking to strip the remains of anything valuable. It was now clear that the Cahmais king no longer considered Ynyover a neutral territory for all the kingdoms. However, the Aberffraw push into Ynyover would be something to sort out later among the leaders of the Kamin world. It would be people like Urith who would fight and die in the coming battles.

As the pair walked back to their original position at the top of the slope, Urith swiftly searched the bodies of the comitatus, retrieving what little rations they carried. The Esterblud knew that scavenging was necessary as spoils gained by those means could be used in and barter for any information or goods during their journey in the hostile land. In the wilds throughout the Kamin world, items scavenged from battles, and the dead warriors were stock trade among the locals providing food and other needed goods for the local farmers who lived from harvest to harvest. Urith traveled the lands of Kamin as mercenary and part of his king's campaigns. At times, bartering with animals and weapons provided information from the locals.

After discovering a few gold koinons on one of the bodies, Urith rose. With a glance back in the direction of Lincus, the money told him that the locals were not necessarily inviting the Aberffraw into their midst. Along with the other evidence he learned, the information would be valuable to his king.

Oslaf galloped back to the shoreline to gather up anything that might be useful from the piles of items he and Urith put together earlier. The Esterblud leader got on his new mount and followed Oslaf across the ridge back to the beach. Coming to the pile, he jumped down and quickly gathered a few swords, spears, and shields onto his mount and the spare animal as Oslaf stood guard, urging his friend to hurry.

"We should get moving," said the young warrior. "I'm not sure how long I can hold out."

"You will continue as long as I tell you, nephew," the warrior said gruffly to him while he tied down the weapons stacked behind his saddle. "You are Esterblud. Now act like it. Go up to the top of the ridge and keep a sharp lookout. We don't give up barter goods if we don't have to."

After he had finished, Urith got on the animal and rode back up to the ridge to Oslaf, who was staring at the Citadel across the bay. The young warrior thought how close they had come but yet so far away from their goal.

"We need to find some back trail away from the Citadel now that our presence is known here. We need to mislead any followers who will be sent to destroy us," stated Urith as he nodded back down the slope to the boulders where they had battled earlier.

"According to our Aberffraw friend, it appears Ynyover is no longer neutral. If I remember our maps correctly, we start toward the Mythroloy Mountains; then, we can double back through that large forest to the south and west." Urith explained. He pointed to the green and blue landscape in the distance. "The path will take us into the backcountry to get around any Ynyover towns and villages. We don't need locals noticing our tunics. We must be very cautious since we left that enemy warrior alive."

"Why did you?" asked Oslaf. "Wouldn't it be wiser to have killed him?"

Urith stared at his young friend for a moment.

"You mean besides the fact it's against our warrior code?" he asked and laughed lightly as the young man reddened. "No, it's a fair question, my friend. I've seen our code twisted to justify what you ask. However, it's like other twisted divides we find on our journeys. Once you go down such a path, it's easy to get lost and never find your way back."

Oslaf did not like the answer from his mentor. "That's sounds too much like those royal skalds you mock."

Urith swung his leg over the high war-saddle, looking down at his new ossane. It was white with just a patch of black in the area around the two-horned face.

"You did well with the ossanes. Good enough for our journey," Urith said as he turned back to Oslaf.

"And, I never mock those skalds too much since they keep our exploits so well documented. It's just they are usually wrong, like the hakras." The warrior his death grin as he ridiculed their king's royal hakra. Oslaf was used to his uncle's sarcasm about the short round man who provided visions to King Penhda. Urith had little use for those who claimed to know the god's intentions.

"Then, we head for the Citadel?" Oslaf asked.

"Now you will learn why the one called Lyncus lives. Our sharp-eyed friend with the broken leg knows we've left. They will have a scouting party coming for him soon. You can bet they will be following us. We will let him believe we are heading back to our kingdom to the east using the narrows pass. Then we swing back around through the woods and highlands following the Ynyover boundary," he explained.

"Can you make it to that woodland?" Urith nodded to the east. "The travel will be tough for you with our injuries, but we need to get some distance before the stars rise. There, we will find medicine to tend your wounds."

Oslaf nodded his head, holding pressure on his wound and looking unsure. "I wish we were heading back home."

Urith relaxed his manner as he agreed.

"As I wish we were as well, but we have not completed our king's charge. We must finish our duty, and you know I'm not one to give up easily. You must always remember that you are the son of Pehnuwick."

The pair of warriors spurred their ossanes down the sloping sandy soil back to the field of boulders, making sure Lyncus saw them as they rode toward the mountains that separated Esterblud from Ynyover. When they reached the main trail that followed the winding landscape, the two riders galloped fast toward the protective cover of the forest in front of them. As they rode along, both men scouted for signs of their enemies. The grasslands in their path appeared to be free of people. Since the trail was close to the sea, only the herders were likely to be found. Fortunately, it was the season for them to be in the highlands with their flocks.

Neither rider noticed a small figure dressed in black watching from the shadows inside the tree line. Only a quarter league away from the trail, the shadow kept still, intently watching as the pair passed by. The figure took particular interest in the black helmets they wore, which now hung on the sides of their mounts. The crest of their helmets matched the visions of the past, but the same images showed the traveler only one visitor, not two. It was a sign that bothered the onlooker. The figure stayed motionless as the warriors disappeared into the green brush in the distance. Then the black-cloaked person swiftly ran over to an ossane tied up to a small tree at the bottom of a ravine. The rider followed the two strangers to Ynyover.

43

Chapter 2: Into the Underworld

Oblivious to the terrible sights and sounds around him, the god of the Sky Realm followed a gleaming white stone path. His trail led through the twisting dark caves into the netherworld home of his rival. It was an odd scene with an immaculate path leading through a pitch-dark underground hole that dripped with foul water. Echoing moans filled the dank air, coming from the very walls around him.

This god made no face from the stench. He walked majestically as a god should, with his back straight and head held high. His long white and gold hair waved along from the fluid movement of his walk. His bare feet touched nothing as his shape hovered above the stone while the entity appeared to stride along. The sky god's human form, covered in an immaculate white and purple robe, portrayed strength and youth with his broad shoulders. His aristocratic face showed a tan from his mountain home. Sprinkled in around the eyes were wrinkles, which gave him an uncertain age.

However, the face cast a sinister expression, which came from the thin yellow mustache that hung down both sides of his mouth past his chin. This expression, when combined with his dark black eyes, provided him with a terrifying appearance which could throw mortals into panic and hysteria if he so wished it. But on this day, the sky god stared ahead, refusing to acknowledge the gathering movement of white shadows around him. A small crowd of wailing souls forced him to stop. He scowled impatiently when they quickly closed around him, begging for his attention.

With an annoyed nod to his consorts, the two rat-faced Vanths swiftly moved forward to push back the souls. The horrible, winged creatures' skin was a mottled black and brown. Each wore long robes of brown hemp. Around their belt, they carried grisly trophies of human fingers, toes, and ears. They were buzzards, collectors of spirits who traveled to places of human death and destruction. Half-human, the demigods led human souls to the underworld for their eternal torment.

As they attacked, the Vanth's sharp bird beaks opened to utter shrill shrieks with an intensity of a hundred *vensars*. They beat back the misty apparitions with the flicks of their beorh-skin whips. Those poor souls struck by the enchanted leather howled in torment while the rest scattered to avoid the excruciating stings. Vanths used their long snake hair, which hung down to their waist, to snap and rip at those souls as well. Any life force caught by the bite of the snake demon venoms would immediately vanish from sight. The spirits would waste away for eons in torment. As quickly as they gathered, the wailing crowd of souls dispersed, pulling at their hair while crying inhuman howls about their terrible ethereal existence. In their retreat, their spectral forms tried to hide in the narrow cracks that ran along the tunnels.

His way cleared, the sky god followed the twisting and turning trail, traveling deeper into the darkness and stench. Eventually, the cave began to widen. No spirit would follow when the path changed to a polished black floor. While solid, the trail now gave the illusion of a bottomless pit below. The deity walked into a large vaulted cavern, bathed in luminous green light. The veins of glowing *tribolrocks* provided illumination for tunneling humans of the Kamin realm.

Inside the underworld realm's main chamber, dark black vault walls of spiraling black and white cubes gave the sickening effect of vertigo overhead. Thousands of faint circles carved into the overhead cubes that stretched into a beehive; each entrance was a handmade cave, the sound of continuous hammering and ringing of hand chisels came from inside thousands of tunnels, echoing down from beyond the dim light. Each shaft was a personal work of the condemned. A close inspection of the walls would reveal the detailed hand-carved engravings showing tortured images of imaginary creatures and dreamscapes of madmen hewn by the countless souls imprisoned there.

The master of the Sky Realm paid no attention as he continued. The spirits were unworthy of the Sky Realm. They would continue to carry out their ceaseless toil. The underworld god viewed punishment for humans as one of his pleasures. A ruthless master enjoyed torment and pain for the inhabitants of the underworld realm.

The sky god, still accompanied by two Vanths, came to the centerpiece of the chamber. A massive black and white throne covered in carvings sat on an elevated platform. Each sculpture on the throne was small statuettes that squirmed and twisted in agony. The throne was alive with souls deserving singular torment and abuse. It was a horrifying display for the visitors to his realm.

As the golden-haired sky god moved closer to the middle of the room, his ugly companions, the Vanths, bowed before the throne of their dark master. They left the sky god as a black mist slowly took a human-like structure above the platform.

"What brings you to my realm, Duwdamon? It has been a long time since we spoke. You must be lost." A hissing voice echoed in the chamber from nowhere.

A part of the figure finally grew visible on the throne. It was a ghostly face peering down at the sky god. The black-skinned deity on the throne appeared relaxed. He had one leg thrown over the arm of the chair, leaning back against a clovelhide rug draped over the back of the throne. When he came into full focus, he revealed high cheekbones on a narrow face with the nose of a vulture and large pointed ears giving a grim expression.

Duwdamon gave a forced smile to his brother god. "No, Caruun. You are the one I wish to speak with since we have something to discuss," he told him.

"You amuse me, brother," Caruun's voice cracked from disuse. "What could I discuss with the supreme lord of the sky? Unless..." He looked down at the god of the heavens, and his yellow eyes narrowed.

"You want to discuss the human realm? If so, you know my answer to that. Humans don't interest me, only their pitiful souls."

Duwdamon showed no emotion to the question, but his form slowly elevated until he came level with the underworld god. The sky god gave a slight nod, and an enormous gilded throne appeared behind him. Duwdamon projected a more substantial figure than his brother god to emphasize his strength.

"Our future is tied to the humans, as you well know," Duwdamon said. "I have received news that you are playing a dangerous game which threatens us all. I'm here to keep this from happening."

"Your visions are mistaken, my friend. It appears that Umcal, your great Sibyl of the future, must be growing weaker." The underworld god waved a clawed hand as he dismissed the idea.

"Don't mistake my calm for weakness, Caruun. I'm here to make sure you realize the Triad is committed to maintaining the balance. I don't believe you are willing to go so far as to have the Triad against you."

The vulture face gave him a frightening smile, and a chattering noise emanated from his open beak. He moved his muscular body to an upright position, tilting his head oddly like a bird. Caruun hated any discussion of the Triad since they were the three gods of sky, sea, and earth who often aligned against his wishes. The god of the underworld objected to their actions as self-proclaimed defenders of the three realms. When he moved forward, his clawed hands clutched the arms of the throne, causing a few of the enclosed souls to shriek and dark liquid to ooze slowly down the side of the chair. Those spirits encased in his cruel throne were his future *beorhs*, his monstrous sub-creatures. Like the occasional bastard children, such as the Vanths, the spirits within the abyss had little choice but to submit to the whims of Caruun and his wife.

Duwdamon may have disliked the underworld god's treatment of his subjects, but said nothing, for such matters remained beyond his realm. The realms of the gods were sacrosanct, and he continued committed to maintaining their order.

"Brother, you come to my realm to threaten me over such a vague vision?" He shook his head in disgust as his crackling voice echoed, spreading his clawed hands wide. "You trouble me with your accusations."

The sky deity focused his unforgiving stare on Caruun.

"The vision of the Sibyl was clear, and you know the oracle is never wrong. It is our future," Duwdamon insisted.

"The Skool will be found. We also know about the humans who search for it. Stories have come to me about gods becoming involved. We both know this will lead to chaos or worse. With chaos, the boundaries are in grave danger. I've come to tell you that we must come together on this for the sake of both our worlds."

The yellow eyes stared back, the cornea turning to a full, dark black at the conversation. Duwdamon knew something was going on behind those eyes. The lower world god still resented how the Sibyl, the single prophet of the gods, came from his realm so many generations before. The idea of a human spirit becoming the prophet of the gods remained a sore spot with Caruun.

"I see," said the deity as he scratched his temple lightly with a claw. "It's unfortunate that you have come such a long way to tell me something that I'm familiar with. Do you forget who of us joined with the gods of the Sky Realm to keep the chaos from spreading?"

"I overlook nothing, Caruun. Despite your allegiance at the time of The Great Passing, I also know that you have no love for humanity," the sky god reminded him. "If it suits you, you would happily destroy the human world to fill your realm. I don't pretend to understand why you carry out some personal vendetta against spirits with such little power in our empire."

Caruun adjusted himself in the seat.

"However true this may be; you need not concern yourself with my intentions. For now, I'm more inclined to let the gods fight amongst themselves. I've always said we should use them as slaves. Since they are only useful for whatever we desire, why worry about their realm? Nearly all of them fail to understand their powers of foresight and rebirth."

"You sound more and more like the old Guardians," the sky god stated to his rival. "You forget the need for balance between the realms. It is vital for humans and the gods to remain in harmony. You know their spirits feed our realms. You helped to send the Guardians into the Great Void for that reason."

"No, just like you, I helped for my reasons," Caruun reminded him. "I've had plenty of time to reflect upon things, and I know you are wrong. Only you and a few other fools think humans are worthy of our care. It's bad enough that I cannot even use my power except when the sad things cry out after death. They don't fear or respect us before their pathetic life ends."

"Your belief is not the view of the sky gods," answered Duwdamon. However, Caruun could tell his words had some effect on his brother god.

"Perhaps not now, but you know what the answer is. It is for us to rule. The pitiful human souls fear me; they will do anything for their keepers and me," he explained. "They grovel at my sight even when I transform them into creatures their human friends would never recognize. We know that the gods have so many ways to keep the humans cowed, forcing them to sustain our needs appropriately."

Caruun gave him his sickly smile again. He ran his claws along the throne of torment, creating screams of despair that echoed throughout the chamber.

"Enough of these rants about the humans!" Duwdamon grew frustrated despite the logic of the argument. "Our bargain among gods decided on the path. Whether you like it or not, the balance between the realms will be maintained. I'm here about your creatures pushing into the Kamin realm. Now, what of the Vanth called Tuulcha?"

Caruun stiffened a bit on the question.

"What of her?"

"Your bastard creature has been seen in the Kamin world within the lands of Ynyover. Tuulcha is only to be retrieving spirits. Your fiendish *scunce* went into Cahmais near Du-Rinell. That is a forbidden land, and I don't believe that is a coincidence."

Caruun leaned back in his chair again with a grunt and waved his clawed hand dismissively at the news.

"Your suspicions are unfounded. Tuulcha was at Ever Clews to lead treacherous spirits into my world after the battle. That is the natural order, as you well know. Where was that bastard daughter, Mivraa?" He smugly asked.

"As I recall, your little daughter's scheming among the humans led to that battle. I suggest you discuss this with Mivraa since you have her acting like your little spy for the humans.

"You leave my daughter out of this," Duwdamon snapped back at Caruun. "We use the best of the human spirits among the sky gods. Unlike you, we see an advantage to those souls even with unforgotten powers. Mivraa's rule of Haligulf meets the bargain of the Great War of Kamin Realm."

"My half-human offspring are useful for taking orders, much like the human breed," the netherworld god scoffed. "They are so unworthy of being a god that even your wife, Unis, doesn't accept Mivraa. Your sons don't recognize her any more than I."

"You forget your manners, Caruun," Duwdamon growled ominously. "Another word about my family, and I'll be happy to call you out. Such insults require a death match in front of the other gods. I'll remove your head and send your foul spirit to join the Guardians in the Void."

The underworld god hesitated at the threat. While he was

as powerful as Duwdamon in many ways, Caruun could never be sure who might win. Now was not the time to call out his brother god before the others.

"You have my regrets for the unintended insult. We should not be fighting, you and me." He changed his tone quickly. "You know I've always held the highest respect for you. Have I not always stated that the gods should always be allies?"

Duwdamon remained stoic at the soothing words.

"As long as the realms stay in balance, we will continue to be allies," he told him. "You may not like it, but you must remember we need the human realm unless you prefer the Great Void?"

Caruun now stood up to look down at the Sky God. Ignoring the challenge, he smoothed his robe.

"Is there anything else you wish to discuss? If not, I would like to get back to the duties of my realm, which I enjoy so much."

Duwdamon stood while his throne dissolved into the background.

"No, we're finished. You know the stakes. Remember my words, Caruun. Otherwise...." He turned and moved back to the entrance, raising his voice a little as he left. "Just remember my words, if you value your realm."

Caruun's ugly face grew fouler at the threat.

"Duwdamon, you are beginning to sound like you believe you control the Skool. It does not allow you to threaten my realm or the other gods. Don't fool yourself; we all abide by the rules following the Great War as far as it suits us."

The Sky God continued to glide back to the entrance, dismissing one of the Vanths who attempted to guide him back out into the lower world tunnel. Caruun turned and followed the bloodstone steps behind his throne toward the darkness, which went into the depths. It was a path that calmed his rage at the sky god's words.

"You know you are playing with fire; the sky god will not let this go. He has too much to lose; more than even you." A female voice purred into the antechamber from the shadows beyond the doorway.

"Alrpan, I see you are spying again. I assume you heard all the conversation." He continued past her. "Rest assured, my wife; I can handle Duwdamon."

The vulture face scowled at his wife in her beautiful human form, thinking about her remarks. She knew he hated her taking the human form around him. Alrpan enjoyed the annoyance.

She moved into the light, her white face and dark raven hair, combined with a very human body, stood out in stark contrast to her husband's quasi-human form. Partially covered in a black fur shawl draped over her shoulders and a long blue tunic, which flowed over the rest of her body, she moved into the light. The underworld goddess liked her excursions into the other two realms. Often, her travels tested the patience of the other deities when she used the abyss monsters in the human world. In her mind, the human was a toy for seduction or torture, even mutilation for her pleasure.

"Do you think that you can stand up against the Triad?" She laughed lightly at his answer, knowing how it would irritate him. "We both know that the sky gods will never agree to take over the human realm. They love tranquility."

"You would think that would be true. However, you assume you know my plans, Alrpan. I'm the one who makes the decisions for this realm. I'm content to see the gods bicker among themselves as the chaos spreads. With the news of the Sibyl predicting the Skool returning to the humans, they will eventually see my way."

"Of course, my husband," the goddess spoke without conviction as she followed him.

"I have suspicions that Mivraa must be causing the Triad, more issues than we know. That's not unexpected given her parentage," Caruun sniffed with the full superiority of a god. "Since I did not send Tuulcha to the Cahmais lands, I know you are involved." He stopped and turned to his wife.

"The Fates saw Uugor in the underworld. Duwdamon's son would not come into my realm without an invitation. I should ask him the reason for his presence." The dark god watched her reaction.

Alrpan knew it was better to stay quiet at this point. She let Caruun continue to work through his ideas. He would soon ask her opinion and accept her words as his own to wreck the human world again. As expected, the question came.

"What do you think?"

"I think such a god from the Sky Realm would be a good ally to have. Any split among the children of Duwdamon would be useful to your cause," she explained. "He cannot keep the realms together without the Triad. If you continue to create divisions among them, your grand plan might come to pass."

He gave her a grotesque smile as he thought about her words.

"That is the reason I keep you around, Alrpan. You give wise counsel for this realm," he quipped.

"I thought it was my powers that you admired so." The goddess smiled back in a tone of sickly sweetness.

"True, but don't mistake my good humor for acceptance of your fun among gods and humans. You may dally among the realms to seek your pleasure, but you will not forget who the master is here," he warned. He watched her face change to a familiar blank expression when she hid her intentions. It confirmed she made a bargain with Uugor.

"The sky god has given me some interesting ideas. In fact, as I think about it further, your lust will serve my needs."

The underworld god's voice cracked a bit as he spoke, giving a sinister echo in the cave. He walked away.

Alrpan continued to stare at Caruun until his form dissolved into the darkness. She gave a soft, amused laugh as she disappeared back through the doorway.

Then, I will continue to have Uugor under my control, my foolish husband.

Shield of Skool

Chapter 3: Through the Forest

After entering the vast Mythroloy forest, the two Esterblud warriors moved quickly. Following a trail that shuttled back and forth, they traveled deep into the densely wooded overgrowth. Their ossanes handled the main trail with experience but hesitated when their new owners guided them along the narrow trail. Oslaf recognized that *duelills*, timid four-legged leaf eater about half the size of an ossane, created the path. The creatures avoided humans who frequently hunted them. It was the thought of duelill meat that suddenly got Oslaf's stomach growling. He hoped they might find one on the way since their flesh made excellent jerky, perfect for this type of travel.

Urith kept a quick pace, trying to ensure they didn't run into roadblocks. By using their trails, the Esterblud riders bypassed small farms that cut into the forest. Locals would turn into bandits when word got out about the strangers crossing their lands.

The green foliage of ancient trees rose high above them, leaving only a few areas of spindly new trees trying to reach up beyond large, decaying trunks and limbs on the ground around them. A few leagues into the forest, the pair followed a trail down into a small valley where they found a creek with good water. Stopping to fill the nearly empty water bag found on one of the mounts, Urith used the time to their advantage. Using the spring water, he cleaned the clotted wound in Oslaf's back, causing it to reopen. He covered the wound with dried sphagnum moss that he found near the stream. Urith asked about the young warrior's ribs. Oslaf told him it hurt some, but the chainmail, which they fixed tightly around his body seemed to dampen the pain. The younger warrior joked that he wished the chainmail had done more to stop the spear. His uncle replied with a laugh that sounded more like a grunt.

Oslaf told him he had seen *Gobmait* bees swarming on a

broken tree trunk downstream.

"Good job," said Urith. "We can use the honey to help your wound, and we'll use it for food as well." He noticed the brief expression of pride in his nephew's face. Urith suppressed a grin. Oslaf was trying to make up for his mistakes earlier. He moved the young man's leather belt higher to cover the wound that he protected with moss.

"Our path leads upstream. I'll take the ossanes over to get the honeycomb," Urith told him. "That should confuse anyone trying to track us. I want you to find dry smoke moss for fire tinder along the bank. Just remember to keep your ossanes in the stream until I return."

Urith led the animals over to the open trunk that held the honey. He made sure to ride on the soft ground where their tracks appeared to be heading toward the Esterblud lands. Jumping off his mount, he quickly climbed the dead limbs to the honeycomb. He was just above the smaller trees surrounding the area. After a brief scan of the area, he turned his attention on the honey. Carefully, he moved toward a dark hole about the size of his head. Happily, he observed the calm black and red bees crawling out of their nest before flying off to their next target. Reaching into the dark hole slowly, he caused a few bees to attack the rough linen canvas covering his arm. Fortunately, none of their stingers pushed through his sleeve while he pulled out the dripping comb. He placed it into a leather bag which he attached to his belt.

Movement in the distance caught his attention, and Urith stared at an animal moving slowly along the trail they came from. It was hard to see in the dense foliage, but he caught glimpses of the ossane with its rider. The Esterblud leader scrambled down the tree and went back to the mounts. Urith led the ossanes into the stream, traveling back to where Oslaf worked. He nodded to the young fighter when he rode up. Oslaf was finishing gathering water in the water bags.

"This stream will do nicely. It has a sand bottom, so if we take our time, we shouldn't leave a trail for any scouts," Urith said. "My view wasn't much from that low tree, so we'll follow where this stream leads and find a spot to camp for the night. Hopefully, we can bypass villages and towns in this area."

Urith dug his heels into the flank of his mount, leading off with the other in tow. Oslaf struggled as he got on the brown ossane he won in their battle. It took a couple of painful tries before he was able to throw his leg over the saddle. Catching his breath from the soreness, the young warrior spurred his mount and soon caught up with his uncle. Looking down at the water streaming behind them, he was satisfied they were covering their tracks.

In the distance, he thought he saw someone in the shadow of a tree, near the top of the valley. He checked again, but he could no longer see the figure. Oslaf stopped his animal momentarily. He scanned the trees, but nothing was in view. Spurring his mount forward, he wondered about telling Urith. He casually glanced over his right shoulder again. He saw nothing unusual in the landscape.

No, I'll wait. It might just be my imagination.

The pair quietly guided their mounts in the twisting stream, slowly continuing to head south and east. After taking so many turns, Oslaf eventually gave up trying to keep his sense of direction. The stream was too narrow for him to pull near enough to Urith to whisper. Besides, he was having trouble keeping his focus. His ribs felt each step of his mount's movement. He remained content to rely on his mentor and kept his ossane close behind his uncle. Oslaf continued to look back on occasion but saw nothing that would indicate someone followed them. Still, he could feel eyes watching them. He kept observing Urith, trying to determine if his uncle noticed anything behind them. The warrior rode erect in his saddle, only occasionally looking up at the sun and at the hundreds of trees near them to get his bearings. From time to time, the Esterblud would look back at Oslaf, making sure he was keeping up. They continued their journey, not really paying attention to the slight upward slope of the land. The Kamin sun struggled to penetrate the dense forest overhead.

His understanding of their route reminded him of his warrior training over the past few seasons with his uncle. Traveling through lands of Esterblud with Urith had developed his abilities as a fighter and traveler. His mentor was fierce and unforgiving at times. However, Oslaf continued to learn and develop his skills. Pehnuwick, his father, would be proud.

The thought of his father reminded him that Pehnuwick was in Regiussa on the other side of the Maflow Sea. Like so many times before, Urith carried the duty to keep Oslaf under his wing. During the many seasons of training and fighting with his uncle, the young warrior became a surrogate for Urith's dead son. He intended to be the same honorable fighter as his uncle. Oslaf understood Urith's ways as a loner, coupled with a dry, biting sense of humor that went along with his violent temper. Few knew the Esterblud leader as well as his nephew.

After the long day of following the meandering stream, the travelers came to an outcropping of striped stone extending from the ground. The formation created a natural stair-step waterfall that flowed down to meet them. Both riders came to a stop, scanning the ground for some way to get by the obstacle. After his ossane slipped, Oslaf realized the rocks under the rushing water were covered in green slime-like moss. Small trees and dark bushes lined the top of the outcropping and down each side. No sure route existed around the waterfall. Urith put his finger to his lips for silence and let himself down from his animal into knee-deep water. He handed the reins to Oslaf, and then carefully walked across the slippery rock, coming to a dry ridge just out of the water. Urith stepped out of the water, looking over the terrain, then he climbed up a waist-high ledge. Scrambling up over the edge, the warrior disappeared through the blue flowering brush.

Suddenly, Oslaf forgot his pain and fatigue as he sensed someone was watching him. The sound of running water overpowered the noise of the forest. He guided his ossane around carefully while keeping a close eye on the shadows in the dense undergrowth along the ridge nearby. In the mottled shadows behind a tree, he spotted a form, a small silhouette. Casually, Oslaf turned his head while keeping the focus on the shadow. After a moment, he saw the form move enough to confirm his suspicions. The sunlight suddenly brightened an area near the tree, showing the person's black cloth in the dark foliage.

The young warrior heard something behind him. Above him, Urith pushed his way through the brush at the spot he entered. He gave the boy a quick whistle, motioning him to come on as he jumped down to the bottom ridge. The young Esterblud hesitated, steeling himself for the oncoming pain, and then pulled his leg over and let his feet slide down into the water. Carefully, he led the mounts to the edge of the stream.

"I found us a trail that runs up to the top," said Urith over the sound of water as Oslaf came up. "But you will need to help me get the ossanes up on those outcroppings and through the brush. Can you do it? The sun will be setting soon."

Oslaf guessed Urith must have noticed his exhausted expression. He gave a weak smile, taking a shallow breath.

"By the gods, I'll carry the ossane that doesn't want to come along."

"You'll be a *Geniht* before you know it." Urith took his reins from Oslaf.

The pair led the animals out of the water and onto the first ridge with little effort as the animal seemed to be happy to be out of the water after the extra effort to keep moving upstream. At the next outcropping they encountered, Oslaf's ossane reared back, unsure of how to get the small jump it needed to make it up. After calming the animal, they coax the mount up to the ridge, and the spare mount followed up. The ossanes pushed through a crevice in the brush.

Urith pressed himself through the brush again led the team upwards through the steep trail. Animals forged the path, leaving their telltale signs of clumps of fur on the limbs of the thorny bushes.

After a grueling journey to reach the near-vertical top, they came over the ridge. The men stood next to the stream, which flowed wide, meandering across the flatland in front of them. From the ridgeline to the plains ahead, the forest suddenly thinned to grassland. They had just reached the highland plains of Horgynys, which led toward the Mythroloy mountains. Ahead of them lay an extensive open meadow of blue and green, which extended far into the horizon of ashy mountains.

The sun was nearly setting behind the mountain range in front of them, leaving long shadows behind the mounted warriors. They pulled themselves back up on their mounts and began heading toward a line of trees to the south.

"Just up to the ridge-line where we can make camp," he said. "From that vantage point, we can watch over the plains below for any of our Aberffraw friends who may be following."

The weariness lifted as Oslaf heard the news and showed his surprise. It also reminded him of the dark shadow that was following them. Oslaf pulled up his ossane to the side of his mentor as they trotted along.

"Urith, I'm sorry, but I should have told you back at the falls. I spotted someone following us. I couldn't get a good look, but I thought I saw the same shadow back when we pulled off the trail and up the rocks." Oslaf kept his voice down just in case their voices would be carried in the wind.

"Don't condemn yourself. I noticed the person before when I was in the tree getting the honey," Urith whispered. "I should have mentioned it before. It was a good catch by you. They are keeping their distance. But I'm sure it's not a scouting party. It's only one rider."

"What do you mean?" Oslaf asked.

"Well, I'm confident that our Aberffraw friends aren't following us. They would have cut us off sooner. I think Lyncus and his friends went the other way at the stream where we got the honey. Our shadow friend must have seen our tunics and is curious. Once we're near a village, the person will be a threat."

While Oslaf thought about the day's events, he grinned at the mental image of the enemy warriors heading the wrong way.

"What do we do? Kill him?" He glanced over his shoulder.

"No, I don't think we have much to worry about for the moment," Urith reassured him. "They are too far away to get reinforcements quickly. I think we might just let them come to us. Remember, it's sometimes better to wait and let things play out."

Urith pulled a water bag from his saddle, handing it to Oslaf.

"Here, have a drink to take off the hunger a bit. We will run a cold camp tonight, so there will be only a honeycomb for dinner," he explained. "I noticed one of the bags you picked up on the spare mounts had Aberffraw wine. It must have come from Lyncus. I guess this might be part of his payment to locals, as well. While not as good as heathmead, it will help you sleep."

After their drinks, the pair rode out the grasslands and up a nearby ridge. They entered a small depression surrounded by a sparse line of trees. The land beyond them extended steeply up into the desolate mountain peaks. The skald's stories claimed the Mythroloy range was home to the underworld gods. Deep below the surface in the bowels of the rock, the unfortunate dead were part of Caruun's realm.

"This is a good spot to see who's following us," Oslaf spoke up as if reading his mentor's thoughts.

Urith just nodded. The two men stopped the animals near a rock outcropping behind the trees where the ossanes could rest and feed. Urith swung off his mount and walked back up to the crest. He peered down at the plains below as the sun was setting, and spotted the lone figure moving slowly along the stream. In the distance, he watched the person inspecting the ground. He sensed whoever followed them was having difficulty. The black-robed figure turned the white ossane toward their hiding place for a while, then hesitate. Finally, their tracker turned their mount around and galloped away toward a small stand of trees near a bend of the stream.

"Looks like our friend will be bedding down for the night," said Oslaf. He fought to stay awake as the shadows lengthened over the water.

"Yes, and it appears the person will remain alone, which is a good sign for us," Urith agreed. "Now, let's make camp for ourselves."

After the pair had shared a quick meal of honeycomb washed down with Aberffraw wine, Urith had Oslaf lay face down on a Vulthnal wool blanket that was among the supplies on the ossanes they took from the Aberffraw. He looked over the wound, taking comfort in the fact the jagged injury was no longer bleeding. The older warrior took some of the remaining honey at the bottom of the bag and spread it over the wound. Urith told the young fighter to lay there and rest while he pulled the saddles and blankets from the ossanes. After he had finished, the giant warrior was able to settle down to watch the sun as it set behind the horizon. He looked out over the plains while he drank some of the wine from the leather bladder.

With the night enveloping them, Urith instantly noticed the single campfire in the distance. The person following them was making sure that any nearby human predators would undoubtedly follow that light. At first, he wondered if the figure was attempting to distract them. Perhaps another group would sneak up during the night. He dismissed the thought.

No, I'd see if another group was following us from here. Besides, they're making too many mistakes.

"Inexperienced and unafraid, that is not a good combination," he said under his breath.

Looking over at Oslaf, who was asleep, he was happy to see him resting. With luck, his nephew would recover from his wounds quickly.

He turned back to watch over the plains as the last rays of the sun disappeared, and the sky above filled with stars. He saw the faint outline of a small herd of duelill as they silently moved along the ridge. Nothing else moved in the distance. Above him, he saw the constellations of Palaphylax and Dame-Apis. The Esterbluds used those stars to navigate across the Maflow Sea.

Urith wanted to sleep so badly. The delayed effects of the deadly storm that nearly killed him and the day's battle pressed over him like a blanket. Every muscle ached. Even though he felt somewhat safe in their elevated perch, the warrior decided to stand watch over the area. After getting up, he grabbed a wool blanket. It smelled of ossane. Urith went over to the outcropping of rock. He removed his spear from the belt behind his back, laid it near his side, and pulled his sword across his lap. He threw the blanket over his back and got comfortable against the boulder as he tried to forget about the stink. Taking another long look up at the sky, he let his eyes close.

I'm a light sleeper.

Urith quickly drifted off to sleep, where he spent his time talking to his dead wife and child.

Below Urith, in the trees along the stream, a small figure huddled in front of the fire. The person was covered with a black robe and a full hood covering the head, obscuring the face in shadow. Sitting with crossed legs, the small figure stared at the flames of the campfire. The flames gave off a red and yellow color inside the hollowed out and rotting trunk of a twisted lellowtere tree. A soft moan escaped from the person as the upper body slowly began to move in a rhythmic side-to-side motion. The sound of the groans caused the nearby ossane to whiny from fear. It pulled on its reins which were tethered to a massive log. After a few moments, the motion from the figure stopped. Suddenly, the figure pitched face forward, ending up in an uncomfortable sprawl across their crossed legs. The hood over the head slowly moved while the figure came out of a stupor. The figure sat up into an upright position, and the hood fell away, revealing a young woman's face. In the firelight, her lovely round eyes cast around the camp in bewilderment at what just occurred. There was a hint of freckles on her cheeks and slightly upturned nose, which gave the girl a natural air of superiority. Her straw-colored hair cut short, just above the shoulders, the woman remained in a slight daze from her self-induced trance. Shivering in spite of the heat given off by the fire, she tugged at the blanket she sat on. She pulled the woolen garment over her shoulder, thinking about the visions.

"We are not exactly done," said a familiar voice behind her.

The young woman twisted around to see a female visitor standing by a tethered mount, lightly patting the animal's long face between its bulging eyes and twin horns.

"Yes, we are," the girl replied defiantly. She shivering now came from fear.

At first glance, the visitor looked to be of the same age as the blonde girl, but the long-haired female's demeanor was cold. The visitor was elegantly dressed in a long flowing white tunic that strategically exposed her striking figure. She was a picture of sophistication, from the raven hair down to her small feet, wrapped in golden sandals. To the men of Kamin, the visitor was a vision of sex and lust.

"It is rather rude to leave one of my visions," said the netherworld goddess as she directed her attention back to the young girl.

"Why to do come to me, Alrpan? I've done your bidding, and now I've lost the trail with no place to go," the girl explained.

The god turned to her and smiled. It was an unsympathetic smile.

"No, as normal you do not understand. You will begin the next phase of your journey soon. You will become part of the group you follow. You are a female, and they will accept you because they don't consider you a threat," the voice of the goddess whispered in her ears.

"However, you seem to forget who I am. I'll decide when you leave my visions. Remember, it is not necessary that you understand, just to follow my visions for you," said Alrpan cryptically.

Rising to her feet, the girl came to the goddess. She was not used to being ordered about, and her face showed the resentment.

"Listen, I've done as you wanted. I have followed the trail you laid out and your vision tonight showed me nothing useful. Besides, my overlord led those men to me. He has shown me much more than you have so why should I follow your whims?"

"I'm not pleased with your tone," Alrpan nodded her head. Instantly, visions of fire and pain struck the woman as if her reality suddenly changed. She fell to her knees in torment. Her mind filled with images that she was tied to a limb above a smoking fire, experiencing the horrifying sensation of being cooked alive. She began choking from smoke and heat in her face. The sensations enveloping her sent her into twisting convulsions, unable to shout or scream. The goddess nodded again, releasing the girl from an illusion so real the girl choked from phantom smoke. She scrambled to her knees and searched her clothes for the fire.

"When we next meet, you will address me with respect, my pretty little human," said the goddess who watched her with amusement. "Since you are young and inexperienced, I will forgive you this time. However, do not expect such mercy again." The soothing tone from the goddess of the underworld gave way to an ominous warning.

"I have special delights for those who betray me. Perhaps I'll bring you into my realm alive as my personal slave. Or better yet, I might give you to the *beorhs* for their pleasure. You may have heard about how much they enjoy abusing and defiling the living."

Alrpan stepped into the twisted tree, and her form faded like a ghost entering the wood. She became transparent.

"Unfortunately, such personal slaves don't last long...." Her humorless laugh hung in the still night air.

Tears welled up in the girl's eyes as she tried to calm herself. Her shoulders sagged as she remained on her knees. The woman knew she needed help, but her earlier pleas to her overlord had met a stony face. Instead, Satres informed her that she needed to grow up and use her abilities to help herself. She remembered his words.

"One cannot aspire to greatness by crying in the arms of your master." Satres was not a sympathetic person, and his words reinforced this view.

Alrpan and Satres pulled her deeper into something she did not understand while leaving the woman with no choice other than to obey. She shivered again, thinking about the threat while she prayed to the other gods.

I just ask for a dreamless sleep.

The woman pulled the blanket around her again. She rolled over to her side, staring into the darkness beyond the firelight.

The woman heard the yapping of the *kuons*, a fierce four-legged predator, nearly the size of a human. The predator ran in packs throughout the backcountry of the highlands. While too far away to be of immediate danger, the sound from the night stalkers reminded her of the many other dangers in her journey. Eventually, the sounds faded away and the day's long travel soon caught up with her. The blonde woman fell asleep.

~~~

Alrpan's passage back into the underworld took a detour
~~~

to a single twisted lellowtere tree overlooking a crippled ship. The mangled bodies of the Esterblud sailors and warriors rolled in the surf. Stripped of all clothing and armor by local scavengers, the bodies would soon be stripped of their flesh by the sea creatures.

The underworld goddess expected to see Tuulcha gathering the spirits of the dead wandering around the site of the disaster. Instead, she found Mivraa nearby. She despised the half-human, bastard child of Duwdamon. Alrpan believed her unworthy of status as a goddess of Haligulf. Also, it was Mivraa who stole the greatest of the human spirits, leading them to the Sky Realm. For a moment, Alrpan watched the demigoddess, trying to determine the reason for her presence. Then, she heard the wails of the dead behind beyond the ridge above her. She silently moved away.

The goddess walked to the top of the sandy ridge where the foul stench of the Vanth reached her. Tuulcha's smell, worse than the scent of rot and death, filled the air. She heard the wails again and turned in their direction. The Vanth led its collection of human spirits which appeared as long wisps of translucent smoke. While the spirits showed little human emotion, their weepy cries filled the winds. They recognized the nature of their journey but could not stop being herded to their wretched end. It was the spirits of shipwrecked Esterblud who shimmered and waves like smoke. Each would be condemned to the underworld since dying outside of battle was deemed unworthy of the Sky Realm.

"You wanting something, mistress?" Hissed the rat-faced Vanth as its black eyes expressed no surprise at her presence.

"Yes, I will need your services for a small job when you return. You need to find a place for several souls I have been told are coming into our realm. These spirits need to be buried deep and out of the way, where they cannot easily be easily found," she explained.

"What say master to this? He makes the decision to punishment." The Vanth expressed no opinion on the question, but the goddess knew what it was asking. Permission from Caruun was expected.

"You don't need to worry, Tuulcha. I'll make sure you bear no responsibility and suffer no retribution," the goddess assured him. "In fact, I'll make it worth your while. You can choose your reward, just name your price."

Stopping the souls with a quick snap of the powerful whip, the Vanth stared at Alrpan carefully considering her words. The creature knew the goddess wanted more *beorhs* to inflict upon the humans for her pleasure.

"I find a place," he said at last. "You let Tuulcha and Actita find living for our pleasure."

The creature's fangs showed white with its hateful smile, and the Vanth didn't wait for a reply as it snapped its cursed whip into the back the nearest spirit which shrieked. The rest of the ghostly figures lurched forward. Alrpan realized the deal was done, and it was a cheap price given. A few live humans would hardly be missed and was a small price to the please the Vanths. Like her, the rat-faced demigods enjoyed using humans as their chattel.

As she walked back to the ridge, Alrpan couldn't notice Mivraa paying close attention to her movements. Mivraa understood that Alrpan conversing with the Vanth would lead to trouble for her. It was bad enough to wrestle away deserving spirits from Tuulcha and Actita who gathered as many as possible for the underworld. Now, Alrpan was up to something. She rarely came in the areas of the wandering dead spirits. With a deep breath of resentment, Mivraa continued to observe the underworld goddess until she faded from sight. As Mivraa stepped into the darkness, she debated on telling her father about what she observed. With a frown, she decided it wasn't worth the effort. Duwdamon would disregard her concerns.

I'd be happy if Caruun ever decides to put a leash on his wife!

<p style="text-align:center">~~~</p>

It was not yet dawn when a dozing Urith heard the ossanes nervously snorting. He jerked awake, his Clovel Sword at the ready, looking around in the darkness.

He saw nothing. Immediately, he wondered if a black *bater* was trying to sneak into camp after the animals. The twin moons of Kamin were waning, lighting the landscape in a pale gray and black. When Urith peered down across the valley, he caught sight of shadows moving. In a line, gray reflections from their chainmail outlined the riders as they slowly led ossanes forward. The riders were following the same path the Esterbluds had traveled earlier. As he watched them, it became apparent the three riders were heading toward the sleeping place of his mysterious follower. The person's dying campfire embers were still seen through the trees.

Ambush!

Urith quickly stood up, starting toward his ossane. Suddenly, he stopped as he saw the sleeping Oslaf.

He quickly considered his options, wondering whether or not they should help, and decided Oslaf needed rest. Besides the person following them was not his responsibility. Since the riders had other prey on their minds.

Let them deal with the spy following us.

While their follower might have information, it was not enough of a reason to take on three enemy fighters. Let alone risk giving their location away to the Aberffraw enemy. Even from a distance, he could feel the menace in the men moving toward the camp where the sleeping figure remained hidden in the brush along the river's edge. However, he could see the outline of the person's ossane along the riverbank. It provided a perfect beacon guiding the predators to their prey.

In the dark, as he watched, Urith wondered why a person lacking the necessary skills of stealth and tracking would be attempting to keep up with two foreigners in the back-lands of Ynyover. He couldn't believe that the Sacred Overlord or Lyncus would send such a person. There were plenty of troops and local militia they might use. Perhaps it was someone who recognized the Esterblud longship and saw their fight against the comitatus. By following the strangers, the person might have thought they could collect on a bounty, which probably existed on the Esterbluds by now. As he took another deep breath to stop the sleep threatening to overcome him, the smell of the damp morning reminded him of the early mornings in his village of Cilgarran. His home village looked over similar broad grasslands.

As the night sky started to lighten, the figures stopped briefly in the lightening morning sky. Urith watched as they huddled. The red of the morning sun coming up in the western sky was about to break over the horizon. Then, he glanced down at Oslaf.

Too bad, but someone was about to learn a deadly lesson!

The young girl smelled the musky odor before she realized the danger, then strong hands grabbed her arms. Two men pinned the young woman down where she lay sleeping. Suddenly terrified and awake, she tried to kick out, but strong hands gripped both of her legs, pulling them apart. A *Gallaeci* bandit with a tattooed face ripped away her tunic after releasing one of her hands. In her frantic struggles, she saw another man with a tattooed face holding her legs. He laughed when his partner struggled to pull down her leather breeches.

The woman grabbed a small dagger from under her blanket to slash at the brute. However, her attacker caught her hand before it struck. The bandit pulled himself on top of her, pressing down with his weight while he squeezed her wrist. With a painful yell, she dropped the dagger. He laughed at her before he savagely slapped her face several times. Finally, she quit fighting him. He grabbed her dagger and tossed it to the side before he stripped her pants away.

The third member of the gang picked up the dagger. He briefly admired the exquisite decorations on the hilt. The man turned back to watch his partner mount the woman who no longer struggled. Her situation was hopeless. She could only pray to the gods that they would not kill her after they finished.

She looked away from the man thrusting into her. His tattooed face leered down, his drool falling on her breast. Suddenly he stopped when he heard one of his comrades cry out. It was instantly cut off.

Seizing the opportunity to push him away, the woman suddenly caught a silver flash out of the corner of her eye. She heard a deadly swishing sound as the tattooed face suddenly disappeared. Instantly, warm liquid splattered across her face, blinding her. She felt the full weight of her convulsing attacker fall on her. Letting out a gasping scream, the woman blindly tried to push off the dead weight on her. Then she heard a man's yell in the background suddenly cut short with sickening wheezing. On her left, she heard the sound of metal against metal followed by a death cry. A growling voice cursed loudly in Esterblud.

"I'll drink from their skulls, damn Vanth scunce."

The frightened woman froze, oblivious to the stinging of her eyes. She listened to the brief silence followed by heavy breathing near her as someone came close. Feeling the weight of the body abruptly lifted from her, the woman blindly slid away while trying to wipe her face with her hand. She listened to the footsteps moving away.

Frantically, the woman wiped her eyes trying to see who was around her. Hearing footsteps approaching from her right, the young woman instinctively tried to cover herself with her blanket she felt under her. Expecting another attack, her eyes started to clear, then she saw the leather leggings next to her. Expecting the worse, suddenly the woman caught a cold splash of water in the face. The stream choked her and caused her to turn over to her side coughing.

"Are you injured or just wanting to lay there for another man to finish this?" A gruff voice above her asked in the Aberffraw language.

Using her blanket to wipe her face, the young woman looked up again, blinking her eyes to focus on the strangers around her. A giant figure of a man came into focus above her, holding her water bag. His scarred grimace gave her the chills as he stood with his black helmet under his arm. She looked over at the other large warrior who stood a few feet away. His left foot placed on a dead body, he pulled his sword from his victim, and it made a sickening sound. A similar colored Esterblud tunic covered him. Still wearing his black battle helmet which covered his face, the man removed it. While he looked as young as her, she noticed that he moved gingerly.

"Do you understand us?" Oslaf asked her in another language he knew. His voice was a bit more sympathetic. He kept staring at her blood-covered naked body. They were the people she was following, and now she was at their mercy.

She flashed hate at his use of the vulgar dialect of the Gallaeci, who had just attacked her.

"How dare you speak to me in such a way?" She answered in proper Cahmais. She hastily retrieved her dagger from the corpse near her. Holding it in front over her, she assumed a defensive position.

"I'll cut you apart if you come toward me."

Urith refused to move. Instead, he looked her over while his expression turned to a sneer.

"Our little bloody bater has claws, it seems," he laughed.

She hesitated at the reaction. The woman realized how naked and vulnerable she appeared before them. They were clearly not intimidated by her actions. Swiftly pulling a blanket around her, the woman tripped over the debris littering the campsite. Oslaf stepped forward, reaching out to help when she snarled back at him.

"Out of my way, you peasant! I'm going to bathe this blood off me," she snarled while waving her dagger.

Instantly, Urith was on her. His large hand dug into her shoulder, and he placed his engraved sword near her throat. His strength forced her back down on her knees as he leaned over to face her. With his face still splattered with the enemy's blood, he made sure to use his snarling sneer to full effect. The woman's wide green eyes showed her panic.

"I don't have time for this, wench. You were spying on us. We just saved your hide," he said with emphasis on the last words.

You don't want us to finish you like your friends were doing," he paused as he glanced over at the headless body near her "Now, you will tell us what you are doing here and why you were following us."

"Don't hurt me," she stammered as she looked down trying to regain her composure. "Yes, I was following you, but it is not as you think." She glanced over at Oslaf, pleading to him with her eyes.

"I was lost and spotted your ossanes leaving the trail at the forest's edge. I planned on trying to meet with you this morning when this Gallaeci scum attacked me." She paused, hoping they would believe her lie.

Urith suppressed a laugh.

"You decided to follow strangers wearing the colors of Esterbluds in the wild country of Ynyover. And you were planning to meet with the two men you don't know." His sarcasm heavy, Urith glanced over to his nephew. "She's just a slave and a liar. That means we can bed her until she tells us what we need to know. That's more fun anyway."

"Please, don't." Her eyes widen at the thought. "I'm not a slave. I'll tell you anything."

"Then, start with the truth, wench." He said grimly. "Who are you? I know you are not a tracker, and your behavior might be that of a noble class."

"You're right. My name is Fedelm, and I'm from the house of Pataric. My family is protected by the Overlord of Ynyover," he stated, watching their reaction. "The overlord will make you regret touching me."

"You might notice your king is not here." She felt Urith loosen his grip slightly and pull back as he considered her family status. He turned to Oslaf, giving him a wink.

"Strange how the threat of a blade and the prospect of being ridden like a slave can bring out the honesty in some people."

Urith turned back to her with a death stare.

"You forgot to tell us why you are here."

"You are not from Cahmais, but you know the language or, at least, the vulgar dialect of it." Fedelm took charge of the conversation. "Why are two foreigners traveling through the highlands?"

Urith stood swiftly, causing Fedelm to fall back on the ground when he released her. Her deflection of his question caused him to grin. A brave woman, he decided, no matter how foolhardy she might be. He liked how she thought on her feet.

"You ask a lot of questions for someone who nearly met death. Why we are just simple Esterblud people, of course!" He smiled at his joke.

A brave woman, no matter how foolhardy she might be.

"Oslaf, we will collect anything of use from this trash," Urith stated as he turned away from Fedelm. He picked up a short sword and tossed it next to the woman. Oslaf hesitated as he watched her reaction. Her shock made him grin as he bent over the body next to him. He pulled the man's leather bag hanging from the belt.

Fedelm sat watching them for a moment, forgetting about the drying blood covering her naked body. The warrior's sudden focus on stripping the dead of any valuables left her confused. It was evident they no longer considered her to be even a minor threat or value to them.

Carefully watching them, she rose to her feet. When she walked over to the stream, the woman half expected them to suddenly charge after her. Afraid of slipping, she treaded carefully into the clear water. The water chilled her as she splashed the water, washing the drying blood away.

Fedelm thought about the warriors behind her and her next moves. She shivered at the thoughts running through her head, fearing what they might do to her now.

Maybe he wasn't joking about turning her into a slave?

Her protection from the overlord meant little for many tribes, especially in this backcountry. In this remote land, people with no protection might be captured for slavery. Moreover, she believed the tales she heard about the Esterbluds. She had no defense against whatever they intended for her. Feeling the rage and tears of helplessness well up in her eyes, she splashed her face again.

No, she decided, I have powerful allies who will help me. Their visions put her in this situation, and they would help her get out of it. She had to believe there was a plan guiding her. This idea calmed her as she looked over to see the Esterbluds rifling through the remains of the dead.

After finding nothing useful on the first body, Urith went over to the decapitated body of the leader. Reaching down, he found a bag on the dead man's belt. He opened the bag, finding it full of gold koinons.

"What have you got?" asked Oslaf walking up to him.

"It looks to be about twenty gold koinons," said Urith as much to himself as his nephew. "Not sure how this bunch got it, though. They're nothing but back-country bandits."

Oslaf was still staring at the gold. "Maybe they stole it from others?"

Both of them heard a gasp from behind as the girl saw the golden objects.

"Are these yours?" Urith asked. She shook her head, covering her cold body with a blanket she picked up. He watched her as she moved over to her ossane. Urith wondered why she seemed so surprised at the coins.

Fedelm reached into her leather bag lying by her saddle. She pulled out an elegant white cloth. Trying to avoid eye contact with Urith and Oslaf, she dropped the blanket and pulled the white cloth over her upper body.

"I should thank you for your help," Fedelm told them. "But I need to know something from you. What are you going to do with me?"

Oslaf appeared shocked by the question while Urith gave her his hideous grin again. An uncomfortable chill ran through her again.

"We will think about this," he said and then moved away. He waved his nephew to follow him. "Oslaf and I will need to discuss. Change your clothes but don't wander too far; it might be dangerous for you."

She hesitated at his apparent warning, then grew livid.

"Very well, I'll accept your invitation," she said with such a superior air of authority that Urith had to suppress a laugh. She turned away as the men glanced back.

"I don't think we can trust her," Oslaf whispered after several paces.

"I agree. But she is a danger either way. If we let her go, the Aberffraws will be around us before we know it," he replied. "I think she is playing a dangerous game. No doubt, she is here to spy on us, which means she saw our ship come against the reef. Or…" Urith considered something before shaking his head as he dismissed the thought.

No, it was impossible that someone could have known they would be on that shoreline.

"You know what I think of spies. My first thought is to slit her throat and leave her with the other corpses." Urith told Oslaf. He waited for a reaction.

"We can't do that. We don't kill the weak and innocent for no reason." Oslaf nearly raised his voice, looking petrified at the thought. Urith sighed in disappointment. He didn't like the fact that the young man was not yet at ease with making such a cold-blooded decision when necessary.

Then again, his nephew was following the code of Heptarc, and it's four values of justice, vengeance, truth, and honor. The outburst gave him pause.

"She is no innocent. We admitted to working for Satres," Urith reminded him. He glanced back at the female putting on her clothes. "You honor my training by remembering the Heptarc code. Perhaps it is wiser to keep her alive and learn what her game is."

"Then, we should let her live and keep a close eye on her. I think she might be worth something to us," said Oslaf. Urith could tell the young man was happy with the decision.

"Yes, I think it's the best for now. Remember what the *satgerts* say about keeping our enemies closer than our friends, so we might know their tricks," he agreed. "Now, let's see how your wound is doing, Urith said, slowly turning the young warrior around to look at the wound on his back.

While keeping one eye on their new traveling companion, Urith examined Oslaf's wound. He was pleased to see that the cut flesh continued clotting up, with just light bleeding from the exertion of the recent fight. He also began appraising Oslaf's skill during the fight. Urith reviewed how the fighter took care of Fedelm's attackers with a swift and powerful blow to the head with his sword. Finishing off the opponent by striking him just under the leather breastplate, the deadly efficient sword work gave Urith a sense of pride. He grudgingly praised Oslaf for his work.

"Your skill showed but don't forget these bandits were not real warriors," he grumbled. "Simple leather armor and short swords are not the same as breastplates and chainmail."

Oslaf smiled anyway, realizing his uncle would not shower him with approval. Esterbluds continually practiced for battle, learning from a young age the necessary skills for a range of weapons.

"How are you holding up?" Urith asked. "You moved like an old lady at times."

Oslaf grinned at his mentor's sarcasm, knowing his uncle was a harsh taskmaster. "I'm still sore in the ribs and my back burns like *Phlege* fire, but I will make it. The rest did me some good."

He nodded toward the bodies nearby. "I didn't find anything on the other body. It's odd; they are not heavily armed, but recently paid in gold."

"It doesn't make sense. They could have gotten better

armor and weapons with that many koinons," Oslaf pointed out.

"I agree," Urith lowered his voice again, turning his nephew toward him. "That leads me to believe they were sent to this spot to deal with her. However, keep it to yourself since we do not know what game is being played here. Only a powerful lord like Satres or Lyncus could afford to spread koinons like that. Anyway, we'll go forward with our plan."

Returning to his normal speaking voice, he continued. "Let's gather up the ossanes as some compensation from our battle this morning. We won't get rich enough to become warlords, but we might have enough barter to get back to our homeland."

Suddenly the young woman appeared before them. She had changed her clothing and now wore long boots of leather that reached her knees, and the white tunic that hung down over finely woven breeches. The tunic was mostly wet clinging to her with long sleeves that came down tight to the wrists. The lower part of the tunic and the borders of the sleeves were trimmed with finely embroidered and beaded bands of red. A leather band encircled the tunic just above her hips.

Nearly dropping the ossane reins he was holding, Oslaf stared at her, the most beautiful woman he had seen. Urith noticed the style of the garments gave away her status. In his mind, there was no doubt she was in a position that provided wealth.

"We will continue on our journey, and you can thank Oslaf that your life has been spared, for I had other ideas," Urith informed her when she looked at him. He paused, thinking she would say something, but she stayed quiet.

"Despite the tales you have heard, you will have nothing to worry about from us now."

The girl looked at him coldly. It irritated that she was not in a position to put him in his place over the tone he used. Rather than argue with him, Fedelm stepped past him toward her mount.

"Shall we go?" she asked, acting very much as her noble status.

Urith turned to a large black ossane he had chosen as his new mount. "Oslaf, you take those animals and meet us where we discussed. While those Gallaeci scum were no warriors, they did know their animals."

The giant Esterblud pulled himself up on the mount, not paying attention to the girl who kept glaring at him. He waited for the girl and his nephew to climbed on their mounts. Urith had spoken with Oslaf as they traveled to battle the bandits. He planned on scouting the area ahead of them. Oslaf agreed to retrieve their remaining ossanes from their hiding spot in the grove. The young man would pack their gear and supplies. Then, he would meet Urith at a line of yellow birken trees near the other side of the plains, near the start of the foothills.

Urith watched his young friend heading off to their sleeping area and wheeled his mount upstream with Fedelm following along. He recognized the girl feared him, so he kept her with him. The warrior hoped she might reveal the truth since she was obviously uncomfortable around the warrior. Also, he had noticed Oslaf's evident fascination with the girl, and he believed it best to keep such temptations away from him for the moment.

The odd pair rode the nearby trail as it wound into the heart of the plains. The hazy outline of the Mythroloy range, which ran between Esterblud and Cahmais, could be seen on their left. Ynyover sat just inside the Cahmais border, hemmed in along the coast. It reminded Urith of the heavy dependence the Sacred Overlord and his people faced when dealing with the Aberffraw king for food. Urith decided to circle back around Ynyover and follow the border until they reached the port of Grimma, very near the Citadel.

From his memory of the maps and the stories told to him by the king's skalds, Urith was able to envision the path he would take through the highlands. However, he knew nothing specific about the distance, nor any landmarks that would guide him into the upper reaches. He also had no knowledge of the mountain passes they would need to traverse to reach the Citadel of Br-Ynys.

"Why are we going this way together?" Fedelm's question brought Urith out of his thoughts.

"I have my reasons. Don't worry; Oslaf will be coming along for a while," he looked back at her. "Why, do you have something to say?" He figured that his question would irritate her, and he smiled to himself when he saw her lovely face sour. She didn't respond.

The pair traveled on as the sun reached its zenith, conversing only on occasion. While they rode, Urith formulated several plans in his head and rejected them almost immediately. He realized he needed allies, but few Esterbluds were known to be in Ynyover. He grew tired of the constant beat of the ossane's hoofs. Urith decided to see where a conversation with Fedelm might go.

"Since we are riding together you should know that we are heading to the lowland city of Grimma, on the other side of those mountains," he explained. "You know we were stranded after our shipwreck upon the coastline back in the Cahmais Magna Bay, and this seems to be the best route while avoiding your friends along the way." It was a partially true statement meant to get the conversation going. It worked.

"Since you know my name, let me ask yours," Fedelm said after a pause.

"I'm known as Urith," said the warrior quietly.

"And Oslaf?" she asked, looking again at the giant next to her. She was suspicious of him, but she relaxed her guard a little now. For the time being, at least, she believed he would not harm her. He seemed to follow the pagan Esterblud code which her overlord had told her about. She recalled his words regarding the Esterbluds and their savageness against enemies, their disrespect for the gods, and their distrust of the hakra, as the prophets were known. What she had observed so far vindicated the words of Satres.

"He is the son of my brother, Pehnuwick, and becoming near as good of a warrior," added Urith. Fedelm heard the pride in his words.

"How does an Esterblud know of the lands through Cahmais and Ynyover to get to Grimma?"

"I've been in this land before. Plus I listen to my enemies' stories," he told her before turning the tables. "How did you end up alone on the highlands along the borders? Don't bother telling me that story from before. Even Oslaf didn't believe it, and he knows nothing of the lies told by women."

Fedelm fought her initial urge to lash out at his comments regarding her trustworthiness. Already branded with suspicion by the nonbelievers because of her abilities as a hakra, she knew warriors held little regard for a woman within the kingdoms of Kamin. She realized he must have a history in Ynyover to know about the area. She instantly realized that getting information from him could be useful to help her cause. Fedelm recognized he would not trust her, regardless of the story she told. In the end, she decided half-truths would be the best solution.

"I recognized your sword. It was described by the skalds who sang of an Esterblud called the Clovel Destroyer," she said while looking at the distant fields of yellow *grambel* grass. He grunted his agreement at his identity.

"I observed your battle with the Aberffraw and comitatus. I was too far away to see much, but I know you, along with your nephew, killed the six riders."

Urith interrupted. "That is only partially correct. An Aberffraw noble led the local militia, and they attacked us. Even the evilest Esterblud warrior would not attack strangers washed up on a shoreline by the gods. And locals in my land would never follow an outsider into battle. That means they were paid just like the Gallaeci who attacked you. The people of this kingdom no longer support the Treaty of Necropa. They have no honor."

She glanced at him.

"Well, that may be, but when you passed my way, I decided to keep a watch on you. At first, I thought you would return to Esterblud, but then I noticed you turning toward the west and back into the lands of Ynyover. I know that you are not simply lost here since it would make more sense to return home. You must have a reason for this path."

"You are correct. However, your loyalties are not ours, are they?" Urith paused a bit before redirecting the topic of the conversation to her.

"Your accent is not of the Aberffraw, and I noticed your clothes are too fine for most in the kingdom," he told her. "And, you wear the scarlet colors of the House of the Sacred Overlord. So where do you come from?"

"My family lived in the village of Ffestini. It is in the land of Eernicia near the coast," she shifted in the saddle as the ride wore on. "Just after I was born, our family was sent to Ynyover as part of the restoration of the Necropa."

"That means your family played a role in restoring the Sacred Overlord. You must come from a noble family of Eernicia."

"Yes, my father is Caestia, record keeper to Satres," she explained.

"Then, your real master is the Overlord of Ynyover?"

"I have no master!" she replied hotly, then caught herself at the statement. "Well, yes, it is true; he is our overlord in these lands. But the Majireef sent me to follow you." Her green eyes flashed at him, and he almost smiled at the reaction. He liked her fire. Plus, he realized his assessment of her was correct, she was telling him only so much.

"How would they know to send you to the location of my shipwreck?" He appeared puzzled by her statement.

Fedelm stared at him a moment as she considered her words.

"The gods speak with the Majireef. In fact, in many ways, they are the supreme hakra," she explained. "The Majireef visions knew of your arrival several days ago. It was foretold by the gods, and your trip was known before you left." She emphasized this knowledge to Urith.

"This council of hakras can foretell my fate? I don't accept such things," he scoffed. "It makes no sense in what you say. The gods have no time for the humans, especially not a shipwreck upon the beach of Ynyover."

Fedelm just kicked lightly at the mount's flanks, spurring it forward to come parallel to him. "The council did not know of your shipwreck, but you will be surprised how much the gods know and intercede, especially when they see a threat," she told him flatly.

Puzzled, Urith looked at her.

"Well, I'm not familiar with the Majireef, but for a few rumors. This must be a recent development." He nudged his ossane back onto the trail as it balked, wanting to go into the grass for a meal.

"I thought you said you traveled to Ynyover before? If so, you would know they were around long before the Restoration of the Necropa," the young girl told him.

"Perhaps this is because it is not common knowledge. No one in Esterblud seems to know about this group. As you know, we're not truly welcome by the Overlord."

"What do you mean?" the girl replied defensively. "The overlord and Majireef welcome all believers, even Esterblud."

"Then, tell me about the Esterblud family who resides there? The last one left many seasons ago because we don't follow the Sacred Overlord's dictates," Urith pointed out.

The girl fumed but said nothing since he was correct about the lack of Esterbluds in the Citadel. In fact, these two men were the first she could remember meeting in her many seasons there.

"It appears you have been sheltered for many *draenyna* among the same group of people. Such a sheltered life can lead you to believe things which others may not," Urith observed. "My guess is you must be connected to other powerful families within Ynyover."

Fedelm was about to respond with a biting comment until she thought about the truth behind his words. As a little girl, she dreamed of leaving the Citadel and traveling among the kingdoms of the world, only to be warned by her father of the dangers within the other lands.

Urith took her silence as agreement with him. If she carried Eernicia royal blood, he knew their beliefs about the gods were much different from his Esterblud faith. In his limited knowledge of Eernicians, he was aware that their *satgerts* spoke against the continued warfare among humans. With such beliefs, their people considered themselves the great diplomats of the Kamin lands. He knew about some of them who were considered highly spiritual people, greatly concerned with achieving oneness with the gods of the Sky Realm.

To Urith is was the simple fact that those from Eernicia lacked the warrior spirit. Their lands were rugged, and their farms poor. Living in such place meant they were traders and they had little history of invading tribes. The Eernicians never saw Aberffraw destroy their villages and towns. That was something he knew too well.

However, Fedelm's thoughts intrigued him. He pressed to learn more about her.

"It appears our ossanes will be ready for a break soon," he said. Getting no response, he continued. "I have seen much in my time, but I have yet to see a god, or an overlord for that matter, worry about an individual human. Even in a battle, demigods like the Vanths come to collect the spirits of the dead only after the fight. Gods never come to aid during the battle. It is against the code of the realms."

"You may not know as much as you think," she replied. There was a smugness that irritated him because she could be right despite his Esterblud beliefs.

"I know this much," he declared. "You were sent to travel alone in these borderland areas filled with bands of outlaws and foreigners. That means you are not well served by your father or your overlord. Your visions didn't help you this morning as you found. Remember, it was Esterbluds who saved you, not your friends or the gods."

Her smugness disappeared when Fedelm considered his words. He was correct. Her dreams did not foretell the attack on her. Moreover, Alrpan had not said anything the night before. She now wondered if that was by design as retribution for doubting the goddess of the underworld. If so, she questioned why she should be trusting in Alrpan.

"Who are you really working for?" Urith noticed her expression and hoped to learn more about her.

Her response was not what he expected as the woman looked down and he heard her softly say, "I told you the truth. I followed a vision that sent me to you. It showed me your dead crew on the beach. That is why I saw you fighting those men near your ship."

Urith reined back his mount at that comment, bringing the pair to a stop.

"Wait a minute. You said the council didn't know of my ship floundering. Who sent that vision to you?"

"I'm not sure, but the gods and others know of your journey," she said cryptically. "They are against you."

She spurred her ossane forward again as the warrior sped up with her. He realized he did not fully understand the extent of those who might be involved. He was in a foreign land with enemies all around him, and now he is told they apparently knew of his plans.

But what did they know?

His simple mission was fast becoming far too involved to be only guided by chance. This knowledge caused him to rethink his plan. He decided they would need to keep her with them for a while as her vision might keep them alive.

"Very well, I understand you must remain loyal to your lord," he said. "Can you tell us what you are tasked with now that you have met us?"

Fedelm gave him a strange look, unsure how far to trust him. "I was only to follow you. Meeting you was a..." she stumbled to find the word, "accident."

Urith heard the doubt in her voice. "And?" he asked.

"I don't know," she lied. "I was just to follow you to the first village and report back. Nothing was shown to me beyond that."

"It appears there are flaws in your visions. For instance, those Gallaeci weren't playing with you for your fun. I would think you are smart enough to guess someone considers you expendable. And it appears your powers of foresight failed to see this." Urith went silent. He decided to let her reflect on his words, making sure she knew how isolated she really was.

The warrior glanced behind to see if anyone was near, but he saw nothing in the plains behind them. He hoped his nephew was not having any problems, but he considered this part of his learning as a warrior.

After a while, Urith turned to Fedelm.

"My guess is we will get to the large river bend near the end of the day," he explained. "Oslaf will meet us there. He will be bringing along the rest of the animals we collected."

"Then what?" she asked.

"When we get to a spot to camp, the ossanes will need water and rest. Then we can discuss how we shall proceed," he said as he slowed his ossane. She slowed to keep pace.

"We've said many things today. We both know only some of it was true. For you to stay alive, you must remember one thing. While Oslaf may not have the stomach for it, I will slit your throat if you bring any danger to him or our mission," the warrior growled out.

"From now on, you will need to convince me how useful you are to our needs."

There was a cruel hardness in his eyes that emphasized his meaning before he spurred his mount forward. He galloped forward through the grasslands.

Fedelm slowly followed behind. She was suddenly

concerned about what the Esterblud might do that evening. She had overheard the young warrior's support of keeping her alive. However, Urith's threat was real, and her protectors were not in sight. Now she prayed to her gods that they would let her see the light of the next morning.

Chapter 4: The Remnants of Dreams

The pair stopped at a shaded spot near the water's edge where Urith tied off the mounts. Fedelm, tired from the long hours of travel, was thankful she no longer had to ride the ossane. She stood watching Urith unpack the ossanes. The woman could not help but notice the gentle voice he used on the animals was very different from when he talked with human company. It was strange seeing him stroke the black mount on the neck as she remembered his killing of its Ynyover owner. She regarded this warrior in front of her as a bit of an enigma. It appeared his vicious nature could be turned on and off as he pleased. He could show compassion that did not fit the concept she had of Esterbluds. The stories she had heard within the walls of the Citadel told of savages who killed with little provocation. Still, Fedelm remained uneasy. She knew he did not believe the answers she had given to his questions. Nevertheless, Fedelm could not blame him for doubting her answers. She was not a skilled liar, and she had growing doubts about what she was doing.

While Urith worked, Fedelm decided to go through the bags, putting together their meager food rations which consisted of a few biscuits the Esterbluds had scrounged from the dead comitatus along with a bit of the honeycomb that remained. She noticed the warrior had given the bulk of his food to his nephew. She went over to her ossane and pulled off a bag which held her own food, adding them to the mix. Fedelm noticed the Esterblud glancing at her covertly.

Yes, I could poison you. Now is not the time. I'll wait until you make the first move.

She gave him a scowl when he looked her way, but his expression remained stoic. His gray eyes seemed to read her mind, and it bothered her that he might somehow know her thoughts. She briefly wondered if he had the power of vision, then dismissed the thought.

No, he is a warrior. Smarter than some maybe, but he's not a hakra.

When he finished caring for the ossanes, the warrior found a shady spot under a couple of trees where he sat to watch over the area. The hot Kamin sun had broken through the late afternoon clouds, streaming shafts of gleaming light over the eastern sky. Fedelm offered some of the food to Urith, who declined. At first, she suspected he believe the food was poisoned. Then, she realized he was thinking about the young warrior he left behind. He had little interest in her now.

As the afternoon wore on, it remained uneventful. However, Fedelm remained wary of him. She jumped when he suddenly scrambled to his feet. He paid her no attention as he began to walk around the area. The warrior took wide laps around their resting place as he surveyed the open plains.

It was late, near dusk when Oslaf finally arrived. Urith noticed the lone rider leading the line of ossanes on one of his watchful sweeps. He returned to the trees.

"Well, here he comes to help now," Urith stated suddenly with friendly sarcasm.

Fedelm looked up to the distant sound of plodding hoof-beats which mixed with the song of a bird above them. As she watched Oslaf leading the captured animals, Fedelm noticed he was still quite pale. His face showed worry as well. He pulled to a stop in front of them, glancing at her, and then looking to Urith.

"Sorry, I'm late. I got the feeling something was following me, so I took a longer route back up through the mounds. I came down through a ravine full of trees and shrubs." The young warrior proudly smiled. "I took so many twists and turns that I almost got myself lost. I'm pretty sure nobody was following me when I came out to the flatlands and got over to the river."

"I see no one following Sing, so you did a good job. Step down and have something to eat." Urith said. "While you eat, we will discuss our path to Grimma. Then, we will try to get a few more leagues in before the stars are out."

Oslaf nodded and slid down to the soft ground. He recognized that the open plains left them very exposed to their enemies. He led the ossanes to the stream to quench their thirst. Leaning down stiffly, he joined the animals at the water's edge after tying the animals to a tree.

When he finished, Oslaf knocked the dust from his long tunic while walking toward Urith. He noticed Fedelm watching him. She smiled at him when he approached.

"Would you like some of the dried *Kilishi*? It will fill your stomach better than those dry biscuits," she told him.

Oslaf, surprised at the woman's generosity, took the smoked fish flesh. Urith gave his nephew a wink of approval. The young warrior sat across from Urith and gobbled his food down. Fedelm observed the ill-mannered way these Esterbluds ate their food as well as their general lack of cleanliness. The warriors seldom washed, but for wiping off the blood after their fights or mending their wounds. At times, it was nauseating to stand downwind from them.

"Well, while Fedelm serves you Oslaf, I'll take some for myself," Urith said with a sneering smile. Fedelm glared at him when he reached into the girl's bag to retrieve a couple of *Kilishi* pieces for himself. He leaned back against a log, watching her closely.

"Alright Fedelm, you are still useful to us. We need some answers," he told her. "I'm unsure exactly how we get to Grimma from here. I've observed at least three major trails which go off in different directions. What route do we take?"

Fedelm blinked at his words, glancing over to Oslaf, who waited for her answer.

"I think—I mean, I know the way," she replied carefully. Fedelm pointed out the well-used trail on her right. "If we follow that path over to that ridge, we will go into the Ranloff Mire where the Great Circle lies. It will lead us to the main road. From there, we would go into the city of Ynys; Grimma is on the other side of the harbor."

"What do you think Oslaf?" Urith asked.

His nephew was visibly surprised at the question, as he usually just followed Urith's lead. He was not often asked for advice, and it pleased him to be involved.

"I'm not sure," he admitted. "We have little information about the highlands. It's not a good idea to travel blind in this country. I guess we have to trust her. I believe she is telling the truth."

Urith rubbed at the stubble of his beard.

"Your reasoning is sound," he agreed. "However, she might be leading us to a trap."

"No, I don't think so, unless she wants to die with us." Oslaf glanced over at Fedelm.

"Well stated," Urith declared. "We will have to trust her. But..." The warrior looked directly at Fedelm again. "We can only trust you so far. For your sake, I hope you remember that."

"I'm not lying to you," She stared back at him. "You have to believe me that it is in my interest to get you to the Citadel of Br-Ynys. My route will get you and Oslaf there as soon as possible. By going through the forest, it will provide cover in case we come upon any other travelers. I thought that would be important to you."

Urith just nodded as he finished the last bit of food. He rose and went to his ossane. Oslaf walked with Fedelm to their mounts. Soon, the travelers were following the path to higher ground in the direction of Ranloff Mire. As he led the way, Urith hoped they would be able to get over the distant ridge to make camp before it became too dark to travel.

The next morning, the sun was just peaking over the western horizon when Fedelm woke with a start. First, she wondered where she was and then she gave quick thanks to the gods for her life. She looked around to see Urith crouched at the fire as he added some wood. He was watching her when she woke, and she must have looked panicked for a moment, as he gave her a sneering grin and rose to his feet. He walked toward her, taking a bit of delight in her widening eyes when he passed by her on the way to the nearby stream to fill their water bags. He knew she expected some violence from him, and he enjoyed keeping her off balance.

Deciding to let his wounded nephew get some extra rest, Urith told Fedelm they would not be leaving until later that morning. The pair did not speak for a long time after that. They were lost in their own thoughts as they watched the sunrise. It was an awkward silence as each desired to know the thoughts of the other. However, their suspicions clouded much of their thinking.

Urith tried to focus his mind on the map to Grimma, a town on the outskirts of the Citadel. His memory of their outdated map was all he would have to go on. Urith recognized the danger grew for them as they traveled deeper in the wild areas ahead. The last he knew, hostile tribes of Gallaeci controlled a large part of this region. He knew Satres used bribes to get information about areas he could not directly control.

For her part, Fedelm kept wondering how far to trust the Esterblud warriors. The young Oslaf looked at her in such a way that she knew he would be receptive to her attention. He was a good target for her to understand more about why they still traveled to the Citadel. However, she certainly did not comprehend the one called Urith. It was unmistakable he could be vicious, and he did not trust her. Most certainly, he would kill her if needed. On the other hand, she recognized his keen instincts about people. He showed the ability to sense the struggles inside others along with something she might almost mistake for fatherly pride toward Oslaf.

Her senses also picked up on something buried deep inside him. She suspected a deep sorrow was masked by his warrior confidence. The mystery strangely intrigued her. Fedelm decided there was more inside this foreigner than she saw inside many of those of the genteel class she knew at the Citadel. Those men around the Sacred Overlord were intent upon finding their opportunities for a proper marriage to advance within the nobility world of their lands. Her father's status was not sufficiently elevated to give a man a chance to greater power and influence which many desired. Instead, Fedelm learned at an early age, such men sought her as a mistress, not a wife. In the end, only Satres made such decisions within her world.

It was not long after Oslaf woke when Urith picked up his bedroll and walked over to the ossanes that grazed on the grass, whipping their long, bushy tails at the flies attracted to their foul smell.

"Bring along the bags and blankets," Urith ordered them. "It's time to get moving."

The Esterblud leader didn't bother to glance back because he surmised Fedelm was staring at him bitterly for ordering her around. Oslaf noticed the glare and grinned while helped her gather their items. As he handed her a blanket from the ground, he told her not to get upset.

"He is used to being in charge," Oslaf said. Urith is a great warrior and protective of his family. I'm the only one left aside from my father." He paused. "However, he is not easy to know."

She turned to him after tying off the blanket, her eyes flashing at him, "I can see that. Your uncle is known in our tales of the Esterbluds. We are aware of the Clovel Sword he carries. However, I'm never sure I can believe all that you have told me. The Cahmais skalds who come into the Citadel say your people are vicious and bloody, destroying everything in your path. You roast Cahmais prisoners over open pits while raping their women."

The young warrior gave her an incredulous look. "Then the Cahmais and their skalds are liars who preach to the fools who believe it. Did you see us attack the Cahmais and their allies at the beach? No! But they attacked shipwreck survivors. What will your lying skalds to say about this?"

He went on. "As for you, did we rape and enslave you after we killed your attackers? How many of these Cahmais you seem to hold so dear would follow such a code?" He stuffed the last of the food items into a saddlebag, jamming it down forcefully at each word.

"It's always the same with Aberffraw lies. They always blame others for their own weakness and treachery."

"Why would they lie? Fedelm asked.

"Why do you think? You do not even know the history of our land. When the Cahmais promised a treaty with us, only to attack us, our King sent them back like whipped *kuon* pups. Urith killed many of those miserable curs when they attacked our village from the sea. The skalds of our kingdom still sing of this, but it seems you only know of the Aberffraw lies. Esterbluds only fight when attacked," he looked up at her with his blue eyes furious at the insult to his people. He didn't catch her softened expression.

"Perhaps, this may be true," she conceded grudgingly. "I've never gone beyond the lands of the overlord since I arrived as a child. I've traveled between the many villages with my father who recorded legends for the Sacred Overlord. This land remembers your people as well."

"Yes, my overlord invaded this land," the warrior agreed, starting to calm down. "It was in response to the Cahmais raids."

"Your uncle seems to have traveled the world," she changed the subject to keep him talking.

"That is true. Our king, for some of the most important duties, calls upon him. I've overheard my overlord tell his advisers that Urith is the most honorable warrior he knows," Oslaf said proudly.

"And he can be as vicious as I've ever seen," replied Fedelm.

"Well, Urith is not a *Geniht* without reason," agreed Oslaf. "The men of the king's guard are the best and most fearless of our lands. He is like a *brokko* with a bone. He will never give up, trying to kill you until his last breath."

With a smug smile, Fedelm thought about this image of

Urith. She had to agree it was an apt description. The *brokko* was a mean forest animal that feasted on small animals and berries. It also stank like carrion. She suddenly realized Oslaf's words had given her, at least, a minor clue about the Esterblud mission.

"I can also see he likes to toy with people, to get their reactions. He reminds me of someone else I know."

"Yes, he does that," he agreed, turning to her. "Who do you know that is he like that?"

Fedelm shook her head. "Never mind, it doesn't matter. Let's get the ossanes. Even with our late start, I believe we can make good progress today."

The sun was past its zenith, and the shadows were getting longer when the trio came to the forest. In front of them were ancient yan-yew and bluewood trees with their overhang of limbs arched above, providing a natural entrance. Patches of green forest-grass grew along the path in areas where the sun streamed through. Low, thick bunches of sweet-smelling locus brush were spread across the shadowed areas they traveled.

The trio learned a little more about each other as they traveled, engaging in periodic conversations. Their primary focus remained on their journey, and the rhythmic sound of the mounts hooves lulled them into silence as they continued along the hard-packed trail. Usually, Fedelm loved watching the green and green-blue foliage sparkle with the interplay of wind and sun. Instead, her mind was on her mission.

The Esterbluds saved her, but to what ends, she wondered? It bothered her that the visions were so vague, lacking the clarity she had known since childhood. Only Alrpan's guidance was clear the night after she met the Esterbluds. During the last few nights, nothing more came to her. Her brief dreams only gave her doubts.

As they rode, she turned her focus on keeping the speed of the riders slow by appearing to be unsure of the directions and paths. She took them deeper into the forest, and the road they traveled grew narrower until it was nothing more than a duelill trail.

"I found it interesting that you know this country so well but lived in the Citadel. Why is that?" Urith suddenly asked.

"As I was growing up, my family brought the work of the council to the village *satgerts*. It was a great honor, given by the Overlord. As part of his work, my father collected the stories of gods and heroes from the local villages. We took many trips throughout Ynyover." There was pride in her explanation.

"However, it's been a while since we've ridden the countryside. This route seems to have changed since I was last through the Ranloff Mire," she lied.

Urith appeared to accept her explanation. He went quiet, his head nodding as if he was trying to catch a bit of sleep. Both Fedelm and Oslaf glanced at each other with grins, guessing the warrior was tired from his late night watch. They both failed to notice Urith covertly watching their looks and movements. He noticed their ossanes were moving slower. It was just a trivial thing and, at first, he wondered if he was mistaken until he heard the explanation from the girl. Her story seemed a little too perfect to him.

"How much longer until we reach a place to camp?" Oslaf asked.

"Not long," she assured him. "I remembered there was a spot not far ahead; a clearing shaped in a circle called Yns Cearcal. It is a place where the skalds and hakras commune with the spirits." Fedelm's nod indicated a place to the north. Green foliage on either side of the trail hid anything beyond their winding path.

"Soon we will come to a rise in this trail, and after that, we will find our camp area," she explained.

Oslaf nodded and appeared ready to say something to her, but then decided against it. They rode on in uncomfortable silence, each wondering what the other was thinking. After a while, they reached a steeply sloping rise. The ossane's grunted at the effort, but they finally broke into the open area. Fedelm reined them to a stop as the men looked over the amazing sight.

"Welcome to Yns Cearcal, the Great Circle," she exclaimed while sweeping her arms out in a grand gesture.

"We have entered Ynyover's circle of the sacred," she told them. "My father tells me that locals will never come to this area without a *satgert* to give them guidance with the gods. It is a holy place used only during the festivals."

As the Esterblud warriors looked around them, their minds slowly grasped what their eyes beheld. They could understand why locals feared it. The trio was on the edge of a giant ring, hollowed out in the middle of the forest. Beyond the scale of the clearing, they were struck by how perfectly round the area was. Just a few furlongs across, it was enclosed; surrounded by a wall of thick trees and brush, but for the single entrance into the area. It appeared that the forest stopped as if an invisible wall held out the foliage. Urith looked down the line of branches and leaves extending into the distance. He realized the limbs and grasses along the way were not cut. They had just stopped growing at the invisible barrier. Even the grass below him appeared to stop at an extremely precise height barely above the hoofs of the ossanes.

"It must be a circle of the gods," exclaimed Oslaf as he looked around like a child during the Gailcca festivals.

"The local *satgerts* and hakra from all the lands come here to give offerings and seek the wisdom of the gods," she told them, her eyes lit up with excitement. "Look around you at the doorway to the realms of the gods. Over there, in the center is the black alter to make your offering to the gods."

The men turned their gaze to the altar, strangely drawn to the starkness in the middle of the field. Urith felt a sudden dislike for the place while Oslaf appeared mesmerized by the view in front of him. Even from a distance, the large rectangular black stone shined like a polished blade in the setting sun. From the size and type of stone, they guessed only the gods could have brought it to this place.

"We should go there now as we have not made any offerings to the gods on this trip," Fedelm stated. She turned her mount to lead the way.

"No! We must move on," Urith hurried his ossane to block her path. His face revealed his distaste at the idea. "This place is not for us. Your gift can wait until the temples of a town."

His mount reared back suddenly, its eyes wide with fear. At the same time, the other mounts began to panic, snorts and whinnying sounds came from the animals as they pulled at their reins, trying to turn away from the open field. The animals heaved and stamped, trying to break from their restraining reins. In growing panic, each creature struggled to exit the circle of the gods.

As he fought to keep himself on his mount, Urith glimpsed a shadowy form standing near the block of stone. His mount circled, its long neck coming around to bite at the warrior's leg. Urith pulled hard on the opposite leather rein, and the ossane came back around. When he looked at the altar again, the figure was no longer there.

Oslaf was having the most difficult time trying to keep the other four animals trailing him from bolting. Fedelm moved into position next to the animals behind Oslaf. She started whistling softly and chanting a song. The soothing sounds began to distract the ossane's. As Fedelm's comforting noise took effect, the terrified animals began to relax; the struggling soon ceased. The frightened whinnying noises turned into nervous snorts. Oslaf and Urith's mounts quieted as well. The men looked at Fedelm with the surprised recognition that she had far more experience and skill at handling the animals than they imagined.

"What happened?" asked Oslaf.

"I don't know. I've never had this happen before. This is a peaceful area." Fedelm replied, her face showing her shock at the animal's reaction. Urith's expression darkened at her words.

"We're leaving," he ordered. "I'm not losing valuable ossanes in this forsaken place."

Turning his mount around, Urith did not wait for them to agree. He spurred his beast back through the opening to the trail. His companions quickly followed him.

Surprised at the warrior's reaction, Fedelm was sorely disappointed. Her instructions never gave her an alternative away from the gateway. She began to wonder if this great Esterblud leader was not as courageous as the skalds claimed. Even so, the sudden change in their path gave her doubt about the visions given to her.

As he followed the woman, Oslaf noticed she was deep in thought. While he was surprised by Urith's quick departure, he suspected his uncle must have a reason. Urith had experiences with the gateways to the realms after his wife died. However, his uncle seldom spoke of them except in passing. Oslaf's father told him once that Urith learned his disgust of the gods and their ways from a gateway in Regiussa. Whatever happened in the circle, he knew to trust Urith's instincts.

The group took a trail to the east, and they quickly rode away from the circle. Fedelm told them they were on the path to Grimma as she pulled next to Urith. The man just glanced over with the same dark expression. She tried to ask when they would stop, but he ignored her. Fedelm let her mount fall back to ride next to Oslaf. The young warrior looked over and shook his head.

"He'll not speak for a while," he told her softly. He recognized his uncle had no intention of explaining. Something was bothering him. When his uncle grew moody, it meant trouble was near them.

Urith paid no attention to his comrades. He continued to focus on the figure he saw at the black altar in the gateway. The brief look at the hazy image appeared somewhat familiar. It nagged at him, but he kept thinking he might have imaged it as well. However, his instincts and feelings remained acute, and they told him the trio was being followed as they hurried along the trail. When they left the Great Circle, Urith had felt like they were being watched. There was nothing in the forest around them to confirm his feeling. Still, many seasons of experience led the warrior to trust his instincts.

As the shadows grew dark along the path, they came upon a small clearing that was near a small creek. The animal tracks along the muddy bank showed Urith a potential hunting spot to replenish their low food supplies.

"Here," Urith finally spoke as he led them into the area. After he had climbed down from his mount, the man took the reins of the spare animals from Oslaf and tied them off near the creek along with his mount.

"It will be dark soon. You two make camp while I scout the area," Urith told them. He quickly turned and walked off into the forest as they watched him go.

Fedelm looked at Oslaf for a moment, unsure at the change in the older warrior. They could tell from his cold manner that something was bothering him. The young Esterblud slid down from his mount, and he remained quiet. Fedelm pulled a blanket from her mount and laid it out while Oslaf tended to the other ossanes, removing the supplies and saddles.

"Like you said, a hard man to understand," the girl declared finally to the silent warrior. Oslaf stopped and looked where Urith was last seen, then went back to removing a pack.

"I think he saw something back in that ring that he doesn't like."

"What do you mean?" Fedelm wondered how much Oslaf saw.

"Did you not feel it while we were there?" he glanced at her. "I could feel eyes were watching us while the mounts were spooked." He turned back to empty the bags as if to help him focus.

"No, I didn't feel anything, really. I think something in the wind just spooked the animals," she lied as Oslaf stopped and turned to her.

"You know if you are being hunted by something you cannot see. It's the way of the dark ones of the underworld that we have fought before," Oslaf said. "That's what if felt like in the circle. I've only felt that way once before during my travels with Urith."

"Where was this?" she asked.

"I'll tell you about it later. But I will say that if he felt this, he will not be back for a while," Oslaf told her.

"How do you know that?"

"He left his shield and spear," he nodded with a glance to Urith's mount. "He is now on the hunt for something in the trees. He must expect it to be coming in close to us after dark. I suspect he is planning an ambush and we're the bait."

Fedelm looked around, suddenly unhappy at the situation. She did not know what could be out there. While she had an idea of what Urith spotted near the altar, it was not the same where they camped. She felt the tension now, and she would be listening to every sound.

Urith traveled in a wide circle around their camp. In the last of the light, he spotted a couple of *feorags* tussling, their bushy tails sweeping back and forth, as they argued over a nut. Too bad they couldn't stay for another day, he thought. A snare trap or two would give them more food for the journey.

The sunlight quick fell from the sky, and the forest grew ominously dark. The warrior moved quietly, carefully taking in all of the sounds and shadows. Starting below the camp near the trail, he took a broad and irregular walk around the area. Urith came through the thin line of trees until the brush thickened. Eventually, he reached the thin creek that ran down by their camp where he stopped for a quick drink of the cold water. While he was squatting at the water's edge, he heard movement in the brush ahead. Urith quickly ducked low among the dark corners of dense foliage near him.

Drawing his longsword silently from his belt, he slid the blade of his sword into the leather baudrik strap on his back for silent, but quick retrieval. Then he waited to see what direction the noise was moving toward. After a moment, he heard a slight rustling coming toward him, then it stopped, and he could tell at least two people were near. Skillfully creeping through the brush the ambushers slowly passed by his position. From his vantage point, he could see the top of worn leather boots about an arm's length away. His muscles strained as he waited. However, he recognized that he had no advantage against the strangers. His movement would be instantly heard. Urith knew he must wait for his opportunity to develop.

The boots turned away from him, carefully moving in the direction of Oslaf and Fedelm. Urith pushed forward to see two dark shadows of armed men in the dim light still available. As they made their way through the brush, he could make out their dark green, long tunics and leather pants, which blended into the brush. Then, he noticed a flicker of white from feather fletching from the arrows hanging on their belts. The men had their sturdy hathrow bows strung over their shoulders. Their heads covered by a brown leather bowl helmet with a thick protective leather flap in the back, which hung down over their shoulders, a trademark sign for these assassins. Urith recognized they were *Fealharan* or death creepers.

His rage grew. These feared men specialized in assassination using either bow or knife to kill as quietly as possible. To someone who honored the warrior code, these Fealharan were nothing more than highly paid scum. Urith continued to watch them as they moved away.

Why are they searching for us?

Urith kept his crouch, quietly following them and using the brush as camouflage. The pair carefully approached the camp where his companions prepared food. Soon Urith heard Oslaf's voice, and he smelled the wood smoke from the campfire. The assassins followed the sounds to a spot just outside of the firelight. One of the killers took up a position from behind a pair of tall, pale green sawhorst bushes. The second man moved off to the right as Urith silently closed in. He watched him climb a short tree to observe the camp while remaining out of sight. Urith drifted closer to the assassin in the tree. He assumed that the figures in green would wait until the moons dropped before striking at those in the encampment. Then, he saw them pull their bows over their heads.

He quietly pulled his long *Sgian* dagger from his waist belt and crept forward. He paused when the figure in the tree looked around, seeming to sense his presence. The camouflage of the tall brush grass around which mixed with the dark shadows provided him with the perfect cover. Urith held his breath for a moment; the figure turned back to stare down at the camp below.

The forest sounds increased around him as night crept along with the warrior to the figure sitting in the tree. He liked how the noise of the *cruicads* filled the air as the insect's sound dampened rustling noise made by his movement in the underbrush. With rapid progress, Urith closed in behind the figure in the tree. The assassin drew back his bow as Urith stepped from behind the tree. With practiced skill, the Esterblud flung his dagger at the man with a smooth swing of his hand. The well-balanced knife made no sound as it traveled the short distance to embed into the assassin's throat. With a throttled groan, the man grabbed at the dagger before toppling down to the ground near Urith's feet.

Thrashing about, the dying man struggled to remove the weapon. Urith fell upon his victim and grabbed the man by his head. Brutally twisting, he heard and felt the neck snap. Glancing at the face of the dead man, Urith pulled out his bloody dagger. The man was young, not much older than Oslaf. Urith felt no pity as he stuffed his weapon back into his belt. He quickly returned to the confines of the dense brush heading toward the other Fealharan.

Fortunately, the sound of the first man's death had been

masked by the forest sounds. Urith drew close, only a few strides away from the man in green. However, when he looked up over the brush, the assassin caught sight of him. Urith leaped forward just as the green-cloaked figure turned. The enemy tried to move to the side, but Urith was too fast. He caught the figure behind the knees with a kick. Both of them fell backward, with Urith partially landing on the assassin. They hit the ground together. Urith felt the heavy punch to his belly, which almost knocked the wind from him. The two men scrambled to get an advantage in their deadly struggle. Urith quickly found his enemy was heavily muscled with large arms that locked onto the Esterblud warrior trying to pin him down. As they thrashed, rolling across the hard-packed dirt, he felt the assassin trying to reach for his knife. Urith hammered his forehead into the man's face while grabbing his Sgian dagger. Despite the head butt, the enemy grasped onto Urith's knife hand, keeping him from pushing the long blade into the assassin's body. The man tried digging his fingers into Urith's eyes. He turned his head slightly and bit down on the assassin's hand. He heard the man cry out as his teeth dug into the bone of the hand. Urith tasted the blood while his enemy tried to pull his hand away. The Esterblud turned his dagger blade toward the man, and then he rolled over on top of his opponent. Using his weight to push the stiletto through the thick coat, Urith forced the blade into the man's belly.

The assassin frantically arched up, attempting to throw the warrior off. However, Urith held the upper hand, and he viciously twisted the blade. He watched the eyes of the enemy grow wide with pain and fear at knowing his death was near. As the assassin weakened, the warrior suddenly pulled out the knife, then slammed his dagger into the man's chest between his ribs. The blade went into the lungs, and the assassin gasped. The man gave one last weak struggle to get the Esterblud off of him. Urith held him tightly and watched the man's brown eyes staring at him. There was no longer light in the eyes, only a blank look of death.

Urith lifted himself up and pulled the dagger from the body Spitting out the blood in his mouth, Urith was breathing heavily from the bloody struggle. Wiping the blade clean on the dead man's clothes, Urith tried to make sense of the assassin's presence. The skilled Fealharan were expensive, therefore usually reserved for the assassinations of high-ranking officials. These experienced killers knew who they wanted. That meant someone was seeking the death of the Esterbluds or Fedelm.

Maybe it was all of us they intended to kill?

Urith stood over the body for a while, catching his breath. A shipwreck and local warriors waiting for them, a spy who was nearly killed by those she should be able to trust, and now they had assassins after them. Nothing made sense to the Esterblud. He understood overlord intrigue and warfare. However, Urith and Oslaf were nothing more than warriors on a simple mission to speak with the Sacred Overlord. His king's mission was not critical enough for these dead men to ambush them.

Then, he remembered Fedelm's statement about the gods and the council knowing Urith and his men were traveling to Ynyover before their shipwreck. While he dismissed the idea at first, now he wasn't so sure.

Before he was able to think about it further, Urith heard movement behind him near the trail and quickly realized other assassins might be coming. He crouched down and moved silently back into the bushes nearby, intending to circle around on the person coming toward him. Light footsteps approached while the warrior remained hidden in the shadows. Near the spot where he killed the first assassin, he heard a light whistle. Then, Urith thought he overheard a quiet conversation.

As he was about to move toward the noise, he heard the sound of footsteps coming directly toward him. It appeared that more than one assassin was still around. A figure soon appeared, slowly moving along the path. The hooded form carried no weapons that he could see when the person walked by the hidden Urith. The dim light revealed this person had a black cloak that reached their knees, partially covering long, leather boots. The fabric of the cape was darker than the deepest night with a type of unusual sheen. Going directly to the dead assassin's body, the mysterious person silently knelt over the body. Seeing his opportunity, he moved quickly and quietly along the path. Coming up behind the kneeling figure, he quickly wrapped his large arm around the stranger's neck. A light curse rose at the sight of his dagger placed at the hooded figure's face.

"How could a man sneak up on me? I should have smelled you a mile away," a female voice said, then cursed again. The figure's hood fell away when he locked his arm tight, revealing the woman's long dark red hair. The next instant, the woman grabbed his arm. With an unbelievable amount of strength, she used her body for leverage and threw him over her shoulder like he was a small boy.

Urith landed awkwardly on his butt a short distance away, dropping his dagger and rolling over to watch in disbelief as the woman gathered herself and gracefully stood with a long silver spear in hand. Urith pulled his Clovel Sword from behind his back as he scrambled to his feet. While the woman knelt before the body, there had been no indication that she was armed. Now, as if by magic, she held a weapon and her hazel eyes wild with excitement. The Esterblud could not shake the feeling he knew this woman as they slowly circled in their attack positions. Each looked for an advantage over their foe.

"You would not be wise to fight me, human. Mivraa does not lose to humans!" she declared.

Before Urith was the demigoddess, who presided over Haligulf, the Hollowed Hall of the Slain. The front of her shawl had fallen away to reveal a powerful woman, her chest and torso covered by a gleaming breastplate of the golden armor. Now, instead of boots, her legs were protected by striking leather leggings covered over in thin plates of the same gold armor. She pointed the silver spear at him. He could only guess it was made of a type of crystal only known to the gods. The weapon had an unusually long two-sided spearhead she could use for thrusting or cutting in combat. He had heard about her deadly fighting skills. However, there was a reason for him to test her mettle.

"You are not the first god I've seen." Urith gave a mocking laugh. "It is known that I don't fear the gods alive or dead. If you are Mivraa, then I will gain much by defeating you." He slowly slid to his right, watching her mirror his movement. The warrior smiled his sneer smile.

"Taking a half-god will spread my reputation far beyond the Maflow Sea," he explained with more confidence than he felt as he watched her smooth motion.

"You dare challenge me!" Mivraa stated as she attacked him, her silver spear aimed at his heart. With practiced skill, the Esterblud slapped the spear away with his sword and pointed his sword at her throat. However, his parry missed its target as she swiftly moved aside. The woman countered with a powerful strike on his wrist with her spear handle, nearly knocking his sword from his hand.

Urith backed away. Mivraa was an expert fighter, and he was fortunate to have avoided the twin blades of her weapon. The demi-goddess initiated the next move with a quick stab of her spear. Urith avoided the initial thrust, but Mivraa followed through by sharply swinging her spear, striking him in the shoulder. The contact was painful as the tip slightly penetrated his chainmail armor. He felt the blood flowing down his arm.

Backing away again, he studied her moves, realizing how her anger might be used to his advantage. Given another sneer smile, he lowered his sword.

"You know, I expected better for a goddess," he mocked her.

Fury filled her face as she instantly went after him. Urith

feinted to his right, then pulled aside as her spear nearly rammed into his middle. As she passed close to him, he capitalized on his opportunity by bringing up the blade of his longsword toward her throat. When she tried to counter his move using her spear shaft to strike at his body, Urith was close enough to grab her long hair from behind with his other hand. He wrenched her head back while he twisted his body around. His foot struck her behind one knee as he pressed her down from behind which caused her to drop to both knees.

Surprised by his quick move, Mivraa tried to turn back at him. Urith pressed his engraved sword blade hard against her exposed white neck.

"Shall I continue?" Urith asked. "The head of a beautiful goddess on my belt might make a great trophy."

Mivraa glared at him with the hazel eyes that reminded him of a black *bater*, a wildcat-like predator. However, she knew even a god could not withstand a sword stroke severing the head.

"No, I'll submit to you for the moment. You have won this match, human." Her voice was low, animal-like. "I might have seen your move coming. You show great skill by exploiting an enemy's weakness."

She stared up at him proudly. There was no trace of fear in her face, only the same excitement in her eyes.

"What do you do now, human?"

Urith cocked his head, then released her. He backed away cautiously as he waited to see her response.

"You are as fine a warrior that I've seen. The skalds sing about you, saying you are a fair goddess," he told her. "Since there is no blood spilled between us, do we need to continue this fight? I'm not sure how I'll fare in a rematch."

The goddess continued to look him over. At first, the human warrior wondered if he made a mistake. However, Mivraa visibly relaxed and stood. Showing her demigod superiority, she placed her spear on the ground while putting the other hand on her hip.

"You're the first warrior to ask this of me," she said. "By defeating me, you've proven yourself to be no ordinary warrior Urith. I'm curious why you attacked me?"

"You know my name? Well, I'm honored," he stated. "I thought you were following us. I'm just a lost traveler in a hostile land."

Mivraa smiled as she leaned against her spear.

"I've heard you say what you think. There are many I meet in battle who do not deserve the glorious death that I have given them," she said. "It takes great courage to take on a god, but even more to let one go as I would be free to destroy you now."

"This is true," Urith agreed. "It might be difficult for me to win a second time. However, I will trust in the words of the skalds who claim your fairness and honor."

She grinned at the compliment, then leaned over to pick up her shawl from the ground. Mivraa patiently waited as the warrior slowly sheathed his sword. Urith carefully glanced over before he went to pick up his dagger. He remained unsure of how she would react, but he thrust his knife back into his belt.

As he watched her, he realized now why she looked so familiar. Her image standing with a spear in hand adorned some of the murals in the temples dedicated to her in Esterblud. But those pictures failed to show the actual beauty of her face and eyes. He recalled the story of her birth in the mountains of Eernicia to an unknown god and a human mother, and as such, she was known as a *Lassas* or demigod.

"I agree with the skalds," he said. "It would be a great sight to see you after a glorious death in battle."

"You also want something when you speak like that," Mivraa laughed.

"Yes, I would ask something of you. There is much about why I'm here that appears to be beyond my knowledge. I want a demigod as an ally if that's possible," he explained.

She frowned at the request.

"That is a problem. The gods don't interfere with the events of humans," she reminded him.

Urith laughed.

"Come now, Mivraa. We're both too old to believe the words of children. What is a goddess doing spying on our camp?" he asked, half expecting her to attack him again. Instead, she grinned

"Since you are not easy to kill, someone had to see how you survive!" Mivraa chuckled roughly at her own joke, reminding him this formidable woman spent time among the coarsest of warriors.

As if to show off her power, the goddess used her shawl to make the chainmail suddenly change into a fine gold cloth that covered her breasts and upper torso. She placed her spear away in the magical depths of the shawl before sitting on a large log. Mivraa watched with amusement at the warrior's shocked expression.

"Even as a half-god, I have some unusual items and powers," she explained. "Now let us talk about what comes next."

Urith relaxed and remained quiet.

"Human warrior, I was not spying, just doing my duty. I've come after your fights before. You are well known within my realm for I have led many spirits you send my way." She stated with a brief smile. Then, she turned sober.

"However, you need to realize that your mission is nearly as well-known as your fame. It's possible that you have friends who could be enemies."

He was surprised at the information.

"That is a mysterious way to describe my plight," the warrior replied.

"True," she agreed. "So, you have questions and, perhaps, I can give you some answers."

"I have plenty of questions, but I'm not sure I'll like the answers. As I see it, the gods have been amusing yourselves at the expense of my friends. And I don't like that."

The demigoddess laughed at him. "And what can you do about it?"

"Well, every god is vulnerable in some ways, according to the skalds. I want to know why so many barriers have been put in my way. You and the other gods seem to know more about what I intend than I do." Urith gave her his sneer smile.

"Since you appear to know everything about this, then why are you here? I've never heard of a goddess picking up the spirits of two assassins. And sneaking around our camp seems to be a trivial business for a goddess."

Her expression turned dark at his words. "This is much bigger than you can imagine, Urith. Do you have any idea why your king sent you on this mission?"

"You should know we were chosen because we are *Geniht*, the trusted guard to King Penhda. We go where the king orders," he replied.

"Yes, I know the *Geniht* warrior loyalty, even to your death," said Mivraa with an air of dismissal. "Still, you speak of the gods amusing themselves, would you feel such loyalty if you were sent to your death for nothing?"

"You are talking in riddles," replied Urith. "You said earlier that you know of our mission. If so, you recognize it is a simple one. Tell me what aspect of our mission that remains a mystery to me, yet the world seems to know."

"Very well, Urith. I can see you must learn to trust me," she concluded. "Therefore, I'll tell you that you were sent to this land of Ynyover on a mission to meet with Satres. You are to start the process to reestablish the Liege Body among the kingdoms. Am I correct?"

He nodded his head in agreement as the goddess continued.

"Yet, this same king told you nothing about the Skool and the certain prophecies of the godhead?" A look of contentment spread across her face when she saw the confusion in his eyes.

"I thought so. Your king knows the prophecies, as does

Satres and his council," Mivraa explained. "By placing you and your nephew in this land between them, you are now a pawn to both."

"How so?" asked Urith, still not fully believing this god.

"The best-known warrior of Esterblud, a man known for fighting, is sent on a journey best suited for your brother," the woman said as she leaned forward with her hands on her thighs. "Suddenly you lose Guthlaf, your best friend, and the rest of your crew in a storm. Now the world appears to come for your hide. Just before we met, you killed highly paid assassins sent to remove you and your friends. Do you believe all of these events come about by chance? Do you find the Fates that unforgiving?"

"No, any chance is out of the question," he agreed, growing grim at the thought.

"I welcomed Guthlaf to Haligulf personally, along with the rest of the crew on the beach only a few nights ago," she continued. "His story was told by the great hearth to the elders of the hall, and he informed them of your battles together. You have no greater friend."

Urith almost looked away as he remembered his friend and their past, but he was able to control the emotion he felt.

"Now, I reason to doubt you. I wish this were true, but Guthlaf was drowned. The gods do not allow a warrior into Haligulf who did not die in battle."

"Really," the goddess gave him a hard stare. "You believe you know how the god's work? Since when do you give offerings like a *satgert*? I thought you to be smarter than most warriors, but maybe not?"

She adjusted herself to a more comfortable position on the log as she considered his words.

"Perhaps, the Esterblud skalds are failing in their teachings? So you may be ignorant of the truth. Either way, the gods decide the worthy based on their deeds in life as well as the manner of their death."

"It is how I learned of your mission," the goddess

continued. "Guthlaf prayed to the Triad, the sky gods, to protect you from those who helped destroy your ship. However, the Triad cannot interfere with human affairs directly. Maybe a demigoddess doesn't consider it as interference when I communicate the truth?"

Urith didn't see her cryptic grin as he peered out at the camp below. He watched the dancing light of his companion's campfire. Occasionally he heard their voices drift up to him, but it was too far to make out their words. Likewise, it was too far for his companions to hear his conversation with the goddess. He knew this news, if true, would be difficult to explain to Oslaf.

"Are you an ally or a messenger?" Urith wondered aloud.

"In a manner of speaking, I'm both. I come because of your friend's request. I know the gods are interested in your travels. When you decided to fight me, I recognized that you deserve those many praises sung your reckless adventures."

Urith gave her a tired smile as he sat down in front of her. "If you met Guthlaf and gave escort for him to Haligulf, then I am sorry for my slight. I will gladly listen and believe your words. He was a dear friend."

Mivraa told him of seeing Guthlaf and his men being led to the underworld. She was successful in retrieving them away from the Vanth by threatening to cut out the heart of the underworld demigod. It was during their journey back from the gateway that the demigoddess learned of Alrpan's agreement with the Vanth from one of the spirits. Living humans were to be taken into the underworld for the brutal entertainment of the Vanths. She finally had enough of the god's tricks and worse upon the humans who worshiped them.

"In some ways, it's like the Guardians have returned," she told him sadly. "If this continues, it could force humans to rise up against the gods.

Urith spoke up when he heard this news. "I know little of the Guardians. When I think that the gods are willing to use the living and the dead as pawns to be used at will, abandoned and forgotten, it makes me want to enter the gateway and remove their heads. You're correct; the humans would give up their beliefs and willingness to follow such entities if they learn the truth."

Mivraa nodded in agreement.

"I too believe this," she conceded. "There is turmoil among the realms, and old alliances are being strained. The rumor is that the Triad is fragile, and the underworld gods are working to capitalize on this. This means you and your friends, like the rest of humanity, are caught in the middle."

"Are you included in this turmoil? Are you part of this?" Urith wondered aloud. The goddess nodded her head slowly as she looked into his eyes.

"I've come to watch you and to see if you are worthy of knowing this truth. We have similarities. My human side rebels at the thought of being manipulated by unworthy creatures. To be used for vain whims and dark plots lacks honor. Your fight with me proved your bravery and your honor."

"I don't understand how the skalds would not tell me about this, unless...." Urith remembered how close the sacred order of skalds was with the king. As if reading his thoughts, Mivraa nodded her head.

"Yes, they know, as does your king. I'm not sure, but he must have other plans, and I believe he may be using the strife among the gods for his own ambition."

"And what would those purposes be?" he asked.

"I would not know this." The goddess smiled. "Can't you identify what he seeks?"

"Yes, I can think of several. Penhda is ambitious and wants to spread his influence over Ynyover," the Esterblud explained, then paused as he thought about this. "I will take Oslaf into my confidence about what you have said. He is young, but a skilled warrior."

"Guthlaf has told me the same. He believes Oslaf to be one of the few fighters who can match you," said Mivraa.

"What of the female who rides with you?"

"Her name is Fedelm. She was following us, spying, until we saved her from Gallaeci bandits in these lands. She is one of my principal concerns as our new partner. Do you know anything about her?"

"Nothing much I'm afraid. I sense she is a hakra which means she could be very dangerous to you," the goddess warned him.

"I agree. However, I don't have much of an option right now. Fedelm mentioned something about the Majireef to me, but I've not heard much about this group. Do you know about them?

The goddess looked at him thoughtfully for a moment before speaking.

"In the dark past, it was said that a small group of hakras and priests used the oracles and spells to allow them to open a gateway to communicate directly with the underworld," she explained. "The Triad believes the council of Majireef remained aligned with the underworld gods. Some think they use this power to help Satres, but to what end, I don't know."

"Are you suspicious as well?" He asked.

Mivraa nodded, her eyes flashing. She kept her thoughts to herself.

"You still have not told me who sent the assassins," Urith reminded her.

The goddess looked at him with disbelief.

"Who would not want you to arrive?" She paused when she realized he still didn't understand her question.

"It's Satres, of course!"

"How would he know we are here," he said mostly to himself. "Unless…" He looked at her. "Apparently I need to reconsider the hakras. I appreciate your help. Is there anything more?" Urith asked.

Mivraa shook her head and rose from the log. "Nothing substantial, just more rumors which may or may not hold true." She paused a minute. "However, I would suggest you might try to contact your lost friend Dughorm. He is someone who might give you more details about the future."

"Dughorm is in Ynyover still? I'd heard that he left, but no one has heard where he went," the shocked warrior told her. He remembered the skalds poem of his old mentor's trip to the Citadel during the Restoration. The great warrior was one of his heroes.

"I understand that he lives in a village called Ynysbeag," she replied.

"Dughorm trained me and fought beside me when I was young. You seem to have a power of mind reading yourself." Urith said with a large smile, visibly impressed.

The goddess grinned.

"I wish that were the case, I just hear many things during my travels among the dead," Mivraa chuckled. "Now, I must go back as I have other duties that I must tend to."

"I hope we can meet again as an ally and friend," said Urith.

"That is entirely possible my warrior friend," the goddess replied as she turned away, putting the shawl hood back over her head, and walking into the woods.

"Take care of yourself and if you need me, merely ask for me in your dreams."

Urith continued watching her until her handsome figure disappeared into the dark. He forgot to ask how she got there and where she was going. He did notice she was headed to the path that led back to the Great Circle. The warrior smiled to himself as he thought about her for a moment. He did not understand why, but he liked her and felt he could trust her. The gods felt betrayed by Mivraa's loyalty to people at times. Perhaps that was why he had confidence in her. Urith suspected she would not have many valued friends. Goddess or not, he knew she was an exceptional warrior and decided she would make a great ally to their cause. At least he had the beginnings of a plan from her visit.

Chapter 5: To Ynysbeag

Urith arrived back at the camp to find his two young companions talking by the flickering light of the campfire. Oslaf was trying hard not to show his attraction to the girl. The pair grew quiet as he entered the camp. Urith did nothing to break the silence. He went directly to the fire and knelt to retrieve his share of cooked fish. The scent of the cooking food had caught him just outside of camp, and he took no time in devouring the meal. Finished, he moved away from the fire to a blanket laid out for him on the grass.

"Well, whoever caught the fish, I thank them. It was perfect." Urith said as he sat across from the fire from them.

"I caught them in a little pool near the creek. Fedelm helped cook them up for us." Oslaf stated with some pride and then asked. "Did you find anything?"

"Well, not as much as I hoped," Urith lied, holding back his encounter with the goddess and the assassins. "I took a long trek through the forest and spotted many places for hunting or trapping. But we're not staying long enough for that." The younger warrior looked closely at his mentor. He knew Urith was leaving something out.

"We thought we heard something up the hill," he told Urith. "It sounded like someone was tramping around. Then I thought I overheard voice. I wondered if you might have stumbled on to something."

Urith forced a grin.

"Yes, well, I did stumble on to something, but it was a *rangifer* that was rooting around for food. You might have heard me talking oaths to the gods to keep it from using its horns on me. Knocked me in the creek," he replied while looking down at his wet tunic. On the way back, Urith took time to wash some of the blood off his clothes, knowing that it would be difficult to explain the blood.

Oslaf gave a half-hearted laugh. He recognized the

damage to his uncle's chain mail at the shoulder. There were fresh blood stains on his tunic as well.

"Well, you must have wounded it by the blood I see. Too bad you didn't kill it. The meat would have been good."

"The meat would have been bad," Urith told Oslaf. He recognized that his nephew didn't believe him.

He hated to lie. However, he didn't trust Fedelm. And he wasn't sure about everything he learned from Mivraa. During the walk back to camp, he came to a decision concerning what he could share about the Fealharans and his strange meeting with the goddess. In the end, he had decided to say nothing for the time being.

As he thought about the encounter, Urith realized needed time to work through all he had been told. His wife had died during childbirth, and since that time, he regarded the gods with much doubt, distrust, and anger. Breaking from his brief musing, he noticed Fedelm was quiet, staring absently at the fire in front of her.

"You are quiet over there, Fedelm. Is something wrong?" he asked.

She jerked up, looking at him. "I'm sorry. I was lost in thought," she stammered.

"Very well, allow me to interrupt your thoughts," he continued. "Does the path to Grimma lead us near a village called Ynysbeag?"

"Yes -- Well, I mean it is not a great distance from the route we are taking. Why does it matter? I thought we were going to Grimma?" She eyed him suspiciously.

"During my wanderings around our camp, I suddenly remembered this village. Now I have a reason to go there." Urith decided to remain cryptic as possible.

Fedelm brightened as she thought about this change. "Very well, we can find the village on the way to Ynys if we take the path through the forest to the east. That will lead us the highland valley," she explained.

Urith took note of her sudden eagerness to lead them to

this town and wondered if he gave away too much information. Knowing he could not take back his words, he decided to be more careful in the future.

"How far away is this village?" he asked.

"I believe we can reach the town in a couple of days of travel if we get a good start in the morning. It's on a back road through the hills."

Urith wiped his mouth with his hands to clean off the remnants of his meal, and then wiped his hands on his leggings. His actions reminded Fedelm again of his uncivilized nature. She hoped that if she made enough biting comments, the Esterbluds might take the hint to bathe in a stream on occasion.

"Did you spend a lot of time at this village?" Oslaf asked as he leaned against his saddle.

"Not much," she admitted. "It is on a trail used by those people traveling to the Citadel who need to bypass the main entrance through Ynys. It is also another route to get to the harbor directly. Some of the people who visit Satres use this path to avoid crowds traveling to the Citadel during festivals."

"Interesting," Urith remarked, standing up. "We should keep you around since you seem to have valuable information." She couldn't be sure if he were serious.

"You two should get some sleep as we will be leaving at first light. I'll take first watch over the camp," he told them. "Oslaf, if you are healed enough, you can relieve me at the peak of the moons tonight."

He looked up as the orbs in the night sky began rising in the east.

"Yes, there's plenty of light tonight," he said as he kicked dirt on the fire until the embers sent up a thick smoke. Taking his lead, Fedelm and Oslaf wrapped the soft wool blankets around their bodies. They settled in to watch the dying embers of the fire.

Urith looked up at the moons and thought briefly about Mivraa as he began a slow trek around the perimeter of the camp. He made sure that his weapons were with him and ready. Nothing appeared ordinary with his journey now.

After Urith walked around the camp several times, he stopped and sat on a log while listening to the night sounds. He went over the events of the last few days, thinking over his options. The words of Mivraa kept running through his mind as he thought about his mission and about his king. He had ridden alongside his overlord during many battles and never felt the slightest indication of betrayal. The Esterblud always felt that he was one of his most trusted advisers. Following his father's death on an ill-fated expedition against the Cahmais, Urith held no bitterness and continued to support King Penhda in all the council gatherings.

If the goddess is telling me the truth, why would the king send me on a path to death in this way?

His mission involved a simple matter to begin the process of restoring the Liege Body. It was something all other kingdoms might be interested in given their common enemy, the sea raiders from the far lands of Regiussa. The kingdoms were constantly under threat from the sea raiders. The bandits came out of isolated harbors along the coast of Vulthnal which were close to the main trading routes for the merchant ships. The sea raiders seized valuable ships along with their crew to resell cargo and slaves on their black markets.

As he turned things over in his mind, Urith was sure the restoration would allow the Esterbluds to influence the needed order among the other kingdoms. He could not believe King Penhda would want his mission to fail. It was this reason the warrior hesitated in fully accepting the goddess. However, he saw no reason for Mivraa to weave such a lie for him.

~~~

During their journey to Ynysbeag, the small group avoided the few farmers and occasional merchant they spotted along the road. They worked out a method of efficiently preventing locals from seeing the Esterbluds. Forced to trust Fedelm's agreement to get them to the Citadel, Urith allowed her to ride
~~~

the trail alone while they rode through the brush and trees of the nearby forest line. They carefully observed Fedelm when she met strangers on the road. Sometimes, they could overhear the exchange she had with the strangers who were surprised that a young woman would ride alone on the trail. They overheard Fedelm explain that her father worked for Satres and that he was coming up to meet her at the next village. The traveler's expressions quickly changed from concern about her safety to fear and mistrust. Bringing in the Sacred Overlord's name into the conversation caused the strangers to hurriedly leave her presence. Urith believed what he observed would be useful information for King Penhda.

Several sunrises later, the warriors watched Fedelm on the trail talking with a bald man on a bright red colored wagon. Urith interrupted Oslaf from his thoughts. He finally told his nephew about the killing of the Fealharan as well as his meeting with Mivraa. Oslaf appeared indignant after Urith explained.

"Why didn't you tell me sooner? I'm not a child," he reminded his uncle.

"I know but I needed time to sort it out," Urith told him. "I couldn't tell you in front of Fedelm. Besides, it's not many times a goddess comes to you, let alone bearing such terrible news."

Urith went on to detail his suspicions and his reasons for heading to Ynysbeag. He also told Oslaf to keep the information to himself.

"You still don't trust her, do you?" His nephew muttered.

"No! And neither should you. Think about it. Since we rescued her, she's never tried to escape or leave. She's playing a game against us." Urith nodded in her direction. Fedelm waved at the trader riding away in his cart.

"Think about why she doesn't ask for help from these people on the trail. They could have sent word for warriors to capture us after we went by. Yet no one follows us," he pointed out. "She is being very cagey about things and only lets us know what she intends."

"Yeah, she sounds a lot like you," Oslaf countered as he spurred his horse toward the trail. He noticed Fedelm motioning for them to come forward once the merchant's cart was out of sight.

Urith hesitated as he considered what Oslaf told him. He had to admit his nephew was probably correct. His ways could be similar to the woman. However, he also disliked the comparison.

I'm a warrior. Fedelm is nothing more than royal chattel.

After making camp, late that evening, Fedelm noticed a strange tension between Oslaf and Urith. Both were unusually quiet. The older warrior eventually rose from the campfire, telling them he would patrol around the camp for a while. Fedelm and Oslaf went back to their respective places to curl up in blankets. Fortunately, while the night grew colder, they were able to have a small fire burning once they pulled off the trail into the forest.

When the pair of moons finally reached their zenith, Urith was ready for sleep. He walked quietly into camp and shook Oslaf by the shoulder. His nephew was in a deep sleep, and it took a couple of shakes to wake him. With the strong moonlight showing the outline of the girl curled up in her blankets, Urith motioned to Oslaf, gesturing for him to follow. They gathered a few steps away from the circle and spoke quietly.

"Now keep a sharp lookout. I haven't seen anything, but something tells me spirits are moving in the night. Something just doesn't feel right," he stated.

With those words, Urith walked away, heading back to the camp. He took a quick glance at Fedelm to make sure she was still sleeping. Lying down on his wool blanket, the warrior was soon asleep.

The twin orbs in the night sky were setting as Oslaf made his quiet circuits around the camp. His mind swam with uncertainty about his feelings toward Fedelm. While he felt his mentor was unfair to the girl, he also had doubts about her as well.

He heard movement coming from behind him. Oslaf quickly turned, crouching instinctively. In the fading moonlight, he saw a person coming from the camp toward the trail. Oslaf immediately recognized Fedelm. Keeping as quiet as possible, he angled his path to meet her. He noticed she was moving in a steady, unhurried walk, her gold hair standing out in the dark forest.

Fedelm exited the brush and stepped onto the hard-packed trail without glancing around. Oslaf was about to call out, but he decided something was not right in her movement. He continued to stay out of sight, remaining in the brush while moving parallel with her. In the light, he could see that her eyes were open wide. However, she had a blank look as she walked. A thought immediately occurred to Oslaf that the girl might be purposely drawing him away from camp. However, as he observed her trance-like walk, Oslaf could not make himself believe this was some type of trickery. Still worried about Urith back at the camp, he decided to continue following her from a distance.

The woman's slow walking movement reminded him of the tales Urith and other elders used to scare the children. During the dark nights of Calanf, the festival to the underworld, Oslaf remembered the stories vividly. Nearly all of the tales were about how the unworthy dead warrior's souls followed the Vanths. The hairs on the back of Oslaf's neck rose when he remembered the sounds the elder's made to replicate the noise of wailing spirits condemned to the underworld.

He seemed to be watching such a procession. Watching her move like the dead caused him to feel the same eerie sensations. Fedelm stopped for a moment, and he froze in his tracks, thinking she might have woken from her trance. Instead, the girl turned and crossed in front of him, heading into an area of thick brush.

Surprised by her turn, Oslaf nearly lost the girl. He tried to catch up by pushing through a thicket of *wstinga* brush. Fedelm continued, somehow missing the sharpened branches as if guided by an unseen hand. The young warrior was so intent on not losing the girl as she moved through the rough terrain that he barely noticed the burrs of the brush scraping his exposed flesh. He was forced to extend himself on tiptoes on occasion to keep her in his view.

Fedelm disappeared as she passed through two larger twisted lellowtere trees which appeared as dark tentacles rising from the ground. Oslaf sprung forward as fast as he could and soon pulled behind her on the same rough trail. As the warrior followed along, he heard a hissing noise like a giant buzzard. He ducked behind one of the small trees where he saw Fedelm standing in the middle of a small clearing in front of the twisted twin trees.

He was about to step out when he noticed movement in front of the girl. Then, he saw a tall, dark figure walked up to the girl. The darkness hid the creature's features, leaving Oslaf unsure whether it was man or woman. The figure led the girl back the way it had come. As they walked, Oslaf stepped from behind the tree, quickly hiking forward. He tried not to lose them in the darkened area where they were heading. Drawing nearer, Oslaf noticed a strange blue light coming from between the twisted trees. He hurried, and half expected the pair to stop at the sound of his footsteps. Just ahead of him, Oslaf saw Fedelm and her unknown companion outlined by the thin blue glow. It appeared like they were approaching a door, similar to a temple. Just several long strides behind Fedelm, he watched as they continued into the light. When the pair reached what looked like the temple door, the light suddenly brightened, momentarily blinding Oslaf. He slowed, trying to shield his eyes with his forearm. The light dimmed, and he looked back at the spot. The figures in front of him were gone! His eyes still seeing the outline of the light, Oslaf leaped forward over the last few paces to reach

Fedelm.

No one was there!

He stopped to listen, yet no sound could be heard, not even the night creatures he had heard earlier. Only a dead silence met him as he cocked his head. He turned around, listening intently. Unwilling to accept that Fedelm and the other figure had disappeared into thin air, Oslaf rushed to look for them. Tramping through the immediate area, he looked for any sign of what had become of the pair. While it was too dark under the trees to see much, he knew something supernatural occurred. The urgency he felt to find them gave way to resignation. She had gotten away. But where did she go and with whom?

~~~

Fedelm came out of her trance inside a dark room. There was a hint of green fluorescence coming from the rough walls. It was cold, and she shivered despite the shawl that covered her as lay on a hard floor. The girl heard a faint echoing sound of water dripping nearby. As she sat up, she felt a heavy chain around her ankles holding her to the wall. Then, she heard a harsh laugh nearby which sent the hair on the back of her neck tingling.

"Yes, my little servant. I believe we need to chat."

"Very well, Alrpan. Start talking," replied the girl as bravely as she could, turning her head in the direction of the god's voice. Fedelm was afraid however she was also growing angry at her treatment as she kicked out her chained legs in disgust.

"Why did you lead our friends away from the place we agreed to meet?" The god's voice echoed in the cave.

"I had no choice. Something spooked the ossanes from the middle of the field. I couldn't make out who or what it was, but there was something near the stone altar. I'm sure that the Esterblud leader saw it," she explained. "If you were there, you must have caused them to leave."

The goddess paused, saying nothing for a moment.
~~~

"Yes, I was there as we agreed. But you should have contacted me."

"That was impossible. They are watching my every move. Even when I try to sleep, the men are on guard around the camp. But you know this as I feel you entering my dreams," she told Alrpan. "Why bring me here?"

"Yes, I've read your imaginings at night. You are here because you grow weak," the goddess stated.

Alrpan moved from the shadows into the pale green light that hovered over the area above where the girl sat. Fedelm tried to stand but was quickly forced to her knees by an unseen force, the chains digging into her ankles.

"I didn't tell you to stand up," the goddess stepped forward. "Now explain why you agreed to take them to Ynysbeag? You failed."

"Urith made this change. It came out of nowhere. How else can I gain their trust?" The girl said as she could feel forms moving closer to the underworld god. She peered behind her into the blackness and thought she spotted vague movement. The human form of Alrpan came next to her.

"Do you know why they are changing their path?" She asked.

"No, they don't trust me well enough yet," replied Fedelm.

There was a long pause as the goddess stared at the girl who could hear the shuffling of steps around her now.

"Very well, you appear to be telling the truth. But your dreams have betrayed you. I told you that you're weak. You grow feelings for the Esterbluds. That is not acceptable." The goddess stroked the blond head of Fedelm who looked up at her. Alrpan's blue eyes showed a wicked gleam, her iris briefly changing to red.

"Your feelings make me think you are not as devoted to our cause as before," she said with an evil smile. "So, I brought along my friends to explain why you should remember whose side you are on."

At that point, Fedelm could finally make out what she

thought, at first, were men. As the creature came into the light, she could see the hideous amalgamation of beast-like features in each of the human forms. The *beorhs* were once human warriors, only to become skeletal, mummy-like monsters of the underworld. Unable to reach Haligulf due to their despicable actions, Alrpan enjoyed turning these man-beasts into her deadly servants of the abyss. When Alrpan desired, the creatures reached out from the depths of the underworld to savagely rape and kill humans.

They quickly circled around the girl, reaching out to touch her warm body, to lust over her living flesh which attracted them. Their elongated hands were now three long claws used to inflict torture and brutality upon their victims. Fedelm turned her head to avoid looking at the hideous creatures. Some of the beasts held their enlarged penises in anticipation while she tried to detach herself from what she expected. One monster held her leg and slowly dug one claw into her leg. Fedelm yelled out in terrified pain.

"Enough," yelled Alrpan, who was still next to the girl. The sound her voice boomed across the room, causing the creatures to stop in their tracks and back away from the goddess. The beast who scratched Fedelm grudgingly moved away, licking the blood from its claw. While the girl grabbed for her leg in pain, the goddess stared down at Fedelm.

"Yes, my dear. Like me, they can't get enough of the living," Alrpan told her prisoner with an evil grin. "Tonight is a warning. Satres asked me to give you this after he heard of your weakness. If I come for you again, you will experience even more fun from my creatures."

"Now that I have your attention, you will take the Esterblud fools to Ynysbeag as they have asked," Alrpan told her. "When you get there, you will take them to a large cave outside of Ynysbeag. It is not a gateway you will lay the herbs upon the fire and bring us out using the ritual Satres taught you. We will deal with the Esterbluds there. Do you understand?"

Fedelm hesitated before nodding her head in resignation to her situation. Suddenly she heard a metallic jangling against the stone floor. The chains fell away from her ankles as Alrpan granted her release. The goddess patted her on the head like a little kuon.

"That's a good girl. Once we deal with this Urith, then you will return in triumph to the Citadel. After that, I'm sure you'll get what you truly deserve," she told her.

The goddess grabbed her hair and touched Fedelm's forehead. A light spark shot from the god's hand and the girl immediately went into a trance, rigidly standing before the goddess. Alrpan turned away and the beasts following their master. Fedelm turned stiffly toward a passage dimly lit by the thin blue arch of light. The dark passage opened for the girl, and she moved toward the blue light.

As the pale light of the morning appeared in the western sky, Oslaf's head nodded from the encroaching sleep. Sitting with his back against a fallen tree near the entry point of Fedelm's disappearance, the warrior committed himself to remain until dawn. Then he would return back to camp with his news about the lost girl.

His head snapped up when he heard a slightly hollow sound near him. Oslaf witnessed an outline of blue light between the twisted trees, and the smell of mustiness hit him. Just after that, Fedelm walked into the visible world from nothing.

Oslaf scrambled to his feet, excited and terrified at what he just witnessed. He was happy to see Fedelm again, but she walked by him, still in her trance-like state. He sprung forth a couple of steps to grab her. He would not allow her to get away this time. She stopped and kept staring off into the distance as he held her arm.

"Fedelm! What's wrong? Wake up!" He stepped in front of her and shook her.

"Wake up!" His voice grew louder, then he slapped her cheek.

"Fedelm, wake up now!"

Her eyes blinked several times and then she recognized him.

"What is the matter?" she asked sleepily, then more forcefully. "Why are you holding me?"

Oslaf released her, stepping back.

"You walked out of camp like a dead one, so I followed you. Don't you remember anything?"

He noticed the girl's eyes widen with memories and then she looked away from him.

"No," she lied. "I just went to sleep, and now I'm here. Where are we?"

"You just came from between those two trees," Oslaf pointed behind her. "It looked like a gateway to another realm." She glanced back, then shook her head.

"Come on," he insisted. "It's going to be dawn soon, and Urith will wonder what happened to us. I have no excuse for letting you walk away from the camp."

He took Fedelm by her hand and quickly led the way back to camp. The girl tried to resist, complaining that she could not keep up. Oslaf looked back at her with an expression she didn't recognize.

"If Urith knows where you have been, he'll cut your throat and leave your body for the *kuons* to scavenge on," he stated. "Just keep up, or you will die!"

He started off at a slow trot, and she sped up. Fedelm's sudden effort to keep pace indicated that she realized her predicament. Oslaf thought desperately of what he could tell Urith to keep her alive. It was evident that something controlled Fedelm. And it meant she could not be trusted. However, she remained the one link they had to the Sacred Overlord. He believed that they needed her. Urith might decide she wasn't worth the risk.

Oslaf debated if he should kill her to save their mission, then he quickly dismissed the idea. He realized if it was anybody else, he could probably do it, but not Fedelm. The turmoil he felt angered him. Oslaf saw through her lie. She was playing him for a fool. This is what Urith said to him the night before, but he was too stubborn to accept it.

The pair periodically glanced over their shoulders at the sky as they continued their trek back to camp. After a while, Oslaf had to slow down as he was not fully recovered. The red sky of the morning mixed with the forest around them. The vivid display of color went unnoticed by the pair lost in their thoughts amid the sound of their heavy breathing. Before they knew it, they were on the footpath which dropped to the stream next to the camp. Oslaf slowed down, holding his finger to his lips, signaling Fedelm to be quiet. She followed along carefully, trying to be silent as well. As they entered the camp, the young pair breathed a sigh of relief to see a mound where Urith lay still covered by his blanket. Oslaf motioned toward Fedelm indicating for her to lie down on a blanket to create the illusion of a regular morning. He moved over to wake Urith when he heard a voice behind him that sent a chill up his spine.

"Oslaf, it's about time you showed up. What have you and the girl been up to?" His uncle asked gruffly.

Oslaf turned to see Urith sitting on a log near the stream, laying out a baited hook to catch breakfast. When Oslaf glanced at the blanket mound before going to Urith, he realized it was just Urith's saddle covered by a blanket. As he reached his mentor's side, he wondered what Urith's reaction would be.

"Oslaf just saved me," Fedelm told Urith as she joined them.

"Really? And how could that be? He was on watch, and you were sleeping." Urith growled lout like the *brokkos* found around Esterblud.

"It was not his fault," Fedelm answered patiently. "He spotted me in a trance-walk and followed me until he could wake me and bring me back."

Urith looked at her and then glanced at Oslaf.

"Is this right?"

Oslaf nodded his head as he stammered out his story. "I didn't see her until she was nearly out of sight and I had a hard time catching up with her. I thought I lost her for a bit, but finally found her."

Urith considered his nephew's words and then he turned to face the creek. He reached down and pulled up two silver fish from the water. A loop of twine ran through their gills to keep them from escaping.

"Well, if you are through running around in the woods, one of you can clean our breakfast while I catch another. Oslaf, you can get the fire started. The sooner we are done here, the better." He turned over the captured meals to Oslaf before returning to his task of providing breakfast.

Oslaf stood dumbfounded by Urith's reaction to their explanation. It was not like his uncle to let something like this go so smoothly. He glanced over at Fedelm, who gave him a smile before bending down to tend to the wound on her leg. Her green eyes told him that everything was alright. However, his heart told him differently. As he moved to a nearby rock to begin cleaning the fish, anxious thoughts filled his mind.

The sun was rising over the highlands in the west as the trio, and their ossanes made it to the base of the steep cliffs of Br-Ynys. While the men had expected to see the Citadel of Br-Ynys at this point, Fedelm explained to them that it would take another day of travel before they could see the fortress high on its vantage point over the sea. She led them away from the main trail which followed the ridge and coastline upward to the Citadel. Crossing the river, they skirted an area between the forest and a steel gray rock wall rising in the heights above them. They could see the clouds with misty rains moving over the range. The men cautiously looked around wondering about the weather above but said nothing as they let the girl lead the way. At a point not far beyond their river crossing, she found the back trail to the village. In fact, it was barely a path. From the tracks, it was evident that local herdsman guided their sure-footed flocks of mountain *starkts* out of the high country using this trail.

With Fedelm in the lead, they pulled into a single column as they followed the hard packed stone and dirt path. Their ossanes moved slowly up the steep trail, occasionally balking by shaking their elongated heads. A fast running stream ran next to the trail. Due to recent rains, there were areas along the way where the rock and dirt became slick. When the ossanes struggled to keep their footing, their riders clutched their hands tightly on the saddle horn to stay on their mount. A few times, Urith and Oslaf prayed for the Fates to remain away.

The group made steady progress as the sun rose higher, exposing dark caves and crevices nearly hidden among the brush and trees. As they came around another bend in the stream, Urith asked how much further to the village as he looked ahead for potential ambush spots.

"Not far. Just above that ridge," Fedelm answered, looking back as she pointed the way above them.

Urith made a sudden stop, causing Oslaf to run into him over as the young warrior tried to control the other ossanes he led. The girl stopped, and then carefully turned the mount around to come back to the group.

"What's the problem?" She asked.

"Nothing in particular, but it's been too quiet. I think I'll take the lead for a while." Urith gave Fedelm his sneering grin as he pushed his animal past her, heading up the trail.

Fedelm said nothing but she fumed at her dismissal. Oslaf sensed her irritation. She carefully turned her ossane and slowed down, allowing Oslaf to come parallel to her.

"He believes you are leading us into a trap," he said.

The girl glared at him.

"Do you believe the same?"

He remained silent for a moment.

"I don't want to," he admitted. "However, as much I

appreciate your help this morning; I know for sure you are not telling us the truth. I've been thinking about the stories I heard as a boy. They were about humans entering the underworld, and those stories never end well. I think your leg wound is evidence of this."

The girl dropped her eyes while Oslaf continued.

"Urith told me you are playing a dangerous game," he recounted. "I believe him." Oslaf paused, coming to a decision.

"I don't know what the Citadel is like, but you should understand that friends earn their trust through actions, not words. Without your honesty, I cannot trust in your actions. Without trust, I will not help you."

He spurred his animal to press past her, leading the other mounts by her as well.

Fedelm watched as the young man spurred his ossane to a trot to catch up with his uncle. She felt tears well in her eyes as she let her ossane slow, falling back from the column. Oslaf cared for her far more than she wanted.

I could live with that but why do I feel like a traitor?

The Esterbluds were the enemy to her future, the world inside the council. Fedelm recognized the time was coming for choices, and she realized that the choices she faced were becoming far more challenging than she dreamed.

Just off a fork in the trail, Urith spotted a cluster of houses not far from a small waterfall that ran down into the valley. Made of stone and clay native to the area, Urith nearly missed the squat buildings that blended so well with the rocky cliffs that rose behind them. At the far end of the village, Urith noticed a small tower. He guessed it was a guard tower waiting to give an early warning to the Citadel. Urith led his mount off the trail, into an area of sparse bluewood trees for cover. He waited for the column of ossanes join him.

"Looks like we made it. Is that Ynysbeag?" Urith asked the girl, who nodded.

"Are we going in?" Oslaf looked at the sprinkles of light

coming through some of the windows as the sunlight faded.

"No, I think we wait a bit," answered Urith. "Our arrival needs to be quiet and uneventful. We are searching for a person who may or may not wish to help us."

"Who are we looking for, Urith? I don't recall any stories about this place."

"No, you probably wouldn't since the skalds never sang of the old ones dying slowly. But if you remember the stories about the Restoration of the Necropa, you have your clue." Urith smiled at his little joke. Oslaf, tired from the trek, disliked his mentor's riddle.

"Come on, what does that have to do with us?"

"Well, think about the Esterblud hero that came to Ynyover." Urith continued grinning. "When did he return to our lands?"

Oslaf thought a moment as he ran through all of the stories and songs he recalled. A glimpse of recognition crossed his face as he glanced at Fedelm.

"Dughorm!" he exclaimed. "You mean he is here?"

Urith turned serious. "I believe so. But the problem is finding him in this village without alerting the wrong people."

"How do I know this name, Dughorm?" Fedelm asked. "It seems familiar to me somehow."

Both men looked at her like she now had the horns of the *Estercetus* coming from her head.

"You should be aware of him. He is a great Esterblud warrior who came over during the Restoration." Oslaf told her, incredulous that she might not know this history.

Fedelm gave Oslaf a glare in return.

"I don't know every little hero from Esterblud," she countered. "I must have heard that name from the early times of the restoration."

"Yes, you would," Urith agreed. "He is a hakra and was instrumental to *satgert* learning since the end of the war. In fact, I heard tales he and Satres were like brothers. That was before his accident. I find it interesting you don't know about how crucial he was to the restoration."

He moved his ossane to get a better look at the darkening village.

"We need to get into that village quietly, and then we can see if we can find him. Any ideas?"

"We could sneak in simply enough. I'm betting the night watchman will be in the meadhouse." Oslaf observed.

"Yes, but we cannot walk up to each house and ask," Urith reminded him. "Perhaps we could hide our animals and armor before going to the meadhouse?" He shook his head at the thought. "No, with our accent's, it won't take long before locals become suspicious."

Fedelm interrupted him. "I can get this information for you."

"How?" he asked suspiciously.

"I've been to this village before, remember? The elder of this village will do anything for Satres. Since my father and I are known to them, I will just ask Wiclam," she offered. "He will know this person, especially if he is a foreigner to the village."

"That sounds like a good plan," observed Oslaf in support.

"Yes, but for one thing." Urith peered back at Oslaf.

"Do you trust her enough to stake your life on it? Even if we can handle the few local warriors, we are too close to the Citadel and the guards in Grimma now. See that guard tower near the back of the village?" He paused and pointed toward the structure. "One person could go there and raise the alarm to the Citadel. We'd have the Citadel guards on top of us before the sun returns. If we try to escape back along the back path that brought us here, it would be suicide without any moonlight to guide us. What is to stop her from alerting the village to our presence?"

"I would not do such a thing," protested Fedelm hotly. "In fact, I'll stake my honor on it."

"Honor!" Urith scoffed. "You've lied to us repeatedly on this journey. Do I need to give you a list or does it even matter to you? You're the same type of female who claims fidelity to one warrior while bedding another."

"You cursed Esterblud!" Her voice rose, scattering the nearby birds into a panicked flight. "I've never given an oath to you." Fedelm swiftly pulled her thin dagger from her belt and pressed her mount into Urith's. Livid at his insult, she tried to strike at the warrior with a sweep of her arm. Urith backed his mount away, trying to control his animal from the sudden onslaught.

Unable to get at him, she continued her rage. "I've had enough of your insults and threats. You can go kiss the ass of Tuulcha for all I care."

Oslaf pulled his ossane between the two riders, fearing for the girl when he saw Urith put his hand on his longsword. He was afraid she might go too far and set off his uncle's quick temper.

"Quiet down, both of you," he exclaimed. "Do you want us captured before we even get there?"

The trio went suddenly quiet, but the harsh glares continued to be pitched around. Finally, Fedelm put away her dagger and Urith removed his hand from his longsword. Urith appeared more surprised than upset at the girl and her reaction. However, Fedelm's eyes still blazed with hate at the senior warrior. Oslaf tried to get back to the reason they were there.

"Now that we're back to the problem, how are we going to find Dughorm?" asked Oslaf.

After a long moment of angry tension, Urith decided to break the ice.

"You're right to get us back on the path." He paused and looked over at Fedelm.

"I was wrong to dismiss your offer. You have not given us an oath of honor before, and I should have taken it as given. I have reasons to distrust, you deserve a chance to prove you are with us in this now."

Both men observed the blaze of hate in her eyes slowly

change into deep suspicion at Urith's words. Oslaf believed he saw an internal conflict going on within her.

"Fedelm, are you still willing to help?" Oslaf interceded.

She looked over, then finally nodded her head.

"Very well, I'll help."

"Great," Oslaf smiled back at her. "Urith what do you say?"

Urith nodded as well, then immediately took over the conversation.

"Fedelm, when you are going to meet with your contact, Oslaf and I will move in close to the village." He caught her glare and took a deep breath.

"It just in case there is trouble with the villagers. We'll be ready to help," he assured her. "Remember, you are alone, and we have many enemies. Besides, are you sure who you can trust? Even that finely made dagger you carry will not stop a longsword."

Urith gave a quick scan over the area.

"Is there a place we can leave the ossanes and still be close without being seen?"

"It's hard to see in this light, but near the waterfall is a clearing with thick brush. Travelers stay there when the village becomes full during the festivals," she explained. "I can walk into the village from there when it's entirely dark."

The men agreed to her plan. Dismounting, they quietly walked their mounts through the sparse woods along the edge of the town. Leaving the ossanes tied to trees at the outskirts of the town, they waited until the sun fell completely behind the horizon and darkness descended upon the valley. As they watched the sunset, Fedelm told them more about her plan. She would go to Wiclam. If the man knew nothing, she would return, and they could decide what they would do next.

Fedelm left the group, covering her head with her brown shawl as she walked toward the village. The warriors watched her until the night enveloped her. They waited for a while, then followed along the trail she had taken. They stopped at the edge of the village, but she was already out of sight. It was too dark to see very far, and the men moved in closer.

Urith nearly fell over the little wall that encircled the village. It was used to control the herds of highland *starkts*, a small long-haired animal the locals used for milk and meat. Climbing effortlessly over the low obstacle, they proceed cautiously as they went toward a nearby building. After sliding against the wall, Urith listened to any sounds coming from inside. The rustle and murmur of a few starkts moving around convinced him the structure was a shed. Suddenly, on the other side of the village, they heard the barking of *wearhs*, a domesticated kuon that is used by the highland locals to herd their starkts.

"Let's see if we can get closer," Urith whispered after the barking stopped. He motioned Oslaf to follow him.

The men crept to the back of another building that appeared to be the village tavern. Stopping with their backs against the wattle and daub back wall, they could hear the roar of laughter coming out of a tiny open window located just above their heads. A dull light came from the hole in the wall as the Esterbluds listened to a few villagers speaking in a highland dialect of the Cahmais language. Urith had a hard time understanding some of the conversations. However, it was obvious the men and women inside were enjoying themselves.

The Esterbluds slid along the wall to the end, then turned the corner going between the two structures. As they crept along the slippery muck, both men could smell the stench from the waste that emptied from the main street through the path they took.

Reaching the front corner, Urith examined the nearly empty street while staying in the shadows. Feeble light emanated from oil lanterns hanging from posts in front of some of the buildings. Despite the nauseating smell at their feet, the two men crouched along the wall watching and waiting. They noticed a man come out of the meadhouse on their right and watched him stagger across the muddy street. As he walked under an oil lantern, they could see he wore the red cloth tunic and red skull cap of the night watchman in Ynyover. His short sword flashed under the flickering light.

"We could make short work of him if needed," Oslaf whispered. Urith only nodded as he continued to watch the street.

After a few moments, they watched as a familiar small figure in a hooded shawl come out of a doorway. Fedelm followed a small man who led the way.

"I think we might have something," he whispered to Oslaf.

"Should we follow?" he quietly asked as he watched them.

Urith shook his head. He continued to watch the guard who was smoking a pipe, leaning unsteadily on the post. Fedelm and the stranger approached the drunken man who turned to greet them. From a distance, the Esterbluds could only make out parts of the conversation. However, they determined that the small man leading Fedelm was called Wiclam. The watchman let the two people pass after the brief conversation, his eyes continuing to follow the woman. While the night watchman remained preoccupied, Urith pulled at Oslaf's arm, and they sprinted across the muddy street. They entered between the two huts. Nearly falling into the muck, Urith slid back to the corner of the hut where he caught a glimpse of Fedelm and Wiclam. They had stopped at a small shack on the far outskirts of the village. Urith led Oslaf around to the back of the hut, then proceeded on a parallel course on the back side of a row of buildings. As they stumbled through the unfamiliar ground, the two warriors finally pulled next to the last building along the main street. The hut where Fedelm disappeared into was across an open area away from the main road.

The men approached the hut slowly, noticing the ray of feeble light coming from the side of the structure. Silently, they positioned themselves under the small window covered with ossane hide. Conversations from inside the house filtered through the window.

"----comes from a highly respected family in Grimma. She is from the house of the clan Pataric, and her father is Caestia, record keeper to Satres. When she came to me this evening, asked for a man whose name I did not recognize. I assumed you might know of this person since you knew of the Esterbluds and their ways. She tells me she is looking for someone called Dughorm, a great Esterblud warrior."

Wiclam paused, and Urith listened intently to the other man's voice.

"Yes, I agree it is a most unusual name for around here."

Wiclam chuckled.

"Yes, I tried to explain that Esterbluds were in short supply in these lands."

Inside the small house, a blind man listened politely to his two visitors. He wore a simple frock of black and had a small blanket covering his legs as he leaned back in his rocking chair. A young child sat near the small hearth. Her brown eyes sparkled through the smudges on her dirty face.

The old man gurgled at the joke before turning to the young woman.

"Yes, I know your father, Caestia. He's a good man. Now, what brings you to our village after one of those nasty Esterblud warriors?"

"Would you excuse us, Wiclam?" Fedelm asked with a sweet smile at the small man who nervously fiddled with his long beard. His brown eyes grew wide, ruffled at the idea of being sent away.

"Uh, yes," he paused. "That is fine. Let me know if you need anything else. I'll stop by to see how you are doing in a little while."

"There is no need, my friend." The old man told him. "I'll be happy to let her stay here if she needs. You know how I keep the strays from wondering off in the village."

"Ok, my friend, I guess you know best." Wiclam looked disappointed as he turned to Fedelm, but he put on a brave face.

"Please let me know if you need anything. And make sure to give my greetings to your father," he told Fedelm. The little man put on his brown cap and proceeded out of the cottage, taking a quick glance back at the dirty-faced child at the hearth.

Urith and Oslaf stayed hidden in their position near the open window watching the little man pass, his boots splashing in the mud as he went by.

"Please, come sit down and tell me how I can help you," the old man told Fedelm. "Don't mind the girl; she is a village orphan who helps me from time to time."

Fedelm sat on the wooden bench near the hearth as the little girl moved over to make room for her.

"Cilgarran, I'm sorry to be so secretive, but I seek this person called Dughorm. I know that the people of Ynyover are suspicious of Esterbluds, so I didn't want Wiclam to get the wrong idea by my visit. Apparently, this Dughorm was part of the Restoration. I was told he came to this village at some point," she explained. "I must admit I don't know much more than that. I've only recently heard of the name, even though I've grown up within the Citadel."

Fedelm looked at the man who remained expressionless, his pale eyes staring in her direction. Cilgarran pulled a pipe from his lap and filled the bowl with a green substance called *ulcath* used by some of the skalds for communicating with the gods. The little orphan handed him a lit stick, and the pleasant sweet aroma soon filled the small room.

"It's not a name that I've heard in a while; I must admit. Can I ask why you are asking for this person?" The old man's expression remained a mask behind the smoke.

"Well, I know of men who asked me to help find him. Wiclam told me you were the one person in the village who might know of this person since you are from Esterblud," Fedelm stated as she looked around the room. Nothing in the hut showed anything of his clan ties. She found this odd since most homes carried, at least, a clan tapestry or symbols of their family ties.

"And who might these men be?" Cilgarran showed a real interest in her words.

"The leader I met says he is Urith. He has a nephew named Oslaf with him. They say this Dughorm is a great hero who can help them," answered the girl.

The old man stopped rocking and sat up straight in his chair as he appeared to look at her.

"Are they near?" he asked.

Fedelm hesitated before answering. "Well, I suspect that they're somewhat close."

"As do I," he chuckled to himself. "Now, to answer your question, I know of this person."

The man smiled, turning his head in the direction of the small girl.

"You can go now, Awerm. Come back in the morning," he told her.

The little girl said nothing but she threw the small stick she was playing with into the fire. Then, she silently left through the blankets that covered the doorway.

"Now we can talk," said the old man. "Awerm is my eyes now. However, her ears are part of this village. The people of the village would not be happy to know the truth about my past."

Fedelm's eyes widen at his comments.

"What are you talking about?"

"Well now," he leaned back into his chair again. "You have brought up memories I thought long buried. The name Dughorm has not been spoken for many seasons in this kingdom."

"Why is that?" asked Fedelm. "Who is he?"

The old man went back to thoughtfully puffing on his pipe, the smoke, giving a pleasant smell to the room.

"That is an easy answer, but very complicated to explain. In another life, I was known as Dughorm."

"Wait a minute. Then, why do they call you Cilgarran?" She asked suspiciously.

"I know I sound crazy young lady. But it's true, I carry two names. And if my senses don't deceive me, you can tell your friends the same if they will come inside."

"What do you mean?" She asked. However, she heard the slight sloshing of footsteps coming around the house. Next, she saw Urith in the doorway.

"Yes, I thought I remembered the voice of an old friend." Urith squinted as he pushed through the tattered long brown curtain that covered the doorway, stepping into the lamplight of the room.

The old man stopped his rocking, turning to the voices coming from the entrance. He pulled his pipe out of his mouth.

"And I recall that voice as well, although it's been many seasons since we last spoke. Please come in, Urith. And bring your companion," Dughorm told them.

"We don't need you noticed by any of the townsfolk. As you know, a small village has many eyes and ears." He waited as his guests entered, filling the small room with their bulk.

Oslaf introduced himself as he moved past Urith and sat next to Fedelm. Urith continued to stand near the doorway, leaning his back against the wall.

"Dughorm, you have been missing from Esterblud for many seasons. No one understood why you never returned. The king would have benefited from your advice," Urith stated. "Only rumors came to us about you. Why are you here now?"

"Yes, it is probably past time for me to explain," the old man let out a sigh as he settled back in his chair again.

"My story goes back many seasons when I came to the lands of Ynyover. Urith, I suppose you have told them why I came here?"

"Yes, I explained you came during the Restoration," the warrior agreed.

"But not anything more," interjected Fedelm quickly.

"I see. Well, the simple reason is I wanted to stay in this land and the only way I could do this was to change my name," the old man answered.

"But why? You are still sung about by the skalds of King Penhda," Urith exclaimed.

"That is harder to explain. You see, during my time here, I grew to love this land along with a particular person who came from here. It was easier to change a name than to change what I desired." He explained to the others before he turned his head in the general direction of Urith.

"Don't you remember a similar desire yourself? I recall hearing news from Esterblud about our great hero marrying a young girl from an enemy kingdom."

Urith dropped his eyes at the question.

"Yes, Earmis was from Cahmais," he said quietly. He didn't notice the shocked expression on Fedelm's face.

"You understand what I'm saying." Dughorm appeared satisfied with himself.

"But why aren't you still part of the Overlord's council?" asked Fedelm. "I've been inside the Citadel for many seasons, and I've never heard your name but in passing conversations. I knew nothing about you having once been part of the council until Urith told me."

"I'm not welcome in the Citadel anymore, or in these lands. Let us say that Satres and I did not part on good terms, so I'm quite sure I was no longer discussed in the proper circles. Now, tell me why are you here? It's unusual to find Esterbluds in Ynyover with the tensions I hear about."

The blind man leaned forward as he listened to Urith tell their story. It was not the full story, and Fedelm occasionally interjected to correct him concerning details that looked unfavorable to her cause. Oslaf sat quietly listening to the stories and wondered how much he did not know about his uncle and Dughorm. He watched Urith and Dughorm, suddenly caught up with the face he was with two of the most prominent warriors of Esterblud. He also realized that he didn't know much about their personal history beyond famous battles. The young warrior listened to the occasional lies coming from Fedelm concerning her travels. It told him that he knew even less about her.

After they had completed their story, the old man leaned back in his chair again, refilling his pipe as he thought about what he heard. He asked for a light, and Fedelm held a burning twig in the man's hand to help him. He puffed on the pipe for a while longer before he started up the conversation again.

"Well, I must apologize that I have no heathmead for us. However, it is an interesting story you tell me, my friends," Dughorm resumed. "I must say, that with so many people against you, I believe you are destined to fail. You have been put on a path by those seeking your disaster."

He noticed Urith and Oslaf remained quiet concerning his thoughts.

"I can tell that you're not surprised by this. But you will be shocked to know there is deeper, much more sinister work against all of you."

"How so?" Oslaf spoke for the first time, and Dughorm laughed with a funny rasping sound.

"I wondered if our young warrior might raise his voice among the adults."

Oslaf scowled, but the old man was smiling at this joke, while Urith gave out a loud chuckle. Fedelm grinned at the joke as well.

"But your question is to the point, my young friend. Let me ask you to tell us more about Fedelm's nocturnal journey. You attempted to follow her." Dughorm stated as he blew out a thick puff of smoke. His words immediately created a stir among the group.

"But how could you know about this? No one here spoke about this before." Oslaf raised his voice defensively.

Again, the old man laughed.

"I thought I was famous for being more than a warrior. Don't you remember one of the reasons I came to Ynyover? I was considered one of the greatest seers in Esterblud. My lack of eyesight doesn't stop me from my visions. In fact, now there is clarity to dreams that I could only have imagined when I was a young man," he explained. "I believe this is something Fedelm can relate to. But I'm not answering your question, am I?"

"No, you're not. Are you saying you had a vision?" Fedelm spoke up quietly.

"Yes, my dear. That is correct. I saw your conversation with Alrpan."

Urith sprung up at this news, and Oslaf turned his head to stare in disbelief. Fedelm's face went deathly pale at the old man's words, impressed with the blind man in front of her. The man was either hakra or on Alrpan's side.

The large Esterblud remained focused on the young woman as he took a step toward her. She glanced up to see the violence in his eyes.

"I knew I should have killed you when I thought about it the first time," Urith growled out as he started to pull his sword. "I'll fix my mistake right now..."

"No, Urith!" The old man interjected firmly, stopping Urith in the middle of his angry tirade. "She is important to you and Oslaf. In fact, her role is vital to everyone. Like you, she is being manipulated by the gods along with their allies. Why do you think the Gallaeci had the gold koinons on them when you killed them while protecting the girl?"

"Wait, you know about that?" said Urith as he turned to Dughorm. "Since when does an old seer know such details?"

"Many things have changed since we last met, my friend," he told him. "Now calm down and listen."

Urith stumped to the other side of the room, confused and angry.

"Those men who attacked her had koinons on them. But, we thought they were just bandits looking for easy prey. You aren't saying Fedelm was a direct target for that scum?" asked Oslaf. Dughorm nodded while puffing on his pipe.

"Yes, she is being used as the rest of you. Things are different now. I've seen it. The three of you are together for a reason. The Fates have seen to that. You have something far more important coming, and you will need to act as one to survive. The number three is important to you Urith. You must believe me when I say that your fates are interlocked."

The trio grew quiet at the news. Each person now felt like they were puppets on the strings of an unknown master.

"I know each of you is surprised at this news. I swear upon the warrior's oath that what I say is true," Dughorm insisted. "Each of you is vital to the events that will come."

"Who is it that takes me for a fool to be manipulated? I would like to meet this person to remove his head personally and stuff it on a spike before my lodge." Urith's voice was cold and deadly.

"This is not entirely clear yet. We have people along with gods who are on separate paths trying to interfere. My visions cannot extend into the reading of minds, Urith. Only a few of the gods have that ability," he reminded his friend.

"Despite tales to the contrary, the hakra must interpret some of the dreams and visions." Another puff of smoke came from the old man. "As such, I'm fortunate to be blind, which gives me much more insight to people and events I see in my dreams."

Urith turned to the window, muttering under his breath. Fedelm spoke up.

"I must admit to you that Dughorm is correct about hakras and my visits with Alrpan. He didn't say it, but that is not the first time the goddess came to me," she glanced over to Oslaf. Her face remained pale. "I know I should have said something sooner, but...." She paused looking for the words.

"Everything has just spiraled out of control. My father was so proud that the Majireef Council chose me for such an important task. The council knew of your shipwreck before it happened. I was told by Satres there would be only one survivor. That's why I followed you, unsure how two people survived." Fedelm paused, her hand twisted the robe she wore."

"Anyway, after Alrpan came to me explaining her alliance with Satres, I was quite confident that I was on the right side. All she told me was to lead you and Urith to the gateway. I mean, how can one refuse a god when asked to help?"

"What would happen to us when we got to the gateway?" asked Oslaf.

"I wasn't sure, but after what Alrpan did to me the other night, I believe we were to be slaughtered by her beorhs," the woman admitted.

"Then, who has the correct side now?" asked Oslaf. He then looked at Urith hoping to get some understanding of what his mentor was thinking, but his stony expression was impossible to read.

"I don't understand what's happened," confessed the girl. "My visions become erratic since just before I was attacked by the Gallaeci. Alrpan has turned me into nothing more than a servant or a spy with her threats. I don't see how any of this helps the council or my overlord. But I know what is right and wrong. And to take you and your uncle before Satres or Alrpan is wrong. It would be suicide."

"Curse the gods and hakras for their meddling in our world. What can we do?" asked Oslaf.

"One thing is sure; we cannot complete our mission for the king," Urith growled loudly. He finally joined the conversation after cooling down. He moved to stand next to the old man, "Tell me Dughorm; what do your visions say about our king?"

The old man stopped rocking, his expression grew grim as he removed the pipe from his mouth.

"Before I tell you, please explain more of your reasons for coming to Ynyover," he said.

Urith took a seat on the floor near his friend and laid out

the mission he received from their king. He started his tale from the day they left his village of Cilgarran. They were to sail to the harbor town of Cuinal, on the other side of Grimma. There, he was to meet with the Sacred Overlord to lay the groundwork which would resurrect the Liege Body among the four powerful kingdoms of the world. King Penhda explained to Urith that he believed that Satres would back the re-establishment of the jointly governing body. After the warrior had finished his story, everyone waited and watched Dughorm. He tapped out the remnants of his pipe on the arm of his chair.

"Since you ask me my thoughts, I will say that I believe your original mission is impossible. Like Fedelm says, you cannot meet with Satres unless it is under his terms. And trust me, you will not like his terms." He paused.

"Unfortunately, I also think your King Penhda has put you in a bind. In my opinion, the actual reason for your coming to Ynyover was not disclosed to you. The king should know well that Satres does not intend to establish anything that will diminish or dilute his power. Because of his network of satgerts and temples, he has always considered himself superior to a mere king. I believe that your overlord thinks an alliance against the Esterblud kingdom is occurring at the Citadel of Br-Ynys. He must have sent you to discover what changes have taken place within the Citadel, and where allegiances lie among those who would head the Liege Body."

"I cannot believe it," stated Urith.

"Consider this my friend; it's the perfect foil for an overlord.   If you return to Esterblud, you will have information about the intentions of Satres.   If you are captured, he has an excuse to find allies among the other overlords to re-establish the Liege Body without the Sacred Overlord. You know King Penhda would not hesitate to use an excuse which can put him in power over Ynyover. It would make him the perfect thorn in the side of Cahmais. Either way, in my humble opinion, you are a sacrifice, my friend."

"You believe my overlord betrays me. Do you really think that?" Urith asked, not bothering to look up while his friend nodded.

Urith continued to stare into the fire burning inside the small fireplace.

"There is something that surprises me," he continued. "You refer to Penhda as my king. Is he not your overlord as well?"

The blind man was silent for a bit, looking down at the hands he could not see.

"It's a fair question, I guess. When I sought to return after banishment from the council, King Penhda would not accept my wife and I back into Esterblud. In his words, I was of no use to the overlord as a blind, old man. In his way, your good king is quite similar to Satres. When I received this word, I decided I no longer had a responsibility to Penhda."

His words struck Urith hard. The blind warrior was right; the overlord of Esterblud had little sympathy for the weak. The more Urith thought of what had been said in this meeting, the angrier he became. His mission was complete betrayal from a man he trusted.

"But Penhda couldn't have known of our ship's destruction that left us in Ynyover. That means gods were involved and knew we were coming," said the warrior grimly as he made his decision. "I'm in agreement with you that we are being used. Now we must determine how we get out of our situation."

He peered over to Fedelm and Oslaf as he continued. "As I see it, we cannot return home without attempting to reach Satres, for our king would never allow us back into our lands. I know Penhda would treat Oslaf and the rest of our family as outcasts for leaving a wrecked ship and dead crew while saving ourselves."

As Urith watched Oslaf carefully for his reaction, the younger warrior nodded his head in silent agreement.

"I say we go to the Citadel. We will meet with Satres,"

Urith said. His partners all looked at him like he lost his mind.

"But why would you go to the Citadel now? You heard Dughorm. If you cannot get to Satres, what is the purpose?" Fedelm's voice rose in shock.

"You just heard we are being used by men and gods who are leading us to dance to their tunes," Urith replied. "I'm not one who enjoys others killing my crew and using Oslaf and me as their playthings. Given a few moments with the right people, I believe we can find out exactly where we stand. I would be happy to use my Clovel Sword to wipe out the majority of that cursed Majireef council."

Fedelm could tell from Urith's tone and manner that there would be much blood and pain once he entered the fortress. She gave a slight shiver at the thought.

"It appears the closer we get to the fortress, the more likely we will be captured or killed," observed Oslaf. "I am not afraid, but I also believe we cannot allow ourselves to be easy targets."

"All the information, all the answers we seek, comes from the people inside the Citadel," said Fedelm. She avoided Urith's gray eyes as he stared at her.

"I wonder. Is there any way we can get into the fortress without an invitation?" Oslaf asked aloud as he looked around. He spotted Urith looking at him with his evil grin.

"I'm not sure..." Urith's voice trailed off as he looked at Fedelm. "It might be possible. Any fortress will have weak points, and the guards who come and go to the village may be more interested in a few koinons than who runs the place. Then again, we have Fedelm. Perhaps she can help on that idea?"

The girl showed her uneasiness at the notion, but she relented. Dughorm admitted his knowledge of the sanctuary and the entrances would be suspect after so many seasons away. He also mentioned rumors he had heard concerning many Cahmais warriors in the area around Grimma and the Citadel. Out of habit, the blind man tapped out the pipe he had already emptied.

"Well, it is getting late, and it won't be safe for all of you to stay here, even if I had the room. You must take the time to consider all that has been revealed here tonight. You can work out the details of access to the fortress and what role Fedelm will play in that. I will also give thought to your situation. One never knows what dreams might reveal."

He smiled as he rose stiffly from his chair, indicating it was time for his guests to depart.

"Where can we meet?" Urith asked. "Our ossanes are on the east side of the village in a small grove near a stream,"

"Downstream just before the trail starts its ascent, you will find a small cave. The locals avoid it because they believe it is cursed. Just be careful no one follows you from the village," Dughorm told them as he confidently walked to the other side of the room. He reached up to a shelf above him.

"Urith, can you stay a bit as I need to give you something?" he asked.

Urith nodded to the others as they moved to the door. He noticed Fedelm would not look directly at him. He guessed she was thinking about his deadly intent against the Majireef Council. Fedelm was worried about her father's safety.

Carefully, Oslaf peered out the brown curtains hanging over the door, waiting a moment as his eyes adjusted to the darkness. Seeing nothing that might indicate they were being watched, he led Fedelm into the night. Urith went over to the old man who turned, handing him a small talisman of carved bloodstone. Surprised by the gesture, he looked at it closely in the dim light. It had the shape of an Esterblud metal shield with the symbol of an X engraved in the middle of the shield. The amulet was smaller than the palm of his hand, its delicate engravings showing the work of a skilled artisan. A small hole in it allowed a length of thin leather to drape the necklace around his neck.

"This might provide some protection from those gods who are not on your side. It has proven useful to me over the seasons. It has unique properties when used with other items."

"Like what items?" Urith asked.

"Only the most valuable weapon you carry. The power of the Clovel Sword will combine with this Bloodstone amulet. Those words engraved upon your sword have significant influence with the right items. Memorize them and remember to use these as a weapon when you need it," He advised.

Dughorm walked back to a small bed next to the wall.

"Also, I would recommend that you keep an eye on the girl. Stop her from taking any more night walks. But don't hurt her. Like I said before, Fedelm will prove vital to you."

He sat down on the edge of the bed.

"Where did you get such an item?" Urith asked.

"Believe it or not, that came from our friend, Satres, as a gift. He told me he found it in the archives of the Citadel, but I never believed him. He uses people to achieve his ends; he does not get his hands dirty with the work. I assumed it came from a *satgert* who gave it in tribute to the Sacred Overlord."

The old man laughed to himself.

"I'm sure he never bothered to find out more about it since he didn't believe it was directly related to the Skool. However, he may soon regret his disregard for the amulet. I was able to learn more about it than he would ever imagine. My friend, it is my gift to you. I wish I could help you on your next quest as I often miss those days." Dughorm explained as he slowly laid out on the cot.

"Ah, Urith, it is an ugly thing to get old."

Urith remembered the stories of this hero and swore to himself that he would not end up like this.

He's right, it's much better to die in battle.

Urith put the amulet around his neck. The stone was cold on his bare skin, but then it grew warm. Hot enough that he looked down at it again, only to dismiss the feeling as a figment of his imagination. He did not see the pommel of his Clovel Sword momentarily glow.

"I appreciate your help, my friend. Get some rest. I will see you after dark tomorrow," he said. "Perhaps, we can come up with a plan that gets me to meet Satres and fulfill my promise to the king."

"Yes, getting old means you look forward to the sleep that comes," the old man murmured to himself, apparently not listening to Urith.

The scarred warrior rose, heading for the doorway. He stopped to look back at the old man again. Dughorm was pulling a threadbare blanket over his frail body. Urith walked out into the night, pausing to scan for any unwelcome eyes observing him. Seeing nothing of interest, he quickly moved across the mud street and disappeared behind a small dark hut. Urith moved silently away into the night, a small figure appeared from between two huts after the warrior passed. The shadow turned and walked slowly back toward the dim lights of the village and the night watchman.

It took only a few moments for Urith to meet up with Fedelm and Oslaf just outside the village. From there, the trio collected their ossanes and walked through the woods to the trailhead. Fedelm wanted to recommend another place to spend the night, but she could not think of a place that was suitable.

It was not long before the group found the cave. It had a wide opening but quickly narrowed as it went deeper into the hillside leaving it suitable to use only the front part of their shelter. They began to settle in for the night, building a small fire with stones around it to take the chill from the entrance. Satisfied their fire would be difficult to see by the villagers, the trio settled in to eat from their remaining provisions and discuss how they could gain access to the Citadel. Fedelm immediately attempted to get them to leave the area and to return to the lands of Esterblud.

"Go back and tell your overlord what happened," she suggested. "I can do the same with Satres. That would stop Alrpan."

"No, the gods don't work that way," Urith stated.

"Besides, it goes against the warrior code," Oslaf interjected passionately. "Penhda would strip us of our tunics and weapons before sending us to wander the wilds like criminals. It doesn't matter if this was a mission designed to fail. May the gods be cursed."

Urith laughed at his nephew's impassioned speech.

"He's right about that," he agreed before turning back to Fedelm. "Now give me details about your conversations with the Majireef Council and Alrpan. I want the full story!"

Reluctantly, she told them how the council came to her with a great mission as proof of her right to become part of these trusted advisors. She knew it was a great honor to be one of the few women invited. The hakra explained that Satres conducted the blessing ritual in front of her proud father. She explained that after the ceremony, her father was sent away on a trip to Grimma. It was then she was told that their ship would be wrecked upon the Ynyover coastline, with one survivor she was to follow. Her information confirmed to the men that people and gods were watching them and manipulating their progress.

She went on to outline her meetings with Alrpan, who came to her separate of the council. The goddess knew much of what was happening. The girl admitted, at first, she was happy to count such an entity as her ally. Fedelm then revealed that the goddess went from acting as a partner who would aid the girl, to a powerful master who threatened her to maintain the cooperation. Finally, the hakra explained how her visions becoming vague, apparently controlled by others. Both men could tell that this part of the experience seemed to be the most troubling to the girl.

At the end of Fedelm's explanation, she nervously waited for Urith to say something.

"You're just another human being manipulated by the gods," he stated calmly. "Now, let's get to the Citadel."

Fedelm showed them the layout of the Citadel with the main corridors and entrances by drawing in the dirt of the cave. With the design understood, Urith outlined a basic plan to get inside the fortress. He noticed the girl stayed quiet, as she appeared to be deliberating something. Occasionally, she would ask a question and appeared happy to point out the pitfalls to their ideas. They failed to notice the girl's periodic glances back into the depths of the cave.

"Once we're inside the Citadel, would you take us to Satres? Urith asked Fedelm. She paused for a moment, considering it.

"Only if you agree not to hurt my father," she told them. "In fact, you should meet with him first."

The Esterbluds decided to talk about this idea with Dughorm the next evening for his thoughts. They hoped he might be able to give them further ideas on this council. Finally growing weary, they went to their respective blankets near the small fire. As they lay there, the group heard the sounds of *kuons* howling in the distance. Neither Esterblud could see the girl staring at the back of the cave as she made up her mind about her next steps. It was time to choose sides, and she hoped she just made the right decision.

In the early morning sunshine, which spread across the valley, a stream of golden light revealed the trio as they slept in the cave. Oslaf woke first, his head popping up with a sudden awareness he was to be on watch. Moving stiffly from his uncomfortable position propped against a large rock at the entrance to the cave, he turned to see Fedelm curled up in her gray blanket. Urith was lying on the other side of the now dead fire. His uncle was beginning to stir as the light brightened the inside of the cave. Oslaf got up stiffly from his place, forced to duck the overhanging rock outcrop which topped the entrance. Standing up, he looked over the valley below. He could see a herder and his two *weahs* guiding a large herd of *starkts* out to graze. The *weahs* barked and nipped at the heels of their herd as they worked the animals to the field. Turning back to the cave, Oslaf crouched again to enter and noticed with some relief that his back was not hurting badly from his wound.

"Well, the day comes early, Urith."

Urith grumbled and nodded as he sat up while pulling the blanket over his shoulders. He grabbed the water bag near him, taking a large drink and using a little in his hand to splash his face.

"Yes, my friend, morning came much too soon." He stretched still shaking off the sleep. "We need to get some food. Unfortunately, we cannot stray too far from this area with the village so close by. Any ideas?"

"I've already thought of it. I noticed several small pools in the stream when I got water for us last night. I think I can come up with fish. I have a net I can use," he replied.

"That's a good idea," Urith agreed. "If you do that, I'll stay here and get a fire going. This highland bluewood will keep the smoke down, and the wind should disperse it well enough." Urith looked over at the sleeping form of their companion. "We'll let Fedelm sleep some more."

Oslaf paused a minute before asking Urith a question. "Do you believe what she told us about Alrpan and the council?"

Urith surprised the young warrior when he nodded.

"Yes, I think she is actually scared about the position she's put herself into. She has more reason to be with us, over those who sent her. However, I don't think she will forget her family and friends who remain in the service of Satres. That's what makes things dangerous for us."

Oslaf nodded thoughtfully, then he grabbed a twine net and began his journey toward the nearby stream. Urith followed him. Stepping by the edge downstream, he spent time cleaning up, before he shaved his growth of beard using his razor-sharp dagger. Oslaf glanced at his uncle before going to the pools of water upstream. He was somewhat surprised by Urith. However, neither man had bathed or shaved since their escape from the shipwreck. It was time.

While he was shaving, he recalled the sharp tongue of Fedelm who stated their smell could be worse than the ossanes they rode. Despite his anger at the statement, Urith had to agree when he entered the enclosed room with Dughorm.

After removing his tunic, Urith steeled himself before he splashed the water across his upper body and arms. Women can sure change a warrior; he thought as he splashed his face and neck, rubbing hard. The water refreshed him, but also sent a shiver through him as the cool morning breeze dried his skin.

Now fully awake, he pulled his tunic back on before he went over to a large dead bluewood tree that overlooked the valley. Standing next to the tree, he thought of Dughorm. Seeing the old man whom he had revered since his youth left him feeling strange. Urith remembered his family telling him of all the old warrior's great exploits. He also recalled the times he had fought beside him as well. Now his hero was living out his final days in obscurity in a foreign land. It was something he never considered possible. He hated the idea that any warrior could end up in such a condition.

Urith took up a load of fallen branches and twigs from around the tree and headed back to the cave, wondering what Dughorm would think of their plan. He suspected the man might have other visions to tell them about. Ultimately, Urith knew he would make the decision on his own, but he held a profound respect for his friend and trusted him as much as anyone he had ever known. As he got back to the cave, he approached slowly to make sure he didn't wake the girl. However, he realized he didn't need to bother as he spotted her moving around in the cave.

"Did you sleep well? He asked as he ducked his head to enter the low-hanging area.

Fedelm was about to snap a sarcastic response, then she realized his manner was friendly. She noticed he had shaved off the growth of beard, which had accumulated since the start of their journey together. He was still wet from his attempt at bathing. His actions surprised her.

"Actually, I slept well for the first time in a while. How

about you?" She watched him, half expecting him to change back into his usual sour mood.

"Not bad, but I think I would prefer a bed like Dughorm's last night." He smiled at the thought. "Oslaf is out getting some breakfast for us. You are stuck with me."

The girl nodded, still surprised by how pleasant Urith treated her.

"Why are you so cheerful? I was waiting for you to threatened to slit my throat again."

He looked at her for a moment.

"I've given many things some thought and realized you are not the full-blown enemy I might have supposed. Plus, you have support from Oslaf. Since he has some trust in you, I must try to keep an open mind," he told her. "Your actions getting to Dughorm confirmed that you can be trusted with your oath."

"I'm not sure how I should respond," Fedelm said carefully after taking a deep breath. "I know Oslaf seems to care for me, and I would not want to hurt him. However, he may be thinking of more than I can give. I'm still not sure what will come. My sleep was dreamless last night, so my visions are of little use right now."

"Well, he is young, so he will need to learn about the world. In ways, your world has been isolated as much as his. Just remember, we live by the warrior code, and I trust Oslaf. I would give my life for him as he would for me. Therefore, I must do the same for you as long as he cares for you in the way I see."

The girl shook her head at what he told her.

"No, that is too much to put on me. I like him, but you and he are still not my friends. There are too many unknowns in front of us. I've seen death and pain when you unsheathe your sword. My family and friends are not your enemies."

"I understand that, but it is enough for now that you know where I stand. You help get us into the Citadel, and you'll never need to worry about dealing with the Esterbluds again,"

Urith told her. "I'll vow not to harm your family if that helps."

Fedelm frowned, then nodded.

"I realize you don't appreciate the code we follow." He continued. "Maybe what we do is hard to understand. But I swear I only want to meet Satres to know what game he plays. We don't kill for the love of killing."

"I want to trust you. However, life at the Citadel is never so simple," she offered.

"That comes from living in the clouds of overlords and gods," Urith smiled his sneer again, but she could see his eyes were bright in jest.

She smiled in return, her green eyes showing relief.

"Alright, it's a truce between us. I'll keep what you say in mind."

"Your word is good enough." He looked up at the sound of approaching footsteps. Oslaf came into sight carrying a string of fish and a large smile. Urith also noticed Oslaf stopped to clean his face and upper body before returning.

"Well, let's get breakfast and prepare for the upcoming trip I believe we'll be taking."

Urith rose to greet his nephew allowing Fedelm to catch a glimpse of the amulet he now wore. She quickly interrupted to ask him where he got such an unusual stone. He told her about his visit with Dughorm. Urith turned back to his nephew, missing the woman's shocked expression as she stared at the talisman. In the sunlight that entered the cave, the amulet showed its color of deep red veins inside a coal black shine.

It was called *Helites*, or Bloodstone, a rock that could provide its wearer with enchanted abilities against humans and gods. A visibly impressed Fedelm stood to join her comrades, convinced the old blind man was indeed talented and probably a powerful hakra.

Chapter 6: Revelations

Narrow stone steps led down into pitch black darkness that the oil lantern failed to penetrate. Sounds echoed up from the blackness; screams and moans which rose from the dungeons where the prisoners of the Sacred Overlord languished as they died. Amid the hideous sounds from the dungeons there came the sound of light, tapping footsteps mixed with the rustle of heavy woolen robes worn by the lone figure as he moved steadily down the stairs. His lantern gave just enough light to see each step in front of him during his dark descent as he considered his options before his meeting.

The figure reached a fork in the path that marked the entrance into a secret level within the Citadel. Following the tunnel as it broke left; he came to a dark alcove where he stopped. He placed his lantern on a small shelf carved into the rock, then feeling with his hands, he found his target, a stone set high and unseen in the dark recesses. As he pulled the stone, he heard the familiar scraping as the stone door opened at the rear of the alcove. Stepping forward, he pushed, and the heavy door reluctantly swung open. Taking his lantern from the small shelf, he passed through the doorway, crossed a small chamber and proceeded down another set of steps into a large room, known as the *sidhera* or gateway room. In the middle of the room was a large round table, encircled by ornate chairs. The tabletop was inlaid with colored stones, creating symbols of the gods of the underworld. It was here where humans and gods could commune, away from the outside world. The man sat down in one of the large chairs made of the same tone of wood as the table. He pulled back the hood of the red cloak to reveal his handsome face. Satres looked younger than his solstices alive, and his thin face had a sharp hooked nose with a small brown mustache underneath that was clipped at the corners of his thin lips. Bright blue eyes darted around the area across from him as if he expected trouble.

"Satres, you are early," a familiar female voice echoed in the air. "I don't normally like coming to the gateway this soon in the day. Is there a problem?"

The man waited, saying nothing. After a bit, his eyes could make out a form moving from behind the curtains at the other end of the room. The curtains hid a small door leading to a favorite room where he regularly met this goddess. As he watched, the pleasing form of Alrpan emerged from behind the curtains to stand across the table from him. She wore a vivid red robe, the fabric of which was woven from the fur of the rare and ancient *scamalel*, a beast long forgotten by humans. It was trimmed in a silken fabric embroidered with a spun-gold thread showing the shapes of mystic symbols of the netherworld. Mostly covering her body, the robe flowed down from her slender shoulder creating a long cleavage line to her waist, exposing her bare flesh underneath.

"Yes, there is a problem. The Esterbluds remain a threat. I've heard they are nearby, but I'm not sure where." The man stared into her exquisite pale blue eyes, finding their intensity unnerving.

"My Fealharan has not reported back to me," he admitted.

"You have reason to worry about your assassins, for they dwell in my realm now," said Alrpan. "Mivraa didn't even bother to keep them for Haligulf. The Esterblud leader caught your incompetent hired hands before they could accomplish anything."

She enjoyed the look on his face that the unexpected news. *You believe that yourself smarter than a god, you fool.*

"However, your girl revealed our enemy's plans to me. They are not a problem. They went into a village called Ynysbeag looking for someone named Dughorm. Their current activities mean little to our plans." The goddess lay back in the giant chair to watch him.

"Dughorm? Are you sure?" Satres eyes widened at her comment.

"Of course, I'm sure. Why? What is this to you?"

Satres' eyes darted away. "It's nothing… well, nothing to concern us. It is not a name I've heard for many seasons."

"Don't lie to me, human. I know you too well. Or don't you remember how close we have been at times?" Alrpan purred at him.

"I'm not lying. He was banished from the Citadel many seasons ago. I expected him to be gone from Ynyover and back in his homeland." The thin man seemed troubled by the news as his fingers began drumming quietly on the table.

"Well, can he hurt our plans?" The female form rose from her chair, coming around the table.

"No, I don't think so. He was an Esterblud, who came to the council as part of the Restoration, so it makes sense his countrymen would seek him out. He is blind and terribly old after all this time. I have no worries about him."

He spoke decisively as if to convince himself and Alrpan. The goddess moved next to him, caressing his cheek with her clammy hand. He felt a lusting surge inside of him, which he had trouble controlling.

"An old blind man, you say. Yes, I can see why you may not worry, but was he not a powerful hakra?" She bent over, whispering in his ear. "I wonder if a superior man could allow such a person to live in the lands he was banished from. That does not strike me as a great leader or one who aspires to rise into the immortal world."

She pulled away, coming around to the other side of the heavy wooden chair. "No, I would think someone who aspires to such greatness would take care of this by using the many that look to Satres for his leadership. As of last night, the old man rests in a village less than a half day away. Why does he mock you by staying? "

He felt rising anger for appearing so weak in front of her. "I had no idea he was still here. While he is no threat, I will take care of this issue."

She leaned down again, exposing more inviting parts of

her body to him. "As long as that Esterblud defiler named Urith remains alive, the Fates may turn against us. If such a human finds the Skool, the chaos he can bring is a threat to you. He is seen in many visions across the lands and now has an influence on your little girl. I told you she was too inexperienced to be the choice."

Satres turned his head away. "But you well know there is no one else, and certainly no man could have been sent to meet Urith. Had your vision of the Cahmais killing this warrior come to pass, we would have no problem now."

"You should not blame your partner, Satres; especially since I've just told you where they are." The goddess pulled away in an overly dramatic huff. "I would think someone aspiring to be a god would fix this."

Satres nodded, giving her the stage. "Yes, you make an excellent suggestion, given how he threatens our plans, my dear. I'll make sure this usurper is taken care of." He reached out, grabbing her hand. "However, I think we have time for other things which you covet as much. Unlike the other gods, you really enjoy the human form." His hand stroked her arm. "And all of the sensations of our bodies."

She leaned over, blowing hot breath lightly into his ear. Again, he nearly melted at the lust that built when he was around this temptress. She was one of the few females who could do this, and she smiled down at him, pulling away from her hand deliberately.

"Perhaps we have such time, but you would be wise not to bet your life on it. I will decide when I want pleasure or pain. Not even another god has the power to force me to do what I don't want." She ran a finger through his long dark hair. "And you are but a human."

He smiled back at her, trying to hold his temper as she walked away, her figure dissolving into the darkness as she exited through the curtains. While he hated how she used him, he told himself it was necessary for the moment. He believed her interests were still his.

"Perhaps! But only for a while," he said as the reply echoed in the room.

The man rose, turning to leave as he masked the anxiety he felt at her words and actions. He shook off the feeling, deciding she must be trusted. In spite of her bravado, she had a great deal at risk; Caruun's wrath against her would not be pretty if her activities were discovered. She was powerful, yet as long as he kept his motives from her visions, he could manage her manipulations and become her master in the future.

"You get what you want, and I get my payment in return. Yes, this works quite nicely," Satres quietly declared as he left the room.

When Satres entered his private chambers later, he told the elaborately dressed warrior at his door to summon Colainn, head of his personal guard. The red-haired giant arrived at his door, breathing heavily from his dash up the stairs to his master's suite of rooms. He was sporting an elaborate purple-feathered, silver helmet and an ornately engraved breastplate. Under the breastplate, he wore the long red tunic, the symbolic color of overlord worn by his guards. He bowed in deference to the Sacred Overlord.

"Your spies have been negligent in their duties, Colainn." Satres looked out windows, glazed with clear crystal, at the lush valley below. In the distance, he could barely see the road heading to Ynysbeag.

The giant appeared shocked by the news. "How is that so, Sacred Overlord?"

"I have news of a traitor called Dughorm still in our territory. He was banished by me before your time. Yes, I hear he is resting comfortably in Ynysbeag, talking with foreigners from Esterblud. Now can you explain why this person still resides within a day's ride of the Citadel? Have we no spies within my lands?"

"I cannot explain this." The giant's eyes were wide at what he was hearing. "I'll send my men there immediately."

Satres turned to the man and gave him a deadly stare. "No! You are not to barge into the village with the entire guard. That will upset the locals."

"Find him with your spies," the overlord lectured him like a child. "Koinons to the right people in the village will disclose the location. I want this Dughorm and his Esterblud friends found and brought to me. This must be done quietly; I don't want the council to know about this. Use our Aberffraw friends to take care of this little matter. That should save your guards from letting anyone inside the Citadel from hearing. Do you understand?"

"I will follow your instructions to the letter," the giant guard bowed again, hurriedly backing to the door.

"Another thing Colainn," the Overlord stopped him with his words. "You have until midday tomorrow to bring the traitor to me, or your head will be placed on the traitor's pole at the gate."

The Overlord walked through a red curtain into a circular room adjoining his bed-chamber. He could picture the guard running panicked to Lyncus about his mission, and it pleased him. The room was adorned with rich tapestries of Vulthnal wool that hung from the tall walls. The fabrics, showing finely woven images of the gods, looked down on two nearly life-sized statues of Alrpan and Caruun, resting across from each other. A small bowl of incense rested on an ornate table, releasing the aroma of scented herbs which aided Satres in his communion with the gods. While not gifted with the insight of a seer, the Sacred Overlord sometimes felt the entities around him. Satres bowed before the statues, then sat cross-legged on a pillow to meditate before them.

Satres heard the sound of the door to his bed-chamber open with the familiar thumping noise of a stick and the shuffling sound of sandals across the stone floor. The Overlord rose from his meditation and walked into his room.

"Welcome Lyncus," said Satres even before his visitor could cross the bedchamber to Satres' altar room. "What brings you to my chambers so early?"

The Aberffraw leader appeared out of breath from his long climb with his injured leg, his body supported by the crutch fashioned by Satres personal *mhoda* or physician.

"I've just heard that Colainn knows where the Esterbluds are and that he is gathering my men for capturing them. You promised them to me," Lyncus reminded the overlord, visibly upset at the perceived snub.

"My friend, you are jumping to a false conclusion," soothed Satres as he stepped forward, putting his arm around the warrior. "He was told to capture a traitor who never left Ynyover. There is a rumor of Esterbluds nearby. I was planning on sending you as leader of the guard, which is why he went to you. Are you strong enough to lead them?"

The overlord steered the Aberffraw warrior back to the vaulted door leading into Satres' chambers. Lyncus looked at him suspiciously but accepted the lie.

"Yes, my lord, I can handle the trip. I'm glad to hear you sent for me. Our mutual interests mean much to the overlord of Cahmais."

"My son, I agree with you. Our people have grown so close over the last season. I trust your judgment more than Colainn, and the last thing I would want is to lose our friendship." Satres kept his arm around the broad shoulders of the younger man.

"I'll make sure you are there when they find the enemy. I'm sure you have much to pay them back for. However, you must not take any chances as you are unable to move about quickly with your leg," warned the overlord. The warrior nodded dutifully as he understood the order from Satres to stay out of the fight.

"That's good," said the thin man happily. "Now when you return, we can discuss your triumph over an excellent cask of wine."

As they reached the door, the Sacred Overlord of Ynyover dropped his arm from the warrior. He told a guard to help

Lyncus to join Colainn and his men before they left. Entering his chambers again, the thin man moved to a wall where an ornate polished silver mirror hung. The man looked into the mirror thinking about the young man while he ran a finger across his brows. He hoped Lyncus would not do anything too rash. It was hard to find such discrete young married men for the things he enjoyed.

The sound of mounts galloping out of the courtyard at full speed soon drifted up to the bed-chamber. The overlord's firm lips turned to a wicked grin of satisfaction as his guards hurried to carry out their orders. The giant man was not very intelligent, but he was intensely loyal and not overly ambitious. He decided that if the big guard came back with the traitor, he might reward him with marriage to Fedelm as he remembered how the big man stammered in her presence. Yes, it was always good to keep the loyal ones by bringing them into his private circle. Such a reward also kept the others interested in maintaining their elite position as protector of the Sacred Overlord.

~~~

Daylight was fading when Dughorm arrived at the cave of the trio. He was led by the little girl called Awerm who, like him, was carrying a large bag of food and drink. They soon laid the feast upon the flat rock at the entrance to the cave. The campfire near the entry of the cave provided enough illumination for the little girl to set out the meal before she left them to return to the village. The old man was in high spirits as they shared the meal of dark bread, *fisheel,* and a local barkmead that Urith nearly spat out as swill. In deference to his friend, he forced it down while they chatted about their past battles together. Fedelm kept asking the blind warrior about his experiences with the Majireef and seemed particularly interested in his associations.

As they cleared away the remains of their meal, the sun was setting in the east, and twin moons came into view. They moved further into the cave, coming around the fire to go over
~~~

their plans. Urith explained their plan to sneak into the Citadel and meet with the Overlord as unexpected visitors. The trio believed that by working with Fedelm's father, they would be able to arrange such a meeting if they lay down their arms. Dughorm listened intently as he puffed on his pipe until they finished telling him about their plan.

Dughorm pulled the pipe from his mouth, his sightless eyes seeming to sparkle in the flickering firelight, "Fedelm, did you have a vision last night?" he asked. Surprised at the question, Fedelm admitted she had no visions.

"Well, that's not unexpected. I believe a god or two are interfering with the natural order. After you had left, I fell into a deep sleep, which is unusual at my age. My sleep brought me desperate premonitions, with regards to my future. It was the most exciting and unbelievable thing I have felt since my last battle."

He paused at the memories rushing through his brain. The group listened dumbfounded by the turn of the conversation. Sensing the silent group staring at him, he continued.

"You must be wondering what this has to do with your plan. Let me explain. This vision became clear to me this morning; it was a moment when my destiny came before me." He turned to Urith.

"Perhaps you remember such times in a battle? When you are struck down; expecting to receive that last death-stroke from your enemy while you are preparing for the end." The old man was growing excited as he spoke.

Urith nodded at his hero. "Yes, I know what you mean. There is clarity at certain points in every battle, no matter the confusion and chaos that surrounds you."

"That is exactly my experience. And now, let me explain how this fits in." He paused again.

"First, your plan will never work as Satres is working to manipulate and control all that has been going on. He will only agree to meet with you to capture you and then destroy you. Lay down your arms, and he will display your heads on pikes at the Citadel. No, you must have another plan."

Dughorm paused to let his companions reflect on what he had said. Oslaf spoke up unexpectedly.

"How can you be so sure? Fedelm tells us you cannot get such clarity from dreams, and now you say our plan is impossible. How can we be certain your visions are the truth? How do we know you are not being manipulated?"

The blind man smiled at the challenge.

"You are wise to ask such a question because it is unusual to get such clarity. But there are blood sacrifices that were foretold to me. It is this sacrifice which will convince you to believe in my words. Be warned that after you know of the truth, you will be forced into drastic actions, and you must prevail. Much of this realm depends on upon your upcoming trials."

"What are the sacrifices and the actions you speak of? I've only heard of such tales about the Gods of the Great Void." Fedelm joined in the disbelief.

"While the premonition of ritual death was very certain, the details surrounding the sacrifice were not. I am sure things will happen very soon. Fedelm, you know from your visions that the gods of the realms are in chaos. Humans have entered into separate pacts with the gods. Alrpan and Satres are working together for something that could alter both the human realm and theirs. You must understand that Satres will be happy to accept you into his Citadel, but he intends to destroy you."

"Therefore, I must tell you about your next steps as told by the visions and no one here will like it. But believe me; the Fates are turning to our side."

The old blind man went silent, dropping his head. At first, Urith thought he might have just fallen asleep. He was about to say something when Dughorm raised his head again.

"*Da Umca Mivwar*," He turned his blind eyes toward Urith. "My friend, you must remember these words. The amulet you have will protect if you use this incantation. Now, promise me you will not forget.”

Urith glanced at the others, instinctively thinking the old man was going crazy.

“Do you understand?” The blind man’s voice rose higher. “*Da Umca Mivwar.* You must give me your warrior’s vow to remember those words for your darkest hours.”

“Very well, I’ll remember as an oath to you.” Urith agreed as he saw the others wondering what was happening.

“Why do you give the spells and such a powerful talisman to someone who is not a hakra?” asked Fedelm. The others looked at her, realizing she understood what the old man was talking about.

“It is for that very reason,” said the old man. “It appears you know well the powers within the *Djeed* talisman. These skills can be used for good or evil, and I’ve yet to meet a hakra who could resist using it for evil or for conquest.”

“Does that include yourself?” Fedelm asked sharply. “You had this before Urith.”

“I know well the potent amulet will remain in the hands of an honorable warrior who follows the code of Heptarc. However, to answer your question was I not blind, I could have been tempted. I know it sounds suspicious to entrust this power to the hands of a person trained to kill and maim at the command of others.” He turned his head in the warrior’s direction with a smile while continuing his thoughts.

“Urith has proven that he is capable of thinking beyond another’s command. I am certain I need not worry about Urith becoming maddened by a natural urge to use such power over others,” he explained. “You don’t understand his past. Plus, he has given his oath to me.”

“Of course, Dughorm. You have my word.” Urith was holding the amulet up in the light, eying it suspiciously.

“Fedelm, when you understand more how much honor and justice mean to my friend, you will know why I did this. Now, someone must tell me how high in the night are the twin moons.” Dughorm asked.

The trio investigated the night sky lit up by the moons and quickly answered they were near their crest.

"Time grows short. And now, you must put into your minds complete trust in yourselves and your friends." He paused to collect his thoughts as he mumbled to himself.

"What is this? Are you coming with us? This is not making any sense." Urith grew impatient at his friend, slowly becoming convinced that he was seeing the twisted ramblings of a mad man.

Dughorm suddenly stopped and turned his head to Urith. "It will come to make sense my friend, for now, we come to our future. You and your friends must escape this land now. For you must seek the Skool now for any chance to save yourselves."

The entire group stared at the old blind man, too stunned to say anything at first.

"Yes, yes, I know what I tell you sounds like the ravings of a mad, blind man, crazy from my visions and age. But it is the only way you can save yourselves and perhaps even the realms," he told them.

"It's beyond crazy," Fedelm jumped to her feet. "No mortal could know where the Skool is. It is even beyond the power of the gods to find. Besides, even if a human were to find it, the very power of it would destroy them."

The old man broke into a smile again. "Those are the tales sprouting from the Citadel of Br-Ynys. But if that were true, how would you explain the Sacred Overlord's many seasons of searching for this very powerful weapon? Ah, I bet you didn't know that. Why would he send an inexperienced and unknown woman to seek out the Esterbluds? It's simply because the others inside of the council would have learned of his plans."

"That's impossible," the girl said hotly.

"Then, explain to us why Aberffraw warriors run throughout the lands of Ynyover? I know you haven't informed our friends about everything that you know,"

Dughorm pointed out.

The girl turned red at the revelations from the old man. Urith glared at her and was about to say something when Oslaf interceded.

"Another lie, Fedelm? Can't you remember the truth anymore?"

"I meant to...," she stammered. "It's just everything was moving so quickly and, at first, I didn't know how to talk about it. Then, it seemed too late."

"Ok, why are they here?" The young warrior asked in a tone that made it clear he regretted the faith he had put in her.

"I was told they were in the lands at the invitation of the Sacred Overlord to help drive out the Gallaeci," she said. "Satres told the council it was the only way since the Ynyover guard was too weak."

"By breaking the Restoration treaty among the lands to drive out a few tribes, Satres risks open war with Esterblud and other lands? I don't believe the other overlords will believe he is that stupid." Urith cursed as he spat on the ground.

"Exactly, Satres is after greater power. But in fairness to Fedelm, I didn't tell you this news last night," continued the blind man. "I had to be sure of her loyalty to helping you. She proved it last night." There was a cryptic grin at the comment, and Fedelm looked at the ground. Before Urith could say anything, Dughorm spoke to him.

"Urith, I give you my warrior oath that the Aberffraw are here, in league with Satres, to find the Skool. I was banished from this land for asking the questions of Satres about his search of the records concerning the Shield. He was surprised by my knowledge, but I still held some power at the time. He banished me instead."

"This is not possible. My father would have told me about such things," the girl cried. "This must be a trick." She looked at the others. "How can you believe these tales of an old blind man?"

Dughorm's voice grew tense. "Listen, girl. I'm still a warrior in spite of my eyes. I don't give my oath to something unless I know it to be true. If you have not asked your father about this, you will get your chance soon enough."

"Let's get back to now and the present." Urith interrupted them.

"I trust your oath, my friend. But you said yourself, this sounds crazy. What about this Shield of Skool and how does this help us? You seem to be leading somewhere, but you are not telling us anything. What is it?" He remained seated on the ground trying to keep control of his rising temper. He didn't want to believe the ideas coming to his mind.

"We don't have much time left together so Fedelm and another warrior will tell you more about your upcoming trip." Everyone noticed that the old man was speaking faster now.

"Wait, you said another," interjected Urith.

"You will see much more as others become interested in your quest," he said cryptically. "You may recall the stories of the skalds who like to sing about the Destruction of Du-Rinell

"Yes, I remember those," Oslaf spoke up. "Wasn't this shield broken up by the Gods of the Great Void many generations ago because the relic would allow humans to be stronger than the gods?"

"You are partially correct, my young friend. It is not known to many, but the Skool gives a human the destructive power of the gods. In fact, it is the very symbol of how the gods and humans are tied together. It is said to have come from the Great Void where all the gods go to their end. Because of that fact, it is the one weapon feared by the gods. They would go to any length to stop any human from possessing it. For they hold power over the mortals, and they see it as a danger to them and as a weapon to be used against their rule of the realms."

Dughorm's face seemed to be lit by the pale moons above them as he continued. "What the skalds don't say is this object is feared by the gods of the Sky Realm. They avoided telling the true story of the destruction of Du-Rinell when the new gods joined with the humans. Together, they vanquished the Gods of the Great Void and the First Overlord. That information was buried deep in the secrets of the Citadel and its keepers. Fedelm will need to ask her father about why Satres does not let this information come to the world."

"What does that have to do with us?" interjected Urith. "I still don't understand why we need to find this object."

"You forget, my friend, that you are now dealing with powerful enemies. How can you challenge the gods without the proper weapon?" The blind man asked as his pale eyes seemed to bore into his companions. He desperately needed for them to understand the gravity in his words.

"You are telling us we need to leave and find this Skool. But how can this object be found now? Was it not destroyed?" Urith wondered as he looked at the group.

"No, the Skool still exists, but recovering it will be difficult. It will be difficult to find and difficult to retrieve by the one person given the task." The old man added.

Oslaf jumped to his feet. "I say we get to the Sacred Overlord and force him to tell us. He would not be able to hold out with the right persuasion."

"No, that will never work. As I've explained, this was what I've seen in my vision." Dughorm said impatiently. "He knows you are here. Remember, he and Alrpan are in this together, and the underworld goddess knows what Fedelm knows. Add to these facts that he has hundreds of warriors and many villages under his command. No, you must attempt to leave this land now."

"And go where?" Urith asked.

The old man smiled as he realized he was getting through to them.

"That's simple," he exclaimed. "Your first trip will be to Du-Rinell!"

The old man stood up, his shaking limbs cause Fedelm to

come to his aid. He told her to pick up the bag he brought, and the two of them went toward the ossanes tied up nearby. Fedelm glanced back at them, trying to understand what she should do. Dughorm acted like he was in a hurry.

"We all must leave here. I have a sense that something is coming our way. You must get to the ruins within the land of Cahmais to find the Skool."

Fedelm and Oslaf followed the old man, unsure what they just heard while Urith looked around into the valley but saw nothing to alert him.

"If the locals are afraid of this area, I see no reason to leave right now," Urith pointed out.

Dughorm continued walking as he spoke. "I don't believe there will be people from the village coming here. I hope you have room on your mounts for a blind man. I'm coming along to get you started to the ruins in Cahmais. Come on, let's move fast."

Urith mumbled under his breath about the madness of entering the lands of their greatest enemy. While Urith remained skeptical, he gathered his items and prepared their long-necked mounts, indicating that Oslaf should do the same. Fedelm helped the old man sit with his back against a bluewood tree and began getting her gear while the old man kept asking when they would be ready. Shortly Urith told him they were prepared to travel. He helped the blind man getting on his mount, and the four started out on their journey toward Grimma. Dughorm's mount was led by Oslaf, who followed Urith. Dughorm insisted that they take a back trail around the large city, and Fedelm agreed that would be the best way to get to the coast, rather than trying to move back down the valley at night.

As they plodded through the darkness, Urith questioned Dughorm about the ruins they were heading toward. Fedelm, leading the way along the trail, and Oslaf, bringing up the rear of their column, strained to hear the conversation and stories that would mean so much to their futures. The old man gave them the story of his life after leaving the Citadel. Satres had banished him back to his homeland. However, Dughorm loved a local girl named Emham. So, on the first night of his banishment, he escaped from the ship which was taking him back to Esterblud. He found it easy to travel through Grimma undetected by giving a few koinons to the right people. His escape succeeded, and he was able to return to his beloved Emham. Even Urith noticed the emotion in the old man's voice when he spoke her name.

"So, you stayed in Ynysbeag?" asked Fedelm.

"No, we traveled around the kingdom of Ynyover in the backcountry during the first five seasons. I was always worried about her safety. You see, her family was well known to Satres. As the seasons passed, we realized her family distrusted the Sacred Overlord, and they would never betray us. When we settled in our little village under our new names, the locals were suspicious. That changed when we had the village satgert perform the sacred vows in the temple, and thus were wed and justified in the eyes of the gods. It was not long before we were no longer outsiders."

"Your wife sounds like a worthy woman. What happened to her?" Urith asked, watching the land around them as the moons gave a good light along the trail.

The old man grew quiet at the question, leaving only the sound of the ossanes hoofs on the trail. Clouds blocked the two moons light as they came to a fork in the trail. Fedelm led them to the left where the trail began to rise gradually as they went around the town of Grimma.

"Where does this path take us?" Oslaf asked Fedelm, now squinting into the darkness ahead.

"We will go past farms until we reach a mead house for travelers," she replied. "We will follow the route past it to the other side of Grimma where we can get to the docks of Cuinal. I'm not sure how we get on a ship since all citrade runs through the *Malhair* house. No merchant can leave without their approval, and I am nearly certain we would be noticed walking around the docks in the early morning."

"A few koinons can fix that," sniffed Dughorm. "The Malhair Guild runs Cuinal just like most of the areas around the Maflow Sea. Satres allows this control because he uses payoffs from guild to help pay for the Aberffraw warriors. I've heard that the overlord, even uses the guild to bribe the Gallaeci and keep them under his control in the backcountry."

Nobody saw the reaction of the girl to this news as she recalled the attack on her by the Gallaeci. Fedelm was convinced that it was Satres who sent them on her trail. Satres saw Urith as a threat, and she was to be killed just like the Esterbluds.

"I've heard rumors of such things before, but I never thought to believe them," observed Fedelm trying to steady her shaking voice. "Perhaps I was too willing to overlook."

"It's difficult to see why the overlord would allow such a thing to happen unless he profits from it. The overlords are no better or worse than any other ruler, even when dressed in the cloak of the gods." Dughorm's voice betrayed his tiredness, and the group fell quiet, each thinking about the future, as they rode on into the night.

Periodically the lights of Grimma showed faintly through the trees as the group skirted village. Rounding a bend in the trail, Fedelm saw a single flickering light ahead.

"I think that's the tavern is just ahead. We made it faster than thought we would," Fedelm told them.

"You might become a scout yet," Urith teased her.

"I'm already better than you, Esterblud barbarian," she shot back in jest.

He gave a snicker while Oslaf and Dughorm said nothing. Urith enjoyed the banter to lighten the mood since the old man was quiet. Silence had again fallen over the group, interrupted by the screeching of a night *krill* cut through the darkness as the creature searched for prey. The mounts began to smell something in the wind and sped up their trotting pace slightly. Urith wondered what they might have noticed. He scanned the area, listening and looking for anything that might be alerting the ossanes. However, he couldn't pick up on what they were sensing. As the group drew nearer to the light coming from the mead house, the behavior of the ossanes and the scurrying of animals in the brush told him something was not right. Urith mentioned it to Dughorm, who said nothing as he seemed lost in his thoughts.

Fedelm noticed movement in front of them, and she slowed her mount to a stop. Her eyes scanned the area when she saw what she believed to be a human form move passed the light just ahead. She looked again, but the form was gone. The three riders, reined back their mounts, coming to a stop behind her.

"Something wrong? Oslaf whispered from behind.

Urith pulled off the trail and forced his mount forward, coming up alongside the girl. Under his breath, he asked what happened.

In the darkness Urith could barely see the girl quickly gesture at the light ahead, "I thought I saw someone over there." Fedelm kept her voice low. "It just passed through the light.

Urith didn't see anything, but suddenly he wondered about the light. Why would there be a lamplight coming from the structure this late?

Everyone should be asleep!

Then, they heard the distant sound of hoofbeats behind them, moving at a slow gallop. Instinctively, the group moved forward, digging their heels into the flanks of their mounts. Urith took the lead, taking them off the trail into an open field. He led them to an isolated structure across the trail from the tavern. As they got close, the group could see the desolate remains of a small cottage, its thatched roof collapsed inside the pale exterior walls. The group stopped, moving to the back of the ruined home while listening to the approaching sound.

Suddenly, there was a yell behind them, a line of

Aberffraw warriors riding armored ossanes poured out of the woods not far from the open field. Their blue tunics hid them well until the rays of first light allowed the Esterblud warriors to see the glint of steel and armor of the approaching enemy riders on ossanes. The Esterbluds, surprised by the sudden onslaught, quickly put on their black helmets, while pulling their spears. Each pushed one arm through the straps on the back of their yan-yew wood shields, using the shield hand to maintain their mount's reins. Pulling alongside Fedelm, Urith quickly told her to watch over Dughorm and to look for an escape route.

"We're going after those Aberffraw warriors and create a diversion," he quickly told her.

Fedelm nodded, grabbing the reins of Dughorm's mount from Oslaf. Dughorm protested, asking for a sword. Urith rode next to him and pulled a comitatus sword from the back of Fedelm's mount. He thanked the gods for the spoils from their earlier battles, before he put the weapon into the hands of the old blind warrior.

"You stay with Fedelm and keep her safe," he winked at Fedelm, his eyes bright. The woman's face remained grim, and she looked over at Oslaf, who was smiling excitedly as Urith. She was struck by the expressions she saw before the Esterbluds raced away to meet the enemy. The woman had heard some of their warrior beliefs, but this was the first time she had seen it so close to her. Fedelm was amazed at their ability to face death with such enthusiasm. She watched them race into battle, severely outnumbered. The enemy line fanned out into a semi-circle cutting the group off from the woods as well as the trail that led to the docks of Cuinal.

Fedelm decided to head back the way they came in and turned her ossane. Her mount turned the still complaining Dughorm's ossane as well. However, the shadowy forms of a small force of Aberffraw warriors coming down the trail blocked to the road leading back to Ynysbeag. Now surrounded, she realized she had to get back to the Esterbluds.

She heard an Esterblud roar as Urith dug his heels into his mount. Partway across the field, he charged at the oncoming enemy with Oslaf moving next to him. Fedelm came back around and rode toward them. As they gallop headlong into the blue line of oncoming Aberffraw riders, Urith had pulled his Clovel Sword which glinted above his head. He had a spear in another hand.

He is excited to die! She thought.

"Hang on. We are following them," Fedelm yelled back to the blind man. She saw no way out but to follow the Esterbluds and hope they could break through.

"It's about time," Dughorm shouted back, obviously excited to be in another battle. "Just lead the way, and we'll see how long an old man can stay on his horse." He dug his heels into his mount. Fedelm had difficulty keeping her ossanes in front of him to guide them.

Fedelm watched Urith send his spear flying ahead of them, followed by Oslaf's launch of his spear. The line of well-trained warriors in front of them kept their formation, even as one of their comrades took a spear in the shoulder that sent him tumbling down in the early morning light.   The girl observed the Esterbluds whipping their swords around when they slammed into a line of Aberffraw fighters. The screams of humans and beasts mixed with the sound of steel upon steel.

Urith nearly ran over another ossane when its rider tried to cut him off. For his mistake, Urith's sword slammed down into the armored enemy's helmet, knocking him to the ground, senseless. The Esterblud swung around to parry an enemy warrior's battle-ax coming at him. The Aberffraw tried to steer his animal into Urith's but succeeded only in allowing the Esterblud within range to slam the man with his shield, knocking him back enough to thrust his longsword into the enemy's belly.

Oslaf swung into the Aberffraw nearest him, using his mount to wedge through the line while using his strength to jam his sword into the rider at a weak point in his armor.

Another Aberffraw fighter came in close enough to throw a spear which struck Oslaf's unarmored ossane in the back hip. The beast stepped awkwardly, coming down on its side with a high pitched scream while sending the warrior tumbling to the grass. As he lay there momentarily stunned, the young fighter noticed another Aberffraw rider bearing down on him with a spear. Sensing he could not react quickly enough, he tried to pull up his shield to defend himself. Just as the enemy rider closed next to him, he glimpsed two riders on ossanes run past him, cutting off the opponent. Fedelm led the old blind man who swung out at the enemy as she yelled for him to strike. The old man missed his target, but he caused the enemy fighter to change course to avoid colliding with the unlikely pair of warriors.

A few strides away, Urith was able to turn his mount into the fray, slicing an enemy fighter just under the chin with his sword. The force of the blow took the man's head off, and his mount raced off with the bleeding body quivering upright, still in the saddle. Urith continued at full gallop into the next wave of warriors coming in. He spotted a spear coming at him and was able to put his shield into its path. However, the spear's metal tip broke through the wood and lodge painfully in the forearm of the Esterblud. The weight of the spear caused the warrior to drop the shield with his rein hand. The action pulled the long neck of his mount in a hard turn into the Aberffraw line. Another enemy fighter was running with him and tried to jab his sword into Urith, who avoided the weapon by turning his mount into a fighter who rushed alongside. The giant man swung his sword, striking the arm of the opponent and he heard a crack of bone followed by a cry of terrified pain. The Esterblud didn't see a fighter who came in close, slamming his sword across the back of Urith's black helmet. The force nearly knocked out the Esterblud while he struggled to stay upright. Then, another rider came in to strike him, his spear catching Urith full in the upper back, high in the shoulder. The blade cut through the mail, and the force of the charge sent Urith down to the ground.

Oslaf was able to get an ossane that had lost its rider. Fedelm and Dughorm circled around him, allowing the young man time to leap onto the mount. He saw his mentor overwhelmed by the enemy, then falling to the ground.

"Follow me through the line," Oslaf ordered them, spurring the beast forward to help Urith. Fedelm led Dughorm as they followed him. Another line of Aberffraw men was coming at them, but Oslaf focused on those surrounding Urith. While he pressed forward, Oslaf pulled a spear hanging from his mount and launching it into the back of an enemy in front of him. He followed up, using his ossane's momentum to push between two mounts, striking at their riders with sword and shield.

The momentum carried through the mass of animals and men as they relentlessly attacked the downed Urith. The big warrior got to his knees, attempting to fend off the enemy strokes with his longsword. He shakily attempted warding off the blows of enemy swords using his crippled shield holding the embedded spear in it. Urith heard his nephew's cursing yells before he witnessed him push through the enemy fighters. Oslaf came in close with his ossane, shielding Urith momentarily. It gave his uncle enough time to use his sword to painfully chop through the spear's long wood shaft. The embedded iron tip remained poking through, still pinning his shield to his forearm. Rising, Urith swung down with his longsword into the legs of a nearby enemy mount. His blade caught the animal just below its armor, sending the screaming animal and rider to the ground.

Urith tried to climb up onto the back of Oslaf's animal, only to be pushed down to the ground when an opponent moved next to Oslaf's mount. The enemy savagely struck the Esterblud leader in the back. Oslaf, swinging wildly, hit the enemy across the helmet. Neither Esterblud saw the man in the golden helmet directing the Aberffraw to capture their opponents.

Nearby, Fedelm and the blind Dughorm tried to push through behind the young Esterblud. The old man swung his sword at any sound he heard. While he didn't do much damage, the charge broke through the Aberffraw line. It caused the enemy warriors to focus briefly on the surprising pair of unarmored fighters. Two riders charged behind the blind seer, striking him in the back with the flat of their sword blades. The force of the blows sent him down to the ground. The girl was quickly overrun by several other Aberffraw warriors, one of which swung his shield into her side, sending her sprawling.

The young Esterblud was still attempting to hack his way out of the enemy group around him while protecting Urith when the other group of warriors arrived. Closing in on the melee, the enemy sent spears flying at the Esterbluds. The young fighter saw one spear coming and was able to duck out of the way, but others struck his mount in the neck and the body while more spears slammed into the two Esterbluds. The ossane died in an instant, dropping to the ground and throwing the wounded young man on to the blood covered grass, next to Urith. Oslaf held on to a spear in his leg, trying to keep it from ripping out as he fell.

During the onslaught of incoming spears, Urith was standing, unable to dodge all of them and took one in the same shoulder as his wounded forearm. The force struck hard, pushing through the chainmail and padded undergarment, sending him down. As he rolled the spear tip twisted in his shoulder muscle painfully and broke away from the wood shaft. The injured warrior was able to come up with his Clovel Sword in time to impale an enemy fighter rushing at him on foot.

There was a brief lull as several of the enemy warriors slid from their mounts to the ground. They moved to battle the Esterbluds on foot while Oslaf pulled the spear from his thigh with a yell as the barbed end tore his flesh. Urith slowly stood and watched the enemy moving in to finish them off. The warrior stuck his sword tip first into the dirt, taking a deep breath and yanked out the remnants of the spear embedded in his shoulder. The pain nearly dropped him to his knees, but he refused to yell out. With a defiant grimace, he spat on the spear and threw it to the side while he pulled his longsword from the grassy soil.

"It is a good morning Oslaf." The Esterblud leader panted as he pulled his wounded shield arm up in front of his bloody body. "We can die like warriors."

Oslaf grimaced as he brought himself up. He crouched to hold pressure on his thigh wound while he readied for his death. Suddenly there was the sound of a horn in the background, and the Aberffraw warriors stopped, maintaining their positions. The Esterbluds watched as ranks of riders opened a hole in the line and a familiar person rode into view on the back of a white mount. Lyncus was sporting a wooden brace on his damaged leg when he pushed through the line of his men. Beside him was a giant man dressed in the golden armor and the colors of the Sacred Overlord Guard on his saddle blanket. An ossane carried their friends. Beaten and bound Dughorm and Fedelm were laid belly down across the saddle. Neither moved much, although Dughorm did look up as if he was attempting to see the battleground. As he tried to say something, the golden giant slapped his head with the back of his hand. Urith had to suppress his urge to rush the man as Lyncus spoke.

"You have fought bravely, Urith. However, now it is time to surrender." Lyncus told the warriors in his native tongue. "Once, you gave me my life, and now I give yours back in return. A fighter's debt paid."

"It is not your debt to give back if I choose to reject it. It would please me greatly to kill off a few more of these women you call warriors, especially that golden girl beside you." Urith replied in Aberffraw as he dropped his arms, saving his strength for the moment.

There was a growl from the group of Aberffraw warriors

at his insult. However, a hearty laugh came from the golden giant as he looked over the Esterbluds, who stood bloody, still breathing hard.

"You Esterbluds act as Satres expected. The Sacred Overlord will enjoy taking you down a peg or two, you yellow water scum drinker." He spoke in the tongue of Aberffraw as well and knew how to insult an Esterblud.

"By the gods, I'll take you down, golden fool." Urith snapped in Aberffraw, giving him a grim sneer. "I see you like to dress up as someone who can fight. But it appears you would rather play as *pitshog* to your master."

The overlord's warrior face turned red with fury as the Aberffraw men sent up a howl of laughter at the insult. Calling any man, let alone a fighter, a queen to be bedded by another man would invite an immediate fight of honor. It nearly worked as intended as the giant guard of Satres started his mount toward Urith.

"Colainn, stop now," yelled Lyncus. The guard stopped reluctantly, his sword drawn. "You idiot; can you not see he wants to take you on alone? Now get back here."

Colainn backed his mount away and rejoined the Aberffraw leader, glaring at Urith with unambiguous hatred and rage.

"Esterbluds, do you really wish to die here?" asked Lyncus. "We have what we came for."

Urith wasted no time in responding,

"Let's get this over with. I have intentions of meeting some old friends in Haligulf tonight."

Lyncus nodded his head and raised his arm to his men. "Very well, we'll do it the hard way. I want their heads delivered to me at the Citadel." He dropped his arm and turned his ossane away, taking his prisoners with him. The gold giant rode his mount near the wounded Esterbluds.

"Twenty koinons to the warrior who brings these peasant's heads to me," cried Colainn to the Aberffraw warriors. There was a roar of approval from the enemy at the prize money.

Smiling, the giant looked down at his enemy.

"I'd rather stay to watch you die, but I'll make sure your skull cap is coated with gold which I will use as my drinking cup. I'll throw the rest of your head in the latrine." The man told them before he turned his mount. Colainn dug his heels into the flanks of his ossane to catch the leader of the Aberffraws. The two riders were followed by a small party of other warriors leaving the honor of finishing off the Esterbluds to the mass of remaining men who were more than enough for two wounded men. However, with their leaders gone, they paused before their final charge as they drew up the courage. They knew, like cornered animals, the Esterbluds would fight viciously, taking more of their friends' lives and perhaps their own. While it was good to die in battle in the Kamin realm, few men wanted death over life.

Urith watched Lyncus leading his friends away. Fury instantly welled up inside him again. The party of riders crossed the field and took the trail back to Grimma and the fortress. As the allies of Satres passed in front of the mead house, the mass of remaining enemy began to press forward to finish off the Esterbluds. Oslaf had moved behind Urith turning forward, so they were back to back. The surrounding enemy warriors pulled up their spears.

"Well, see you in Haligulf." Oslaf's voice cracked a bit.

"Not until we crack a few of these girls' heads," Urith growled. "Stay close to me. I'm getting thirsty and wouldn't mind a drink with Mivraa."

Suddenly Urith yelled the Esterblud battle cry of the *Estercetus*, flying into a line of Aberffraw warriors in front of him as Oslaf quickly turned and joined with him. They hacked into the enemy who was surprised by the sudden attack from the wounded men. Urith jammed his shield into the helmet of one warrior while slashing another next to him, the force of his longsword cutting into the padded leather and chainmail over his shoulders. Both men went down screaming. Oslaf struck another Aberffraw, who was running his spear toward the exposed side of Urith. The young warrior's longsword landing on the man's back with a weighty blow which sent the dying man, face first into the ground.

The sudden rush of the Esterblud warriors into the line of the enemy caused the ossanes behind them to back away, creating a natural opening. Urith seized the advantage and ran as fast as he could into the side of one rider. He jammed his sword up under the mail tunic, into his victim's unarmored belly. Just as the man screamed, Urith lifted up his sword, shifting his stance and used man's leg to help pitch him off the saddle. Oslaf deflected a spear with his shield and tried to keep up with his uncle as the swarm of enemy warriors regrouped against the Esterbluds.

None of battling fighters saw the cloud of white mist swiftly heading into the battlefield, coming down the valley like a surging tide of gray clouds. The wall of fog fell upon the mass of bodies enveloping the area, darkening the sky and soon leaving the battlefield in a bewildering murkiness. The dense mist grew so heavy that the men couldn't see the person next to them. Urith grabbed Oslaf by his shoulder and pulled him into a thick fog bank near them. The fighting came to an abrupt halt as a deathly quiet descended upon the field. Only the occasional screams of the dying and wounded were heard. Soon, prayers came from men begging for mercy from the gods. The two Esterbluds slowly turned in a circle, unsure of their position. The shadows of enemy warriors appeared and disappeared like ghosts in the mist as fear suddenly gripped those blinded by the impenetrable fog.

Urith crept along and stopped when he heard the nervous shrill coming from an ossane. He followed the sound and stopped near one of the Aberffraw riders only an arm's length away. He was nearly run over by Oslaf, who almost lost him in the mist. Urith could just make out the outline of the rider who slowly guided his mount away from them, calling out to his comrades. The Esterblud warrior sheathed his longsword and pulled his dagger as he carefully approached the mounted rider from behind. The fog grew worse, but he was able to step next to the warrior before the enemy realized he was there. He pulled down hard on the Aberffraw shield, thrusting his dagger into the man's exposed throat before his prey was able to respond to the attack. Urith let the body fall past him to the ground as he grabbed the reins.

"Come on," he whispered out to his friend. Oslaf was hanging on to the ossane's long, bushy tail.

Both men scrambled onto the ossane, guiding the mount away from the sounds of the enemy fighters. Oslaf was sitting behind Urith, trying to stop the bleeding of his leg as he pressed on the wound. Urith guided their stolen mount by leading the animal away from the eerie noises coming from terrified men and animals. He slid out his sword, carefully listening to the sounds carried across the battlefield as Aberffraw warriors sought to find friends and comrades. The occasional sounds of fighting erupted when groups of Aberffraw would run into their comrades. Urith kept leading the animal away from the sounds, and eventually, the two Esterbluds made their way into the woods.

They pushed through the brush until they stumbled upon a path made by the duelill. They stayed with the trail. After what seemed like a full morning of travel to the men, the path led deeper into the woods. Eventually, the echoes of men and fighting died away behind them. The fog suddenly lifted around them, and the Esterbluds found themselves among forests of ancient trees on an up-sloping land. They followed the trail as it led up the slope until they came to a crest that overlooked the still fog-shrouded valley behind them. Weary and feeling the wounds sapping their strength, they came to a stop in front of large boulders.

"I wondered when you might arrive." Mivraa came around from the other side of the rock riding a black ossane. She gave them a broad smile.

"Neither of you don't look ready to join me in Haligulf

yet."

The pair nearly fell from their mount when they jerked it around to see their visitor. Oslaf slid off the back, groaning as his leg hit the ground. Urith slid his sword back into the belt and carefully swung his leg over the animal's back to keep the shield still pinned to his arm from striking the high saddle. The pain of his movement caused him to grimace, and he paused for a bit as his breath caught in his chest. When his boots touched down on the soft grasses under him, he looked back at the mount at the goddess.

"If you aren't here to take us away, then you must be heading down below," he surmised.

"Eventually, I will be. However, I thought you might take advantage of some help if offered." Mivraa explained while she continued to look down at them from her black mount, but there was a note of sympathy in her voice that both wounded men took notice of.

"Then, join us as we mend these wounds." He turned to his nephew who sat on the ground, his back to the boulder watching him remove his battle helmet.

"How's the leg? Is the spear tip still in there?" Urith asked.

"I'm in good shape; the tip came out of the muscle. I don't think it got to the bone." He gave him a thin smile. "I must admit I'm getting tired of all the wounds."

"Well, you need to move quicker," his uncle jokingly sneered and groaned as he bent down closer. "I see your bleeding is nearly stopped. We'll find some dry moss to get on that. I expect there should be some around here."

Mivraa joined them.

"Here, I brought you some Galicia wine from my mount." The goddess held it out to Oslaf, who stared dumbfounded as she continued. "From the way you two look, I believe both of you could use a drink of the god's wine."

"I..I thought you were just a dream at first," Oslaf admitted to her, accepting the leather drinking bag. He took a drink before handing it to his uncle.

"Urith was right, you are beautiful," he told her.

The woman bent down to him; her face lit up with a mischievous grin at his words.

"Did he now? I would suspect that was an unexpected compliment coming from him. Now, let's get you cleaned up," she said.

Mivraa motioned Urith over to rest next to his nephew. He hesitated, but now his adrenaline was gone. Urith knew he needed help with his wounds. He sat down and removed his battered helmet. The sweat, combined with the blood from several scraps, left trails running down his face. Mivraa looked over his arm first, carefully feeling for the broken spear point which remained stuck in his forearm, holding the shield in place. The spearhead had penetrated the muscle and hung between the bones, the tip penetrating out the other side. As designed, the spine of soft metal bent on impact and kept the shield hung up on the wood handle connected to the spear tip.

"Let's get the spear away from the shield, break it off, and you can pull the tip on through. Hopefully, it doesn't catch too much coming out," Urith said wearily.

Oslaf adjusted himself, moving around in pain to help hold down the warrior's arm. Mivraa waited until Urith took a deep breath and nodded as he held the metal tip while the girl slowly turned the wood handle. Her powerful hands got the handle out of the metal shaft, straightening the shaft as well. The wood fell away, leaving just the shaft in his arm, blood pouring out from the wound. Holding the spear point, she then slowly pulled the spear and rod through the wound while the Esterblud leader inadvertently yelled out, cursing the gods. After grabbing his arm when she finished, he realized what he just yelled against the goddess in front of him.

"Sorry, bad habit," he explained awkwardly. His face was pale as he thanked her. It was a gesture she prized.

Mivraa snickered at him as she handed him a cloth from her bag to wrap the wound. She soaked the wound with a clear liquid from a long crystal vial that she had pulled from the bag.

"No need to apologize. I hear much worse from those spirits I lead to the gateways. When they meet the Vanths, they suddenly realize they are not going to Haligulf," she said as she poured more clear fluid on his arm, before pouring more on other open wounds.

"Use this cloth to staunch the blood. This is healing water from the Exyts spring. If it can keep the gods young, it will heal you. You will not need the moss."

The goddess gave Oslaf a vial with the liquid as well as some cloth, telling him to use it on his wounds while she helped Urith wrap the cloth around his forearm. The wounded warrior felt a soothing relief wash over him. The woman's hazel eyes met Urith's as she tenderly dabbed another bit of damp cloth on his wounded shoulder.

As she worked, he took a deep drink of the *Gailcca* or gods wine. It tasted sweeter than the heathmead he preferred, but the healing effect was almost instantaneous as the warmth spread through his body. It didn't intoxicate like the mead would, yet a calm euphoria enveloped him. He quickly understood why the gods would drink such elixirs, as well as their interest in keeping them from humans.

"You can be my healer anytime," Urith told her with his scarred grin.

"You fought bravely today. I wondered for a moment if you would be joining me in Haligulf when I arrived." Her voice was as calming as the healing cloth that swathed his severely wounded arm.

"Yes, we came close. We were lucky to get away. However, my new friends were not as fortunate. They have been captured by Satres' men who must have them in the Citadel by now."

Mivraa smiled, nodding. "What do you do now? Do you return to Esterblud?"

Oslaf looked up at her words, but before he could speak.

"By the gods, no!" Urith spoke up. "Our path has changed since we last spoke. Now, we must regroup and find our way into the fortress."

Urith's mind was racing as he wondered how much to reveal to their goddess friend.

"I owe this to Dughorm," he explained.

Mivraa stood up, still leaning over him and smiled. "I'm not surprised. You fight as a hero worthy of the tales that are sung about you. Yet, you continue to surprise me when you don't trust those who would help you."

Urith nodded his head, resting it against the rock behind him. "Yes, this is true. But you have helped me far beyond what I could expect. I assume you had something to do with keeping us alive, able to escape the battle. Why?"

Mivraa did not reply as she moved over to Oslaf, kneeling to look at his leg. When she pulled back the cloth, the young man stared in amazement at the wound, scabbed over and healing.

"I told Urith before, we have some interesting items at our disposal," Mivraa sat down cross-legged between them.

"Urith did mention that, but I scarcely believed it. Now, I cannot doubt the abilities of the gods," Oslaf replied.

"Don't go too far, you have reason to doubt. That is why I'm here," Mivraa's face clouded. "Well, at least partially."

She continued, "We have much to accomplish together. Urith, you asked why I helped you and your friend? Well, it's very simple; your friend Dughorm asked this of me."

"Wait a minute, how could he do this? He is not dead, is he? They just sprung upon us."

"No, he is not dead. He showed me his visions through his dreams last night. He is a great hakra, probably one of the greatest. It is part of the reason why he was sent away by Satres and why he was taken back to the Citadel. He had known before he left his village that such things awaited your party." Mivraa sat erect, her gaze shifting between the warriors as she explained. Oslaf did notice she liked to stare a bit more at Urith and a thought crossed his mind when he considered her half-human nature.

"Dughorm knew, yet he didn't tell us, and you were not able to interfere," Urith concluded.

"Perhaps he told you more?" Mivraa observed. "His visions revealed a new path for your journeys."

Urith looked embarrassed as he nodded his head in agreement. He decided that, as Dughorm had shown the goddess his visions, it would be wise for him to explain their decision to seek out the Skool. Mivraa showed no emotion at the news, only taking in the story and the plans they had made. She only interrupted at one point to ask how they felt as the zenith sun began to beat down on them. Both warriors admitted that while they were bruised and battered, they felt good enough to take on another army.

"I don't understand why Satres would need to capture Dughorm," Urith stood.

"Satres needed to show that he controlled Ynyover. I have no doubt that his allies in the underworld had something to do with it," she stated. "Dughorm showed me Alrpan in the visions."

"What you mean is, we let Alrpan discover Dughorm, through Fedelm," Urith stated, watching Mivraa nod reluctantly. "Then, it's time we get Dughorm and Fedelm out of the Citadel."

"But how?" Oslaf asked. "We have one ossane, and we don't know how to get in there."

"You seem to have forgotten about me, young warrior." The demigoddess spoke up. "Remember, I said that we have much to accomplish. Now if you two are done lying around, let's get moving."

The two Esterbluds looked at each other, unsure what they just agreed to. They had never heard of a god of the Sky Realm intervening in the affairs of humans.

As the trio took the trail back toward the battlefield, Mivraa explained her ideas to get inside the stronghold of the overlord. She described that the visions of Dughorm were sent as a series of dreams that she could not ignore. She told the warriors that when she put her dreams together, the demigoddess realized she must intervene. Otherwise, the realms between the gods and humans would disintegrate. She refused to tell them what she saw and withheld her concern that they may already be too late.

Mivraa led the way as they traveled down the ridge, with the men following on their mount. They planned to retrieve enough Aberffraw armor from the battlefield to disguise the Esterbluds, then enter the fortress through an underground passage Mivraa told them about.

During their journey back to the battleground, the demigoddess told them that King Asgurd of Cahmais was now ruling over the Sacred Overlord.

"That confirms the Treaty of Restoration is in tatters," Urith stated. "War will be coming. King Penhda will send men against Ynyover."

"That's not the worst of what Dughorm is telling me. Gods have started to turn against humans. This will bring ruin to everyone. There has been a rumor that, across the Maflow Sea, villages have been destroyed in the wrathful destruction by Uugor," she explained. She decided not to mention that it was the same deity who destroyed Urith's boat and killed his crew.

"The underworld seems to be pushing chaos into the human world. It will bring the gods into conflict."

"Do you know what villages were destroyed in the god's wrath?" Urith asked when he thought about his home in Esterblud.

"Don't worry, my friend. It was on the Vulthnal coast; your village is safe."

Urith first wondered how she could be so certain, momentarily forgetting who she was and the powers she held. He couldn't help but stare at her red hair and profile as they rode. The man wondered briefly about her human mother and whether her mother had the same striking features.

As they neared the site of their earlier battle, Urith asked the demigod what she knew about the Skool. She did not respond, and he wondered if her silence meant she hadn't heard him, or if she was choosing her words. Finally, she spoke.

"It was in the vision. To be blunt, it nearly kept me from joining this cause of yours. Ultimately, this could bring death to some of the gods."

Urith looked at her, surprised by the statement. "How so?"

"Quite simply, this weapon of the gods could destroy the world we know. The boundaries between the gods and human can be broken down by the complete Skool. In the wrong hands, it could be used to destroy all the realms, leaving nothing. Why do you think Satres is looking for this weapon? Control of the Shield means control of the Kamin realms. And I'm quite sure he and some of the gods have thought of this."

"I don't understand." The fighter looked worried at her response. "Why would this be?"

She sighed.

"You already know that the Shield was the weapon used by the human hero called Heptarc to cast out the Gods of the Void. He was able to call forth others from the Great Void and convince them to join the humans to help bring peace to the realms. No person was able to do this before or since. However, it's not widely known that the Skool was not completed demolished but broken into four pieces which scattered across the human world. Those gods cast into the pit of the void cursed the lands where the pieces lay so no deity can enter the boundaries to discover such a weapon. It is said, only a human who worthy enough to find the pieces can put it back together."

"That seems pretty simple," Oslaf interjected. "Just find the four areas gods cannot enter and get someone to find it. What did this thing look like?"

Mivraa smiled at him.

"Simple enough, it seems, except only one place is known which has the power to keep the gods away," she said. "No curses hide the other areas that are known only to the Fates."

"We must start with Du-Rinell," said Oslaf.

"Correct. Yet, what is left of the shield is not really known. I have heard it said it was like metal which flows like a river. When fully formed, it carries the words of the Guardians. However, for someone like Satres, the Skool is not to be used in the care-taking of the realms. He will want control over those realms, including gods and humans alike," Mivraa told them as she rose.

"Satres now aligns himself with gods who think they can use his work for their own purposes while he has plans of his own. We are searching for something of immense power which can recreate the worlds we live in." Mivraa stared at Urith while she continued. "Now you understand better why I must travel with you to the Citadel."

Urith thought about the explanation for a moment.

"It appears that you are torn between your god world and Kamin world. I am worried about what will happen if it comes to pass that you must take one side. Which side will you choose?"

She turned away and nodded.

"I am worried as well. Our paths are not set."

Chapter 7: Into The Lair

Arriving back at the scene of their earlier fighting, the warriors, and the goddess found the bodies still lying in the grass. Fortunately, the wounded had been carried away by their comrades after the fog finally lifted. The weapons, shields and other items left strewn across the battleground during the confusion. Urith guessed the fog must have kept the nearby villagers inside, too afraid to venture out into the mist-shrouded battlefield, even for spoils. As if she read his mind, Mivraa told them the fog had just lifted.

"Did you create the mist?" Oslaf asked. "It was thicker than I recall seeing anywhere before."

The goddess smiled at him. "I heard you were like your uncle, always full of questions about the gods. No, I didn't do it. It was difficult, but I persuaded my father to do this using his command of the weather. I convinced him to counter Caruun's push for chaos. If Satres wanted you dead, then it would be best to let you live."

"Your father is a supporter of our cause?" Urith wondered aloud.

"We should move quickly as the villagers will soon develop enough courage to come to this place to scavenge." Mivraa changed the subject. "I'll keep watch. There might even be lost Aberffraw fighters who may drift back into the area."

The men got down from their mounts and fanned out looking for discarded items that would transform them into the enemy. From the number of discarded items and bodies, Urith knew quite a few of the enemy were killed or wounded by their own men during the chaotic battles. Working quickly, they pulled off their identifying Esterblud garments, making sure to store them in their saddlebags. Urith rolled up his distinctive sword with their bedding. Both decided to let their black helmets dangle from the mounts like trophies.

Trying on several of the less bloody, but serviceable blue tunics over their chainmail, the Esterbluds finally found clothing that fit over their large frames. Mivraa reminded them that they would have to remove their baudrik belts since the Aberffraw warriors did not wear them. Urith also scrounged up two curved swords, much shorter and lighter than their longswords. Finally, they gathered shields and helmets which carried the symbol of the Clovel. Standing by their single ossane, each man dressed as their Aberffraw enemy, making sure to put the enemy shields on the back of the mount. They kept their own battered shields covered with a blanket which they put on Mivraa's mount.

"We can purchase another ossane in Grimma," Urith said as he adjusted the canvas padding inside his new helmet to get it on. "But we will have to stop along the way to clean off some of the blood on these tunics to avoid questions." He put the helmet on and looked up at Mivraa.

"I'm still unsure how we can sneak into the Citadel with a lovely goddess at our side?"

His voice was gruff. However, Mivraa smiled at the compliment which seldom came, especially from a human. She might be worshiped as a goddess, but many times the warriors only concerned themselves with reaching the final state of drunken oblivion in Haligulf. She felt more about Urith than she thought possible, especially a man who was not immortal.

"Well, I like the compliment. But don't you worry. I assure you I can get us into the Citadel," she told him. "And we won't be going to the front door."

From the back of her saddle, she pulled out her black robe. She mumbled a few words as she put the cape over her while lifting the hood to cover her red hair. In the blink of an eye, the robe changed from a black sheen to a roughly woven brown covering. Incredibly, it transformed her appearance into an elderly peasant. Even her upright stance changed to a slumped old woman with a large hooked nose who gave them a toothy grin. Both warriors stared in amazement at what they saw.

"Sometimes, it's good to have exceptional gifts," she said, her voice crackling like an old woman.

"How do you do that?" Oslaf asked as he tried to recall the skalds tales.

"Every god as a different power," she explained. "In this case, the cape comes down from the Guardians, allowing someone to transform their physical being. It is another powerful apparatus of the gods."

"Most of the gods are no stronger than me in their various abilities. They can manipulate the elements and, sometimes, the people. But we must all submit to the reality of the realm we exist. While some, like my father, can master the elements, they cannot fly as a human or override the realities of your realm," she explained. It was clear to Oslaf that Mivraa enjoyed talking with them. Urith and Oslaf get on their ossane.

"For me, I can see spirits upon their passing. Thus, I can move them between dominions of the living and the dead. And with the help of this robe, I also have the power to transform into almost anything that comes into my mind. Few other gods can do this." There was pride in her tone.

"Now, we have to move. Urith, can you lead us into Cuinal?"

The warrior nodded.

"Good, I'll stay behind as this old lady keeping up with strong warriors for protection on the trail. I think we can make it there just past sundown," she continued to outline her plan. "You can stop by the Malhair House and see about passage out of the port. We can sell off some weapons if we need more koinons. Find us a boat leaving tonight. We'll need a way to exit this area quickly. If the ship is traveling to the coast near Cahmais, it would probably be best."

Mivraa spurred her mount, and the men followed her to the road.

"Why would we do that?" Urith asked.

"Don't you remember? It was part of Dughorm's vision," she told them simply as she held her ossane back to pull in behind them. "It's where the Du-Rinell ruins are."

The men took the lead following the trail to the Citadel as they were softly reminded by Mivraa that they should only to speak in Aberffraw. As their mounts trotted along, heading to the dreaded lair of their enemy, they felt the oppressive mixture of obligation and anxiety.

~~~

Inside a nearly dark room of the Citadel, lit only by a few lanterns, the sound of footfalls approached Dughorm as he hung by chains from the stone wall. He tried pulling his head up, but his neck muscles shook at the effort, injured in the attack earlier that day. The dampness of the wall that touched his back reminded him he was in the belly of the beast, and the footsteps had the familiar gait of the Sacred Overlord. Dressed in his red robe, the thin man entered the room holding his hands together as if he was entering a mystic trance.

"I'm glad you are back with us Dughorm. You have been quite inconsiderate leaving me with nothing to do." Satres give him a wicked smirk.

"You are lucky I'm chained here, my friend. I would give you my personal greeting, just like last time." The old man looked toward his enemy's voice, enjoying the memory of his savage beating of Satres many seasons before.

The overlord walked over to an open hearth which held multiple red-hot pokers and pincers to extract confessions from the miscreants and freethinkers of Ynyover. After their confessions, they were executed. The heads of the condemned were mounted on poles at the entrance to the fortress.

"Well, you will not be as lucky again. I have other plans for you. You will tell me your visions and what you told the Esterbluds you had met with before they died. Yes, I know of your discussions. It seems the child you called Awerm told
~~~

us all that she knew. It's too bad, she was unable to last very long. It seems the Aberffraw was too rough on the child in your village. They were in too much haste to follow you. She died quite painfully, as you will.

Dughorm cursed and spat in the general direction of Satres. As a grizzled warrior, he well knew the use of such barbarity over his many seasons. However, he wanted to strike out at Satres again, to weep for the quiet little girl who he treated as his own child.

"Call yourself an overlord, while not man enough to be a warrior. I welcome the terrible death coming to you."

The thin man stirred the coals in the pit as he nodded to a big man who entered the room.

"Yes, yes, I've heard you before. However, let me introduce you to Colainn, who will continue your discussions. You would be wise to tell him all you know. Your suffering will be far less, and your death will be quick, I promise. If not…well your mind will give up before your body does."

Dughorm put his head down in resignation to his fate. "Satres, like normal, you fail to realize that I've seen this coming. Whatever happens to me is of no consequence now. I know I will go among the gods happy that you will be destroyed by the very choices you make here," he growled. "Too bad I can't piss on your dying body."

Satres laughed at his challenge.

"And you, old man, fail to realize I have the gods on my side, no matter what your pathetic visions tell you."

He turned and walked away as the giant called Colainn pulled out hot iron, walking over to the old man. Satres shut the large, dense arched door behind him, walking toward the end of the tunnel-like corridor when he heard the tormented screams of the old man echoing through as if they came from the very stones around him. He went through the next set of doors, closing them as well, which shut out the echoes. As he continued down the darkened way, he could still hear the screams of his former friend in his head. He tried to forget the hideous noise by reminding himself of his ambitions.

As he walked back to his suite of rooms, he recalled his early friendship with Dughorm. It was at the time of the Restoration of the Necropa when both men became part of the Sacred Order upon the agreement among the lands to end the War of Succession between Cahmais and Esterblud. Both countries fought over control of the Citadel, home of Sacred Order, and control of these lands was still a goal of both Kingdoms. It was the Restoration which brought Satres and Dughorm together as rival leaders tasked with restoring the Order as the home of *satgert* learning.

While competitors from competing lands, at first, they were good friends and helped establish the Majireef Council. Beyond that, they worked as brothers to stamp out the dark rituals and blasphemy that had become prevalent. During the war, some human rulers implored their *satgerts* to use unnatural rites to send hordes of monsters into the lands of their enemies. Dughorm and Satres worked tirelessly to send their allies, and loyal to the Citadel Order, to the temples scattered through the domains. Their work brought order to the rituals of the temples and sacrifices given to the gods. Immoral practices were banned as the Citadel achieve supremacy over other worship practices by winning over the richest kingdom's sacred leaders. Influence and stability began to calm the ambitions of the overlords of Kamin.

Dughorm's illness led to his blindness which changed everything between the men. Satres viewed invalids with powerful disdain. And he was not alone in his position. Even when the incredible foresight powers within the Esterblud came to be known, the council saw no value in continuing their friendship. Beyond the loss of a friend, Satres discovered his mission in life when he stumbled upon a long-forgotten archive about the Great Passing of Gods and the First War of the Kamin Realm. Although written in the age's past, in an instant, he realized those fragile parchments were the key to his future.

Satres entered his elegant rooms, nearly forgetting to close the door. Walking into his antechamber, he stoked the bluewood fire and poured a small drink of Aberffraw wine, enjoying the scent of lavender flowers. He hoped that Colainn would be able to get the needed information from Dughorm. But looking over the room at the ancient writings he gathered and stored there, he was confident even if the old man died, he could still collect the necessary information about the Skool from his archives. It was these manuscripts found in the hidden rooms around the Citadel that brought Alrpan to Satres. During his research, he found the rare manuscript of *Necrow Menato*, the book of the talisman. This is where he discovered the gods' vulnerabilities, including Alrpan's love of the human form and all human sensations. Satres knew well the power of information, and he used this information to bring her into his plan. But, for all her vanities, he also realized she was a dangerous ally, someone that could kill him or help him, depending on her mood. Yet, the prize he sought was worth it, and he successfully used her vanities as well as her hatred of Caruun to shape his plan.

His subtle manipulation was working. The underworld goddess convinced Uugor of the Sky Realm to destroy villages along the coasts. Soon, Duwdamon would interfere against the underworld, further eroding trust in the gods and between the realms. The more the gods lost control, the more he could move toward control of the human world through his allies. With the Skool, he would hold the god powers he believed were rightfully his. He knew his limited visions allowed him to have it all, even if it meant stepping over the bodies of his former friend or any others that got in his way.

~~~

That evening, the two Esterblud warriors had entered the port town of Cuinal and made their way to the Malhair House, which was situated near the docks. The Malhair house was a small building where the Trade Guild had an office. In the Kamin world, the Guild controlled both the sea trade, and
~~~

banking between the lands, and as such, it was the primary means of securing travel between ports. Other, lesser guilds kept secret alliances with the Guild, using those associations to exert control, bribing overlords and destroying their enemies.

Leaving the Malhair House, the warriors made their way back to the stables where their mounts were tied. Their plans were going smoothly. First, their disguises worked well, and as the presence of Aberffraw warriors was not unusual in the neutral kingdom, few locals paid any notice of them. And now they had just managed to secure passage on a small Vulthnal cargo cuggle that would be sailing with the early morning tide. The ship was bound for a small port called Hyropda which lay in the eastern portion of Cahmais, deep in enemy lands. From there they would travel into the Eilginn Mountains where the Du-Rinell ruins lay. They spoke quietly, careful to avoid being overheard.

"Do you think they are still alive?" Oslaf asked.

Urith nodded.

"Yes, they wanted them both for some reason, although I'm not sure even Mivraa knows why. I suspect that Dughorm holds the key since he seemed very sure of our path. Perhaps Satres knows this and wants more information? However, this is speculation until we get there."

He stopped talking and changed the subject using the Aberffraw language as he saw someone approaching them.

"Fear not as we will soon dine on the best meat," he thundered to make sure the stranger heard him.

He didn't need to bother when he realized the figure was only a drunken old man staggering to another mead house. The man mumbled incoherently before moving into the shadows. The men continued on, and Urith finished his thought.

"I believe Fedelm will be safe as well since they should still believe her to be on their side. Plus, her father is still in the Citadel. But if not, we will find out when we get there."

He quickened their pace back to the stall.

The pair of disguised Aberffraws had already purchased another ossane, and their mounts were still tied to the rail outside the shed when they arrived. The Esterblud weapons they left with Mivraa. Urith handed a gold koinon to the large man who came out of the shed as he expressed disappointment they were leaving so soon. Urith believed the money was enough to keep the man from asking too many questions about two warriors arriving on a single ossane.

Getting on their mounts, they moved slowly out of docks following the road toward the Citadel. The dark path was occasionally outlined by the dim light of oil lanterns coming from the ships and boats in the harbor and occasionally from the buildings along the road. They kept a slow, deliberate pace, on the lookout for any guards. Knowing they might have problems if they came upon guards who came from unfamiliar clan associations and customs, the men held their collective breath at anything they heard.

They reached the outskirts of the village where they found Mivraa waiting for them in her disguise. Jumping on her mount, she told them to follow her, and they pulled off the main road which led to the Citadel gate. Instead, she took them along a small trail that narrowed to almost a footpath. The path ran parallel with the edge of the cliffs overlooking the dark sea below. Mivraa found an area with brush and small, windblown trees where they could leave their mounts hidden. They collected their weapons, and the Esterbluds pulled out their longswords to replace the shorter Aberffraw blades on their belts, adding their battle axes as well. They knew they might not come out of the Citadel alive and wanted their best weapons for the fight.

As they followed the demigoddess, the Esterbluds remained close to the rock wall while being lashed by winds that swept through the trees that hung low over the footpath as it led upward. It was a long climb, and they moved steadily as the foreboding Citadel loomed dark and tall over them, as if watching their approach. The group moved cautiously, stopping at sounds that carried through the darkness, but no enemy guards appeared. After a while, Mivraa stopped at a rock outcropping, and the Esterbluds knew they were coming in a secret entrance to the Citadel that the goddess had told them about. It was from that point they hoped to get by the guards. She led them to the side of the path which had a row of nasty prickly bushes with finger-long thorns covering the rock face.

"We enter the cave behind the bushes here," she whispered.

Using his shield, Urith forced the brush apart to get through the hole with just a few scrapes. While they watched Urith pushing through, Oslaf asked Mivraa how she knew of this place.

"This place is well known by both the Sky Realm and underworld realm. The Citadel is a meeting place for demigods and humans at times. In the past, we needed places to enter and exit without the prying eyes of humans. Some of the demigods can bend the plants to their will, so it's easier to get through."

"Where do we find our friends?" Urith asked.

"That will be the simple part," she replied. "We will capture Satres and ask him. You will find he is not well protected inside his home since he assumes full loyalty among those who call him overlord."

"Then, I will break his head for all of this," muttered Urith, his voice echoing back out of the tunnel. As the Oslaf pushed through the opening, he silently hoped Satres would give them the information before Urith grew impatient with him and his trickery.

Once inside the two Esterbluds waited for Mivraa to take the lead. The goddess stopped, nearly causing the two men to bump into her. In the pitch black, they heard her fumbling in her shawl. Soon a light glowed in front of her, illuminating the tunnel with a soft green glow. Urith recognized the tribolrock she held. They were used by the miners of the Neewar Mountains in his homeland.

Looking around him, Urith noted the tunnel walls appeared carved from the rock using hand tools. "Is this end of the tunnel guarded?" he asked the woman.

She shrugged her shoulders, looking back with the green light on her face.

"It's doubtful since there is no reason to guard the room. But we cannot be sure."

She led the way as all of them hunched over to keep from striking their heads on the low ceiling. To the warriors, they seemed to be going into the bowels of the underworld itself as the dimly lit tunnel wound through the rock. Finally, they could see the light in the distance, and Mivraa put away her stones. As she did, Urith pressed past her, taking the lead.

"You are a great warrior, but remember these are our friends," Urith quietly stated as he moved past.

At first, the goddess appeared annoyed, but she said nothing and let him squeeze by. The warrior pressed forward slowly and quietly, his leather boots making only a slight noise on the damp floor. He soon reached an open doorway to a small room. The room was dimly lit, and he entered slowly, listening intently. Hearing nothing, he crossed the room and discovered the light came from a torch sitting in a sconce a few steps up a staircase that wound up from the basement floor. Urith went up a few steps to try to see how far the staircase rose. Turning, he saw Mivraa and Oslaf enter the room. Coming back down the steps, he spoke quietly to the goddess trying to conceal his embarrassment from taking the lead.

"Alright, you will need to lead the way since you've been here before, but I need to know where we are heading."

Mivraa walked past him with a sly grin on her face, heading up the stairs as she spoke. "As I recall from my few visits, these stairs lead to the main level. We will need to get across the passage to the stairway that goes to the rooms above. That is where the overlord and his advisors will have their chambers."

They followed the warrior goddess up to the next level, halting at the sound of people passing nearby. Mivraa pulled a weapon, choosing her short sword, rather than her spear since it would work better in close quarters. She threw her back against the stone wall, using her arm to push her partners back. Peeking carefully around the corner, she spotted servants passing the entrance as they walked along the grand hallway. The hall rose with large vaulted walls majestically holding the colored crystal windows up to a wooden roof. From her position, she could see the passage was covered with large tapestries and banners that hung from lancet arches high above. Other massive curtains carried the colors of the Sacred Overlord and hung down to the floor, lining the sides of walls. The yellow light which flickered through the hall came from decorative oil torches that lined the walk at the base of each arch, stretching up to illuminate the ceiling above.

Mivraa looked around, then she hurried across the passage, hugging the shadows. The two warriors followed behind her, having pulled their longswords from the scabbard on their belts. The trio moved up the next stairway, quietly climbing the stone steps until they reached a long hall at the top. The goddess stopped and then motioned them along, pointing below a massive door that was banded with iron. In the crack of space where the door met the floor, they could see shadows moving in the room. Mivraa moved close to the door, listening in while Urith motioned Oslaf, pointing for him to watch other doors across the hall. The Esterblud leader then came up close with the goddess to hear the voices coming from within, while keeping an eye on the stairway behind.

Inside the door, Satres paced back and forth in front of the large hearth, visibly upset as he went over what Colainn told him.

"You cursed fool. I ought to have your head for this. I didn't tell you to kill the man," said the Overlord as he turned to Colainn. "His visions were needed. What did he say to you?"

A scared giant stumbled to get out the words for his master. "I—I never saw anything like it—it was like he suddenly stopped screaming and went limp. I backed off, and slapped him, thinking he passed out, but he was just smiling at me." Colainn's red tunic showed the dark stains of the blind man's dried blood.

"I didn't ask you how he died," snapped the overlord.

"But he just looked up at me and smiled; like he could see into my eyes. He just told me that he died a happy, man, knowing –," his voice trailed off.

"Knowing what, you fool? Go on." The overlord stared into the fire, thinking about this setback.

"The old man just told me he was happy at the vision of your death, and he died in my arms, just smiling at me."

Satres had no time to respond as the door burst open with Urith slamming headlong into the giant's back. Before Colainn had time to answer, he was face down on the floor. The Esterblud pressed his sword to Colainn's throat while Mivraa had her sword pointed at Satres' face, pressing a finger to her lips to keep him quiet.

"Did you kill Dughorm, you gold *pitshog*. You have one chance. Yes, or no?" Urith growled in the man's ear.

The giant could not speak due to the pressure on his throat. He choked, coughing out a yes while he tried to spit out his regret. Urith would not let the man get the words out. He slammed the enemy's head down while pulling up on the Clovel Sword with his other hand, using the tip of the long blade for leverage. There was a sickening sound of gurgling and the snap of bone, and the Esterblud stood up with the dead giant's head in his hand, oblivious to the blood flowing across the stone floor. He spat on the head and threw it into the fire, before turning to Satres. A primitive savageness in the warrior's eyes made the Sacred Overlord suddenly feel mortal terror he had never experienced before. He began to pray to

Alrpan for help.

"Urith, No!" Oslaf and Mivraa shouted at the same time.

"We need him to find Fedelm," Oslaf was halfway into the room.

The vengeful man stopped. However, his muscles shook at the effort, and he slowly moved over to the other side of the room just to keep himself from destroying the thin, putrid excuse for a man. He nodded to Mivraa, who pushed her sword slightly into the overlord's throat.

"Now, to make sure you understand, I'm Mivraa, and if you wish to live, you will talk true. Where is the hakra called Fedelm?" Mivraa gave the overlord a deathly stare.

Satres' face grew pale when he realized the demigoddess of Haligulf was in front of him. His mind raced as he understood that the Aberffraw warriors had failed in their battle and those who returned lied about the deaths of the Esterbluds. Trying to regain his composure, he told the goddess the girl was fine.

"She's with her father," the man shakily told her, his eyes, trying to avoid staring at the sword at this throat. "I have no reason to harm her."

"And you had reason to kill Dughorm?" Urith came toward him again. "You sent that the Fealharan filth after us, I should kill you for that alone," Urith's voice rose, and the Sacred Overlord cringed at the expected attack, trying to back up as he was stopped by the hearth.

"I didn't want him dead, I swear it," the man pleaded. "I needed Dughorm alive. I only needed to find out about his visions. I was about to have that stupid fool executed." He pointed to the body on the floor as he backed into the stone wall. "Dughorm was my friend."

The Esterblud warrior stared at him.

"You will take us to Fedelm. If she lives, then we will decide what your fate is."

"Urith, I believe we should kill him now," Mivraa interjected. "We can't trust him."

"No, we need him!" Oslaf spoke up. "I know we can't trust him, but we may need him to get out of here alive."

Urith nodded as he grabbed Satres and put his sword to his neck. "You will take us to Fedelm. If you make any mistake, I'll be happy to remove your head—slowly."

The Sacred Overlord nodded, visibly frightened by the warrior. Mivraa led the group out of the room and back to the stairs. They moved quietly down the staircase, coming to the great hall where Satres indicated they should cross. They crossed in pairs; Urith crossed with Satres, whom he held tightly by the back of the neck. They soon came to another stairway that followed the circular sweep of the outside wall, to a hallway with many servants' chambers as well as rooms used for satgert learning. The oil torchlights along the path lit their way, showing off the beautiful tapestries that hung down the walls with large beams of wood between. Satres now led the group, still held by Urith, as they passed a pair of decoratively carved wood doors, entrance to a large hallway. At this time of night, they met no one and heard no sounds coming from the staff quarters. At the end of the passage, they came to a heavy wooden door that bore a striking similarity to that of the Sacred Overlord's chambers. Mivraa stopped them, moving in front of Satres.

Urith looked for light coming from beneath the door, and seeing none; he nodded to Mivraa, who opened the door. The unlocked door made a slight creaking noise coming from the iron hinges as the door swung wide. The light from the hallway gave them a dim picture of a large bed in the room with someone in it. Pressing forward, Urith held out his sword as he whispered over at Mivraa for her to retrieve the light rocks. The girl pushed Satres against the wall next to her, keeping herself in the doorway, then pulled out the glowing rocks which she handed to Oslaf. The young warrior moved up to the bed, and the soft light revealed an aristocratic face sleeping alone. His long gray hair spread across his white pillow. Urith dropped the flat side of his sword blade down on the man's chest, which was covered by a fine red wool blanket. The man didn't respond so Urith dropped the sword again, harder this time. The man began to blink his eyes; then he gasped as he realized he was not alone in his room.

The man tried to sit up in bed. He was stopped when Urith pressed his blood covered sword to the man's throat. The man felt a sharp point and froze.

"Who are you? What do you want?" He demanded, staring up at the two large shadows in front of him.

"Shh," Urith pressed his finger to his lips. "We brought you a visitor."

Oslaf pointed his glowing rocks to show Satres near the wall. The man could see the blade of a sword point, held by Mivraa, at his overlord's chest.

"Satres, are you injured?" The man's eyes widened as he was now fully awake and grasping the danger in his room.

"No, Caestia. I'm fine. I've brought these people for Fedelm." The thin man moved slowly to his left along the wall, staring at the point of Mivraa's sword.

"What do you mean?" Caestia's blue eyes turned to the warriors at the side of his bed. "Fedelm is not here. What are you talking about?"

Mivraa was watching Caestia, and there was a quick movement by the Sacred Overlord. She turned just in time to see the thin man closing a small door barely outlined on the dark wall. The group heard the latching of a lock and opening of another door behind the wall.

"Curses," the goddess snapped as she ran to the door, trying to open it. "Where does this door go?"

Urith pushed his sword into the man. "Tell her now!"

"It is a passage that goes to the stairs below, back into the great hall," he stammered, and then realized what had happened. "Why is the goddess of Haligulf after the Sacred Overlord?" He asked in disbelief.

After a couple of quick tugs on the latch, Mivraa turned to the Esterbluds. "He's gone, and this door bolts on the other side.”

"It is too late to catch him now, thank the gods. The Sacred Overlord is now safe from you, whoever you are." Caestia's usually confident manner emerged.

"Now, you can put that sword away as killing me will do you no good." The man was staring at Mivraa. "I cannot understand why you are here. The sky gods don't join with humans against other humans."

Urith prodded the man a little harder with his sword as he spoke in his native tongue. "I'll be happy to mix your blood on my blade with Satres' guard if you don't shut up. Mivraa, watch the hallway while I help our friend out of bed."

"You are not Aberffraw, are you? You must know you will be captured and taken to be executed; I have no doubt. Now, what of Fedelm?"

The old warrior grabbed the man by his white linen undergarment with his free arm, nearly tossing the older man across the room. The man landed on his knees with a cry. Grabbing him by the back of his bed-cloths, Urith pushed him out into the hallway, and into the arms of Oslaf.

"Tell us, where is Fedelm?" Oslaf questioned him as he caught him by the collar. "Your daughter told me you are one of Satres counselors, a guardian of the archives. You know where she is!"

"What are you talking about? My daughter is not here. She hasn't been for many days," he insisted.

Oslaf narrowed his eyes. "Your master captured Fedelm and Dughorm this morning, using his Aberffraw cronies. How do you think we got this armor?"

"Satres' warriors brought them back here as prisoners, and now Dughorm is dead by your master's hand. My friend Urith will be happy to avenge his death with yours if you continue to lie to us."

The dignified man suddenly deflated at Oslaf's words. "Urith! By the gods, that is the name of the one Fedelm was seeking. This is not possible. I would know if she was here.

Satres would have told me."

The group had been moving down the hall, and now Mivraa stopped the group at the landing of the stairs that lead down to the main lobby. The sound of yelling and running footsteps came from below.

"We need to find another way out of here." She turned to Caestia.

"Listen, we don't have much time. Think about it. Why would we take your master hostage if we were not sure that your daughter is somewhere in the Citadel? Where does your loyalty lie?" asked the goddess.

"This so-called overlord left you with us and saved himself. Is your loyalty to your daughter? Or do you follow the overlord who dishonors himself and your trust? You need to decide right now," Urith growled through clenched teeth.

The man stared back and forth between the men and the demigoddess. Finally, he motioned that they should go back down the hall toward his room,

"Come, we can use another stairway that will take us up to the battlements," he said. "From there we can go down into the undercroft below the castle."

The warriors glanced at each other before Urith finally nodded. "If you are leading us into a trap, you will not see your daughter again," he reminded him grimly.

Caestia nodded absently, turning to lead them to a door in the hallway near his quarters. Inside, the group quickly ran up the circular staircase, coming out on the inside parapets near the top of the Citadel walls. Fortunately, they didn't see any guards. But they could see lights moving as people ran across the courtyard below, and an occasional shout echoed up from the guards and staff milling around. Even with the darkness and the distance, it was evident an alarm had been given as the lights were rushing toward the extended tower they were just leaving. The group followed the overlord's record keeper as he led them along the top of the battlement wall into a circular tower. From there, the group descended a stairwell to another level. They hurried through several doors into a small arched hall that was dark as night.

Pausing, Caestia told them they would be heading into a wing of the Citadel used only by the council members of the Majireef who controlled the temples of the lands. Mivraa brought forth her tribolrocks, giving the dim green light to the hall. He noticed their suspicious faces in the faint light and the small man explained he was trying to get them to the rooms of the ancient writings. The man told the group there was another passage into the underground caverns.

"If Fedelm was brought to the Citadel, this is the only place she could be taken, and I would not hear about it from the servants or the guards," explained Caestia. "Only a few know of its existence, and nobody spoke about any prisoners brought in today. I would have heard," he said confidently.

Unconvinced, Urith nodded to Mivraa and Oslaf as he allowed the small man to lead them through a large vaulted hall to a set of wooden doors. They cautiously entered the next room after dousing the light rocks. Inside they found tables covered in documents and tall shelves holding rolled parchments that filled the room with a musty odor. The room had a few lanterns still lit, but the room was empty. Caestia led them past the tables to a section of bookshelves in the center of the chamber. After reaching between two sections of shelves, the group heard a metallic sound, and one section opened slightly. The gray-haired man pushed the shelves open, and the lantern light revealed the tunnel. Mivraa pulled out her light rocks and moved forward with Urith. Oslaf pushed Caestia forward with his sword and pulled the bookcase closed after they entered. Unlike the burrow through which they entered the Citadel, this shaft was dry and the walls smooth. They passed areas that showed elaborate and grotesque carvings that looked to have been etched by deranged artists. The path they followed descended steeply into enveloping darkness.

"How far?" asked Mivraa looking back, past Urith to the

smaller man.

"It is not far. We are close to the gateway to the underworld."

Mivraa stopped, turning to Caestia. "You know we cannot go into the underworld without the permission of Caruun. What trick are you trying to pull?"

The man tried to hide behind Urith. "It's no trick. The room is a sidhera, a plane between the realms. It's only known about by a few hakra from the ancient texts during the Great Passing. I swear by the gods that humans and demigod can come and go into this sidhera."

Mivraa paused, thinking about his words. "I've heard rumors of such a place in the Citadel, but my father never spoke of it. I thought I knew them all." She looked at Urith. "What do you say?"

"If I can remove the head of the Sacred Overlord, I'll follow him to the throne of Caruun just to get the chance. However, we must be cautious as we could bring the hordes of the underworld upon us."

"Very well, let's go," said the demigoddess. She led the group as they continued down into the dark tunnel while Oslaf continued worrying about Fedelm. For Urith, his mind focused on the vengeance he wanted to inflict on Satres and those who worked with him.

~~~

Inside a cavernous room which glowed with a pale misty-yellow light, a biting cold struck the waking woman. Fedelm lay naked on a cold black slab, shivering as the stone seemed to suck the warmth from her body. A wave of modesty struck her, and she tried to gather herself, but couldn't move due to unseen bindings holding her in place. Instantly she thought of Alrpan as she spotted movement around her in the dark shadows. She turned her head around looking for anything familiar, but nothing revealed itself. She struggled to free herself while trying to determine her location. Only a glimpse of a large arched doorway on the far wall was seen from her
~~~

position.

"Welcome to my realm, Fedelm." A familiar voice echoed from the shadows.

"Alrpan, what are you doing? Where am I?"

The goddess slowly moved toward the girl from the shadows with an evil grin. Her eyes slowly scanned the woman and she licked her lips.

"You have been given to me for my pleasure. You are no longer needed by the Sacred Overlord. He once considered you to be a suitable wife for one of his guards. However, you disappointed him with your attempted escape with Dughorm. He decided to give you to me as a gift."

"No, you promised me the vision of greatest hakras if I helped you," the girl now shivered from the thought of what Alrpan might have in store for her. "I've done as you have asked."

The evil creature laughed.

"When you failed to bring us through the cave at Ynysbeag, I knew you betrayed me. Even Satres decided you could no longer be trusted. Then again, I've never been one to hold with agreements made with mere humans."

The goddess took a deep breath as she came next to the restrained woman. The feeble light inside the room grew stronger.

"I can smell the fear coming from you, my dear. You wonder, yet you know the tales. Pleasure and pain are my special gifts."

As the evil underworld goddess spoke, the girl saw the hideous forms milling around, moving closer to her. "I told you I would return with my pets," said the goddess. "I understand their needs. It doesn't matter to them what they mate with.   Male or female, young or old, they enjoy the screams and depravity. It excites them. I believe it brings back vague memories of their warrior days of rape and pillage. Just like those Gallaeci who I sent to kill you."

Fedelm turned back to Alrpan. Her shocked expression

changed to bitter hate.

"I'll help them remove your head," she spat out.

Alrpan laughed and ran her sharp nails along her prisoner's inner thigh. Fedelm cried out in pain.

"Little girl, you'll be much too busy pleasing me along with my pets. You forget I've seen your dreams and I've felt the powerful yearnings in your loins and your lip."

Fedelm looked away, but the face of a grotesque half human leered at her, licking its lips. Her eyes came back to the goddess as she leaned over the frightened woman. Alrpan kissed Fedelm on the cheek, her hot rancid breath sent a wave of revulsion through her body. Alrpan placed a caressing hand on the girl's breast.

"I'm going to let you in on a little secret. This is why I enjoy the human form so much. While you are pitiful, weak creatures, your senses and feelings are exquisitely intertwined." Alrpan held Fedelm's jaw and kissed her on the lips.

"That is what we gods crave. We have never known feelings such as pleasure and pain. We feel nothing but the emptiness of the void. Some of my fellow gods fear to use your human forms, thinking they will lose power and control. What those fools don't understand is, this human form allows us to experience the passion that comes from torment and craving."

She kept her smile while at the struggles of her prey. "Over the seasons, I've learned how to prolong the terror and pain for my pleasures. It mixes so well with sexual gratification."

The beorhs moved in close, watching excitedly as their master raked Fedelm with her thick, sharp nails. The beasts paced around giving whining noises, enticed by the screams coming from the bleeding girl. Alrpan continued her entertainment by climbing on top of the woman and painfully scratching Fedelm's breasts. Her ugly face lit up as she let her monsters claw the screaming human.

Alrpan's entertainment came to a premature end when the large arched door at the far end of the cavern burst open. The excited monsters were so focused on their prey; they didn't see the demigoddess and the Esterblud warriors enter. Mivraa saw Alrpan on top of the table, surrounded by her beorhs. She pulled her spear from her shawl, intending to confront the underworld goddess. Several of the beorhs immediately started toward Mivraa. That's when the rest of the group noticed Fedelm under Alrpan.

Oslaf surged past the demigoddess, his sword already in his hands as he slashed across the chest of the first beast to reach them. Urith rushed forward as well, impaling one of the creatures with his longsword before slamming his fist into the face of another. The creature screamed, backing away before the Esterblud ended its life with a downswing from his famous sword.

Oslaf slashed his way through the fiends and was nearly halfway across the room when he felt his body covered with searing pain. He believed himself enveloped in flames. Dropping to his knees, he yelled to the gods for protection. Mivraa was fighting off two more of the *beorhs*, jabbing her spear into the single eye of one of the beasts before pulling back and using the other end to slam into the head of the other. She suddenly felt the same pain streak across her body, causing her to collapse. Alrpan was using her power of illusion, but Mivraa was unable to stop it. She began to groan, feeling like she was being roasted alive upon a spit while the monsters attacked her.

Urith noticed his comrades drop to the ground, catching the hideous grinning face of Alrpan looking over at him. Suspecting the experience coming to him, he steeled himself and rushed toward the goddess. He pushed and sliced through the remaining monsters coming at him. The blast of a terrible phantom pain nearly took him to his knees. It was beyond the worst torture he had ever endured that swept into his bones. Still, he stayed on his feet, although significantly slowed by the sudden feeling of flames crawling up his body. Another beorh came at him. Urith nearly forgot the pain as he sliced into the once human form with a quick uplift of his sword. As he moved closer to the goddess, the agony intensified.

Alrpan could see the Esterblud still coming at her, and her eyes widened with each step that the human was able to proceed against her powers. She could not believe any human capable of such a thing, especially against her powerful illusions. However, she didn't realize that Urith was coming near to the end as his mind could no longer turn away the agony. As his energy slipped from him, he remembered the words of Dughorm and the Djeed talisman.

"*Da Umca Mivwar*," he croaked out as he fell to his knees a few steps from Alrpan. Unable to lift his sword as a beorh started ripping at his armor.

In an instant, the bloodstone talisman hanging from his neck glowed an intense, fiery red, temporarily blinding several of the beasts next to him. The agony enveloping his body suddenly vanished. Regaining his feet, he instantly killed one of the beorhs as it moved between him and the enemy goddess. He heard another beast cry out it's last as Oslaf was suddenly freed of the illusion. Mivraa stood up as well, tossing one of the beasts into another before impaling her thin shiny spear through them both. Sensing the danger, Alrpan rolled off Fedelm. She dropped behind the altar and backed away. Shock filled her as the humans pushed through her powerful spells.

Urith pressed his way forward, grasping at the goddess who was now yelling for protection from her monsters. The Esterblud fell when he was struck by a monster, but he was able to grab her ankle, twisting it as a beorh landed on him. The goddess screamed at the unaccustomed pain, unable to leave her human form to vanish from the realm. Urith hung on despite a monster ripping at his flesh as the beorh dug its claws into his back and legs. He was crawling up her naked leg, dragging her down to him. For the first time in her existence, the goddess panicked at the thought of a human overcoming her. She lashed out, kicking at the man, but she was unable to inflict any damage. Alrpan looked up to see some of the monsters stop their attack on the humans, the remnants of their human minds suddenly confused by the sight of their master's vulnerability. Oslaf ran into the pile of beasts, heading past the Mivraa and the Esterblud. He pushed his way through those beorhs who quit the fight and put his sword to the throat of the goddess.

"Call them off before I take your head. God or not, you will no longer exist," he smiled triumphantly at the goddess.

The goddess gave the beasts the order, her eyes turning red with fury at the human who dared humiliate her. Alrpan's mind raced to come up with a plan of escape. While he stood so close holding his blade at her throat, she would be unable to change from her human body. Somehow, the amulet worn by the other warrior seemed to have drained her powers away. As if he could read her thoughts, Urith pushed through the remaining beorhs who backed away, attempting to return to the shadows. Urith's eyes were cruelly assessing what to do with the naked deity in front of him, his permanent sneer showing her the look of death. The goddess could see in those eyes the same look that her husband gave those human souls he wished to torment. For the first time in her memory, she was feeling an emotion she didn't recognize. Fear was something she always considered a human weakness.

Caestia ran through the beasts, and he reached his daughter. He released her from the bindings. Fedelm was curled up, tightly holding her legs with her arms and her eyes wide with shock. Her fearful eyes stayed locked on the fiends moving into the shadows. Caestia covered her with the finely spun wool cloak left on the floor by the goddess.

Mivraa watched the scene. Even with all of her dealings with the dead, the demigoddess felt a pang of sympathy. However, she recognized the expression on Urith's face as he looked at Fedelm. The Esterblud glanced down at his black blood covered sword. Mivraa could almost read his mind. He was about to exact revenge on the goddess. It was an act that would lead to a bloody realm war between gods and humans. The demigoddess ran to the side of Alrpan, planting the end of her bloody spear down on the stone floor in front of her.

"Urith, stop!" She commanded him.

The warrior was about to swing his weapon. He stopped.

"I see your thoughts on your eyes. You cannot destroy this goddess of the underworld." Mivraa yelled out.

"After what this scunce has done. Time to end this now!" He insisted. "Out of the way."

"No! This will make it worse," the goddess remained steadfast. "What do you think Caruun will do to the humans of the world? He may not care for this loathsome goddess, but his pride will lead to vengeance that can only be satisfied by more blood than even you and I could stand. He will send his beasts out to wipe whole villages off the face of Kamin. He would have the underworld rise up and scatter their evil into this world. Do you believe humans can overcome the gods and their monsters?"

Mivraa stepped closer and reached out to touch Urith's arm, lowering her voice.

"Do you really want all that suffering? All of that death just because of this Clovel scunce?"

"How dare you speak to me that way, you *Estercetus* offspring? I don't fear any human." Alrpan spat her slur back at Mivraa. The goddess of the underworld was offended at being called the demeaning term of the female anatomy.

"Only a half-breed would beg a human. You're not worthy of being called a god," Alrpan voice rose in anger.

Mivraa moved her spear tip closer to the goddess as a warning.

"You should watch your mouth. I might decide to help Urith remove your head. Or would you prefer that I inform Caruun about your interference among the humans? He'll have something special in store for you if he learns you nearly started a war between the realms."

The goddess stared bitterly at Mivraa, forcing herself to keep quiet. Urith watched the exchange, still believing he should end this now.

Before he could make his decision, the room was filled with the echoes of heavy boots coming from the tunnel door. Urith turned toward the sound and could see the outline of blue-clad Aberffraw warriors and Citadel guards dressed in red tunics coming down the passageway toward the open entrance.

"Oslaf, keep your sword on her neck and remove her head if she moves," ordered Urith.

"Get Caestia to find us another way out of here. I'll hold them at the tunnel," he told Mivraa. Before the demigoddess could speak, Urith raced forward to the large open doors. Mivraa hurried over to Caestia.

While Urith tried to close one of the doors, two Aberffraw warriors sent spears flying toward him. They missed, their weapons impaling into the wooden door as it closed. More Aberffraw rushed to the entrance as he tried to push the other door shut. The force of their charge knocked him back. Urith used his shield to slam back at the warriors coming at him. During the struggle, the warrior thought he caught a glimpse of Lyncus, hobbling in the background and leading the guards in their charge. With the mass of bodies pushing forward, he jumped back with his longsword at the ready.

While Oslaf had moved behind the underworld goddess, holding his sword on her shoulder to let her know he was in control. He dug his fingers into her bare shoulder with his shield hand. His skin crawled at the coldness of her skin, feeling as if he was touching the dead flesh of a drowned person.

"Mivraa, is there a way out of here?" He yelled at the demigoddess who got Fedelm to her feet. Appearing in a daze, Fedelm still stared dumbly at the beasts in the shadows. Her eyes suddenly widened, and she backed away.

Oslaf spotted movement out of the shadows as several beorhs moved into the light chattering something intelligible. He saw the remaining beasts coming out of the shadows. Instead of attacking, they were quickly converging upon the entrance where Urith stood with his back to them. Oslaf yelled out a warning to his uncle. However, one of the monsters ran past the Urith and leaped on an Aberffraw guard coming through the door, tearing at the man's eyes with its claws. The other beasts followed, crashing into the mass of men coming through the entrance.

Urith was frozen for a moment, stunned by the sudden, unexpected help. He could only guess that whatever humanity was left in the beasts must have regained control. Once fighters, they must have remembered their battling instincts. An instant later, Urith joined the foray striking down one of the armed guards who managed to get past the beorhs. The mass of humans and beasts whirled around the tunnel with the creatures keeping the enemy from entering the room.

Caestia led Mivraa and his daughter to a small door behind a tapestry with embroidered images of the underworld gods which was hanging down the sidewall. He caught Oslaf's eye with his movement, and the man looked back to wave him over. Before following, Oslaf pushed the goddess toward the melee in the tunnel entrance. Alrpan resisted at first, but the warrior dug his fingers hard into her shoulder.

"Move it, scunce. You will be our protection for now."

Pushing her forward, they were soon alongside Urith. Seeing his nephew's hostage, Urith began backing away from the mass of beasts and warriors who fought in bitter combat. The sounds of screams and animal chattering echoed throughout the room.

Seeing the naked woman as a type of hostage, some of the Aberffraw guards stopped advancing for the moment. They believed Alrpan was a noblewoman of the fortress. While they decided, Oslaf pushed the beautiful woman into the group of remaining beorhs still fighting the guards. Some of the beasts saw an opportunity. Before the goddess could disappear, they jumped on her, dragging her down to the ground.

Coming into the room, Lyncus saw what was happening. He recognized Alrpan and ordered his men to rescue the underworld goddess.

"Come on, we need to catch up with the other. We have to leave now," Urith yelled out as he pulled Oslaf away.

Oslaf remained to grin at the just punishment he witnessed for Alrpan. He turned and joined his uncle.

They ran to the back of the room, where they reached Caestia. He held open the small door into another tunnel. When Urith looked back as he shut the door, he could see many of the sub-humans scratching and trying to mount the naked goddess as she screamed and ranted in rage. While he didn't want to leave her still alive, he felt a wave of satisfaction at the revenge exacted. He knew, with the Aberffraw trying to rescue the goddess, the beorhs gave them time to escape.

Urith used his battle-ax to help secure the small door from the inside by jamming the wood shaft through the latch handle. It would take a while for the enemy to rip down the door. Following the green light, they saw in the darkened tunnel, Urith and Oslaf soon joined the small group. Caestia's rage was clear when he learned that the Sacred Overlord had given his beloved daughter to Alrpan.

"Caestia said we have a way out," Mivraa waved them forward. "Come!"

Oslaf helped Fedelm, but she remained quiet and shaky. He led her through the tunnel.

Mivraa led the way down the tunnel with her light rocks in one hand and her spear in the other as the rest of the group followed. The tunnel led them to the opposite side of the Citadel, far away from where they had entered. As they moved along, Mivraa told them she believed they could work their way around the base of the walls, which should keep them safe from any alerted patrols. The demigoddess pushed on with her green rocks, moving quickly through the large tunnel to a much smaller tunnel. After entering, the group hurried along hunched over, occasionally hitting their helmets on the rough tunnel ceiling as they went. Finally, Mivraa stopped and put away her rocks, before pushing through a small crawl space out into the night air. Urith followed her and pushed back the brush wedged up against the hole, allowing the others to exit a little easier.

The Esterblud warrior looked into the darkness above, which revealed the waning moons. He could hear the waves crashing below them as Mivraa crept forward along the edge of the cliff, looking for a footpath. After the others had joined them, Urith moved to the other side of the ledge where looking below he saw a path that trailed out of sight as it led around to the opposite end of the Citadel. He found no guards on the pathway. However, he remained concerned that their armor might reflect the moonlight, sending more guards their way.

Mivraa nodded agreement, saying they would have to risk it. Urith felt the goddess hold his rough hand for a bit longer, and he smiled at the touch.

Oslaf, who had moved ahead a little way, motioned the group to him. As Urith approached with Mivraa, his nephew pointed to an area, nearly hidden, where footholds stair-stepped down the side of the cliff face.

Mivraa nodded approvingly.

"The guards built a way to move up or down this area when they are patrolling around the Citadel. We will use it for our convenience as well."

The group carefully descended to the footpath. They only stopped on occasion when they heard sounds coming from the battlements above. After a long trip, stumbling through near darkness, the group came to the place where they had tied the ossanes. They hurried to the animals which nearly spooked by the swarm of people coming upon them,. Oslaf was able to get to his ossane first, quickly calming it and the other animals. Mivraa had Fedelm sit behind her while Caestia doubled up with Oslaf. Urith led them down the mountain toward Cuinal.

The waning moonlight, they moved along the road carefully on the lookout for patrols. Urith and Oslaf could hear whispers occasionally between Fedelm and Mivraa, but neither warrior could make out what the women were discussing. Oslaf could make out Fedelm's ashen face. He noticed that she moved like she was in a stupor since her rescue.

Just outside of Cuinal, Urith trotted his mount ahead in his Aberffraw armor. When he came upon the light of a campfire, he saw several guards milling about. The warrior decided it would be better to enter the village quietly from another path. He waited for the rest of the group outside of the reach of the campfire.

They abandoned their mounts, tying them off behind a row of trees near an open field. Urith talked them into splitting off into two groups before proceeding into the village. They agreed to meet up near the dock before they boarded as a group. Urith reminded them that their ship would leave at high tide, right at daybreak so they would need to gather before then.

After pulling off the saddlebags and blankets from the mounts, they carried what they could in their bags and on their shoulders. Oslaf, Fedelm, and Caestia worked their way along a footpath to the beach where they could follow the shoreline toward the dock. Urith and Mivraa decided to follow the road and bypass the guards with a wide swing through the field. Before they left, Mivraa untied the mounts and shooed them away. The animals only ran a few steps and stopped to eat at the plants in the field. Urith lamented the fact they would be leaving the saddles and ossanes which would be good trading barter, but it would be too risky to keep the mounts with them.

As Urith and Mivraa walked along the road to the village, she told Urith that she was returning to the Sky Realm.

Mivraa planned to tell her god father about Alrpan and her meddling in human affairs. The warrior nodded his head, feeling a bit disappointed. Still, he was surprised the goddess had stayed with them this long and pleased she would accompany him to the docks.

The pair had little difficulty getting around the guards by staying in the shadows of the trees along the road. As they passed by, the pair were close enough to hear the complaints of a comitatus guard who was upset with the Citadel overlord's orders. The couple learned the local militia was stopping everyone on the roads. The guard complained to his friends that he could make better use of his time.

Urith and Mivraa paused, listening to the man, who gave away the orders coming from the Overlord. Anyone unknown to the local guard would be suspect, and taken prisoner. The faceless voice went on to wonder what the price would be if they captured these fugitives. The pair pushed on in a hurry to get to their destination.

After they entered the town, the odd pair bypassed another guard patrol as they worked their way through the deserted streets. Mivraa led Urith to the docks, taking care to keep them both in the shadows. They found a bench next to an upturned rowing skiff that was awaiting a hull cleaning. Silently, they watched the morning light give the horizon a purple glow. As they sat watching, Urith felt a weariness seep into his mind. The need for rest beginning to take hold. Taking off his Aberffraw helmet, Urith focused his thoughts on Dughorm. Lost in thought, the warrior paid little attention to the fisherman working to mend nets and preparing for their day in the small boats that lined one side of the dock. He felt Mivraa touch his shoulder, then lean in close to whisper, the scent of her bringing him back from his reverie.

"I promise you, I will find Dughorm, and he will get to Haligulf, I swear." She told him.

Urith stared ahead, nodding.

"I know you will do what is right. However, I'm also

thinking of the future of the gods and humans among other things."

"Perhaps, you are thinking about gods and humans? Or maybe just one in particular?" She gave him a playful tweak on the ear lobe.

Urith looked back at her and spoke gently.

"Yes, I was thinking of you. It's been a while since I've found someone to show my affection for. You are both a fighter and a beautiful woman. I wish I had met you many *Draenyna* ago," he confessed.

"Then, why are you so hesitant?" she asked. "I have the same feelings as well. We can find a secluded spot while the dawn rises."

The man touched her cheek with his rough hand, smiling his sneer smile as he looked into her eyes lit up by the morning rays.

"While I'm not hakra, I'm afraid we may be forced to choose different sides soon. I'm not very smart, but I can see that there is a storm coming. You know about this as well as I do," he replied with a tired smile. "I've seen your fears about what's coming from the look in your face at times. By letting Alrpan and Satres live, I'm afraid it's now inevitable."

Mivraa placed her hand on his larger hand, holding it.

"You could be right. But you must not think that Alrpan or Satres can control what is coming for all of us any more than you or I can control the cycles of the moons."

She turned to look at the dock. "But you must remember this; I will never betray you. You and I will always be on the same side."

Urith turned his head and unexpectedly kissed the goddess on her cheek. "That means more to me than you know. Now, what's next?"

"Well, you and the others will need to find the Skool." Mivraa seemed slightly taken aback by a kiss from this man, but pleased as well. She turned her head and kissed him on the lips.

"You should have taken me up on the secluded spot," she admonished him lightly. "I see your ship is getting ready to undock."

She nodded to the cuggle halfway up the dock as the sailors were moving about the deck. Their trade ship was fitted with a single mast and a square-rigged single gray canvas sail which they began to unfurl for the morning tide.

"I will return to let the sky gods know what is happening." She continued. "Perhaps my father will have answers for me when he understands the rumors hold more truth than he first believed. I'll return as soon as I can."

Mivraa gave his hand a squeeze before letting go.

As the sunrise broke into the day, Oslaf and the others arrived.

"It looks like your nephew has a few tricks like his uncle." Mivraa rose from the bench.

Urith looked at the young warrior, and he could not recognize him at first. The Aberffraw armor was gone, replaced by some sort of gray merchant's wrap-over coat with a gold hood and brown canvas leggings didn't fit. He carried one white bag like a sailor over his back along with his other bag. There was a rolled up blanket that clanked with his footsteps. Fedelm and Caestia had removed their elegant tunics as well and now wore the black woolen robes of the *satgert*, trimmed in the scarlet color of the Sacred Overlord.

Urith smiled approvingly at the change. Any locals who spotted Caestia and Fedelm would immediately know their authority under the overlord banner. Locals were unlikely to ask much of them while they traveled. Fedelm walked behind the group, but her father was no longer assisting her as they walked. The father and daughter waited near the docks for the Esterbluds to join them. Oslaf was smiling as he came up to Urith.

"We found some clothes along the way. I figured we might find it a little easier to board if we don't look like those who left the Citadel. We ran into a laundress shack near a creek and borrowed these. I think I have something for you as well."

"You are planning ahead, my nephew. I'm impressed."

The Clovel Destroyer moved between the upturned skiff and a line of netting to change his clothes while Mivraa and Oslaf went over their plan. Removing his Aberffraw tunic, he decided to keep it, along with the helmet which he put into the bag Oslaf gave him.

Mivraa snickered when she saw the giant warrior trying to fit a tunic that was obviously too small over his chainmail. Fortunately, Oslaf had another tunic, which did fit the older fighter. However, none of the leggings would fit Urith, so he put on his own Esterblud gaiters. Only an experienced warrior would know the difference. Oslaf had wrapped their captured weapons in a blanket, carrying them over his shoulder. Urith used a blanket to wrap his Clovel Sword along with his baldric belt and the rest of his armor. Like Oslaf, he kept on his chain mail and swung his shield over his back, which he covered with an oversized coat. It worked reasonably well in the morning light as long as he carried the rolled-up blankets and bags over his shoulders. While he changed, Urith listened to changes necessary to get on the ship now with their new identities.

Fedelm and Caestia would go aboard as *satgerts* from the Citadel of Br-Ynys heading to Hyropda. Urith and Oslaf would act as their personal servants and guides. While the bigger men did not really look the part of merchants, Caestia believed the captain and ship's crew would not care much as long as they were paid. They would be paid well enough to bypass the Malhair House, which might get word back to the Overlord. Any suspicions of the captain would be soothed by the fresh weight of coins in his pocket.

Mivraa stayed in the lightening shadows near the skiff as the group walked to the ship where bells were clanging. Sailors began working the lanyards and sails. She waited as the group went aboard and could just see Caestia and Fedelm talking with the captain of the deck. Eventually, he must have accepted the money as the crew pulled up the gangway and the ship was untied from the dock. The demigoddess watched until the ship had slipped out of the harbor and into the calm sea before her shape changed into an old hag. Mivraa hobbled along toward the village square which would lead out of the village and to the lellowtere tree she spotted just off the main trail when they first came to the village. The twisted tree would provide her gateway back to the Sky Realm, and hopefully, answers to the future.

Chapter 8: Flight to Cahmais

The trip through the western passage gave the weary group time to catch up on rest. Heading toward the village of Hyropda, they soon realized that the ship they took had its problems. Urith recognized the unruly crew was led by a lazy captain. He overheard that the crew came from debtor's prisons controlled by the merchant guild. It left them in a dangerous situation. Urith told the group to stay in their cabin as much as possible. To help, Caestia paid the captain and his boy, a lad called Mokee, to serve them meals in their cabin. The little red-haired boy took a liking to Fedelm and spent time chattering to her about the happenings on the ship and conversations of the crew. Since the group was staying to themselves on the voyage, the boy's youthful talk gave them valuable information they wouldn't have otherwise come across.

For his part, Urith enjoyed getting back to the sea and away from the smell of ossanes. As the days progressed, the warriors gave Fedelm and Caestia the full details of their escape from certain death with the help of Mivraa. While they talked about their battle and how they got into the Citadel; the men kept the discussion away from discussing Dughorm or Alrpan. While Fedelm was getting back to her old self with her biting comments at Urith's expense, everyone sensed an underlying strain within the girl. Her father was very protective of her, and both he and Oslaf kept a careful eye on her when she went on deck. She appeared alright as she walked among the sailors while she took in the fresh air and sunshine.

In conversations with her father, Urith learned that Fedelm's mother was a hakra as well, chosen by their Eernicia overlord to go to the Citadel. She was excited at what she considered an adventure and, reasoning that it would be a welcome change from the doldrums of their small village convinced Caestia to accompany her. It was evident to the Urith that Caestia was still deeply in love when he saw the gray-haired man's eyes glisten from the memories of her death. It was an emotion he well knew and kept deeply buried.

Urith's eye caught Oslaf, who struggled to communicate with Fedelm. His uncle could see by his expression that the young warrior was frustrated by her distance and inattentiveness to him since coming aboard the ship. For his part, Urith didn't fully understand the change either. However, he knew people reacted differently when they suffered. In his seasons as a warrior, he had been in many battles and had seen the abuse and defilement of men and women, young and old. Despite the warrior code used by many overlords, cruel things happened in war. He knew well the inhumanity of men. However, he had never witnessed such acts committed by beasts and gods upon a helpless human. While she was not his child, he still felt the rage that went through him when he saw what happened. Urith remembered the vow against Alrpan that he gave himself. The warrior already had reason to hate the gods. However, his desire for vengeance against the gods grew on that night.

During the second morning of their trip, Caestia took Urith aside in the early morning as the others were sleeping. He and the Esterblud spoke about Du-Rinell and its history. As a former counsel to Satres, the gray-haired man told Urith much about the council. He also explained to Urith that, while he was proud, he never really wanted Fedelm to become part of the Majireef's mission. Urith remained silent as he let the man talk.

"I never expected Fedelm to become part of this," he confided to the warrior. "I was one of Satres' trusted confidantes, but not a seer within his council. I handled the archives and records of the Citadel, so he came to me for information. Satres was keen on knowing about the myths around Heptarc."

"I knew of Fedelm's visions, of course. It was the same

with her mother, a curse handed down from her family." He looked over at the sleeping girl. "But my girl considers it a gift she can use to help the family. She believed that if she could become one of Satres' council, it would be a crowning achievement. She knew I was proud of her, but not because of the council. I had reservations how Satres used the group."

"You knew she decided to follow Alrpan? Urith asked as he looked out the small porthole at the blue and green sea, wishing he could get more time on deck.

"No, I did not know this." Caestia shoulder's slumped. "I found out about it when Fedelm told me just before she left to find you. I never let her explore the world beyond Ynyover despite her pleas. I think Satres used her ambitions along with manipulation from the goddess herself. The overlord has great influence over others, more than you can imagine."

Urith nodded in agreement.

"I can see that. With all the Aberffraw warriors running around in Ynyover, I assume that King Asgurd is tied in with Satres and Alrpan as well." Urith sat down on a small bench in the cabin. He leaned his back against the hull, enjoying the rolling ocean.

Caestia sat next to him.

"Yes, the King and the Overlord have held many sessions in council. I don't know much about what was discussed in those conversations. A small group of hakras and advisor handled the arrangements. I was able to find out a little bit when I overheard the private conversations of Satres and Lyncus. I also overhead the guard's rumors about Lyncus and Satres spending their time together." Caestia paused, his face bitter.

"When King Asgurd placed his Aberffraw warriors in Ynyover as a presence to keep his influence there, he also promoted Lyncus, his son, as leader of those troops. They use the Citadel to help keep a watchful eye on the people of Ynyover," he explained.

Urith shook his head in disbelief.

"To think that I had the son of our worst enemy before me, and I let him live." He didn't bother to explain to the confused Caestia but asked him why Asgurd and Satres were in partnership.

Fedelm's father considered his question for a bit.

"Well, my guess is Satres believes that reforming the Liege Body would make it too difficult for him to expand his powers. While Satres is too weak to send the Aberffraw warriors away, he and King Asgurd are very much alike in their desires. I would believe they will continue to be allies as long as they need each other. But I don't know what they have agreed to. Lyncus is probably the only person who would be privy to any agreements."

"If you are correct, I think I should be heading back to my king to let him know the tide that is coming. I believe he has little knowledge of the threat to Esterblud." Urith stood and began to pace in the small cabin, keeping his head down due to the low ceiling. He looked over as Fedelm turned over in her sleep, but her breathing remained deep and steady.

"It is a tough decision," agreed Caestia. "I don't envy you. For what it's worth, I believe you are making the right choice in following Dughorm's path. I briefly knew him when he was at the Citadel, and know his visions were entirely accurate. From what I know, he was a great hakra and a warrior. You have my sympathy for his death. I'm sorry I didn't know he had been brought to the Citadel. Perhaps…." He hesitated. "Well, I like to hope I would have been able to help him."

Urith nodded absently.

"Thank you, your words are appreciated. But I have a question for you. What will you and Fedelm do now? You must realize that you and your daughter traveling with Esterbluds will be dangerous," he pointed out.

"I don't think we have much choice but to stay with you." Caestia smiled grimly at his words. "You and your nephew have uncovered something that was meant to remain unknown." He saw that Urith was puzzled, waiting for an explanation.

"You see. Satres is not very discrete at times. I have seen and heard things he didn't intend others to know. Now that I understand clearly what that brute is capable of, I believe Fedelm and I should help you and Oslaf." The record keeper stopped and lowered his voice. "However, don't get me wrong, while I thank you for your help, I don't agree entirely with any human controlling the Skool. It was meant to be destroyed. Its power will corrupt the person who finds it."

Urith thought about his words, remaining quiet for a while. The sounds of sails flapping outside came through the porthole near them.

"Your thoughts about the Shield weigh on me as well. However, I must follow Dughorm's instructions, for I believe his path must be the correct one." The warrior looked at Fedelm. "What about your daughter? We can't expect anything to be easy anymore."

"She is getting better," the older man said. "She told me that her dreams with Alrpan have stopped. It appears the control over her is gone. Fedelm told me of her intent to help you and your nephew."

The Clovel Destroyer nodded as he watched Oslaf finally struggle out of his hard bed.

"We're partners now. Since you look more of a merchant than I do, see if you can get an idea from the captain when we get to the port and what time we should arrive. Then, we can decide how we get to the ruins of Du-Rinell."

They broke up the conversation as Fedelm and Oslaf stirred; the freshening wind was pitching the cuggle in the swells. Urith found himself thinking of Mivraa and when he would see her again. He drew a deep breath to clear his head. He needed to think about Dughorm and the stories and visions he had shared. He put on his merchant cloak over his chainmail and went up to walk the deck.

For the rest of the day, they remained quiet and thoughtful.

Urith and Oslaf found themselves on the deck listening to the stories they overheard from the sailors who told of terrible events happening throughout Kamin. The sailors spoke in hushed tones about the ships disappearing and whole villages swallowed by massive tidal waves. Oslaf overhead a story about a fleet of ships held up by unending beds of thick seaweed across their paths. Another sailor spoke about his conversations with local fishermen who complained about the difficulty in getting a full catch for his family as the schools of fish seem to have disappeared.

When Urith and Oslaf returned to their cabin, they agreed that the gods were somehow angered and taking out their punishment upon the world.

"The sailors are nervous about the signs they see and hear," Urith stated. Then he mentioned a grizzled old man who spoke about a God of the Void called Kriell only to be loudly interrupted with cries of dissent at his foul heresy. The old Guardians were not to be talked about aboard ship. It was an insult to their god of the sea, Uugor, and would put the whole ship at risk.

While they spoke, Oslaf sat near the open window, not far from Fedelm. She was mending clothes to pass the dull day, but he knew she was interested in the conversation. He watched her, seeing her eyes light up at the discussion. Her face grew dark when the talk turned to the Gods of the Void. While she looked like she wanted to say something, Fedelm avoided eye contact with him. He tried speaking to her many times during the trip, but she ignored him or talked to others in response.

Finally, Urith and Caestia decided to leave the cabin to check on the progress to their destination, allowing the young warrior a chance to speak with her alone.

"Why are you avoiding me, Fedelm," Oslaf asked, his voice quiet after they left. "Since the Citadel, you have hardly spoken to me or even acknowledged me."

Fedelm stopped her work, sighing uncomfortably.

"It is not you Oslaf," she kept her eyes on the cloth. "I've failed! I'm ashamed to be around you. I could not see my hand in front of my face. Used by two people I trusted, and I've achieved nothing but the death of a kind man. I nearly got you and your uncle killed. You cannot know of such failure. I don't understand why you continue to want to speak with me."

"No Fedelm, I recognize how you feel entirely," he reassured her. "Trust me, I felt as you did when I woke on the Cahmais coast, saved by Urith yet again. And I told him things that I'm ashamed of now. But he set me right, and he has continued to believe in me, even about you." He moved over to sit next to her.

"All you have done was trusting the wrong people, which is nothing to be ashamed of. My uncle told me, I must learn from my mistakes."

Fedelm looked up at him; her eyes were holding back the start of tears but could say nothing. Pain and sorrow filled her face. Oslaf wrapped her in his arms. She didn't resist as she quietly cried out her sorrow. The woman wanted to tell him so much, but she held it in, only taking comfort in his strength.

The pair was still sitting there when Caestia and Urith returned. Her father scowled at Oslaf, and the young warrior released the girl, his face turning red with embarrassment. Urith just smiled.

"The captain just gave your father the news, Fedelm. We land tomorrow in the high tide."

"And what's next?" Fedelm spoke, wiping her red eyes. "I've got nothing to give you from my dreams at this point. No visions have appeared in my dreamless sleep."

"You are too hard on yourself. We have enough information to start, and we can hope that the Fates give us a chance." Urith replied. "Besides, your father told me he was familiar with the area, so we won't need to rely on the locals."

The woman remained unconvinced but kept silent. Oslaf asked about the weather. He noticed the wind was freshening throughout the day. Caestia told them that the captain believed they would make port well before the storm arrived. If all went as planned, they would be off the ship and into the village before the rains came.

"We'll get ossanes at the village," Urith explained. "Caestia would pose as a representative of the overlord, traveling to meet with a *satgert* who lived in a nearby village called Turqew. That should keep local gossip down. Maybe even throw off any Fealharan who might be following us."

A light knock at the cabin door broke up their conversation as the ship's boy arrived with their food for the evening.

That night Oslaf kept the first watch for any unexpected visitors sneaking in from the crew. Considering the makeup of the crew, they might come looking for valuables, only to discover everyone's real identities.

Urith fell into a deep sleep, sinking deeper and deeper into the black before an image of Mivraa appeared to him, and he felt the comfort of her presence. Then, a vision of Fedelm came to the same dream, and he could hear them speaking with each other about the past and the future. While he listened in to the conversation, he recognized the musky scent of the warrior goddess and the smell pleased him. While Urith kept telling himself it was a dream, Mivraa spoke to the Esterblud.

"I have come to you as a warning, my dear friend. While you are not a hakra, I must bring you visions that will help guide you on your quest. Remember, that Fedelm can help you. Seek her advice." Her voice drifted off, and only the image of young Fedelm stayed with him.

Next, a vision from Mivraa splashed in front of them, showing the Sky Realm as they never envisioned. The whiteness of the temples that spread across the horizon blinded them for an instant. They could see the Sibyl, the god's oracle, talking to the sky god. Fedelm and Urith listened to the news about the Triad's leadership becoming fragile. Uugor, bewitched by Alrpan, flashed across their minds. Other images flashed across his mind as well. He saw his shield, but somehow it was different. It glinted with a light, bright silver flash that struck his eyes, making him squint. Then, along with the image of his shield, he was given a vision of his longsword, as well as the amulet given to him by Dughorm. Three items of his, all shined with an unbearable light, making him turn away in his sleep.

"The gods grow divided. Uugor is using his powers against the coasts of the human world. The sea god is supported by Unis, the wife of my father." Mivraa's voice trembled in his mind. "I'm sorry, but I'm unable to stop this damage inflicted upon the human world. The relationships between the gods of the earth, sea, and sky were now fractured. And my father is focused on healing the rift among his sons, so he does nothing to stop this. He does not listen to me now."

As the visions continued, they drifted through the temple of the Sky Realm, showing images of the gods bickering amongst themselves. Following the golden halls that shot upward into the blue sky, the vision came to the throne of her father which was empty. Suddenly his vision disappeared, and Urith heard the voice of the goddess fill his head.

"Sleep well. We will meet soon."

It was early when heavy swells caused the ship to shudder, waking Urith. He looked out the small porthole, confirming that the ship was indeed turning into the harbor. The others felt the change as well, and were soon up and dressed, following Urith out to the deck of the ship where sailors climbed up into the rigging, scrambling to shorten the large primary sails as the wind pushed against the ship. The craft lumbered low in the water toward the port of Hyropda which was now visible in the distance. A long, wide mooring jutted out to them, welcoming them as they raced the white caps. Several cuggles and fishing vessels lined either side of the dock. In the distance beyond the village, the mountains of Mythroloy rose up into the clouds. The purple and gray outlines gave the mountain range a majestic look even as the clouds cut off the mountain tops from view. In the distance, they could see a great white squall line heading their way. The ship's boy ran by, stopping briefly to update Fedelm with a big smile, his long bright red hair blowing in the wind.

"The captain says we will make it past the breakers in plenty of time, but it might be bumpy as we come into the mooring inside the harbor." He looked at the young woman intently. "I hope you aren't a boat-sick person?"

Fedelm smiled at him and assured him she would be okay. The youngster ran off to his duties, his eyes glancing back at the woman. Urith scarcely noticed the boy, as his eyes were on the thick line of low, dark clouds in the distance. What he saw made him very uneasy. He was no stranger to sea travel and the storms that suddenly sprang up on the ocean. But this storm he saw coming looked particularly threatening.

"We must gather our belongings and be ready to move quickly once we get into port." He turned to the others. "I've never seen a line of water and rain like that before. I think there may be more behind it. Perhaps the gods have something in mind for us?"

"I've got our stuff packed, so it won't take long." Oslaf volunteered as he ran inside the cabin, followed by Caestia. Fedelm remained to observe the storm coming.

"You know I saw the visions Mivraa brought. We shared the dream," she said as she moved next to him. "Like you, I believe something is coming after us."

The warrior acknowledged Fedelm's thoughts with a nod. Urith felt sick in the pit of his stomach as he could only watch the oncoming storm while looking at the sun-bleached wooden dock in the distance. The pair heard the captain yelling orders to the crew as they scrambled across the deck. Urith recognized they would be cutting it close before the squall line was on top of them. Fortunately, the wind was pushing the ship faster toward the harbor, and they finally passed the breakwater.

"You know our escape would not have reached Hyropda already," she commented. "Father should be able to get us through any Aberffraw guard we find. He asked me to pool our remaining koinons for the animals and provisions we need."

"Let's get out of the way so the sailors can bring the ship in," he said as he handed her a small leather bag. "I want everything ready."

As they entered the cabin, they heard the crew yelling for lines from the dock, and the grunts of men as they heaved on the lines, dragging the ship toward the berth. Soon the cuggle slid up with a bump against the bundles of thin *chickle* wood strips that lined the dock for protection.

After the gangplank had been lowered, Caestia and Fedelm led the Esterbluds, still dressed in their gray merchant tunics and hoods as they pushed into the crowd of traders who waited at the dock for the cargo on the ship. The incoming crowd of finely dressed merchants and interested villagers filled the wooden wharf near the ship, pressing in close to see the latest trading goods brought in. Urith watched for thieves who found such dense crowds as opportunities to rob passengers of their bags. A loss of such items would spell disaster for them, giving away their disguise. Urith whispered for Oslaf to keep an eye on Fedelm, who was unperturbed by the crush of people. Caestia stopped one of the merchants, asking the fat man for the best ossane trader in the village. The man bowed before the fake satgert and directed them to the other side of the village. Following the gray-haired man, the group continued down the dock.

They were near to the shoreline when they felt the dock sway them. At first, Urith thought something hit the pier, but then he realized something else was wrong. He pushed Caestia and Fedelm forward and told them to run as the first major shock of the earthquake hit the dock sending them to their knees.

Another massive tremor shook the dock. Oslaf grabbed

Fedelm, and they jumped clear of the splintering wood as the pilings of the pier fell apart. Caestia and Urith leaped into the surf, landing in water to their knees, and then staggered onto the beach. The group ran into the village trying to follow the road amid the chaos of frightened people and animals. The earth continued to shake and pitch as the group stumbled up the street trying to avoid the small stone houses and shops as they fell apart, sending debris across the road. The sidewall of a two-story shop fell, slamming down into a small house next door, silencing the screams of the inhabitants inside. With his purple sock cap falling into his face, a local watchman struggled to calm the villagers who surrounded him. Urith watched as the watchman assembled a small group of men to help rescue two children from underneath a collapsed roof. Screams of pain came from a fallen wattle and daub building nearby, and the older warrior made his decision.

"Get to the ossane trader and find us some mounts, even if you have to steal them. We'll be right behind you." He shouted to Caestia in the Aberffraw language.

The gray-haired man looked at him and reluctantly nodded as he took Fedelm by the hand. Oslaf hesitated briefly and then followed Urith inside the collapsed building, searching for the source of the yells of pain. The warriors came to a large support beam angling down from the rubble that used to be a wall, pinning a fat shopkeeper and his wife. Urith got under the lower end on his hands and knees, pushing up while Oslaf pulled the brown-haired woman from the beam while she groaned from her leg injuries. Trying to be as gentle as possible, the young warrior picked her up and carried her to the street where he grabbed another woman to help her. Quickly, he ran back inside as Urith pushed up again on the wooden beam. The man was yelling in an accented Cahmais dialect that Oslaf had trouble understanding. Finally, he realized the man had an arm pinned under the beam. He dug around the arm, finally able to get it free and slid the screaming man away from the beam while telling Urith to let go. Urith crawled out from under the beam to help Oslaf carry the victim out of the rubble to where his wife was waiting, nursing her injured leg. The shaken couple clung to Urith and Oslaf, thanking them. They pulled free, and Urith warned them to leave the village immediately.

"Come on, we have to move fast. The sea is leaving the harbor. We don't have much time before it returns." Urith told his nephew as he looked over the harbor with an odd, desperate look on his face. Urith noticed the ships that had been moored at the docks now lying at various angles in an empty harbor. He knew the gods had drawn the water out to sea and would send it back to shore with terrible force, wiping out everything in its path. They had to get to the high ground!

Urith and Oslaf struggled through rubble, past groups of people as they made their way to Fedelm and Caestia at the edge of the village. Finally, the chaotic jumble of people thinned out as the men got near the stable, which was still standing. Caestia and Fedelm were on their mounts, but they were having trouble keeping the animals from bolting in fright as the ground still trembled occasionally. Urith said nothing, just jumped on the first ossane, while Oslaf quickly climbed on the other, slinging their blankets and bags over the tall saddle horns.

"We have to ride fast and get up the mountain now. No time to explain," Urith dug his heels into the flank of the beast which took off.

Others in the group didn't hesitate; they just followed him up the trail toward the distant peaks as fast as their mounts could gallop. He avoided the main road which ran along the coast; instead, he rode straight into the mountain gorge along a steep, narrow trail that followed along the edge of a ravine covered by low hanging tree branches and dense brush. The trail climbed toward a long rocky shelf of red and brown rock that jutted out and led into the clouds. Fedelm looked back just before they entered the forest and spotted a dark black and blue line of water coming in from the sea. She understood the danger immediately and got her father's attention, pointing behind. He glanced back, and she saw the fear in his face when he spurred his mount on.

The four pressed on following twists and turns as the rough path steepened, forcing the ossanes to slow as they traveled higher into the Eilginn Mountains. Nearly impenetrable foliage surrounded them, and the group felt a surge behind them. Soon, the sounds of the mounts huffing along with the noise from their cloven hoofs beating on the forest floor were drowned out by a rising roar that echoed up from the seashore. Urith spurred his ossane on faster, but the animal was getting winded, and it struggled on the slippery rocks.

As the roar behind them moved closer, they were suddenly buffeted by the wind that pushed them while a wall of water surged into the valley from below. The barrage of water and debris toppled the brush and trees like a giant scythe. Almost immediately the group was overwhelmed by a rising surge of water and forest debris which struck them.

Caestia was knocked from his mount by an uprooted tree, becoming tangled in the limbs which pulled him under. Oslaf jumped into the surging water after the old man as Urith grabbed his saddle to keep from being thrown from his mount. Branches, thick as a large tree, pushed into the warrior and his mount, pulling them both under the muddy water. As quickly as he went under, Urith struggled to the surface, a hand clutching his arm, helping him as he came up for air. Fedelm was beside him, pushing her mount through the water as she helped the Esterblud leader climb up the side of the animal. Desperately, Urith hung on, catching a glimpse of his own mount craning its long neck above water as it carried his longsword and other weapons away from them. Urith suddenly released himself from Fedelm's saddle, determined to let the water surge take him to his struggling mount.

Oslaf had pulled Caestia to the top of a debris pile nearby and was yelling for them to head toward his position. Fedelm was able to steer her animal through the swirling water to the reach the debris pile where Oslaf held the animal for her to dismount. He was visibly impressed by her courage in rescuing Urith.

The seawater surge finally reached its highest point as Urith overcame the swift current to get to his mount. Urith thrashed around in the chest-deep water, suddenly running into the dead body of a large *rangifer* which shot up from under the water. The body still stunk despite the water bath, its snout face and fat black body spinning around like a log. The warrior pushed it aside and was able to reach the giant bluewood tree where his panicked ossane was entangled. Urith pushed through in branches of tree limbs where the mount struggled, its eyes wide with fear. The Clovel Destroyer, talking gently in his gruff voice, pulled himself alongside the animal, stroking its neck and head. He freed the animal by cutting the reins with his dagger; holding on to the shortened leather straps. He was able to coax the beast toward the others, struggling through the chest-deep muck.

By this time, the water surge reversed course, moving back down the valley toward the ocean. Urith tied off the animal and scrambled up the haphazard mound, where he joined the others. They checked over their remaining items after Urith had ensured his weapons and armor were still attached to the saddle of his mount. Fedelm told him that the animal that carried her father also had much of their food. Oslaf went through the wet bags on his mount and found the rest of their grass flour and panbread was ruined by the sea water tidal surge.

"Well, we will need to tighten our belts some on this trip, unless we can find another village or farm," said Oslaf. "We might be able to find some animals higher up in the highlands as well. But, I still have my weapons so we can thank the gods for that."

"Damn the gods!" Urith exclaimed bitterly as he shook the muddy droplets of water out of his long sandy hair.

"On the one hand, we are supposed to thank the gods for

getting through this alive, I guess. However, at least, two gods just wiped out an entire village and nearly destroyed us. I say curse the coward gods involved."

Urith's bitterness to the gods grew as he reflected upon the morning's events. Fedelm was shivering despite the warm sunshine as she remembered the visions from Mivraa last night. She, like Urith, had failed to understand the warning. Uugor, the god of the sea, and Ecarca, god over the earth, had just tried to kill them. Both Fedelm and Urith were convinced this was not an accident.

"I'm not sure I fully agree with you, warrior," Caestia stated philosophically while he sat next to the warrior. "Perhaps one of the gods just saved us?"

In front of them, the torrent of water now streamed back to the ocean. High trees, uprooted by the massive force of the giant wave, twisted and bobbed as the water rushed back down the mountainside to the sea. Occasionally, the group would see an animal carcass, or a human body swept along with the debris. One corpse still held on, remaining eerily upright in a tree he must have climbed in an attempt to save himself. His sightless eyes stared up and one arm, caught in the branches, raised a grisly salute to the cruel gods.

Oslaf thought of the couple that he and Urith rescued earlier. He wondered if they had somehow survived.

No, they're dead!

The thought made him curse at the gods as Urith had earlier. He hated the helplessness of dealing with powers beyond his abilities to stop.

It took until the sun reached its zenith for the travelers to restart their journey. From their vantage point, looking below they could now see the valley was stripped bare of the vegetation and many of the trees. Caestia told them they would need to head back down the valley to an old trail which connected the ruins with a small village called Turqew. Caestia was given another mount to lead them to Du-Rinell. Oslaf smiled brightly after Fedelm offered the back of her horse to him. Her father and Urith just looked knowingly at each other before they proceeded.

With the trail in shambles, they followed a different path to the valley ridge, their animals stumbling through the muck and wreckage. The riders were forced off their mounts at times, to lead the animals around mounds of trees, boulders, and other debris.

At the top of the ridge the travelers, clear of the area damaged by the waters, got back on their animals and followed the arching slope as it rose up into the highlands of the Eilginn range. In the distance, they heard the echoes of rumbling thunder, adding more misery to the valley, as a storm front moved in. After several leagues of exhausting climbing, the forest thinned out, and the travelers finally entered a large mountain pass. Lightning struck a tree nearby, causing the ossanes to rear up at the sudden flash and harsh clap of the thunder. Caestia yelled for them to follow him to a large outcrop of rock which formed a cavern.

The group pushed their tired animals on as the blue-black clouds turned the day to near dusk. They arrived at the shelter as the first rains began to fall, sending down large water drops, followed by a torrential downpour. Lightning flashes jumped across the dark sky as the travelers tied off their animals on one side of the cavern, next to wet green sawhorst bushes. Fedelm and Caestia helped Oslaf remove the wet bags and saddles from the mounts. Urith gathered what dry wood he could find near the tree and used a pair of strike rocks and dry tinder he found to start a fire near the back of the wall. Fedelm and Oslaf hung the still wet contents of their bags and blankets on the wall while Caestia and Urith continued to look for wood.

"How long until we get to the ruins?" Urith asked after Caestia ran in from the rain, holding a few pieces of wood.

"I'm not really sure, my friend. I believe we will reach the road to Du-Rinell soon. If we don't run into delays, we should get there by the end of the day tomorrow."

"That's good, but we don't really have any idea what we are looking for."

"Well, Fedelm and I should be able to help. With my knowledge of the old stories and legends, along with her capabilities, we should be able to find it, the gods willing."

"That remains to be seen. Despite your confidence, this whole journey is more confused the further we go. But I'll be cursed if I have any other ideas."

Suddenly, the storm seemed to increase in ferocity as if the gods were listening to them. The few trees near the overhang provided them with little protection as the wind blew mist from the rains into the cavern to where the group was sheltered. After night had fallen, the storm gave up its ferocity as it rolled up into the mountains. The group watched the lightning streaks fade into the clouds and listening to the roll of thunder move away before they lay uncomfortably on the cold hard ground. Shivering from the drop in the temperature, they wrapped themselves in the damp blankets and were soon overcome with sleep.

Early in the morning, Urith scouted out the area ahead and soon found what he thought was the trail described by Caestia. He was dressed in his tunic over his chainmail and had wrapped the merchant clothing in his bedroll, tied off behind the saddle. When the others arrived, he nodded approvingly to Oslaf, who had put on his Esterblud clothing as well. Even though they were in enemy land, both fighters felt rejuvenated by putting on their own colors.

Caestia confirmed that, from his memory of the maps used by the Citadel library, Urith had found the correct road. He reminisced about how he showed his wide-eyed little girl all of the maps they had on the Kamin world. He smiled as Fedelm turned slightly red. Sitting tall in his saddle, Caestia nodded his head decisively, stating he was sure the road led to the deserted ruins of Du-Rinell. Urith watched with a grin as the gray-haired man took the lead, apparently envisioning himself as the scout of their group.

As they followed him, Urith thought of Mivraa, and although he hadn't expected her to come in his dreams, he had hoped for it to occur again. He told Fedelm and Oslaf about the fact he had no dreams during the night. Fedelm, who was quiet all morning, answered with a grim smile.

"Well, she came to me last night. You guessed correctly. Two gods sent the storms and earthquake to kill us."

"What else did she say?" Urith asked her.

"The dream was hard to decipher, but I think she was telling me that Duwdamon hasn't been able to bring the gods together. She also showed me things about the Skool that make no sense. Right now, they are pieces like a large puzzle that are hard to understand. I'll have to think about them a while."

"I never understand why the gods cannot just tell us what they mean," complained Oslaf with a gruff agreement coming from Urith. Fedelm just smiled patiently at his thought.

"Who knows? Come on, we need to catch up with my father before he leaves us."

Smiling now at the thought of her bookworm father excitedly leading the way, the girl dug her heels into her mount, leaving Urith behind to think about her words and his quest that was coming.

During the rest of the morning, the travelers followed the old road through the mountain pass, making small talk along the way. Despite the rising elevation, the sun grew warm. It was coming into the planting season, called *Brydon* on Kamin, and the chilled air was leaving the mountain valleys. However, the snow remained year-round on the highest peaks. The seasonal change meant the farmers would soon fill the valley areas below, tilling and planting their crops of *zeam*, *vulgere* and other grains used for bread and feedstock. Shepherds would move their highland *starkts* into the mountain passes to graze.

The sun reached its zenith as the group cleared the top of the plateau, and the road leveled off into a small highland plain. After the lushness of the valley behind them, they were surprised to see how sparse and barren it was. The wild yellow tinged grambel grass was spotty, showing more red dirt than plant life. A brackish creek meandered slowly next to the road. Fedelm looked up to try to see the source of the water and was dazzled by the view. She could see places where water glittered in the sun as it trickled down from blue slate cliffs that rose in dizzying vertical lines, seeming to pierce into the heavens above. In spite of the beauty of the scene, the water flow was not sufficient to create a fast flow but instead ended in the narrow creek with water that was not fit for drinking. Far ahead, within the area surrounded by the spectacular cliffs, she noticed two round towers and mentioned it to the group.

"Don't be fooled," Caestia warned. "The cliffs and the towers appear closer than they are due to their immense size, but we still have a long way to go."

The group followed the trail to the ruins. It was evident that the humans who had once inhabited the area had abandoned it, leaving the land to return to its wild and desolate state. As they rode, they passed a few abandoned houses, each decaying into nothing more than some white walls of cast stone with roofs long ago collapsed. The only signs of life were large bushes that pushed through the doors and windows of the derelict buildings.

It had taken the rest of the morning before they reached the outskirts of the long-abandoned village of Du-Rinell. A single twisted lellowtere tree stood by the side of the road, not more than a league away from the twin towers that marked the entrance gate to the town. The tired travelers could see the first visible signs of the destroyed city. It had been hard to see from a distance but, as they neared, they could see that it had been built in an area next to a small lake, long since dry. Not much remained since it had been mostly leveled by the forces of destruction that happened so many seasons ago.

They came to a stop where the squat towers, joined by an

entry arch, still stood sentry to the town. Made from the dark blue-gray rocks of the mountain cliffs nearby, they held steady, showing little decay. However, the wooden walls that stretched around the town had long since crumbled. Rock mounds and remnants of walls covered the area where the buildings and shops had once stood. As the ossanes approached the gate, they grew nervous, recoiling their long necks in fear.

"It looks like we enter without the mounts," observed Caestia, his face showing the concern he felt. "This is the closest I've ever gotten. One of the inhabitants of Turqew I met at the Citadel told me a story of this place. He said they never come to this place out of fear that the Gods of the Void will reach out to grab them and drag them into their world."

"Every place gets a reputation. I think it's more likely that a pack of *kuons* will catch them while they sleep," Urith dismissed the idea.

"Perhaps, but I seem to recall you didn't believe much in hakras at one point." Fedelm reminded him.

"Well, even a grown man can learn if faced with evidence. Right now, I see no proof that the gods of the Great Void have the power to reach us," he replied, giving her a sneering grin. "We need to focus on our biggest problem. Have you figured out the meaning of your visions?"

"Just this, I remember that Dughorm told us that you are needed to find the Skool. My visions from Mivraa confirmed that you will find it."

"How could you know that?" he asked.

"In my vision, I saw you alone with a shield."

"That makes no sense," the Clovel Destroyer responded. "Dughorm said we three must act like one."

"He was protecting you," said the hakra. "Why do you think he died protecting your identity? The Sacred Overlord has no idea you are the one. Satres is trying to kill anyone who might be involved."

Urith thought about her words. "Tell me what you know

about the Skool. What should we look for?" Urith asked, resigned to what he felt must be true.

"I don't know. And my uncertainty is made worse by things my father told me regarding stories told by the skalds."

Urith eyed Caestia. "And what was that?"

The gray-haired record keeper was just getting off his mount and looked over the animal at Urith.

"Understand that I wasn't invited into discussions that Satres had with various skalds. But from the various conversations I overheard, I'm pretty sure you cannot be searching for it, at least not as you might think. The tales I heard from Satres spoke of a hero who would find the Skool, but no human could find the Skool while looking for it."

"Curse the gods!" Urith was visibly upset at the riddle. "Have we wasted everything by coming to know this is impossible?"

"Perhaps not," the girl interjected as she thought over the riddle. "Right or wrong, the stories handed down seem to be true, just like our visions. We just have to figure out the puzzle. If the rest of us fan out looking around for signs, perhaps you will just come across it."

"What do you mean? Don't look for it and somehow it will find me?" The old warrior stared at her skeptically.

"Something like that." Fedelm slid off her mount. "Look, you stated the gods like to manipulate us, right? This seems to be another way for them to work their will. So, then you don't look for it. Just look around the area without trying to find something. I know this sounds crazy, but it's not any crazier than all the other things that happened to us so far."

"Ok, I'm trying to understand. You look for what?" Urith asked as he got down from his ossane mumbling curses to the gods. He stopped himself short, deciding he would give special thanks to Mivraa for all she had done for him. While the warrior mumbled under his breath, Oslaf got down from his mount and handed his reins to Urith, smiling.

"Well, uncle, it seems that something used by the gods

would be special and, from what I remember of Dughorm's story and Fedelm's vision, it would be as part of a large shield. I'm betting; it's like a sphere but laid out flat like a shield."

Oslaf continued, "And now since you get to be the lookout, it looks like you can tie up the animals and follow us in." The others could tell that the young man was enjoying the temporary change in status.

Urith couldn't help but grin at his nephew's joke as the others entered the ruin through iron gates which hung from broken hinges, sagging against the towers on either side. Meanwhile, Urith tied off the animals in a field near a small mound of rocks before entering the town ruins. Looking at the desolate highland plain, he was happy they would be able to spot any potential trouble from a safe distance away. He joined his friends at the center of town near a once majestic fountain where all the streets converged. The travelers split up, each going in a separate direction, pushing back the flat brush and picking up odd pieces of debris. At first, Caestia seemed to be more interested in looking at the various inscriptions engraved upon the broken blue tablets which littered the area before he looked back at Urith and grinned self-consciously. Throwing down the carved rock, he began looking around again for anything that might look like a broken shield.

After the others had gone out of sight from the fountain area, Urith wandered around, trying to decipher the layout of the town and looking for any unusual items that caught his eye. The water fountain was encircled by a road, creating an intersection of four primary streets. Urith noticed that the main road leading from the main gate went directly to the fountain, then rounded it, before continuing to the other side of the town. The cross-street came through and rounded the circle in the same fashion. Each street made of the same polished stone used in the towers. Each of the streets came to an end where the wooden wall once stood as it encircled the town. The warrior took a stick and bent down in the dirt, drawing a rough map of the city's layout. As he stood up, he realized the town would have looked like a large sphere surrounding the symbol of 'X'. From above, the town's layout would be just like the amulet symbol he wore around his neck!

Convinced they were on the right path concerning the visions, Urith wandered around. He looked down a street where he noticed the small figure of Fedelm, who seemed happy moving about the ruins nearby. Occasionally, she broke out whistling when she spotted something. The girl had removed her thick woolen shawl and now wore a thin tunic top and tight canvas pants which accented her body. While he enjoyed watching the cute woman, his thoughts turned to Mivraa. He suddenly missed her more than he wanted to admit to himself.

Shaking his head, he turned away from the view of the girl and looked down another street as his mind went back to the thoughts of the town design which intrigued him. He wondered how much Dughorm might have known and why his old friend didn't explain more to him.

His mind turned to the stories he had heard about the battle in the town which occurred so many *Draenyna* before. He pictured the deadly Guardians locked in mortal combat with the new gods while great human warriors joined in to assist in driving the ancient gods into the Great Void. He could hear the songs of the skalds as they gave him a mental picture of vicious lightning strikes taking down warriors and gods alike, obliterating them in an instant. He could almost feel the fury of combat as the new gods, and the heroes fought against the Guardians and their monsters, while one great human hero, Heptarc, opened the gateway between the realms. Urith always wondered how the mortally wounded warrior used the Skool to strike at the Guardians forcing them into the void for eternity.

As he absently changed his position to look back at the main gate, he slowly backed to the fountain and sat on the flat circular blue rock edge of the basin. The sound of running water calmly cascaded into his ears and left him feeling sleepy in the heat of the sun. He turned slightly and looked at the fountain and into the water. Thinking about it, he was surprised the water still flowed from the stone pipe. Although the water in the basin was thick with dense green moss and debris from seasons of disuse, water still gurgled from the narrow column that pushed up in the center of the pool. Looking more closely, Urith saw that the water coming from decorative spigots on either side of the column appeared to be fresh spring water. Urith took some in his hand, sniffing it first and tasting it carefully. It was clear and clean, perfect for the heat of the day and his thirst. Pulling off his shield and spear, he set them aside against the basin wall while he splashed the cool water on his face and gave himself several long drinks.

Refreshed, he stuck his head under stream a bit and pulled it back up, letting the cooling drips run down his back and shoulders as he arched over the basin. The Esterblud spotted something silver gleaming in the pool below and to his right, and he moved over for a closer inspection. Bending down, he lost sight of the glinting object as the thick moss waved from the slight current created by the splashing of water from the spigot as he refreshed himself. Feeling around, he soon came up with something that appeared to be a broken medal or strange medallion about the size of his palm. He looked at his prize briefly, noting the curious inscription, before he placed the item on the ledge next to the shield. He noticed Caestia coming toward him, and the warrior told the record keeper the water from the fountain was good for such a hot day.

It was much later, and the sun was beginning to set in the east when the group came back together with the disappointing news. Fedelm and Oslaf carried a few pieces of metal of various sizes, none of which seemed likely to be part of a weapon of the gods. Caestia found no items which might fit the Skool. However, he did find a nest of *staryl* eggs, which they planned to dine on in the evening. They rested in the shade behind the fountain sitting cross-legged as they considered their next move.

"Well, I'm not sure what we should do now," admitted Fedelm as she and Caestia went through the pieces of debris.

"Nothing here looks to be supernatural. I can make out no writing on any of these things," Caestia tossed a rusty part of a metal plate on top of the small pile. "Nothing to indicate any of the gods was here that I can see; just vast, empty, and very dead city."

The statement struck Urith, and he climbed to his feet, going to other the other side of the large fountain. He looked around the edge of the basin near his equipment still propped against the stone. It was not there!

"It's not here. Did anyone see a piece of a silver metal lying around here earlier? Urith stared over the water to the group, confused. "I found it in the fountain basin."

All of them shook their heads looking at each other with the same confused look. Urith looked around a while longer before deciding he must have imagined it during his thirst.

"What was it?" Oslaf asked.

"I don't know," the perplexed man said. "I noticed it gleaming in the basin, pulled it out and I remember putting it next to the shield here. It had engravings on it which I couldn't read. It was Caestia's words that reminded me of this."

"Do you need any help," offered Oslaf.

"No, it must be gone," he said discouraged.

Urith picked up his shield and spear, carrying them back to the group. He followed the curved basin around to them, and he heard a collective gasp from them. The warrior stopped, then followed their stares to his shield. The circular planks of green colored wood bolted together with iron cross plates had a shiny coat of silver metal covering part of it. As he turned it around, the others in his party scrambled on their feet, staring at the shield.

"By the gods, your shield front has changed," Oslaf said as

he came up behind Urith, peering over his shoulder. "Is that what you found?"

"No," his uncle replied in shock. "It was much smaller; it fits in my palm. It looks similar in shape; however, I didn't pay much attention to the engraving or the words. I just put it down on the edge of the fountain and forgot about it."

"Yes, something has happened while our backs have been turned," agreed Caestia. "It must have attached to your shield somehow." He grew excited as he thought about it.

"By the gods, look at the wording on the silver metal now. Can you make it out?" he asked his daughter.

Fedelm moved closer, leaning next to Urith and squinting to make out letters and symbols on the shield. She read the letters out to her father who peered over her shoulder attempting to decipher them as well. After some discussion, they agreed the name *gcothrem* was the word engraved on the silver part of the shield.

"Vengeance," breathed Urith to himself. He was convinced now that some mystical power was at work when the gods battled for this place.

"But have we found it? What does it do?" asked Oslaf, his eyes widened as he overheard his mentor.

He looked at Fedelm as she seemed caught up in the excitement of the moment. Then, she remembered something in her vision from the night before. In her dream, she saw a shield with gleaming silver metal, held by a terrifying creature. The creature was attempting to pull itself out of a black pit. She felt if the creature were able to get out of the pit, then the world would be turned upside down. Then a blinding flash struck the creature, shattering the shield. That is when Fedelm remembered the shape in her dream. It was the same shape as the one on Urith's shield.

"I've seen it before in my visions," she said. "Now I'm sure Urith has the Skool. Look at the symbols of the Guardians next to the word. They were cast out using this shield. We have it."

"Well, at least, part of it," Caestia reminded the group. "We are not finished. Three more must be found."

The sense of relief that flooded across everyone in the group was soon replaced by a question that no one wanted to ask. Oslaf and Urith continued to examine the shield, with the old warrior showing the younger one a series of moves to use in battle as he tried out the balance and weight of the revamped shield. He noticed how the armor seemed lighter to him now. Fedelm and Caestia discussed her visions quietly a few footsteps away. They came back to the fighters, deciding to ask.

"We were wondering. What now?" Fedelm wondered. "My father and I were discussing what we do now. It seems we are at a crossroads, and we are not sure where we go from here."

Caestia spoke in agreement, "My daughter has told me of Dughorm's vision from your time with him. It seems to me his revelation is complete now."

Urith cocked his head.

"Perhaps, but somehow I am not convinced this is complete."

He looked at the sky of fading sunlight, then continued. "It will be dark soon. Let's find some cover for the night. We can eat and perhaps someone will get a vision tonight," he winked at Fedelm, who smiled knowingly back at him. She was getting used to his ways and his sarcastic sense of humor.

The group began to make preparations for the night. Fedelm went to the ossanes to get the bags, and Oslaf followed along to help. Urith and Caestia left the fountain as well, looking for a place to set up camp. They decided upon a place under one of the few trees, near the main gate. The former record keeper convinced Urith to keep their watch inside the fragments of walls encircling the town when he pointed out that any gods and their monsters could not cross the boundaries since the Great Passing. The former record keeper said he had concerns that the gods might wish to capture the relic Urith now carried. To help prevent the gods from coming for the shield, he suggested they make their camp inside the ruins under one of the few trees near the main gate. The sky showed purple as the sun fell behind the highland horizon and the sound of chirping cruicads began to fill the air, highlighting the calm that settled over the plains.

~~~

In the early morning darkness, near the twisted lellowtere tree just outside the town, there was a faint glow of blue light that flashed for an instant. After the blue light, the only starlight covered the area, where a movement could be seen among the branches. A short figure emerged from behind the dark, twisted wood, looking around before moving away. It is hard to see the black silhouette as it ran parallel to the remains of the town walls, occasionally looking to its left at the red glow of a dead fire near the main gate towers. The figure halted when the ossanes began to stir from the new scent in the area. The dark figure changed course, taking a wide arc around the town ruins until it was downwind of the animals. Waiting until the animals calmed down, the shadow profile crouched as it crept toward the ossanes who shook their horned heads slightly before going back to their standing sleep. The figure used the mound of rock debris where the animals were tied to hide its shadowy form.

Reaching the base of the small knoll, the creature slowly crept to the top, staring down at the standing ossanes several long strides away. Bright yellow eyes took in the faint light seeing the animals as if the sun was at its height, making sure it remained undetected. Satisfied with its target, the beast lowered its arms revealing long claws, which dragged on the rocks, inadvertently creating a slight scraping sound. Without another sound, the figure swiftly jumped from its perch onto the back of the first animal. In an instant, the monster had sliced the ossanes throat with those long claws, nearly decapitating the animal as it died instantly. Before the creature hit the ground, the figure had leaped to another,
~~~

repeating its attack with deadly accuracy. The last mount tried to rear back to bolt from the fearsome beast with a panicked whinnying sound. However, its reins held it in place for the monster to jump toward the mount while the animal tried to pull away. There was another whiny sound that was cut off by a gurgling noise as the animal lay dying in its own blood, next to the other ossanes.

Sounds from the camp caught the monster's attention, as a large human came running to check on the animals. The dark creature crouched and backed away behind the mound, waiting for the foolish person that raced its way. The saliva drooled past long, exposed teeth as the beast smelled the human coming down the path. The scent mixed with the stench of animal sweat and blood. The heavy breathing from the warrior was music to its thin, reptilian ears as it remained crouched in the darkness. The crunching sound of footfalls on the rough ground got closer and then slowed to a stop. There was no exclamation at the sight the human must have stumbled upon. Oddly, the monster could not smell the overwhelming fear it expected. There was a touch of fear scent in the air. The monster breathed in deeply, noticing the scent of its prey drew closer. There was another feeling it didn't expect either. It was a sudden understanding that the human was hunting it, which confused its primitive brain.

The cruba decided to come around the other side of the mound to surprise its prey. Silent as the night hunter it was, the monster crept along, lightly sniffing the air. When it came back around to the bodies of the dead ossanes, it didn't find its prey as expected.

It stopped!

Confused rage caused the creature to whirl its massive head around sniffing through the lizard-like nostrils. The monster could smell the human nearby, but it could not place the direction of its victim. Turning, the cruba lifted its reptilian head, opening its massive jaw to help draw in more scent. Pulling its long arms away from the dark cowl covering the body, the cruba readied its long, deadly claws which gleamed slightly in the waning night. The claws were about double the length of a human hand, sharp and hard as flint.

Slowly, the creature continued around the mound, expecting to pick up a closer scent of the person. Smelling the stronger human scent, it quickly spun around at the sound of something moving behind it. It found nothing there. Suddenly, there was a slight rustle from the top of the mound, causing the beast suddenly to cock its head while it looked up. The monster felt the instant pain when the Clovel Sword pierced its eye and entered its brain. The blade came out of the other side of the creature's skull, driven through by the strength of Urith's momentum after jumping from the top of the mound. The cruba collapsed to the ground, the sound of its short, squat body flopping around as the small brain died. Urith stepped off the edge of the rocks where he landed, walking over to the body of the evil beast. He calmly placed his leather boot on the head of the monster and yanked his longsword from the creature's skull. Bending over, he wiped the foul-smelling blood of the beast from his sword using the rough cloth the cruba wore. Cursing under his breath, Urith turned back to the camp to finish his watch.

Chapter 9: Out of the Ruins

The yellow rays of the morning sun were crossing into the highlands when Urith spotted the young Esterblud warrior stirring. Oslaf had strategically placed himself across from Fedelm so he would be able to see her face in the morning. However, on this morning, the back of the girl's head was facing him, the slight morning breeze lazily moving her golden hair. Still, the young man was pleased to see her lying there, and a feeling of contentment drifted over him. At least until Oslaf noticed the giant shadow of Urith standing over him. He looked up at him and noticed the grim expression on his uncle's face. Urith put his finger to his lips, motioning for the young man to follow him.

The two walked several paces away, and Urith kept his voice low as he informed his nephew about the killing of the ossanes by the cruba.

"I've only heard of such a thing in the stories told by our elders to scare the children," explained Urith. "It was my fault we lost our ossanes. I didn't move quickly enough. It's a cursed beast, but not very bright and can be outsmarted if we ever run into another one."

"Do you think there are more?"

"It's a creature of the underworld," Urith told him. "It didn't just show up and kill our mounts on its own. This was the work of our enemies."

"Why didn't you wake us?" Oslaf asked.

The scarred warrior shook his head.

"No need, it was over before it posed a danger to the rest of the camp. I decided there was no reason to get everyone upset. It's better to be rested for what's coming."

"What do you mean?" Oslaf noticed his uncle's raised eyebrow at the question.

"No, wait. I get it. This is a setup for an attack. We discussed this tactic before. The enemy removes any chance of our escape before they attack," he told Urith.

His uncle nodded.

"Excellent, you're learning. Now, if I were planning this, I would have attacked right after the cruba showed up. My guess is they are waiting for more warriors or worse, maybe more of those beasts."

The Clovel Destroyer looked over the open ground around them.

"As you can see, it will be difficult to sneak up on us with this open prairie. It would appear that they aren't worried and probably have overwhelming numbers coming for us."

Oslaf felt the pit of his belly tighten.

"Should we tell the others that a fight is coming?"

"After breakfast," said Urith. "No need to die on an empty stomach." He slapped his nephew on his back and walked back to the camp.

As the others awoke, Oslaf stoked up a fire from some dry wood nearby. Fedelm used the last of their supplies to make them a meal. While they ate, the two warriors let the father and daughter know about the attack of the cruba and their isolation within the ruins. Urith also explained what he expected to happen next. To his surprise, Fedelm and Caestia took the news calmly. However, he did notice the girl bite her lip slightly during the conversation. He felt sorry for her. However, there was little they could do at this point. They could leave on foot; trying to get back to the coast by the way they came. Caestia pointed out they could not outrun ossanes. Plus, going back to the devastation of the Hyropda would gain them nothing.

Oslaf asked about returning on the trail to reach the village of Turqew. Caestia stated it would be two sunrises before they would reach the village.

"We could try," Urith agreed, "but we might have difficulty getting there."

"Why?" Fedelm asked.

"Because, if you look down that road, you will see the dust

rising." Urith stared at the road behind the others. "I guess that dust comes from a long line of our Aberffraw enemy heading to our camp." Urith calmly told them. "You can bet that no merchant traveler will throw up that kind of dust with a cart." He slowly stood to get a better view of the oncoming enemy.

"Oslaf, we'll use the main gate and towers to make our stand. Gather what supplies we can, especially water and weapons," he ordered.

Fedelm jumped up first, quickly grabbing various items, while Oslaf scrambled to help her. They soon had armfuls of blankets, bags and what weapons they could carry. Urith retrieved all of their pillaged arms before heading toward the main gate towers. Caestia grabbed the water bags, hurriedly filling them at the fountain.

When they got to the entrance of the town, Urith laid one hand on the blue stone wall preparing to climb the steps when he heard a familiar female voice.

"Are you ready for my wrath?"

Alrpan, the goddess of the abyss was flanked on either side by the Vanth twins, Tuulcha, and Actita. They stood across the road from the twin towers.

Urith dropped his armload of items, whipping out his sword. Oslaf drew his longsword nearly as fast while stepping up next to his uncle. He handed Urith his black helmet. Caestia and Fedelm hurried to gather the dropped items before taking them inside the tower.

As three figures from the underworld approached from the twisted lellowtere tree, the Esterbluds prepared for the coming battle. Oslaf put on his helmet and pulled his shield from the sling on his back. Urith left his shield hanging from his back, preferring to hold his battle-ax in his spare hand. His gaze remained fixed on the creatures approaching.

While the goddess was unarmed, dressed in the white flowing gown as though she was going to a temple gathering, her companions were heavily armed. Each Vanth was holding long halberds casually in their hands. It was a weapon designed for holding off swordsman; the long pole was topped with a spike and ax blade. Since the Vanth seldom needed to use the weapon against humans, Oslaf wondered at their fighting capability. However, their ugly rat face along with their long snake hair sent shivers down Oslaf's back. He guessed that was a typical reaction when they met others after death.

Urith noticed the Vanths seemed uncomfortable in the heat of the sun, wearing brown hooded cloaks tied at the waist with whips of *beorh*-skin. The covering was necessary to protect their mottled skin and night eyes. However, Urith recognized these demigods would be tough and very dangerous, even if inexperienced with weapons.

"I see you didn't learn your lesson the first time, scunce," Urith told her, grinning intentionally to show his sneer. He intentionally described the goddess by the worst Aberffraw term for a woman. "By the time I leave here, you'll be missing your head."

The goddess and her companions stopped a short distance away. Alrpan's eyes went red with fury at the insolent human.

"I'll watch happily when my Vanths skin you alive. When they are through with their fun, I have unusual ideas for what to do with your spirit."

On the trail behind them, the rising dust of the mounted Aberffraw warriors told the group that the goddess would soon have many allies joining her. Urith thought about their position for a moment and spoke to Oslaf in their native tongue as he backed up slightly, "Remember the famous story of about King Geniht when he was becoming surrounded by the Helter tribes?" he whispered. "I do believe it's time to do this again."

Oslaf whispered back that he understood. From within the tower entrance, they heard Caestia respond in the Esterblud tongue.

"It's not just warriors that remember that story," the record keeper interjected. "I'll watch Fedelm."

With the plan made, Urith took a deep breath and suddenly let out an Esterblud yell, attacking the first Vanth, who seemed to sense something was coming. The clash of Urith's sweeping longsword against the underworld pike rang out in the morning stillness. Expecting Alrpan's tricks to start, the Clovel Destroyer spoke the words of his amulet protector as he swung.

"Da Umca Mivwar"

He parried the stick of the pike with his battle ax which he swung with his other hand. Urith didn't feel the amulet around his neck warm when he invoked its power. He struck at the Vanth called Actita with another blow of his sword. The other demigod stepped in, attempting to jam his spear into Urith's chest. The demigod received a glancing blow from the warrior's sword that caused the Vanth to stumble backward. Actita came at Urith again, aiming at his exposed midsection.

From the side, Oslaf sprang into action as he slammed into Actita, sending the Vanth off course. The body blow caused it to miss its target. The young warrior was about to land a blow with his sword when he felt the fire suddenly enveloped him. It was not the same burning sensation he experienced before. Now a fire wrapped around him. Oslaf couldn't see Alrpan's red eyes focused on him while he tried to fight the flames while fending off the incoming blows of the Vanth. He screamed out from the pain, struggling to stay on his feet.

Urith glimpsed his nephew's struggles when he struck at Tuulcha using a hammer blow of this battle ax. Breaking the handle with his blow, Urith watched his opponent back away. Urith suddenly turned and rushed headlong into Actita who was raining blows down on Oslaf. Momentum from Urith's rush into Actita carried them toward the main gate of the ruins.

As Urith pushed by with the Vanth, Oslaf felt someone knock him down from behind, trying to cover him with a cloak. Caestia grabbed at the burning Oslaf, pulling him to his feet. He guided the warrior back to the ruins while Fedelm used the cloak she had thrown on him to put out the flames. Caestia yelled at him to seek the protection of the ruins. Suddenly, the fire of Alrpan spread outward to strike those helping the warrior. Fedelm felt the flames spreading across her back and caught the smell of burnt hair. Struggling, the trio of burning people managed to get just inside the main gate and the flames they felt suddenly disappeared around them, leaving smoke rising from their burnt clothes.

While the others were running back to the towers, Urith kept up the blows on Actita. He glimpsed the fire surrounding his friends and realized that his amulet was not powerful enough to cover all of them. When he saw the flames die out on his friends, Urith suddenly realized the connection. Out of the corner of his eye, he caught Tuulcha coming on fast to join its twin against him. Recognizing his peril going against the two Vanths, he saw his coming opportunity. Urith parried a blow from Actita, then he deftly sidestepped the oncoming Tuulcha, who just missed him with his pole weapon. Urith grabbed Tuulcha by the coarse wool robe and continued pushing the demigod forward.

Using the stumbling creature's momentum, Urith and Tuulcha ran headlong into the cursed invisible wall surrounding the ruins of Da-Rinell. As they passed through the invisible barrier, the Vanth could only screech out in pain and surprise. The demigod instantly dissolved into a red mist that covered the Clovel Destroyer. Urith didn't think about what happened as he continued running toward his friends who were still recovering from the burns. When he reached them, Urith saw burn blisters forming on Oslaf's exposed arms.

Still breathing heavily from his battle, Urith coughed at the sickening mix of burning hair and wool. He turned his head to keep an eye on their enemies.

Actita, the remaining Vanth, stopped in its tracks. It made loud guttural noises from its rat-like mouth, trying to understand its twin death. There was nothing left, not even a spirit of the demigod. The shield around the ruins destroyed completely. Even Alrpan looked perplexed at what she had just witnessed. She focused her deadly gaze upon Urith, contemplating her next move as the dust rose behind her from the Aberffraw warriors as they rode toward the ruins.

"These gods forgot about the boundaries left by the

Guardians," Caestia as he observed Urith watching the goddess.

"It appears we are in a draw. The goddess and the Vanth cannot come in, and we cannot leave," he continued.

"Well, momentarily anyway. The Aberffraws coming down the road will have no problems passing into the ruins to kill us. Do you have more fight in you?" Urith asked Oslaf softly.

"As much as needed to kill that scunce," Fedelm spoke for the young fighter.

"I'll live Urith, but I can't take another blast from Alrpan. She has too much power. She will kill the rest of us without cover from your amulet," Oslaf told him quietly when he got to his feet.

"Agreed, my friend. Since I'm somewhat protected, I'll go after Alrpan and her beast of a son. You defend inside the tower when the rest of the enemy arrives." Urith nodded to the turret that kept most of its stones during the Guardians fighting so many generations earlier.

Caestia had joined them, carrying a smaller sword he picked up from their supplies. Urith looked at him, nodding as he accepted the help.

"My friend, we'll hold out in the tower behind us. The Aberffraws cannot climb those stairs with their mounts. They can send only a few at a time, which will help us hold out for a while," he explained.

"For how long?" The record keeper asked.

"Until we win or die. Get the water into the tower and have Fedelm carry it up with you." He looked at her father. "Expect the worst. These enemy warriors will give no quarter if I guess right about Satres. I think our hides are worth a lot of koinons to his mercenary fighters at this point."

"Then, they had better be ready to meet the gods," said the gray-haired man.

Urith grinned at him. He considered the man as brave as any warrior he knew. He turned to Fedelm who showed him a fierce determination in her green eyes. She picked up two of the water bags.

"If you have any ideas to help, I welcome them," Urith invited the woman.

"I'm working on something with my father. I've explained my dreams to him. Hopefully, the Fates will show us the way." She continued her task, and he could see her jaw was firmly set while she forced her way past the dead brush at the dark entrance to the tower. Urith realized that she had the courage of her father, but there was a fire of vengeance burning inside as well.

Urith took a deep breath, then turned toward Alrpan and the Vanth. He could now see the line of Aberffraw warriors far in the distance galloping steadily toward them. Judging the distance from the bulk of the warriors coming, Urith hoped he still had time to take down his underworld enemies. He gave mental thanks to the goddess Mivraa.

Soon, I'll be joining her!

Urith walked through the invisible boundaries of Du-Rinell, heading for the goddess who stood erect with her hands on her hips. Her lovely human facade was now fully ugly, unable to hold back the venom she held for Urith. The rat-faced Actita lifted his long pike, readied for battle.

Several long strides away from the vengeful goddess and her ally, Urith pulled out his shield which still hung behind his back. Sliding it over his right arm, he began a full run into the two underworld fiends waiting for him. He felt the flames suddenly started to wrap around him, and the agony of the illusions both real and imaged as Alrpan focused her power on the Esterblud. She understood his full intent was to kill her.

"*Da Umca Mivwar!*" Urith ordered.

He ran toward the goddess at full speed, oblivious to the growing pain he felt. The pain lessened, and the flames died down but not entirely as the goddess continued to focus on him. Still, the warrior pushed forward, using his sword to counter the pike as the Vanth struck out at him. Actita anticipated the move and hit him with the other end, striking him in the knee. The move sent the Esterblud tumbling down to his hands and knees. As the Vanth pressed his attack, Urith was able to slam the edge of the shield into the leg of the creature. His action brought the creature down to his level as Actita grabbed at its leg. Urith struck out with his sword, aiming for the throat of Actita. He missed, catching the demi-god in the shoulder.

"Uncarum dewaih!"

Urith heard the words from Alrpan an instant before he could react. He was hit by her curse, a full blast of heat and fire that struck. The force sent him tumbling back, falling away from the Vanth.

The spell overwhelmed his amulet's power, and he felt as if his skin was being scraped off by the flames. Collapsing in the dirt, he managed to land on his side where he caught a glimpse of Alrpan mouthing a spell to send another blast of her infernal flash to finish him off. Reacting instinctively, he raised his shield in defense.

"Uncarum dewaih!"

When the blast struck him, Urith felt a flash of heat. Suddenly strange energy entered him. With a blinding light, the shield instantaneously sent the goddess's curse back to her. Dazed by the flash of light and blast he felt, Urith couldn't see what happened when the ricochet struck Alrpan. The immediate shrieking of torment rang in his ears. He struggled to his feet looking for the source of the terrible sound. A light breeze sent the dust around them drifting away, and in the haze, he saw what he thought was a fragment of burnt bone and flesh where Alrpan once stood defiantly.

The Goddess of the Abyss screamed from the agony and fear while she grappled with the aftermath. The hideous creature that lay curled up on the road felt the agony of raw, exposed nerves. Her flesh gone, Alrpan's appalling body was racked in torment as her brain sought to transform her image. Each attempt caused her to shriek while her figure twisted into ghastly profiles.

Urith stared at the thing just a few strides away; his mind shocked at what he saw. The creature was a goddess, the wife of Caruun, now as vulnerable as any human. Alrpan was covered with leathery, mummy-like flesh, dark brown and pulled tight over a small skeletal body. Her venomous red eyes, dulled with pain, peeked from behind her dark clawed hand she held over a hideous face. The tormented creature appeared part monster with short pointy teeth inside a lipless mouth. Exposed, desiccated muscles stretched across the face and body, giving the impression of hideously carved wood with remnants of rough skin that clung to her skull, adding to the horrifying visage.

Actita moved with surprising speed to sweep up the goddess, leaving its pike behind while it carried the whimpering figure in both arms. The Vanth's long legs swiftly took Alrpan to the twisted lellowtere tree by the road. The pair ducked under low hanging branches, a blue light suddenly flashed, and the two creatures of the underworld disappeared.

While Urith grappled the amount of power on his arm, he slowly pushed himself to his feet. The sounds of galloping ossanes broke the silence, announcing the arrival of the Aberffraw as they moved full speed toward the ruins. In a daze, Urith felt Oslaf shouting for him as he grabbed his uncle. The two warriors sprinted back to the main entrance where Caestia was waiting. No one had time to think about what they had just witnessed coming from the Shield of Skool. Instead, they moved to defend themselves just inside the archway alcove at the stairway entrance of the blue tower. Urith and Oslaf stood there, waiting to see what would happen next.

Satres, dressed out in his splendid red cloak which hung over a golden tunic, pulled his ossane to a halt. He wore a red conical cap with the top laid forward toward his brow. The Aberffraw warriors following him pulled up along the edge of the road a short distance from the main gate. Their ranks were an impressive display of force. The Esterbluds instantly saw Lyncus as he pulled close, his gold helmet gleaming in the sun. The men watched as the two enemy leaders conversed briefly, then Lyncus gave a brief nod. Urith looked over the enemy, resplendently dressed in their silver and gold kettle hat helmets and brown tunics laced in blue. He focused on archers among them and rightly guessed that the Aberffraw warriors planned on meeting a larger force.

"Well, good thing we will be fighting out of the tower," said Oslaf. "I checked, and the tower should hold out against fire arrows from the archers since the roof at the top is gone, little timber remains in here."

"I'm more worried about the number we face. Against that many, we will not survive this without help. Unfortunately, we can't expect that. Maybe the Fates will set the sun early," Urith joked grimly.

The Aberffraw warriors listened to the orders coming from their leader and soon swept out into smaller groups, moving around the main gate to get behind their enemy, cutting off any chance of escape. As the band of archers got down from their mounts, a line of armored men mounted on armored ossanes took up positions to the side of the Sacred Overlord and his ally. With a quick signal, the first line of warriors got off their mounts, pulling their swords with a precision that caught the eye of the fighters. Such military precision was unexpected from the Cahmais forces. It was apparent that this group was different and totally committed. Satres had no intention of taking anyone alive.

"You are too late, overlord. I just sent your scunce back to the underworld," Urith yelled out.

Satres ignored the comment; his beady blue eyes were fixated upon the shield that Urith held at his side. His firm mouth showed a bit of a grin as he looked at Lyncus.

"We seek something much more powerful, now don't we? Lyncus, please have your men remove the Skool from this Esterblud heathen." The thin man moved his mount out of the way of the warriors coming closer.

"I care not how you do it, Lyncus but bring me the shield," he continued. "Your warriors can do what they want with the defilers."

Urith casually propped up his longsword at the entrance in a show of defiance. He slowly rested his free hand on a spear next to the shield. Oslaf noticed what his mentor was doing, and he casually slid closer to the entrance of the tower where several spears were already positioned for quick retrieval.

"Lyncus, make sure you let those old women understand the koinons you pay is not worth anything when they are dead," Urith spoke loud enough for the Aberffraw to hear his words.

Urith smiled his sneering grin while he listened to the men grumble at his insult. A few of them rained colorful curses at him. With a sudden, fluid movement, the spear Urith had been holding flew toward the Sacred Overlord. Satres caught sight of the spear just in time. He was able to pull his mount hard to the left with the reins while ducking. The iron spear tip found his cape, catching it and nearly unseating him from his ossane.

Lyncus didn't hesitate. He sent his warriors forward. The line of Aberffraw men charged as Oslaf sent a spear toward Lyncus. One of the archers accidentally stepped in front of his leader, and the man took the spear tip in the neck. Oslaf sent several more before he backed into the front entrance of the tower. He struck true, but he was unable to see the damage amid the crush of fighters.

"A few down and too cursed many to go," he yelled out with grimly smile.

Urith released another spear into the chest plate of the first warrior coming then he joined Oslaf at steps leading into the tower. Their defensive position just inside the entry forced the enemy to come forward in singles and doubles. The Esterblud used this to their advantage at the moment.

Another enemy ran forward with an archer following close behind him. The archer shot an arrow into the archway. Urith was able to move aside, and the arrow struck the stone behind them. The armored warrior tried to push forward, but he was struck by Oslaf's last spear. The body fell to the floor just inside the entrance. The warrior behind him tried to jump over his body, only to be cut down. Urith swung his longsword down across his metal helmet which caved in the man's head. The two bodies piled up in the doorway slowed down the oncoming rush momentarily. However, arrows began to fly from the bows of archers into the opening. Without spears, the men were forced to back up the stairs.

The Esterblud fighters tried to keep out of the direct line of fire as they backed up the curved staircase. Two Aberffraw warriors charged up the stairs only to meet vicious longsword attacks from the Clovel Destroyer, their dying corpses tumbling down the stairs. The bodies obstructed their comrades trying to move up the narrow path.

Outside, Satres and Lyncus watched their mass of men pushing into the tower, remaining confident they would soon have the prize they sought. However, each man had a different vision who would keep the Skool. As they casually chatted about the brightness of the sun and the unusual heat for the highlands, the men guided their mounts over into the shade of the tree. Sliding off their mounts, Satres and Lyncus glanced over at the spectacle of battle while their men, both dead and dying, were pulled from the tower entrance while others filled in behind them. In this game of numbers, the enemy leaders knew that the Esterbluds, and their allies inside, were living on borrowed time.

Satres ordered his aide that he and Lyncus would have their lunch ready soon.

"In the shade of that lellowtere tree," he stated. The Sacred Overlord paid little attention as his attendant scramble to get others to accommodate his order. One of the overlord's guard directed a few of his men to the pack animals that carried the overlord's personal items, including food and drink. Soon, the men were leading the ossanes to unpack for the feast.

As the men approached the tree to lay out wool blankets, they caught a glimpse of blue light which they thought was just a reflection of the bright sun. To their astonishment, a woman, dressed in gold armor and wearing a black cloak, stepped from behind the tree. The guard tried to pull his short sword, but before he could even unsheathe the weapon, he was impaled by the silver spear the goddess pulled from under her shawl. Watching the unarmed aides of the overlord scatter back to their master, Mivraa sliced off the strap holding the overlord's bags on the mount, spilling clothes, food, and wine across the hard gravel. Throwing her leg over the animal, she turned the mount around, spurring it toward the mass of warriors surrounding the main gate.

Satres was leaning comfortably forward in his saddle, listening to the yells and screams of wounded men among the sound of clashing weapons, when an aide ran up to him, shouting a warning. The Overlord turned to observe the galloping ossane coming full bore past them, carrying a beautiful and determined female warrior. Lyncus spotted her about the same time and jumped on his mount, shouting orders to organize the men around the tower area. None of the Aberffraw understood that a demigoddess had now sided with the Esterbluds in defiance of the other gods. Mivraa slammed into the disorganized group of Aberffraw archers closest to her. She struck down several of the lightly armored men who failed to move quickly enough. Using her short silver sword in one hand while holding her infamous spear and reins in the other, the female warrior cut through the lines trying to close on the tower.

Inside the tower, the warriors were now backed up near the top of the stairway. Even though they had killed and wounded many Aberffraw, the length, and intensity of battle had them at the point of exhaustion. The constriction of the passage and turn of the stairs permitted the Esterbluds to keep their attackers from sending more than a few men up the stairs at any one time. Blood and gore spilling from the dead and dying caused the stone steps to become slippery as well. However, both Esterbluds carried several bloody wounds which sapped their strength. Breathing heavily, they gathered their strength before the next push from the enemy. During the fighting, Urith took a spear in his lower leg, and his upper shoulder was severely bleeding from a sword stroke that broke through the chainmail. Oslaf was in slightly better shape, with a stab wound near his chest, and the other arm having been injured when he was forced down during a particularly vicious fight with two Aberffraw. Even Caestia and Fedelm jumped into the middle of the fight, helping to fight off Aberffraw fighters who nearly overwhelmed the Esterbluds.

The group welcomed a brief lull in the battle while the

Aberffraw cleared the stairwell of their casualties to mount a stronger attack. Caestia was able to repel one injured Aberffraw, who attempted a suicide charge during the lull. Fedelm took the opportunity to hurriedly bind their wounds with scraps of cloth. Urith noticed the girl's steady, firm hand pushing the material under his chainmail along his shoulder. He also saw her father, the record keeper, was smiling at him, his adrenaline from the battle surging. Urith sent the man back up to the top of the tower to find a way to drop stones on the enemy.

Finished with Urith, Fedelm immediately helped with Oslaf's wounds. Urith noticed she carried a short sword, stuffed inside her belt along with her dagger. Oslaf noticed her weapons as well and understood she was determined to go out fighting, rather than waiting for her death in the room above.

Caestia suddenly yelled down. "Mivraa is here! She has arrived. She is fighting the enemy outside the tower."

"Urith, that's the sign," Fedelm stated suddenly. She left Oslaf's partially dressed wound, then hustled Urith to his feet.

"I put together the vision sent by Mivraa last night," she explained hurriedly. "You need to use the Skool to get us down there to help Mivraa."

The Esterblud leader looked at her dumbfounded. "What are you talking about?" He glanced down the stairs and saw fighters coming up the stairs.

"You have the amulet, the Clovel Sword and the Shield of Skool," her eyes held his as she patiently explained. "All three together form a triad. The power of the gods is wrapped in the three weapons. With the strength of all those items together, you can even destroy a god. It is more than a shield; it can be used as a weapon. This is what Heptarc knew. Do you understand now?"

The Aberffraw fighters drew closer, their weapons striking the stone. Urith stared at the girl thinking of her words.

"Try to use them together," she suggested.

Nodding, Urith put his engraved sword in front of the shield. He pulled his amulet from around his neck held in his hand behind the shield. Then, he crouched and leaned back against the stone wall. As he heard the warriors nearing the top, he saw the coal black polished bloodstone suddenly show red veins through the amulet. The pommel of the sword lit up as well. A line of four Aberffraw fighters broke into a battle cry as they ran up the last few steps to reach their enemy. Urith stood up as Oslaf pressed passed him going forward to meet the enemy. The swords of the enemy struck against the Oslaf's sword and shield. Urith pulled up behind his nephew, positioning himself to attack when he felt the hand of Fedelm holding him back.

"Wait until more get up here," she told him, and Urith stopped.

They didn't have to wait long as several more of the enemy arrived, filling the stairs below him. Urith felt the girl slap him on the back.

"Do it now! Say Dughorm's words."

"Oslaf, fall back," Urith yelled out as he positioned his shield toward the enemy.

Oslaf retreated; rapidly pulling away from the fighter, coming next to Urith, who said the words and held his breath.

"Da Umca Mivwar!"

Urith felt the energy surge through him, and a blinding flash shot from his shield into the crowd of Aberffraw warriors coming up the steps. In the blink of an eye, the men were gone. There was a large hole blown through the wall of the curved, blue tower. Screams and shouts from outside rose up from the shocked group of warriors below. At the top of the stairs, the Esterbluds and their companions were stunned with the power the Skool unleashed as well. However, Urith recovered quickly and seized the advantage. He charged downstairs toward the enemy fighters who were out of the path of the blast, dazed by the blast above them and the debris that came down. Oslaf was right behind Urith, followed by Fedelm and her father.

Urith slashed down the first warrior he met. The man fell backward, tumbling into several of his companions. Those who couldn't get out of the way fell from the stairs. A crescendo of deafening noise followed as the men's screams combined with the falling armor and swords. The wounded and dying men landed on the blood-slick entrance floor. Two Aberffraw fighters tried to enter the tower when they ran into Urith, who rushed past them. Right behind him, Oslaf quickly cut the men down before they could react.

Urith hobbled through the terrified warriors running from the tower. He saw Mivraa galloping toward him. Fearing that she was too close to the invisible boundary, the Esterblud jumped in front of her animal, yelling to her to not enter the ruins. As the goddess slowed her mount, an enemy galloped up on her blind side. Diving out of the way as Mivraa turned her mount, Urith rolled back to his feet and struck the Aberffraw's mount with his shield. The animal screamed in pain, slamming into the ground. Its human cargo fell face first into the rocks, instantly killing him.

Mivraa's attacks scattered enough of the Aberffraw warriors to create an opening for everyone to get to Urith. Oslaf pointed out that remaining enemy fighters were regrouping near the main gate. Almost immediately, archers sent arrows toward the exposed group. Urith ordered them to follow him behind the large pile of rubble and stones of the fallen tower.

Fedelm suddenly shouted to her father. The old man hesitated, failing to see the spear coming toward him. Urith heard the spear cutting through the air, followed by the familiar thump as it entered flesh. He stopped moving when he saw Caestia fall. While holding the shank of a spear, stuck in his chest, the gray-haired man as he slid to the ground. Urith and Fedelm quickly pulling him to cover behind the rubble.

Mivraa yanked a piece of cloth from her belt and had just removed the vial of healing water she carried on a cord around her neck. When she looked up, the demigoddess stopped. Caestia's eyes were glazed over in death. Mivraa watched the man's spirit rise above his body, floating in disbelief at his new state. The goddess said nothing to Fedelm, who was on her knees, holding his hand. Mivraa, staying low to avoid the incoming arrows, placed her hand on the girl's shoulder and gave a gentle squeeze. The demigoddess told her there was no time to grieve until they finished the battle. The young lady nodded slowly.

Oslaf, looking down at the dead man, turned his gaze up to see the murderous Lyncus outside the main gate now shielded behind several lines of his warriors. The Esterblud had seen the enemy leader throw the spear at Urith, missing him and striking Fedelm's father. He told Urith what he witnessed. Urith looked over the pile of rubble and spotted Lyncus.

"Next time, I won't leave him alive," Urith vowed.

The regrouped line of Aberffraw warriors began moving forward to finish off their enemy. None of them understood what happened inside the tower. The enemy was sure they could destroy the two Esterbluds, along with the unknown woman warrior.

Satres and Lyncus understood something was wrong when they recognized the Haligulf goddess. They knew despite their overwhelming numbers; the presence of the goddess could mean the gods were taking sides. Nevertheless, the Sacred Overlord barked orders to his guards as he steered his mount away from lines. Lyncus heard the orders, then sent word to the men, directing them to get ready for action. The Aberffraw leader looked over at Urith standing next to Mivraa. He grew concerned when he overheard several of his men whispering about what happened inside the tower.

Perhaps the tales from Satres regarding the power of the Skool were true?

Still, Lyncus could not let his men give up on two easy targets and the Skool.

"The men who bring me the head of the Esterbluds will get a cask of wine," he yelled out as he sent his men towards the enemy.

Mivraa wondered what Urith was waiting for as she ducked the steady stream of arrows keeping them pinned down. The Esterblud kept looking up over the stones as calmly watched. When the rows of enemy warriors rushed toward them, he looked down at his sword pommel, still glowing from the closeness of the triad of items.

"It's a waste of good men," Urith said aloud. Mivraa suddenly realized what he was doing when she overheard him repeat Dughorm's words.

For an instant, a light brighter than the hot sun flashed, striking the mass of oncoming enemies, instantly vaporizing them as their bodies, clothes and armor seem to blow apart like swirls of dust in the wind. The echoes of their fierce battle cries were immediately cut off. Behind them, the powerful shock wave from the blast struck the Scared Overlord and Lyncus. Their mounts were knocked over, hurling both men from their ossanes. Behind him, Urith heard Mivraa's cursing exclamation under her breath in amazement of the power she just witnessed.

Those Aberffraw enemies who survived the Shield of Skool were stunned and deafened by the blast. Suddenly one warrior panicked as he looked at Urith holding his Shield of Skool. The first man dropped his sword as he turned to run away. Soon, others joined him. They scrambled to find any ossanes that were scattered across the road. The enemy who was attacking from the sides halted during the blast. Now, seeing their friends retreat, they too backed away. Those still mounted on their animals skirted around the tower, while those on foot tried to keep up, their armor and weapons clanking as they ran.

Urith wasn't finished yet. He headed toward Lyncus and Satres as he hobbled across the road. Mivraa followed as she wondered how far she would go to help then realizing she didn't have much choice now. While Urith tried to catch their enemy leaders, Satres was able to regain his mount. Throwing his leg over the animal, he sped off, leaving the others to protect him. The overlord's unarmed aides scrambled among the fighters to find their animals, creating chaos as Lyncus positioned his remaining guards in a defensive line, leaving orders to hold the area for the retreat. He grabbed his mount and followed the Sacred Overlord, galloping fast to catch up. Urith came to a stop as he realized the battle was done and he would be unable to catch his prey. He didn't have enough help to take on the enemy. He heard Mivraa coming up behind him.

"Why did you stop?" she asked breathlessly.

"We need to help Fedelm, and I will not use the Skool on a few men protecting their friends."

Urith yelled out to the Aberffraw in front of him, telling them to leave in peace. For his gesture, one of the enemies acknowledged it with a hand held up giving thanks. The Aberffraw and Esterblud warriors turned away from each other, leaving the battlefield. Urith and Mivraa went back to their friends while the enemy began their long trek back to Turqew. While they walked back to the main gate, Urith remained quiet, thinking about what he now held in his arms.

Anticipating his thoughts, Mivraa spoke, "You impress me with your wisdom. With the power you now have, it takes an extraordinary person to let your enemy go."

"No, I'm not wise. It was the right thing to do. They were just doing their duty." He paused. "However, it does strike me as odd that I hold something that is too dangerous for a person to have." Urith looked over at the woman, starting to feel the pleasure of her return.

"I will escort Caestia into the Sky Realm when you leave," she said to him. "I've seen his spirit, and I feel him waiting in the tower for guidance."

"Yes, he deserves nothing less. He fought bravely today. However, I'm not sure how Fedelm will take this." He noticed her face grow thoughtful at his words, but she said nothing.

"You will not be coming with us?" asked Urith.

"No, I must return to the home of my father. It will be known that I've interceded with the humans in a battle to help. This is not done."

"Why? It is no different than Alrpan working with Satres," said the warrior as he limped along. He was oblivious to his pain as his thoughts were entirely on Mivraa and how her actions would be received by those in the Sky Realm.

She smiled at him as they walked.

"You are a good man, but you don't understand how gods

think. Caruun and others only went along with the Great Passing and the banishment of the Guardians to the Great Void for his own purposes. It was hoped he would follow the rules set forth by the new gods. But now it appears he is going by his own criteria, and my father has high concern for the path he seems to be taking. Duwdamon has become set in his ways and doesn't see the other gods for what they are or have become. They interfere more and more in the Kamin realm. This is the chaos my father is concerned about, but he doesn't realize it comes from both the Sky Realm and the underworld." Mivraa was visibly upset as she spoke of this.

"What will you do?"

"I'm not sure," she said as they returned to the pile of blue-stone rubble where they had taken cover. They found Fedelm standing over her father's body. "I suppose it will depend on upon how Duwdamon takes this news."

She and Oslaf had laid out Caestia's body to be buried. Oslaf had found a shovel in the items strewn around the ruins and he attempting to dig a grave for their new friend. Urith noticed that the injuries to Oslaf were making his job of digging the grave difficult. Mivraa told Urith to sit down so she could heal him using the Exyts spring water she carried with her.

"I seem to do this a lot recently," she told him as she removed the dried cloth from under his chainmail, kneeling close enough for their eyes to lock.

"Yes, too much," he agreed, suddenly wanting to hold her, but knowing too much was left to do.

"We'll need to leave here before darkness comes," he said, changing the subject. He spoke to Oslaf. "Once Mivraa is done, I'll take over so you can get your wounds healed."

Mivraa nodded and told Urith she would round up some ossanes for them.

"Don't forget about the boundary," Urith warned her.

"Urith, you worry too much," she teased as she finished tying a cloth dampened with healing water around his leg. "Besides, I know something you don't. You stopped the curse and ability of the barrier to affect anyone when you used the Skool.”

She helped Urith up from the ground, saying, “I wish I had brought along some of the god wine.”

The warrior groaned slightly from the leg, still sore despite the quick healing from the Exyts Springwater.

“So do I,” he agreed as he stepped over to the tiring Oslaf. “Here, let me finish it, you get patched up.”

Oslaf took Urith’s extended hand and dragged himself up from the hole. The young Esterblud went to Fedelm, speaking to her briefly before going to Mivraa. Urith took a deep breath and began to finish the grave. Looking at the lengthening shadows, the Clovel Destroyer realized he would need to hurry so they could get out of the area in case he misread the retreat of the Aberffraw enemy.

It didn’t take Urith long to finish what Oslaf started. He helped Fedelm carry the body of Caestia to his resting place. Mivraa had finished up with bandaging Oslaf, and they came over to join the burial of their friend. Fedelm sang a sad song in Eernician, something she called a *duain* which their countrymen used to help their spirits find peace in the Sky Realm. Given the excellent voice and sad song he heard, Urith hoped such a tune might be sung at his death. After she had finished, he told Fedelm his thoughts. She smiled briefly and thanked him for the words.

“My father told me of his great respect for you. I’m indebted to you as well for your help at the Citadel,” Fedelm said. “He asked me to make sure you got through whatever happens. In his honor, I promise to see this thing through, come what may.”

“I welcome your help. Your father was as brave and wise as any warrior I’ve known,” the Esterblud told her. “Caestia will do well among the warriors of Haligulf.”

The girl gave him a curious look. “He was never a fighter. He was a keeper of history. That is not something he would want.”

“Yes, but he died like one. It is a great honor.” Urith insisted.

“Maybe to your beliefs,” she said. But an Eernician, especially of royal blood, would never consider such a thing. A great Eernician will go into the Sky Realm among the gods as counselors and aides. They would not associate with warriors."

"I'm sorry," the man said. "I thought I was helping."

Urith turned and walked away, suddenly unsettled by the fact that other beliefs conflicted with his own. He knew about such beliefs in other lands, but this was the first time he had become friends with those of differing views on the gods and existence in the spirit world. The events during his trip to Cahmais brought him tremendous powers, which he didn't understand, and now he wondered about his beliefs that would put souls in places they didn't belong. It was too much for him, and he wondered if he could get guidance from Mivraa after they traveled away from the ruined city.

Oslaf followed Urith wondering what was on his uncle's mind as he had never seen him in such a state. Typically after a battle, the old combatant would be focused on his mission. Now, the Esterblud seem distracted. When he caught up to Urith, he walked along with him for a short distance, then asked him about the remaining wounded that were lying nearby. He told his uncle that he counted four men too injured to leave on their own. Urith stopped momentarily. Without looking at his nephew, he told him to make the decision whether they would live or die by his hand.

"Urith, that is not fair," exclaimed Oslaf. "I cannot make such a decision. The warrior's code will not allow us to kill wounded."

"You are correct, and you have your answer," said the Urith grumpily. "It was an easy question. However, if you remember something in the code to help me, please let me know."

"Something I've realized today is that I now have great power over life and death of mere warriors like us," he confided in Oslaf. "I don't like this burden. It makes me too much like those cursed gods who toy with us."

Oslaf stood not knowing what to say as his uncle turned away, grumbling under his breath that such responsibility should be left to the gods. He watched Urith limp to Mivraa, who was leading five ossanes to the entrance of the ruins. Oslaf decided to go talk with Fedelm about helping him with the wounded.

Mivraa sensed the troubles Urith felt. He told her about the conversation with Fedelm and his words to Oslaf. The woman listened to him, understanding the feeling of overwhelming frustration. When he finished, she remained silent for a while as he took the reins of some of the mounts and walked with her to the main gate

"We'll give a couple of ossanes to the Aberffraw wounded to return to Turqew," he explained.

Oslaf helped several of the Aberffraw bind their wounds the best he could as a non-healer. His short discussion with Fedelm made it clear she had no stomach for helping the enemies who had killed her father. Urith arrived with the ossanes, and they helped the wounded Aberffraw enemy get up on the two spare animals. Fortunately, two of the fighters were able to hold onto their more grievously wounded comrades. Apparently, the Aberffraw expected to be abandoned to a slow death.

One of the abandoned Aberffraw thanked them for their assistance, telling them he was from the Cahmais coastal village of Barean. His name was Flacanus, and he commented that he seldom saw fighters offer assistance to the enemy wounded, despite the warrior code.

"It's not like the old days. Like you Esterblud, I follow my overlord's commands. But maybe we older men can get others to remain committed to our code of honor as well." Flacanus said as Urith quietly nodded agreement with the Aberffraw warrior.

"Too many times, our leaders use us as fodder to achieve their goals," observed the older warrior in his native tongue. His mount snorted at the weight of the two riders and stamped its feet, impatient at standing still.

"While we must remain enemies at this point, perhaps this may change. If so, you will be welcomed as honored guests in my home," Flacanus dug his heels into the mount as Urith bid him farewell. As the men rode off, Urith silently agreed that it would be good to meet as friends rather than enemies. Soon the group was out of sight.

The Esterbluds, fully recovered with the help of Mivraa's

healing water, proceeded to gather up all the supplies they could find around the area. On one of the dead ossanes, Oslaf found enough food and wine to last them for days. Scavenging other items from the dead warriors and ossanes, the three mounts were fully packed as the sun dropped in the sky, creating long shadows. Fedelm returned with Mivraa, who took Urith aside. The goddess told the warrior that she talked to the girl about Caestia's spirit and his path into the Sky Realm.

"I will go with him to the realm of my father after I take others to Haligulf. Perhaps he can help the gods to see the disaster coming to their world," she told him as she saw the flicker of disappointment in his face. The warrior goddess smiled, giving him a kiss on the cheek as she began to understand his thinking and reactions.

"When I return, we will talk about many things, I promise."

Soon, the trio was mounted, having decided they would head toward the mountain gap of the Eilginn range. In their brief discussions, the demigoddess told Urith and Oslaf about back trails through the mountain pass which would lead to the Maflow Sea. Together, they agreed to travel to Eernicia to make an offering to the Temple of the Triad with its sacred grove and open-air altar. As the group spurred their ossanes to the road, they left Mivraa standing next to the tower. She would wait for the darkness to close around her before setting out to the other realms. Watching Urith as he rode out of sight, his long hair waving in the slight breeze, she smiled to herself. When she could no longer see the group, she turned to gather the spirits for their journey to the Sky Realm.

Chapter 10: To the Maflow Sea

On the tenth morning of their journey, the trio of outcasts broke through the dense forests along the Eilginn range. At the top of the ridge, they looked over the broad expanse of ocean that lay on the horizon. The view showed they still had a long way to go. However, the trio felt a sense of relief at their progress through the dense forest. The warriors wore the gray overcoats with gold hoods, the same ones they wore on the sea voyage from Grimma. They hoped that anyone they might encounter would dismiss them as merchants. Having taken a series of paths used by animals, the travelers met no travelers along the way, and they were confident they were not being followed.

During their journey, Fedelm had opened up from her shell and told them many things about her father and even brought up interesting facts about her mother. It was apparent from the conversations that the girl was sharing her life with friends, rather than strangers. Oslaf still tried to coax the girl into private conversations when Urith was away on side trips for food or water, but he still found her to be distant from him. In fact, she paid more attention to his uncle, which he secretly resented.

Urith paid scant attention to Oslaf and Fedelm's discussions as he was distracted by the missing demigoddess. As they traveled, he found himself hoping she would suddenly show up. Because there was no sign of her, the scarred warrior remained moody and grumbling most of the time. He complained about the weather, forests, bugs, and anything else which bothered him. Oslaf and Fedelm noticed the change as they traveled with him, but they only looked at each other with bemused smiles. Urith had even asked Fedelm if she had any vision from the goddess, but the girl responded that there was none that she could remember. She admitted to them a fear of trying to contact those within the other realms. The words didn't relieve his anxiety; in fact, it made it worse.

They understood Mivraa traveled to the Sky Realm to speak with her father about her role in their battles. Urith told them that he feared Mivraa might have met with the sky god's wrath for her betrayal. Despite Fedelm's assurances, Urith retreated into his thoughts once more while the group followed a relatively easy trail to the coast.

That evening they found themselves in a field near the main road coming down from the mountains and leading to a village they could see in the distance. The field was filled with the long-haired lowland *starkts*, and the trio proceeded with caution to avoid encountering any herders who might be in the area. The trio decided to make a cold camp in the woods that lay nearby. After they had found a small clearing, Oslaf suggested they might be able to sneak into the village during the night to determine their location and check on means of travel across the sea to Eernicia. Fedelm agreed the idea seemed reasonable and worth a try. Against his better judgment, Urith approved as well, knowing they needed news and information as much as anything at this point.

"No doubt Fedelm will have an easier time of appearing as a Cahmais with her ability with the language and dialect," he told them. "However, I'm pretty sure Oslaf or I will get people's attention with our accents despite our disguises. That is something we don't want from locals right now. We are still in the land of our enemy."

"I think you are right," said the hakra over Oslaf's protests. "I'll go into the village alone and see what I can find out. It will be fully dark by the time I get there. The tavern will allow me to stay overnight and come back in the morning."

"Very well, but I would suggest you have a good excuse for traveling alone. Do you want us to follow you until you reach the village?" Urith paid no attention to his nephew who spurred his mount away to look over the village. He remained upset at their decision to send Fedelm out on her own.

Fedelm gave a grin at Urith's worry before she rode off toward the road. Urith turned to follow Oslaf into the forest just past the stand of trees. The young Esterblud stopped at a small clearing, jumping down from his beast. He said nothing as he unpacked his mount.

"Leave the saddle on," Urith warned him. "We might need to get out quickly if Fedelm gets caught."

The words caused the young warrior to stop.

"Do you still not trust her," Oslaf fumed through gritted teeth.

"No, I trust her completely. But if she is captured, she can be tortured to reveal where we are. Or they might have worse punishment for her. I think that Satres will have a high price on our heads now."

"What do you mean worse? The young man asked, his attention now turned to the danger Fedelm faced.

"If I were Alrpan, I would be looking for vengeance and who better than someone like Fedelm, who has turned to our ally." Urith stood at his ossane's side, looking over the saddle at his friend.

"The gods can be much crueler than humans. You might not know about Kestra, personal hakra to King Penhda. Before you were born, he found the sky god, Unis in a sidhera. He didn't realize who she was, but the goddess seduced him. The story is Unis drove him into madness to keep him from telling her husband." Urith explained. "You've already seen what that bitch Alrpan could do. The gods can dig into our minds or rip at our souls. We can no more trust them than our human enemies. We need to be watchful of Fedelm."

Oslaf said nothing as he thought more about the danger Fedelm faced. It took much more courage than he realized at the time for the woman to stay with them. As he spread out his blanket on the needles and leaves that covered the forest floor, he gave a prayer of thanks to Mivraa. He hoped she would watch over the girl he loved.

~~~

Deep inside the large sidhera room at the Citadel, Satres drummed his fingertips nervously on the dark wooden table where he and Alrpan met so many times before. The thin man could not temper his edginess as he waited. This was a time that he wished that Colainn was still alive. He felt the need for
~~~

protection during this unexpected meeting. Still, he hoped that his upcoming meeting with the god of the abyss might go well. If Caruun was coming to talk, he doubted it concerned Alrpan. The underworld god would hardly set up a meeting to discuss such a thing.

It wasn't long before the god arrived, his typical hideous form repulsing the human in the room. Caruun's yellow eyes peered down upon the human he held in open contempt. His black mottled skin was covered with a dark red robe which fell to the floor. Satres noticed a Vanth accompanied Caruun. The demigod watched the human with suspicious, beady eyes.

"I've come to make you an offer, human," said the god, looking around the room as if it was beneath him.

"Yes, my lord. I cannot imagine what type of offer you could give me?" asked the surprised overlord.

"Well, for one thing, your miserable life," said the god. "You are in league with my wife, of course. She explained everything following your failure in the ruins of Du-Rinell. The was after my Vanth learned of the deaths caused by the Skool," the deity looked over to the Vanth, who bowed to his master. He left the room.

"I was not happy with what she told me," Caruun said. "It appears your incompetence has extended into my realm. You can see for yourself."

Satres didn't see the Vanth quietly return as he was focused on survival. He expected something violent directed at him. When he looked over at the entrance where the god nodded, he saw Actita carrying a naked, skeletal body covered in dark brown leather-like flesh. The creature stared at Satres with its venomous red eyes, expressing a recognition that the Sacred Overlord didn't understand at first. In the next instant, he realized he was looking at Alrpan. He visibly recoiled at the sight, which brought a smirk to the vulture face of the god of the underworld.

"You see her real figure now, human. While ugly in your world, I'm glad she has come back into my world. Her power to transform is gone. The human hero you left to live inside the ruins has seen to that."

Satres remained silent.

"Do you have nothing to say? I would think you would be offering your greatest gifts along with human sacrifices to stop what I have in store for your kingdom. I don't hear any regrets for allowing this to happen to a god, let alone a god of the underworld. Should I send my beasts to ravage your lands? Perhaps bring them in this door behind me instead, to feast upon your bones. I can even think of several ways in which I'll shred your spirit when my monsters are through with you."

Realizing his meticulous plans were spinning out of control, Satres tried to speak in his own defense. However, the netherworld leader stopped him.

"As for myself, I wondered what I should do to such an insignificant worm who allows my wife to be treated in such a way. It appears you are quite weak since you cannot even stop a few people with swords." The cruel face of Caruun stared down at the thin man. "I hear nothing about the death of these blasphemers who so abuse a god. I would think their heads would be given to the temple as an offering to me. Must I release the hordes of the underworld upon your realm for satisfaction?"

Satres face drained of blood as he thought quickly to come up with a reply.

"You are correct, great one, in all you say. I swear that I did not realize the extent of Alrpan's injuries until now. However, I've not been negligent in my duties against those who injured your wife. You know that we lost many men at Du-Rinell against a weapon of the gods if your Vanth was there. These Esterbluds have as much power as my armies."

"I don't want to hear your excuses, little man." Caruun walked behind the chair where Satres sat. The god drummed his claws on the back of the chair, and Satres felt his stomach tighten into a knot.

Satres continued, sensing the deity was making up his mind about his fate which the man was powerless to stop.

"My lord, I promise you I'm taking action against those who

have injured your wife. I have already notified King Asgurd of the obscenity committed on his lands, against your realm. His army will be your ally in punishing the Esterbluds as they try to escape. My militia is actively hunting them at the border should they try to cross. It will not be long now."

"This helps me not," said the vulture face grimly. "And I don't want them dead. Killing those traitors now only sends them to the Sky Realm, along with that half-breed Mivraa. A god can not hold the Skool, and I cannot allow a human to control it."

"Perhaps not, great one. But with the right strategy, it may be possible to capture those who dishonor you. If they were handed over to you alive, there would be no need for the Sky Realm to know what you decide to do with them. You have the means to make them pay, alive and dead." The overlord grew more confident as he spoke.

"I believe the death of the chosen warrior would allow another human - say a person fully under your power - to be your instrument of control and use of the Shield."

Caruun sat down across the table from Satres. He scowled over the idea. In his mind, this pitiful creature was beneath contempt. But the god recognized the devious nature of the overlord and believed he could make a convenient ally. Once his fool wife Alrpan explained her plan to control the Skool, the underworld god decided he would take charge. He might be able to salvage something from her meddling with the humans.

"I agree you might have some use for me now," Caruun continued. "Perhaps I can give you what you seek. I understand that you wish to become immortal like us."

The Sacred Overlord looked back at the creature called Alrpan. "What are your terms, my lord?" he asked Caruun, knowing the answer in the pit of his stomach.

"For now, you will continue to hunt the defilers. Reach out to your *satgerts* in the temples across your world. You will use any means necessary to retrieve the Skool. However, you will now follow my direction in all things of importance," said the god as he stood up. As he approached the entrance to his realm, he didn't bother to turn his head as he continued.

"You will hear from me when I want your services. I expect more than you have shown me so far and you don't want to disappoint me."

~~~

Fedelm entered the village as the night fell, just as the twin moons were rising in the sky. She wondered how much she might find in such a small hamlet. A few small huts surrounded two larger buildings which she rightly guessed were a mead hall and a shop for trading goods. She pulled up in front of a small cabin with a wooden fence that held a few animals. The sound of her ossane coming to a stop in front of the railing brought a stooped thin man out of his nearby hut. Scratching his head, he looked up at the young girl with suspicion in his eyes.

"Stopping here?" he asked, pulling out his long Cahmais pipe from his large lips.

Fedelm nodded. "Yes, if there was a place to sleep." She spoke in Aberffraw.

The little man looked at the ossane carefully and then pointed across the road to one of the larger buildings.

"Above the tavern," he said. "Tell the old widow Jyeeth you need a room and she will help you. Not many folks stop by here since the gods destroyed Hyropda. How did you get here?" The man raised his eyebrow as he stared at the girl's elegant clothes.

Without missing a beat, Fedelm told him she came through from Turqew. He seemed to accept her lie, merely taking the reins from her.

"It's two koinons a night, in advance," he told her. She reached into her small bag hanging from the leather belt and handed the man the coins. Sliding off the mount, she grabbed her saddlebag and walked across the road as the man stared at her for a while before taking the mount around the hut.

Coming to the building, Fedelm paid little attention to the figure which stood looking down at her from the second story window of the building. Inside, she found a few men huddled in the center of the room. Dressed in the brown cloaks of herders,
~~~

they sat by the great hearth which held a fire. Their conversation came to a halt as the cute girl in her stylish clothes entered the building, each man drinking in her figure with their eyes while they swallowed their heathmead. Fedelm looked past them to the fat lady sitting on a rough board. Perched next to a cask, she was pouring herself a drink when Fedelm approached, asking about a room for the night.

"My little one, we're happy to accommodate you. It's been rough around here since the gods took it in their heads to wipe out towns." The big woman got to her feet, complaining about her ailments since the devastation down the coast. She made sure to curse the sea god, which she emphasized by spitting on the dirt floor. Fedelm was happy to let the woman talk while she was led to a small dark stairway at the end of the room. She followed the woman who took a candle holder from a worn table to light their way. The girl felt uncomfortable from the staring men who followed her movement but decided that the old farmers presented her no real danger.

"I have a good room and only one person in it. Don't mind the woman in there; she comes through our village on occasion. Word is she is a rock trader, but I never heard tell of a lady traveling alone doing such work. They say she trades in tribolrocks to the miners in those Eilginn Mountains along with the fishermen along the coast. Sometimes she comes with an ossane, other times she just walks in."

Jyeeth turned to her, smiling with rotting teeth.

"She may act strange, but nobody pays attention to her anymore," she explained.

Fedelm thanked Jyeeth, giving her a koinon as she opened the door to the dimly lit room. The woman nodded, acknowledging the payment, then turned away, leaving her with a warning.

"By the way, don't get the old lady angry. I've seen her run a sword through a local boy who tried to rob her." With a cackle, the innkeeper left her at the ramshackle door.

When Fedelm entered, she noticed there were, on either side of the room, two mattresses that were posing as beds, the straw contents spilling out on the floor. At the foot of each was a rickety chair. In the middle of the room, near the open window, was a table with a nearly finished candle. On one bed was a mound covered with a shiny black wrap. Assuming the person to be asleep, Fedelm went to the table near the window thinking.

"Well, my little girl. Don't you talk to old ladies?" The sound of a chortling voice came from the bed as the figure sat up. Pulling back the hood covering her hair, Mivraa smiled at the hakra, who could only stare in disbelief.

Getting over her initial surprise, Fedelm found her voice again, "Mivraa, what are you doing here?"

"Waiting for you, of course. I was told by the *Sybil* you would be here. The god's oracle said you would get there today, so I arrived the last sunset. It is one of my regular stopping points when I travel in the land of Cahmais. As you heard, the locals are familiar with my strange behaviors, and they pay me no attention."

"Why didn't you reach out to me," the girl asked the goddess. "I've had no visions since leaving the ruins."

The demigoddess lowered her eyes. "We need to discuss that with the others. Where are they?"

"Just outside, along the road to the hamlet. I came alone to figure out our location and to hear any news or gossip."

"Very well, we'll have to wait until the sun rises before we can meet with them. I'm back from the Sky Realm, and your father's spirit is in good hands, I promise you."

Fedelm eyes filled with tears, but she remained stoic as Mivraa continued. "When you arrived, I noticed you left your mount at the stable across the road. If we leave now, we will attract attention, and the locals might talk. We don't want any attention because there are spies throughout the land."

The goddess reached into her pack, pulling out some *weamater*, sun-dried slices of salted duelill flesh. Fedelm stepped forward accepting a slice as the smell made her stomach growl. As she sat down next to the goddess, she took a bite, savoring the taste.

"So where are we? She asked.

Mivraa smiled as she explained they were in Cacoon, on the main road to Uugaraa.

"You're not far from the home of the Aberffraw king," she told Fedelm. "We can get passage out of the lands from there."

"That means you travel with us?"

The red-haired woman nodded.

"I have no choice, but we will discuss that with everyone else. We will leave separately with the sunrise."

As she spoke, she pulled out a simple peasant's woolen gown and threw it on the other bed.

"I found this during my travels here," the goddess laid back on the mattress. "Your clothing is too smart, and it shows the marks of the Sacred Overlord. Given what has happened, we need to blend in, especially in this land. Now let's get some rest since we have much to decide with the men before we get to Uugaraa."

Fedelm wanted to ask more, but she realized Mivraa would not discuss it without the Esterbluds. She went to the other bed, moving the woolen gown Mivraa had given her, noticing the straw in the mattress emitted a musty odor. Blowing out the candle the girl lay down to try to get some rest. She listened to the chirping of the cruicads outside. The sound reminded her of happy times with her father when they took trips into the countryside. Drifting off to sleep, she could see her father standing at the side of Duwdamon, feeling sadness but also a calming peace. It was a sensation she missed and the night washed over her as she smiled.

It was just after sunrise and Urith was just pulling the last of their dried meat from a saddle bag when he heard hoof beats coming. Lifting up his spear from the leaf covered ground; he stepped forward to see two riders on one ossane coming his way. He immediately recognized Fedelm who road in front, but he had difficulty understanding who was behind the girl. As the long-necked animal moved its head to the side as it galloped up, he recognized the other rider.

Mivraa!

His quick smile caught the attention of Oslaf, who tried to suppress a smile of his own. It was becoming obvious about Urith's infatuation with the demigoddess. Still wearing his grin as the two women on the ossane came through the first line of trees, Oslaf got to his feet to greet Fedelm.

"I see you found someone," Urith chucked as the women pulled up to the camp.

Mivraa jumped down from the mount, coming to Urith and placing her hand on his shoulder.

"It's nice to see you, my friend," the goddess tried to appear formal. Oslaf and Fedelm just grinned at her effort. Oslaf stepped toward Fedelm, who was still sitting on the ossane, asking if anything happened after she left. The young man shook his head.

"No, everything was quiet. I wish I could have gone with you."

"No, it was best you didn't. The people in that hamlet are a suspicious lot, and you would have stood out. They weren't sure about me. That's alright. Mivraa was waiting there for me, and she has news. Besides, I brought some heathmead for you both."

With that, the girl slid off the mount and pulled off the water bag containing their favorite drink, giving it to Oslaf. He accepted with a smile and took a long drink. It was stale, but he found it refreshing. He thanked her, turning around to share with Urith. His uncle accepted the bag before settling down on his blanket which was still spread out on the ground.

"From the look on her face, I believe our goddess friend has something we need to know," the Clovel Destroyer stated as he leaned back on the log. Sitting next to Urith, Mivraa paused while the others moved to sit across from her, their faces showing the curiosity they felt.

"It's a long story, but I'll try to make it brief. As suspected, the agreement between the gods is falling apart, and the unity of the Triad no longer exists. I went to Duwdamon and told him what I saw and what I know," said the demigoddess.

"Unfortunately, he refuses my advice. My brothers have more influence. They want to follow their own paths. Uugor has some loyalty to Alrpan. He's killed many with his powers."

"Do we have any gods working for us?" asked Oslaf.

"I doubt it," admitted the goddess. "I suspect Caruun may be behind much of the hatred toward humans. He made it clear to my father that he holds all of Kamin responsible for the injuries to Alrpan."

"Why not me?" interjected Urith as he sat up, "I'm the one who did this to his wife. He should be seeking vengeance against me."

The demigoddess shook her head, saying she didn't know. There was a pause in the conversation as the group thought about the battle and their future.

"I think Caruun is after bigger things," Fedelm spoke up, her green eyes wide at her thoughts. "I believe he is using the chaos to his advantage."

"How do you know?" asked the goddess. "While it makes sense, no one but Alrpan is close enough to know such a thing."

"I'm not sure," The hakra looked confused, shaking her head. "I just feel it somehow."

"Well, that's good enough for me," said Urith.n"We need to assume the worst. And since we've had the gods against us for a while now, what does it matter?" The Esterblud warrior gave a quick wink to Mivraa, who punched him playfully on the arm.

He continued. "So, on to the next problem. Where are we and how do we get to Eernicia?"

Mivraa explained that the road they were on led to Uugaraa.

"We must enter the harbor town and find some means of passage to Fedelm's homeland," she said. "While the city is home to King Asgurd, leader of the Aberffraw, once we get in they'll have a hard time finding us with all the people around."

It turned quiet for a while until Urith spoke up as he got to his feet, bending over to get his blanket.

"Well, it's time to get moving. We'll keep in the trees as much as possible while we follow the road to Uugaraa."

With his words, the group broke up, and the two Esterbluds packed their mounts for the ride while the women got back on

Fedelm's ossane. Starting out from behind the trees, they waited until the road cleared, then trotted over to the other side, working their way around the hamlet. Soon, the group of travelers was out of sight, heading for the harbor where passage to Eernicia could be obtained.

It was two evenings later and nearing the time of the *Draenyna* Festival when Oslaf crested the top of a ridge behind some small dreathtrees. Scouting the area ahead of the others, he waited for the others. The tempting scent of the ripe green fruit of the trees caused the young warrior's stomach to growl, and he pulled down a fruit to eat before turning back to signal the others. He wondered at the stories he heard about the festival dedicated to *Draenyna,* the height of the growing season. It was known that the city would come alive to honor the sky gods in tributes of food and drink. He questioned whether the stories of the rampant voyeurism and debauchery that occurred during the festival were true. It was something he hoped they might be able to see. He knew that was an impossible thought as long as they were hunted.

The others soon joined him and rested. They looked down at the scene before them. From their vantage point, they could see the twin towering spires of the Aberffraw king's castle in the distance, as it stood sentinel over the great city of Uugaraa. A wall, built to protect it from enemy attacks bordered the town as it spread down to the sea. Directly below the high ridge where they now sat, they observed a colorful stream of people traveling into the city, following the main road as it twisted toward Uugaraa.

"Well, looks like we're nearly here," said Mivraa. "I don't think you two Esterbluds can enter dressed in your armor."

Urith agreed, telling Oslaf and Fedelm they would have to arrive at night, bypassing the watchtowers and main gate they could see in the distance.

"Do they close the main gate at night?" Urith asked.

"Yes, we cannot just sneak in," she warned while noticing Urith was particularly interested in a *pagyn,* or merchant wagon stopped below them. When she looked closer, she saw one wheel was removed, and a bearded man was working on the axle. The yellow flickering of lights could be seen in the city as the sun set, giving the eastern sky a purple hue.

"Looks like we might need to use other means to enter the city," Urith told them. He peered up at the waning light. "I don't think our friend in the wagon will be finished before night falls. We should pay him a visit after dark. Who knows, perhaps he would be interested in a trade?"

The others looked at him as he grinned while sliding off his mount. Fedelm and Oslaf glanced at each other before getting off their animals to wait until the sun fell behind the eastern sea. The group moved out of sight from their perch while Urith briefly outlined his plan for them to get into the city. Oslaf watched the road, paying close attention to the wagon which remained by the side of the road. He noticed how the throngs of people, animals, and wagons dispersed as darkness crept in. Even within the relatively secure lands close to the capital, the roads could be unsafe after dark.

"Let's head down to chat with our merchant about his wagon," Urith said. "Let's hope he is reasonable."

He slapped his nephew on the back, then stepped over the top of the ridge and down to the road below. Oslaf quickly caught up with him while the women stayed behind, where they would act as lookouts while using Mivraa's power to keep them both unseen. Silently the men crossed the now empty road, keeping their distance from the wagon and watching the man moving around in the light of the campfire. They heard the man cursing in Gallaeci, a dialect of the Cahmais language. That meant the man was from one of the hostile tribes inhabiting the isolated forests of Eilginn highlands. Hearing his accent, Urith thought of an idea which might get them into the city.

"Hello, in the camp," Urith called out in Gallaeci. "Can we approach?" Oslaf grabbed his arm, but the older man softly told him to play along. From the camp, they heard the man call back.

"Any friends of Spanca are welcome here, come ahead," replied the voice.

Catching the code word about the Gallaeci's favorite god, Urith approached the camp with Oslaf nervously trailing behind. They came up from behind the wagon, carefully scanning around for any others they might have missed while watching from the ridge above. As they passed the cart, Urith was able to see the wheel had been fixed.

"Welcome," said the man facing them as he crouched in front of the campfire. He put on another log. "What brings you here in the night?"

The wagon owner had a full beard and he was a large man, nearly the size of Urith, but with a big belly hanging over his lap. His shirt was an unusually bright yellow, with a high collar and Urith noticed the man was missing several fingers on his left hand. A heavy blue wool trader's cape hung on a branch of a small tree nearby. Near his side, a wooden cask sat on two pieces of wood to keep its spigot out of the dirt. Both warriors could see the man's dark eyes watching suspiciously. Urith tried to put him at ease.

"We spotted your fire. We thank you for letting us enter. I'm Urith, and this is Oslaf." Urith spoke in Gallaeci making sure they didn't move too close.

"Interesting," replied the man as he sat down cross-legged on the other side of the fire from them. "You know our language. Tell me how do you know of our ways?"

"I've traveled much over the seasons," said the Clovel Destroyer, "so I've learned some of the beliefs of the Gallaeci." Urith kept his eye on the man's left hand where he held a large flask. The Esterbluds noticed how the man kept his right hand out of their sight. Evidently, the man traveled dangerous roads in his journeys.

Eying them for a moment, he offered them a place at the fire. "Please sit and share a flask with me. My name is Atheern."

The two warriors sat down on the other side of the fire. Oslaf took the flask from the man who leaned over, handing him the ceramic vessel. The young warrior took a drink of the ale and honey mix.

"Aye, interesting indeed," Atheern said with a twinkle in his eye. "I don't often meet Esterbluds in Cahmais."

Oslaf nearly spat out the drink at the words of the man. Urith tightened his grip on his Clovel Sword, hidden under the rough brown cloak he wore.

His deep laugh boomed into the night when Atheern saw the reactions of his guests.

"No need to worry friends. Please relax your hands from your swords I see under your cloaks. I have no quarrel with the Esterbluds or anyone for that matter. Most Gallaeci would not know an Esterblud from a Vulthnal or any other foreigner. However, I'm not most Gallaeci. I'm a trader of heathmead to the Aberffraw king."

His words made Urith more nervous as he tried to look around for the trap he expected to fall anytime. Atheern's booming laugh roared again as he caught Urith's eyes.

"I know it makes no sense to a foreigner does it? A Gallaeci serving an Aberffraw king and his castle their favorite drinks. Makes for interesting discussions back home, I can assure you," he said with a smile.

The man reached over and took back the flask back from the still stunned Oslaf.

"You don't drink much, do you son?" showing disappointment at the young man. He then topped off the flask from the cask next to him and reached across to Urith, who took it, still not convinced about the man. However, he enjoyed the taste as it felt warm going down.

"Good drink," Urith says, impressed as he looked down at the foaming vessel. "Are you traveling to the castle?"

The Gallaeci smiled, proudly. "Yes, they are my only customer. Don't need any others since I'm the only one that can get heathmead out of the Mythroloy Highlands."

"I can see why, that's some of the best mead I've had," the warrior complemented the trader. "You must have quite the connections with the trading guild in Uugaraa?"

Atheern quashed up his face in disgust, spitting on the fire.

"Nah, those vultures are no good to me. They only work for their Cahmais friends. They control the sea trade."

"You must be lost. The Aberffraw are not your friends. Where are you traveling to, my friends?" the merchant shifted the conversation.

"We're looking for ship passage to Vulthnal," Urith lied. "Since the destruction of Hyropda, we had to come this way."

The large man shifted his weight as he took the flask back from Urith.

"That is a problem for you," he replied, thinking aloud.

"Obviously, as we are foreigners, we need to get into Uugaraa without the city guards asking too many questions," conceded Urith. "The king might decide to throw us in his jail."

"You come to me for what?" asked the merchant. "Am I to help you and lose my only customer? I don't think so."

"Look, we are only looking for a ride in the back of your wagon. We have some ossanes and some koinons to make it worth your risk." The Esterblud leader explained. He took another drink and burped loudly.

"Besides, do you really think guards would bother the only man who can get heathmead from the Gallaeci to the Aberffraw king?" Urith smiled with his sneer as he watched the big man consider the idea for a moment.

"Very well, my new friend. It will cost you twenty koinons and your animals, I will not bargain on this." Urith made a show of considering the idea.

"Good enough, we will bring the ossanes as down payment and pay you once inside the city," said the warrior as he finished the flask. He stood up.

"Do we have a deal?"

The man nodded his head, his eyes twinkling as he thought of his profit.

"Good, we will be back when the sun rises."

Urith turned and walked away as Oslaf scrambled to catch up with him. As they walked back to the road, they spotted the women waiting for them, looking at them expectantly. Putting his finger to his lips, he motioned for them to follow him. Once he was sure they were far enough to not be overheard, he spoke, but still quiet. He told the women of the agreement that had been reached as they crept back to where the ossanes were tied. Mivraa said they overheard most of it, but she questioned whether they could trust him.

"I get the sense he is much more interested in getting paid with a minimum of risk. I guess the Fates might be with us on this," replied Urith.

"Or they are helping the gods lay a trap for us," said the demigoddess.

"If that's the case, let's get a good rest before we find out," he answered smugly.

Mivraa just shook her head at Urith's comment.

They arrived at the top of the ridge. The mood among them was lighter as they pulled out blankets to catch some rest before going back to Atheern's wagon before the sun rose. Urith skipped getting a blanket as he told Oslaf he would stay up for the first watch as normal. He walked back to the ridge, deciding to keep an eye on the road below, as he wondered if he was correct about their new friend.

Oslaf woke Urith and the others as the first rays of the sun started to lighten the western sky. After keeping watch on the road all night, Urith and Oslaf were convinced the heathmead trader would help them into the city. They packed their belongings so that they could carry them, knowing they would not be using the ossanes much longer. The group led the animals over the ridge to the road below, on the lookout for early travelers who might be coming down the road.

When they reached the road, the sun was just peeking over the horizon. Atheern's *erba* were already harnessed to the front of the wagon, snorting through long muzzles as they shook their large heads. Their massive bodies, covered in brown and black striped hair stood nearly as high as the seat of the wagon. As the group approached, they saw Atheern putting his bedroll into the back of his wagon, flopping down the green canvas covering the load of barrels inside. He was not pleased to see the group.

"You said nothing about women coming with you. It is too dangerous," the man spit on the ground when they walked up. "And those ossanes aren't fit to pull my wagon. No, this is a bad deal."

Urith was about to say something, but Fedelm placed a hand on his arm.

"Perhaps to an average man," Fedelm beamed her sweet smile at him speaking in his language. "I was told you are not like most Gallaeci. You are the great trader of heathmead to the Aberffraw king."

Atheern's face turned red then he burst out laughing as his belly shook. "I like this one," he announced before his face turned serious.

"Come, we don't have much time. Tie off those mounts and put the saddles and bags in the wagon with you. Except you, lovely lady. You will sit up with me."

Oslaf was about to protest when the trader stopped him with a stern look.

"Guards looking at a pretty girl will not be looking in the back of my wagon," he explained.

Fedelm took the man by the arm and led him to the front of the cart. He told her about his trade while the others tied the ossanes to the back. In the back of the wagon, they placed their bags and bedrolls in front of the casks. Finding a place to sit or lay down was difficult among the casks, but they were able to use the saddles as a type of bench for each to sit on. Urith positioned himself just behind the seat where Fedelm sat, which allowed him to peer between the canvas and side of the wagon. The hidden group heard the man snap a whip, cursing at his *erba* which slowly pulled the wagon back onto the road heading to Uugaraa.

The sun had reached its zenith when the cart arrived at the main gate to the city. As Atheern expected, the guards at the gate paid little attention to his wagon while they spent their time trying to get the attention of Fedelm. Now dressed in the plain clothes of a peasant girl, she was a good pairing with the trader as they joked with the sentries. The guards finally waved them into the city without bothering to look in the back of the wagon. Those in the wagon didn't see the stooped, thin man who had come up behind the ossanes. He stared at the mount that Fedelm and Mivraa rode. The man walked up near the driver's side and caught a glimpse of the girl on the other side. His eyes widened, recognizing her as he pulled his long Cahmais pipe from his mouth, exhaling a puff of smoke. When the wagon pulled away from him, he casually began to walk behind at a distance, making sure to keep the cart in sight.

Following the winding streets of Uugaraa, Atheern stopped his wagon at a stable just down from the Malhair House. It was a good position for them to get to the Malhair House, the place of business where the guild controlled the trade in and out of the city. The house was actually a small hut with a thatched roof. On either side of the structure were large warehouses that followed the street leading down to the harbor. Fedelm noticed several ships lining the docks past the end of the road. Jumping down from his seat, the man looked around as Fedelm came around from the other side, her ears still ringing at the constant chatter the big man kept up during the trip. The trader untied the animals from the back of the wagon, turning them to provide some cover for those in the back of the wagon. After a couple of children ran by, shouting to each other about the next ship leaving on the tide, the man told the hidden travelers to hurry out of the back.

The trio quickly climbed out of the wagon, happy to get out of the tight and uncomfortable space. Urith thanked Atheern for his help as he handed the big man the twenty koinons as promised, while the rest quickly pulled out their bedrolls which held their extra weapons and saddlebags of food and drink.

"We left those saddles for you," said Oslaf as he pulled out the last of their gear.

"It was good doing business with you," the trader said as he put the money into a leather bag that hung from his belt. He led the ossanes to the stables.

"You can join me on my trips when you get tired of your

adventures," he told Fedelm as he went by her, winking. "Otherwise, I suggest you get off the streets soon. Your two big warriors aren't going to fool many of these people."

He waved to them after tying up the ossanes in front of the stables and walked inside to work out the sale of the animals. Dressed in her dark cape which hid her armor, Mivraa told the others to follow her as she headed down the street. They followed her to a long row of warehouses with shop fronts that lined the street heading toward the harbor. Before they reached the first shop where a few men were unloading a cart, the goddess turned into an alley along a fence that separated the guild house and the warehouses. Turning behind into another alley that ran along the back of the buildings, they immediately came to a door which barely hung on its iron hinges. The door creaked in protest as it opened, then Mivraa sent everyone into the dimly lit room while she looked back down the alley to ensure they hadn't been followed. After a while, she was satisfied and followed the others inside.

"I've been to this city many times, so I know some of the places to get lost," she explained as she sat on the bench next to Urith.

"This room is part of the warehouse, set aside as one of the sailmaker's shops used for sewing and repairing sails when boats are in port. As you can see, it's usually empty during the *Draenyna* season when the sea is warmer. The fishermen remain at sea most of the time."

Around them in the small room were dusty wooden crates and stacks of rope and canvas, while iron tools hung from the low beams above them. Gaps between the outside panels on the walls let in the rays of sunlight showing the swirling dust coming up from the straw floor.

"Why would you know this?" asked Oslaf, who was next to Fedelm. "This city is nowhere close to a battlefield."

"Do you think the battles are only fought by warriors? In my experience, humans fight for power, or honor, even for scraps of food nearly anywhere." Her face appeared almost ghostly in the dim light coming in from between the boards along the walls.

"This area of Uugaraa is known for gangs of thieves who prey on the sailors coming from the docks. Some think the guilds allow it to happen with the support of the king. I've had my own battles among these alleys," she explained.

"I guess we stay here until we can get passage out of here. Is that the plan?" asked Urith, knowing the answer.

"Unless someone has a better one," replied Mivraa, looking around. "Fedelm and I will get the passage on the first ship out of here, hopefully at night, which will keep the prying eyes away."

Getting up, the goddess motioned for Fedelm to follow her. As they got to the door, Urith handed the last of his koinons to Mivraa telling her if they needed more, they would find a trader for some of their weapons. She gave him a smile and left, following Fedelm into the alley. Urith and Oslaf sat down, occupying their time sorting through their belongings, preparing for their trip. As he was going through their items, the younger man began thinking about how much had happened to them since they landed at the seashore. He also wondered what lay ahead for them, as he thought of the changes he'd seen in his uncle. While still a fearsome fighter, if not more vicious, Urith was showing a side that the young man hadn't seen in many seasons. Since Urith's wife died in childbirth, his uncle remained distant to anyone beyond him and his family. Now it was evident his feelings for Mivraa were similar to what Oslaf felt for Fedelm. And he had to admit the thought worried him. His biggest concern was how his uncle would be able to handle the power of the Shield of Skool. He knew of his uncle's anger of the gods. The young warrior wondered how a man could not want vengeance against those gods he blamed for the death of his family. It made the situation difficult for Oslaf to talk with his uncle about.

It was near dark when Mivraa and Fedelm returned to the sail maker's shop. An agitated Oslaf met them at the door asking if they ran into any problems while Urith continued sharpening his sword with a small grindstone. Fedelm gave Oslaf a tired grin.

"It took a while to convince the man in the guild we were the ones planning the trip. Seems he only wants to deal with men. Mivraa had to convince him otherwise."

Urith looked up at Mivraa.

"What did you do?" he asked.

"I grabbed him by the collar of his dirty little shirt and told him I would rip out his throat with my sword if he didn't find passage for us."

The Esterbluds burst out laughing at her description as Mivraa smiled at their reaction. Even Fedelm was laughing when she remembered the man's petrified face. The demigoddess went on to explain the two women got the guild papers to the ship called "Shackle," sailing after dark on the high tide. While they spoke, Oslaf gave them food and drink as Urith finished sharpening his sword. After the women had finished eating, they settled down, waiting for the time to pass.

Green light given off by the tribolrocks filled the room as the night came when the group heard the far off sound of the watchman announcing the incoming tide as he walked along the docks. Packed and ready to leave for their ship, the warriors put on their gray merchant cloaks to cover their shields that hung on their backs. They loaded their bags over their shoulders while Mivraa put away the glowing rocks. Urith opened the creaky door slightly and then moved out into the darkness. As he looked around the corner to the alley, the others came out behind him. Suddenly he stopped, causing Mivraa to run into him.

"Back inside!" he hissed while he pulled his sword.

From the passageway in the darkness, they could hear the jangling sound of armor as men came running down the alleyway. They could hear the same sound coming from the other side of the warehouse. Scrambling, they ran back into the dark room. Urith and Oslaf lifted and pushed the heavy wooden crates in front of the door, and Urith stacked other boxes on top as moving red and yellow light shot past the open gaps in the wall boards. Outside, they could hear the shouting of the Aberffraw guards as they surrounded the warehouse, followed by pounding on the door.

"Come out, foreigners! We know you are in there. Surrender or we will kill you," yelled a hoarse voice from near the door.

"It must have been that trader," said Oslaf to Urith.

"No, they would have come sooner," he replied. "Somehow, someone must have followed Mivraa and Fedelm."

Outside the flaming torches lit up the room as they looked for an escape route. There were no other doors and no windows in the shop. The ceiling was made of heavy timber. Oslaf moved to the interior wall across from the entrance, looking for anything they could use to escape. Urith saw a shadow near the entrance, and suddenly the door was being pushed in. The Clovel Destroyer pushed his back against the crates as he felt the thumping pressure of men running against the door. Mivraa abruptly grabbed Oslaf and pointed him to a spot in the corner while she went to help Urith where the wood was separating away from the timber frame. The young fighter took a step back and kicked at the wall with his foot which sent several boards flying back from the wall. Several savage kicks later, there was a dark hole large enough to crawl through.

"Come on," Oslaf grabbed Fedelm, talking close to her ear to be heard over the noise, "go through and look for a way out. I'll send Mivraa after you."

The woman looked at the dark hole, took a breath and entered. Oslaf moved to the door, telling Mivraa, who was pushing back on the crate with Urith to follow as he pointed to the girl exiting through the hole. Nodding, she let go as Oslaf took her place. The goddess ran over to the hole, fumbling for her tribolrocks. Urith heard the wood being ripped from the thin wall to his right, and he turned his head to spot a guard trying to push into the room. Swinging out his Clovel Sword as he heaved himself away from the crate, his savage upswing nearly sliced through the man's face at the neck.

"Let them come through now," he yelled to Oslaf as he pulled on his shield.

Nodding, the younger warrior let loose of the crates which came tumbling down as the door pushed open. Two guards fell into the room when the door suddenly opened. Oslaf ran his sword through the back of one while Urith killed the other. Two more guards carrying spears followed their comrades through the entrance, forcing the Esterbluds to back away while fending them off with their swords as another entered with his torch. Backing themselves to the dark exit behind them, the men were powerless to stop the others coming into the room. Fortunately, the area was small, so the fighters were able to use their swords and shields to keep from being overwhelmed by a large number of guards. Urith yelled for Oslaf to crawl through the hole to where the women were, and find a way out of the building. Hesitating, Oslaf knew if he left Urith could be overwhelmed.

"Go now!" Urith ordered as he stood in front of the younger man. "I'll be right behind you."

Oslaf dropped down and pushed his way through, his broad shoulders and shield, forcing the thin wood out of the way. As the young man pushed his way through, Urith caught sight of the guard standing with the flaming torch. Suddenly, he used his shield to push a smaller defender out of his way, sending him tumbling down. He rushed the man with the torch, impaling him in the chest with his sword. Pulling back, the Esterblud glanced with satisfaction as he saw the flames already spreading on the floor as the dry canvas and rope provided fuel. Barreling into the guard standing between him and the dark hole, Urith sent the man flying, and before any other guards could react, he scrambled through the hole in the wall. Once inside the dark room, Oslaf was waiting with a lit rock. He told the warrior the women were looking for a way out.

"They better find a way out soon, before this whole warehouse goes up," Urith said. Back in the room that held the sailmaker's shop, men were shouting as they scrambled to get out.

"Come on, let's find the girls." Oslaf led him through the maze of stacked goods in the warehouse. Listening to the sounds of yelling and footsteps pass by, they tried the other side of the room that fronted the street, but the large wooden door banded in iron was locked from the outside, and the smoke was making it difficult to breathe.

"Well, on to the next. They must be somewhere close," said Oslaf.

As they pushed through the door that connected the next building, they ran headlong into Fedelm and Mivraa. Mivraa led the group through another warren of aisles stacked on either side with tall racks of smoked fish. They finally reached a door at the other side of the warehouse, near the back alley.

"It's locked from the outside. I didn't want to force it when we heard the guards talking outside," she explained.

Urith nodded as he listened to another wave of yelling and the sound of people moving away from them and toward the fire. Thick smoke began to fill the room as they looked at each other in the green light.

"I don't think we have any choice at this point," Urith said. "We leave and hope for the crowd to cover us, or we die here. I won't use the Skool on people trying to save their buildings," he explained. "If we fight it will be with our swords and spears."

The others nodded their understanding.

"Mivraa, you take Fedelm and escape with your disguise and get through the crowd," Urith ordered. "Oslaf and I will hold them off, and we'll meet at the ship."

"Don't be a fool," Fedelm objected. "You'll die with the Skool in your hands. You escape while the rest of us hold them off."

"She's right," Mivraa agreed. "It's better to die in battle, isn't it?" There was a cocky smile on her face.

Realizing he would not win the argument, Urith put his sword and shield away, telling Oslaf to do the same.

"Alright, we'll go out and take as many as we can," he said, starting to cough. They quickly covered themselves with their large cloaks.

Urith took a step back and plunged forward, slamming himself into the door, nearly breaking through the hinges. The sounds of chaos and yells continued to fade. But the fire drew closer and the smoke became unbearable. Urith slammed into the door one more time, causing it open wide. The group spilled out into the alleyway, each gasping and choking.

Surprised there was no one around, they discovered that they were in the alley behind the warehouse. Dimly lit figures milled around at the other end of the alleyway, trying to fight a losing battle with the flames as they spread. Retreating from the area, Urith led the others through the alley and across the unlit roadway. The docks were only a stone's throw away, and they saw dark vessels that lined the port. They slowed as they came upon a small group of sailors who stood around, watching the blaze. They were Vulthnal sailors who debated whether they should help the citizens. Mivraa, covered in her black shawl, stopped another sailor coming down the dock to join his comrades. She asked the man the location of the ship called "Shackle," and the sailor pointed to the small single-mast cuggle, lying low in the water preparing to get underway. The group hurried down the dock, Urith telling the goddess to lead them up the gangplank.

Soon, after paying a bribe to keep the captain silent about their journey, the group was standing on the bow of the ship watching the fire glow red in the night sky as the ship slipped its mooring lines. Sailors, in their gray canvas breeches and red wool shirts, worked on the deck, dropping the square sail, catching the wind to guide the ship gently out of the harbor. Urith moved slowly along the starboard side as the ship turned its bow toward the open sea. They picked up speed as they passed the breakwaters, watching the moonlight highlight the white swirls of the waves catching the rocks. Urith kept looking the lights from the town of Uugaraa until they grow dim. The fighter wondered about his choices that got them there and if he was the man his friends seemed to believe he was. The Esterblud warrior heard the demigoddess come up beside him, but he said nothing, lost in his thoughts. He felt Mivraa slip her rough hand into his and, for the moment, he was pleased.

~~~

As the ship plowed into open water, a dark skeletal figure moved within the depths of the underworld realm; stopping in front of an obscure, unused entrance blocked by an ancient stone wall. With the entrance hidden from view, the gods and spirits of the depths had long forgotten the passageway behind the wall. However, the skeletal creature standing at the wall remembered reading about this passage in the journals of the Citadel of Br-Ynys and used the ancient words, hissing them into an echo that filled the area. At first, there was nothing, and the figure slumped, but soon a dull rumble started and grew, shaking the ground until the wall split open revealing narrow passageway. Entering the dark passage, the figure hobbled along, its skinny legs moving painfully, while it's glowing red eyes revealed all despite the pitch black that enveloped it. Stale damp air didn't bother the surreal form as it focused upon its vengeance. Its clawed feet gripped the slimy rock floor as it steadily descended through narrow corridors that had not been used since the time of the Great Passing. Behind the figure, the rock reformed itself, as the traveler moved on.

Following the winding passageway down, the skeletal figure stopped at the end where a small cave was hollowed out in the rock. On the far wall from the entrance was a mural of a hideous creature not unlike the one passing through. Upon entering, a luminous glow filled the chamber, outlining a rock slab at the foot of the mural. The oblong rock was polished black about the length of a human and raised from the floor by the same polished black stone legs. Limping around to the side, the figure could see a small trench cut in the slab, running from the middle to the edge. Below the trench, engraved on the rock floor was a bowl-shaped depression.

The grotesque figure reached down, taking the bowl to place it on the slab while it tried to make out the ancient symbols around the item. Satisfied with the words it read aloud, the creature pulled a flask from under the robes, pouring the congealing blood from a human sacrifice into the bowl. The
~~~

unfortunate human man had wandered too close to a lellowtere tree when the creature struck him down. After pouring in the red liquid, the hideous being held its wrist above the bowl, slicing across the thin arm using its claws on the other hand. Black blood spilled from the arm as the red-eyed god hissed unintelligible words in pain and waited, staring at the mural. Soon, the painting seemed to move a little, like a tapestry in the early morning breeze. However, the smell that filled the room was suffocating, and the creature turned its head, coughing and wheezing at the unbearable stench. When it turned back, the area of the mural was now black like a starless night.

A dark mass slowly came forth from the Great Void. The skeletal underworld goddess stood before the creature coming through, her wretched body aching with pain and an insatiable desire for vengeance upon the human who caused this. She wanted her lost powers to transform into a human figure at will. Then, Alrpan would use the ability to control and manipulate her human serfs to inflict devastation throughout Kamin. By unlocking the hidden key to the Great Void, she could now align with a powerful god to restore her power and her plans. Her wretched husband would no longer be able to hold her back from her rightful place as the owner of the realm.

It was hard to tell she was smiling as thick black appendages, covered in serrated suckers, crawled across the slab, tasting the blood she spilled on the altar of sacrifice. Ancient words and ritual used to open the portal.

The shadowy nebulous blob came into view from the eternal deep, although it was impossible to tell what creature it was that slid out through the portal. Apparently satisfied with the offering, the creature's tentacles reached out into the room squirming and writhing as its body felt the rough walls, pulling entirely onto the slab. Covered in a thick, slimy secretion that reeked of the dark pit of emptiness, the creature had no features to distinguish what it was.

Sure of her success, Alrpan whispered thanks to this powerful god, knowing that soon, she would become a master, and vengeance against the humans would be hers for the taking. She could feel the soothing touch of the suckers working around her weak legs as they latched on, but she didn't move. Greedily another sucker arm latched on, causing the goddess to begin to back away, but another appendage quickly wrapped around her like an octopus around its prey. The tentacles were pulling her into the blob on the slab of rock. The goddess tried to scream as she grasped what was happening to her, but her hideous face was wrapped around another limb of suckers. She fought the slimy mass; her repulsive body trying to move around but the quick absorption by the blob was inevitable. Soon, the frantic movement stopped, leaving a black mass with a vague outline of a two-legged creature.

After a while, the black began to fade, and the form slowly grew and transformed into a human body very familiar to those within the underworld. The stench slowly subsided as the copy of Alrpan stood. Red eyes opened, looking around as the entity processed the memories of the goddess it had just taken over. Alrpan's entire being and powers were now part of this stronger life-force, which was one of godly punishment and revenge.

Kriell, the spirit stealer, had returned from the Great Void.

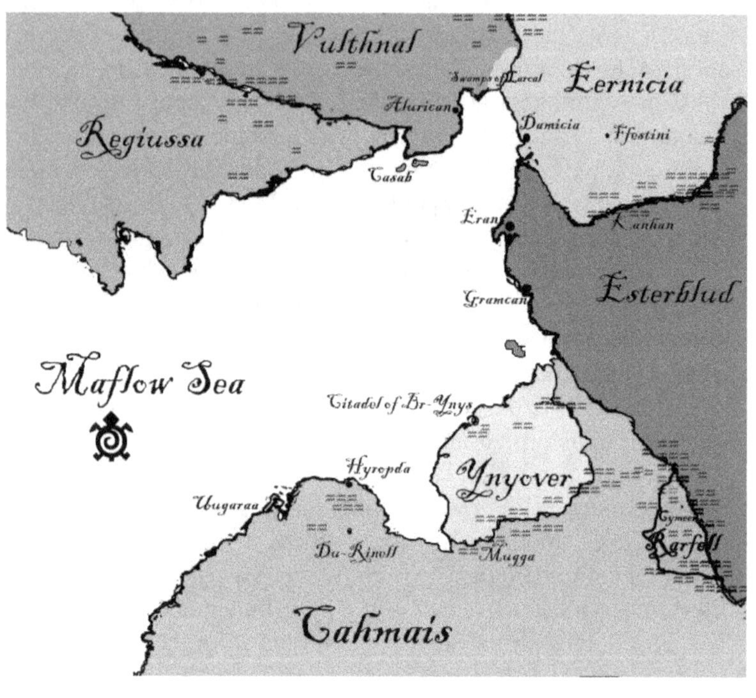

Vulthnal
Swamps of Larcal
Eernicia
Alurican
Damicia
Ffostini
Regiussa
Casah
Eran
Kanhan
Gramcan
Esterblud
Maflow Sea
Citadel of Br-Ynys
Hyropda
Ynyover
Ubugaraa
Gymee
Du-Rinoll
Mugga
Barfell
Tahmais

About the Author

Gordon Brewer is the pseudonym for a professional geek, history buff, and full-time dad who took up a challenge from his son to finish his first novel and enter the world of writing. Raised on a farm in Kansas, the author spent nearly five years in the US Navy traveling to 12 different countries during this time. After his discharge, he received his BS degree with majors in History and Political Science.

Over the next twenty years, Gordon focused on the business and IT world. His experiences left him with a need to explore wide-ranging interests in multiple genres, each with historical consideration given to the characters and settings.

Residing in Tennessee, he often uses his family and friends as unfortunate guinea pigs, where they listen to his tales, no matter how poorly conceived they may be.

You can find out more about the author and upcoming books, along with his other works at www.gordonbrewer.com.